THE INTRUDER

BY HELEN FOWLER

THE INTRUDER

WILLIAM MORROW & COMPANY
NEW YORK

To Mrs. V. Bennett

*whose gentle but persistent encouragement
has urged more than one of her protégés
to efforts they would not otherwise
have made.*

THE INTRUDER

1

FRIDAY AFTERNOON

I

IT WAS almost half-past four when Paul Quentin stepped from the train at Ambara, and whereas the day had been nondescript in the city, here it was unmistakably autumn. Forcing himself to pass through the little wicket gate without touching the railings in groups of two—so often he had to cheat when the number was uneven, sometimes inventing an additional one, sometimes ignoring the last one—he walked across the little red-gravel square, around which the shops were grouped, and stood under the branches of a large cedar, its leaves unstirred by even a faint breeze. He was trembling a little because of the incident with the railings, but he felt a sense of triumph; it was only a small victory, but perhaps it was a beginning. He was momentarily elated, joyful; he took off his hat and wiped his damp forehead with a handkerchief, and then, as he replaced his hat, he realized that it had happened. He had tapped twice with two fingers on his thumb. He always had to do this if things didn't work out in the right patterns, but this time he thought he had been able to stand firm. Dejection seized him and tears came into his eyes; he looked hard at the ground, the muscles in his face twitching erratically. In a moment he was calm, but with the customary feeling of apathy. He looked about him, leaning on the barred fence of the railway line, his dark eyes narrowed against the light, his thin brown face alert and attentive; then he propped one foot upon the bottom rail of the fence and leant more comfortably, with all the casual grace of the very young and the very tall.

Across the line, paddocks stretched uneventfully to the low ring of hills. How gently green and gold it was! The sunlight was not merely light but coloured light—light coloured deeply gold. Not red-gold as it was in high summer, but just softly yellow-gold. And the green of the trees and the grass-covered fields and hills was a sensible green, a green wherewith one could breathe freely of pure air, not a mad, savage mass of green steaming up evilly from a poisonous soil, not pressing down on one's brain and throwing out mouthing, writhing tendrils into it, not the sickening, amorphous foliage wall from which a dead face gazed sightlessly, with down-dropping jaw . . .

"No!" he said violently, aloud. Then he shouted "No!" and started away from the fence, standing in the open space at the edge of the square.

Gradually the trembling passed, and he looked anxiously about to see if anyone had noticed. The ticket boy in the little station had come out and was staring towards him, but otherwise there was no one near enough to hear, he felt sure. A surge of relief sent him back to stand under the cedar tree and he managed to light a cigarette in an easy manner, for the benefit of the still-staring ticket boy, who at last turned and re-entered the office. He felt that he'd had a narrow escape, but it was perhaps fortunate that it had happened because he was forearmed, now. He had been too optimistic, he'd felt that it would be easier than was actually the case; now he would go very carefully, take no more risks, attempt no great effort. He again turned to his surroundings.

Nothing had stirred; the cows standing here and there in the paddocks had perhaps moved infinitesimally, and the smoke from a chimney had drifted a tiny distance. Small sounds came from a long way away; far down the line towards Sydney there was a little farm and from somewhere there he heard a horse whinnying, and there was the distant, bell-like sound of a flock of turkeys from the same direction. The farm had a round silo of apricot-coloured bricks; the little silo had a dark brown roof and was standing beneath a gum so faintly green as to be almost

2

colourless. He looked back to the hills, their green sharply broken by the dull red of the roads twisting up from the flat. Up on the skyline was a group of buildings, half hidden by very massive gums. Yes, yes, he thought, stretching up to see more clearly, that was it: that was Laing's dairy. Adrian had told him just where it was—just there. Eagerly he looked for further landmarks. Adrian had told him that they used to ride across the bridge over the creek—Bannerman's Creek, he'd said. Suddenly his eye caught the line of the creek, weaving in and out among the paddocks, almost at the foot of the hills. Its thick line of heavily foliaged trees, its masses of blackthorn and feathery she-oaks, made it easy to follow when once he knew where to look. And there was the bridge with the two white posts and the great, white-stemmed gum bowing across it. Yes, by Jove, just as Adrian had told him.

The feeling of familiarity made him happy; the dreadful lostness, the greatest of all his discomforts, was fading. He began to feel at ease again, and he sat up on the top bar of the fence, whistling softly. All at once he realized that Adrian was there beside him, sitting on the railing. Incredulous joy swept over him and he began to talk excitedly to Adrian; and though he received no reply, he felt happily reassured, for the very fact that Adrian was here with him in the daytime meant that he was pleased with Paul, that he realized that at last Paul was actually beginning his task in earnest. Adrian had come back, and perhaps now he wouldn't come at night. Now that Paul was keeping his word Adrian would let him rest at night. . . . But his mind shuddered away from the thought. Of course, he didn't mention any of this to Adrian, for they both knew the reason for this return. He didn't in any way blame Adrian for coming at night. No, that was necessary. If he hadn't come like that Paul might have let things drift, might have neglected his task. No, he knew the old boy didn't want to torture him unnecessarily; it was just that Adrian knew that he, Paul, needed to be kept up to things, and Paul was really grateful for being reminded, for the sooner he fulfilled his promise, the sooner he would be free—free to enjoy Adrian's company like this. So he kept the conversation to cheerful subjects; he talked about his

3

journey and pointed out the various places Adrian had described to him, showing him that he recognized them. After a while he was aware that he was alone again, and though he was slightly disappointed, yet he felt wonderfully content.

He had known that it was wise to come, and here was the proof of it; it had been impossible to convince them at the hospital place, and then at home he hadn't felt able to explain it at all. But he knew he had been right, and thank God they'd agreed at last to let him have this week end to himself, to do what he had to do for Adrian. They'd only given way after a long while, and then only because the psychiatrist had persuaded them. He was a nice fellow, Duncan, even if he was a psychiatrist. Paul remembered, with a grin, the conversation he'd overheard between them, between Duncan and his mother.

"But, doctor," his mother had said, her troubled voice filled with misgiving, "couldn't one of us go with him? We'll go anywhere he wants to go and for any time. But alone . . ."

And Duncan had replied soothingly, "It's a waste of time, Mrs. Quentin. The last trip you made with him was a failure, wasn't it?"

"Oh, yes, it was terrible. He was worse than ever when we came back; but we couldn't have dreamed of letting him go alone then—he just couldn't get about."

"No," Duncan's voice broke in. "No, that's true. But that was several months ago, and the treatment he's had since then has done wonders. I think that this obsession of his may completely work itself out now, and I think he is quite sufficiently master of himself . . ."

And at length she'd given in. Thank God, thank God! Because now he was sure he was right; he was back with things he knew, not desperately struggling to exist in a world where he knew no one and was not known. It was nearly three months since Adrian had left him and had come only at night; and Paul had known why. He had been terribly afraid that he had left it too late, that Adrian would not return, that he was too disgusted; but Adrian was always supremely understanding, and he would have realized that it was just because Paul couldn't get away that he'd had to postpone it. And now he was back in a country-

4

side where Adrian had walked and lived and breathed and they were together once more; the relief made him madly happy, but the tears began to come again. He stood up, shook his head and twisted his mouth frantically for a moment, and then walked slowly towards the creeper-grown cottage that announced itself to be, not only the post office, but the Commonwealth Bank of Australia.

II

Mary Carmichael lifted her head as she counted the strokes of the chiming clock in the hall. Two, three, four, five. That meant that she must go in; but she stayed a moment longer, squatting in the pathway as she tugged at the weeds in the corner by the steps; then she knelt on one knee and raised herself, a little bulkily, to her feet. It had been hot working in the windless air, though there was little heat in the sun at this time of the year, but her time in the garden was so precious that she always worked feverishly while she was there. She propped herself against the big square stone at the base of the steps while she pulled off her gardening gloves and took off her hat. She looked with satisfaction at the bed she had just weeded; it looked better, the rich black earth soft and healthy round the plants she had left. She bundled up the little pile of debris and took it down to the already burning heap just inside the orchard gate, and before she turned towards the house she leant a moment against the white railing, letting the scent of burning leaves blow over her. The essence of autumn, an unbearable concentration of nostalgia. Surely no human spirit, however insensitive, however complacent, could withstand this powerful reminder of the dying of a season; even if one were wildly happy it would penetrate. No season really died except summer, she thought; autumn slipped unnoticed into winter, and spring and summer were born into the year. Only summer died, and though its passing was immeasurably beautiful, yet it brought a sense of mourning, a yearning to return, a looking backward rather than an anticipation.

5

Dusk was deepening as she went back up the path, and there was darkness lying in the wistaria grove at the side of the house. Just as she turned to enter it she saw him. He was fumbling with the gate, and the young wattles half hid his figure, but she knew he was a stranger. For no reason she could think of she felt alarmed, and her heart beat heavily and thickly for a moment; then he came through the opening between the giant monkey puzzle tree and the widely spreading, yellow-laden lemon tree and she saw him clearly. He was tall and very thin, and he seemed preoccupied, for he didn't notice her until he was quite close and then he stopped and looked at her without speaking.

He's young, she thought, and he's ill—or he's been ill—and there's a strangeness about him. Suddenly the melodrama fell away from her and she was just Mary Carmichael, who liked young creatures and was liked by them; she smiled at him and his thin face changed, looked reassured.

"I'm Paul Quentin," he said. "I knew Adrian. I knew him . . . well."

She said nothing for a moment, but stared at him. Dear God, she thought, will I never, never get over it! Will I always be shaken by this mad, sick rush of feeling to my heart whenever I hear his name suddenly! Then it was gone, and though the usual weakness followed, the weakness which made it hard to walk for a moment and even harder to talk, she was able to think of what she must do for this tall young thing with the sensitive lips and the deeply searching, uneasy eyes.

"I'm glad you came," she said evenly. "It was good of you."

"I would have come a long time ago," he said eagerly, "but— but . . ." His eyes glanced away and his brows knitted, as if the explanation was beyond his ability to describe.

"But you've been ill, haven't you?" she asked calmly.

"Yes," he said, almost happily. "Yes, I was ill. . . ."

Incongruity! she thought. Here are we two, talking gently together, surrounded everywhere by beauty—of scent and sound and scene. Behind his head the last faint light touched the hills softly; above them birds rustled and muttered tinily in the wistaria; Johnny snuffled quietly as he cropped the grass in the

6

paddock behind the orchard; a rabbit bobbed rapidly on its
irregular course to the line of young gums down by the gate.
And he has known frightfulness and seen savagery and filth and
torture, she thought wildly; and Adrian died of it and I will
never forget.

"I'm Adrian's mother, of course," she said. "I hope you have
come to stay awhile with us, Paul. It will be a great pleasure to
us all. Will you come inside with me now?"

"Yes, thank you," he answered happily. "Yes, I'd like to stay
—for a few days. You see, Adrian . . ." He broke off and looked
at her urgently.

"Yes?" she prompted.

"Oh, no, really—but I'd like to stay, if I may."

She took his arm and together they went round to the front
of the house.

"It's a beautiful house," he said.

"Yes," she answered. "It's an Australian house."

They stood at the foot of the steps, gazing upwards. Yes, he
thought, an Australian house: veranda on three sides, the
sloping red roof broken by four gabled upper-storey windows,
a central hall at the top of the white, outward-curving steps, a
hall on either side of which the rooms were placed. On their
left lay the orchard and, closer to hand, the wistaria grove.
Behind the wistaria a kindly cedar towered over the house, and
over to the right lay a smooth, grassy paddock where there
were tall gums, merely colourless shapes now in the misty dusk.
Gracious and tranquil, he thought; a house that was more than
protection from wind and heat and storm, a house where one's
mind, as well as one's body, might shelter safely.

"Come inside and we'll talk to my husband," Mary said.

Together they walked up the white steps and entered the
dark hall.

III

Anthea Carmichael drove slowly once the car had ascended the
hill at whose base Ambara lay stretched out before her. It was

her aim, each evening, to arrive here before the dusk took all the colour from the scene, but there was so much to do now that it was becoming difficult, and when the winter evenings came she would be cheated even of this tiny moment of peace. Sometimes she pulled up on the slope and smoked a cigarette while she watched the day end down there in the valley, and always she felt triumphant, as if she had had the last word. No matter how much bitterness that day had brought her, it had to go, the sun must set on it; she had lived through it, she had prevailed against it and finally conquered. But tonight she could not stay; there were a dozen things to do at home to prepare for the children tomorrow, and then, later on, she must drive down to Thornfield, for a visit with Mary and James and for what had, of necessity, become her almost nightly business discussion with her father-in-law. What an endless overexertion her life had become. Suddenly it occurred to her that the most melancholy factor in the whole situation was that she felt thankful for the necessity to strive endlessly, that without this unbearable effort her life would indeed be unbearable. Oh, what a curse a mind was! If one could only turn it on or off like a wireless set or a gas tap! What heaven to be able to say, "That's enough thought for tonight." And then click! and the mind a blank until morning!

There was the long whiteness of the house at Cedar Hill, clinging, limpet-like, to the hillside, its two terraces cutting sharply into the steep, green slope. "A dachshund of a house," Adrian had said. "If it had a tail it would wag it joyfully as we come round this curve."

Joseph had opened the gates as usual, and Anthea drove slowly down the steep driveway; as she stopped the car in front of the porch and swung herself stiffly from the driver's seat, Cassie came hurrying out.

"'Ere you are at last, lovey," she said in her soft, slightly breathless tones. "I seen the car over the 'ill, so I run and put the bath on. And there's some tea made fresh for yer. Now you get into your bath. . . ."

As she lay in the soothing hot water, she reflected on the number of people who would envy her her material comfort. If

8

she had been poor she would have thought that people who enjoyed such freedom from drudgery as she did were so much to be envied that, if they were ever unhappy, it was merely the result of wicked, idle discontent; that beautiful surroundings, wealth, a car, servants, luxurious clothes were a cast-iron protection against unhappiness of any kind. And perhaps she would have been right. If she had been forced to bring John and Libby up on a widow's pension after Adrian's death perhaps she would have had no time to indulge in melancholy—but then, if she had been poor, no doubt the whole nightmare would have been undreamed.

Beautifully soft, huge bath towels, subtly perfumed talc, little velvet slippers, and, over fresh satin underclothes, her rich, burgundy velvet house gown. A cushion under her head, Anthea lay on the padded window seat and gazed out over the misty flatness of Ambara, its lights winking plentifully now, its smoke threads still and sluggish in the calm air. Cassie brought in the tea and lit her cigarette, and then sat down on the window seat for a moment.

"Anything happen today, Cassie?"

"Nothing much, lovey. Joseph got ten eggs today, and so I made a cake. Oh, don't mind the bit of butter—didn't use much. And we're 'aving all our own vegetables tonight. . . ."

"Joseph's a wonder and so are you, Cassie dear. I'm going to stay here for ten minutes, and then can we have dinner? I must be quick tonight—I've got to get over to Thornfield early."

"Okay, lovey. I'll go and let yer rest and then we'll 'ave dinner straight off."

"Turn the radio on, will you, Cassie? You know—someone talking."

"Bloomin' thing," said Cassie, turning the dial. "Blessed if I know why y' always want to 'ear 'em talk. There's only music—no, there's a feller tellin' the prices of vegetables. That do?"

"Lovely, thank you, Cassie."

"Why on earth yer want to know the price of cabbages . . ." Cassie finished her sentence outside the door.

Yes, Cassie dear, but you don't realize what a slow, insidious drug the radio is, and how it interrupts and stultifies thought.

9

Anthea kept a table model by her bed and often, at night, or when she woke early, she turned it on softly, thankful for cheap, silly music, for preposterous advertising claims, for the sound of a human voice—anything that came between her and thinking. Less harmful, physically, perhaps, than sleeping tablets, but just as habit-forming, just as useful in keeping reality at bay. She lay still and waited for Cassie to call her to the night's activities.

IV

When the five-twenty train pulled in to Ambara station Megan Carmichael jumped out and hurried down the platform to the white gate that served Ambara for a ticket barrier. Little Harry Slade, important in a new peaked cap, scrutinized her ticket efficiently and she remembered that Sid Beck, who had adoringly permitted her passage through the gate for the last three years, had, this week, been promoted to the ticket office at Mitcham. It was a pity to be deprived of the pleasure of throwing someone into a stammering flutter merely by smiling brightly at him. And then swiftly, remorsefully, she realized that she was cruel. Perhaps she meant as much to Sid Beck as Julian did to her. Heaven help the poor thing if I do, she thought.

As she began to cross the square she altered her course suddenly and walked farther over to the right, where she would be in the shadow of the cedar trees by the railway line, for just ahead of her, in the deepening dusk, were her sister Honor and Hester Laing. As Megan skirted the edge of the square, unnoticed, Hester Laing climbed into her car and Honor shut the door and then, her school case and hat on the running board, leant her elbows on the side of the car and went on talking earnestly. So Honor was going to risk being more than ordinarily late. Oh, well, it was her own lookout and Megan had more urgent things to think about than her sister's emotional life; anyway, Honor would do things in her own fashion and it was no use imagining that she could be turned or dissuaded from any course she had decided upon. Honor had long ago convinced them all of that, just as she had apparently convinced herself not only that Hester Laing needed a champion, a protector who would shield her from Ambara's none-too-covert disapproval, but that she, Honor Carmichael, was the one to do the protecting. If Honor would only leave the woman alone she'd draw much less attention to her, Megan thought; and in any case, anyone less in need of a protector than that calm, self-possessed, clever Hester Laing, one couldn't imagine.

Megan turned off the road into the bush track. It would be a bit dim and stumbly this evening, but she'd need all the time she could save; she wanted to bathe and change before dinner so that she could get away quickly afterwards. It was going to be glorious to tell the news to Julian; but it was going to be very difficult to get him alone: that appalling woman never gave her an opportunity to talk to either of them alone, though it didn't matter about Alec. She could tell him at any time; in fact, she was reluctant to tell anyone but Julian. She'd worried all the way home in the train about the order in which she was going to tell everybody; she had even toyed with the idea of keeping it a secret, but she had realized that that would be impossible. The honours lists would be in the paper on Monday morning and the special awards, prizes and scholarships, would appear on Tuesday; and even if she had been able to refuse this afternoon, when dear old Hemsley had told her, she realized that the university authorities would not have omitted her name from the list with such unseemly haste. Regretfully, she thought how good it would look to see it there: *Proctor Travelling Scholarship, Megan V. Carmichael*. Yes, in other circumstances it would have been rather wonderful, and it was queer to remember, now that she was so anxious to be rid of the honour, how she had slaved to achieve it during the last four years.

It was dark now, and the heel of her shoe turned sideways, sending her lurching into the trough that formed the middle of the track, where it passed through the cluster of paperbark trees at the back of Armitage's place. Megan said "Damn!" in a forlorn voice, and the imprecation applied not only to the twisting, rut-ridden path, but to all the vexing tangle in her mind. She faced the thought that she just didn't know how to deal with

11

this situation, that it was too much for her; the thought of hurting and disappointing everybody by refusing her well-earned scholarship, the dread of trying to give some painfully inadequate explanation, the misery of being at odds with all those who wished her well—these were hateful reflections. They would be bewildered, all of them, from Professor Hemsley, the dear old sweet, to Sid Beck and all the other people in Ambara who liked her. And how to answer their amazed questions? How could she conceal from them the fact they were quite mistaken about her, that she was not just pleasant, agreeable Megan Carmichael, of whose prowess in the field of literature they had been proud since the days when she used to win prizes in the Children's Corner competitions in the Sunday papers? Supposing they discovered that, instead, she was a deeply emotional woman, passionately in love with a married man, devoted to him, prepared to give her future, her success, her whole life to him? "What!" they'd say. "At twenty? Why, you're only a baby. You don't know your own mind. You'll be in and out of love a dozen times before you marry. Don't be silly, child."

Megan kicked gloomily at a stone for a few yards as she emerged from the bush track into the light of a street lamp at the side of the road that led past Pritchard's; she crossed the road to the paddock where the old pear tree stood, whose pears Johnny insisted on eating, even when Megan was in a frantic hurry. She was halfway home now and still she had decided nothing; anyway, she wouldn't tell them tonight; tomorrow would do, and then she'd have all night to make her plans.

Fortunately they'd never guess that she knew; it was quite by accident that she had met Professor Hemsley at the university this afternoon, and it was out of the simple kindliness of his heart that he'd invited her up to his room and, beamingly, told her the news. She hoped that she hadn't let him down by her reception of the highly confidential communication. It was not completely unexpected, of course; she should have been prepared for it, for she had always been well in the running for the scholarship. But lately these things had slipped into the back of her mind; after all, it was more than three months since she had done the exam, and it was, tonight, just three months and four days since the night when she had known she was in love with Julian. Still, Hemsley had probably attributed her rather inane remarks and her silences to an appropriately overwhelming modesty; he really had been awfully nice to her, and it would have been pleasant, if her mind had been undivided, to revel in his quiet praise. He had always been kind to her; perhaps he had felt something of her admiration for him and his work, or perhaps it was just that she was a good student and Hemsley loved his women students to distinguish themselves, for he held firmly to the view that women had more to contribute to literature than men, but that their subservient position in society had prevented them from producing their best work. He was going to be deeply disappointed in her, for she felt that he had plans for her future; he had delicately hinted that, if she returned with a first from Oxford, the academic world would be open to her if she chose to enter it. As things were, of course, she would have to make do with some ordinary job, and there was little offering, save teaching, for a person with an Arts degree, even a brilliant one—and she knew she'd hate teaching.

It was all very unfortunate and complicated; but, painful as it was, it was as nothing compared with the dread of leaving Julian for two long years. Of course, nothing would ever happen to bring her closer to Julian; he would for ever be beyond her reach; but all she wanted was to be somewhere where she could, by little stratagems, see him at least a couple of times a week. He was not unaware of her, she felt sure, but, naturally, there was nothing overt between them. How could there be, with Veronica Kyles so overpoweringly present? Megan remembered often, with shame, how she had pityingly agreed with the others that he was henpecked. She wrinkled her nose at the distasteful term. But that was before she had come to understand and love Julian, before she had realized that it was the fastidiousness of the artist in him that made him reluctant to provoke the crude scenes which would follow if he opposed his wife's intentions. No, ever since that night, just three months and four days ago, when she had met him by chance in the city, when he had taken her to tea and then, to her amazed delight, to a film they had both wanted to see, when he had talked to her about his

13

painting over supper and then again as they had walked home through the hot, dusty air of the January night—since then she had known Julian. She had seen in him the soul of the artist tortured by lack of understanding in his home, saddened by the disappointment of having a brilliant son who was crushed by illness. She knew that he was a great artist, that he was too good for the humdrum position he occupied as art instructor at the Technical College, and, fervently, she had vowed that she would do what she could to help him, even if it were only by the warmth of a distant devotion.

Since then she had lived a secret life, and no one had guessed, she felt certain. Sometimes they met in town, and often she visited the Kyleses' home; no one had thought the visits strange, for her companionship with Alec was of many years' standing, and though Mrs. Kyles always jealously kept watch while Megan was there, she made no objection to her visiting Alec, whether he was lying in his chair under the trees, or working in his studio, or whether, as was too often the case, he was in bed. And nearly always she saw Julian once or twice during these visits and always she could feel the delicious, blissful certainty that there was something precious but unspoken between them, something that he would have put into words if he had not been so fine, so aware of his responsibilities. And, of course, it could not be otherwise, and she was proud to be thus devoting her life to him with no thought of reward; but, somehow, she felt sure that, when she told him tonight of her decision, it would stir to life and flame the embers that were smouldering beneath the surface of their—their love. Her heart beat high at the word, and she quickened her step as she opened the gate of Thornfield. Perhaps Julian would walk home with her, as he sometimes did now if she didn't take the car—and the moon would be bright tonight.

Megan broke into a run when she had stooped to go through the arch that the boughs of the lemon tree were beginning to form with the monkey puzzle. She could see, dimly, the results of her mother's afternoon in the garden, and the smell of burning leaves was still coming from the orchard; the front door stood open and she raced up the steps, her hat in her hand. Suddenly

14

she felt that something was different inside the house, and she paused a moment before she walked quietly into the hall and stood at the big double doors that opened into the living room.

The three of them turned as she stood there, and there was a moment of immobility; then the man, the stranger, rose slowly, and her mother said, in her calm voice, "This is Paul Quentin, Megan. He is"—almost she altered the tense but stopped herself in time—"is a friend of Adrian's. He has come to stay with us for a little while. Megan is the elder of Adrian's sisters, Paul."

Megan came forward firmly. Calmness in difficult situations, composure in the face of the unexpected, had always been her mother's criterion of the cultivated, socially adroit person. She remembered suddenly that Adrian had once said that Charlotte was his mother's pattern of correct behaviour—Charlotte, who,

> . . . when she saw his body
> Carried past her on a shutter,
> Like a well-conducted person
> Went on cutting bread and butter.

As Megan came to Paul with her hand outstretched, the sound of Adrian's voice, absurd with solemnity as he quoted, came vividly to her mind.

"How do you do, Paul?" she said. "It's just a bit of a shock to be brought quite so close to Adrian again, but when I get used to it I shall be awfully glad if you will talk to us about him."

Good girl, she's a good girl, Mary Carmichael thought exultantly. Nothing insincere, no polite mouthings; just the right amount of self-control. How madly proud of children one could feel! A moment such as this repaid one a thousandfold for enduring all their annoying, aggravating ways. They'd never failed her yet, not one of them; and she loved them, all of them —no, both of them. If she hadn't coughed suddenly, a sob would have forced itself into her throat. She rose and went through to the kitchen.

2

FRIDAY NIGHT

I

SINCE James Carmichael's illness the carving and serving of the meals was always done by Joady and Mary Carmichael in the kitchen; then Mary took her place at the head of the table in the dining room and either Honor or Megan brought in the plates, while Joady took James's dinner and her own to his study. James had insisted on this arrangement, for his attempts at eating with his still slightly paralysed hand were unsuitable for the public gaze, he maintained, and he would allow no one but Joady with him at mealtimes. It was many months since Mary Carmichael had consciously felt the bitterness that his choice of Joady, rather than herself, had roused in her, for there was wisdom in the arrangement and all of them had probably been spared a good deal of embarrassment because of it. At times, however, she thought that there were worse things to endure than embarrassment; also, what had begun as a temporary measure seemed to be hardening into permanency and she felt that perhaps James might have made greater efforts to regain his control over things if he had been forced to manipulate them before his family.

However, James wanted it this way, and, of course, no one could resent Joady. She was fat and briskly efficient, her hair and her apron equally white, her smooth face and forehead unlined by violent emotions. She had come to Thornfield as Mother's help when Adrian was born, and since then she had seldom left it, except for occasional duty visits to ailing members of her family. They had called her Joan then, but Adrian had

16

christened her Joady with his first few distinguishable words, and this name had clung. None of them could remember a time when they hadn't needed Joady; she never betrayed any deep feeling for any of them and her strict impartiality and lack of sentiment had made her the perfect adjudicator in the innumerable struggles that she had been called upon to settle. Her one weakness, a passionate devotion to the Carmichael children, she had effectively concealed beneath a dourness which was only skin-deep, but which was sufficient to maintain the strict discipline without which she would have been an easy prey for them. She never "poor deared" or "there, there'd" either the children or their parents; they could be sure of sound advice, never-tiring effort on their behalf, and severe but just criticism from Joady, and so, when James had developed this hypersensitivity about his awkward attempts to eat and to wash and to carry on all the activities that are necessary for a stricken person to remain clean and wholesome, Joady's apparently unemotional acceptance of his disablement had been heart balm to him. She had a lively mind and an interest in an amazing variety of subjects, and the mealtimes were never dull; at breakfast they generally went over the main items in the morning papers, at lunchtime they talked about the books they had read (no one guessed how often Joady woke herself while it was still dark to finish or to skim through some book of which she was making rather heavy weather), and in the evening they listened to the dinner music on the radio and talked and read accounts of the lives and works of the composers.

"Lord Kitchener!" Joady exploded to Megan one day, shaking with mirth. "If this keeps on much longer I'll be educated, that's what I'll be—and I'll go to the university and get myself a degree, like some other people I know round here who think themselves very high-falutin." And Megan had given her a solid whack with the egg-slice she was drying.

Tonight Mary was thankful for James's plan, though she would have been glad of his expert assistance in handling a difficult conversation. Still, the girls would help; thank goodness they were not the dumb, staring, giggling type; there were times when they all deplored Honor's assured self-possession, but

17

tonight it would be useful. She had sent Megan to knock at Paul's door when the dinner was ready, and, as she stood by the sideboard, pouring the sherry, he came slowly into the dining room. He smiled at her and looked about the room.

"It's pretty, isn't it?" he said, with a little stumble in the words. "It's a pretty room."

"Yes," she said. "I think it's a lovely room."

It was lit by an amber-shaded standard lamp; the dark wood of the table, dotted with its lace mats, threw up the brilliance of the green bowl of nasturtiums in the centre, and the fire burned brightly in the red-brick fireplace. Mary Carmichael seated herself, indicating Paul's chair on her right; opposite him, against the wall on her left, stood a tall Dutch dresser, warmly reflecting the winking flames from the fireplace in its polished blackness; the room ended in a huge casement, flanked by undrawn curtains of dull green velvet, and the windows opened on the orchard.

The girls came in with the plates and seated themselves, and Mary braced herself to the task of carrying this meal through; the main thing was not to ask too many questions, not to try to make him talk, and yet to see that conversation brought them all more closely in touch with each other, so that the feeling of his being a stranger among them should disappear as quickly as possible.

"This is Paul Quentin, Honor," she said. "My younger daughter, Paul."

"How do you do?" said Honor. "Will you have pepper and salt, Paul? And there's mustard in that little pot thing. I adore mustard—I could eat shoals of it, couldn't you?"

"Well," he said, consideringly, "I like it in moderation. I should think you'd need to get acclimatized to it, wouldn't you?"

Oh, thank God! It was going to be easy. Both Megan and her mother felt a wave of relief.

"Honor is notoriously immoderate in her enthusiasms," Mary said easily, the strain already smoothing out of her voice, "and she's never sufficiently constant to become acclimatized to anything."

"Abuse is one of the chief methods of argument here," replied

18

Honor calmly. "Thank goodness I've never had to descend to it yet."

Heavens! The composure of the creature, Mary thought. When I was sixteen . . . Everyone was easy, smiling.

Suddenly he said, tentatively, "Does Mr. Carmichael—I mean, doesn't he dine . . . ?"

And then they were all able to join in the explanation, to tell him about the stroke which had paralysed James two years ago and from which he was now greatly recovered; they were able to talk about Joady, to recall anecdotes about Joady, to enumerate her excellences and so to give him briefly a sketch of the family background. He turned from one to the other, listening to each in turn with, seemingly, a deep interest. Then Megan began to tell him about Joady on Adrian's wedding day, when Anthea . . .

As the story proceeded Mary felt a difference in his attitude, and, carefully careless, she turned to observe him. Yes, his expression had changed, the lightness was gone from his face. As she watched him, he folded his table napkin in two, then across again and then again; when it became too bulky to fold any more, his fingers became frenzied in their efforts. Then they were still. Suddenly he tapped twice with two fingers against his thumb and his hands relaxed; but there were drops of perspiration on his upper lip, and quickly he wiped his forehead with his handkerchief. He slumped back in his chair, looking spent, for a moment, and Megan's little story ended heavily. Both girls turned their eyes to her but she frowned at their discomposure and said quietly, "I'm afraid that that fire is too warm tonight. We're inclined to hurry into making fires too early in the year, Paul, because we love the look of them in this room."

Then, as he still looked vaguely at her, she went on quickly, "Honor, will you take Paul's plate? And Megan, bring in the dessert, please. Put the fruit bowl on the table as you come in. Honor. . . ."

By the time they had reassembled he was back again with them, but the atmosphere had changed. After a moment he said, inquiringly, "Anthea? Yes, of course; she is Adrian's wife. He—often spoke of her."

19

"She's lovely," said Honor. "She's the most super thing!"

"What abominably inaccurate terms you use," said Megan.

"Isn't she, Mother?" Honor asked indignantly. "Wouldn't you say Anthea is super?"

"If you mean that she's near perfection, then I agree," answered her mother. Turning to Paul, she went on, "It would be difficult to tell you how much Anthea has come to mean to us. She was everything to Adrian, and she has been a perfect mother to his children; throughout this terrible time, in the midst of her own suffering, she has inspired us all. More than that, she came to our aid when my husband fell ill and took over the running of his entire business, which she has managed excellently for over two years, now. It's all the more wonderful because Anthea has never had any special training for business work; her family are wealthy and she led a very sheltered easy life. She has had a tremendous amount to learn and she has worked night and day to learn it. She even parted with the children. . . ."

He started so suddenly that Megan, sitting beside him, jumped and stared at him.

"The children—aren't they with her? Aren't they here?" he said tensely.

She was so taken aback that she paused a moment. Before she could speak Honor said easily, "Gosh! You must be keen on kids. Haven't got much time for them myself, but then, *chacun à son goût*, as we say at St. Anne's."

"And you say it with the most execrable accent," said Megan.

Mary was able to carry on, now.

"The children are weekly boarders at a coeducational school in Mitcham," she said evenly. "They come home on Friday night, generally, but they're coming on Saturday morning, this time, so you'll see them tomorrow. You'll see Anthea this evening, though; she's coming here after dinner to see my husband."

Dear God! she thought, whatever is going on in his mind? If only I knew. . . . But it's just that he's in a highly nervous state, no doubt, and it must be overwhelming to meet people whom, so far, he has known only through Adrian. That must

20

be all . . . yet she discovered that her hands were quivering and she pressed them firmly on the table as she stood up.

"We generally have our coffee in the living room with my husband and Joady," she said. "If you girls will clear away here you can bring the coffee in as you come. Will you come with me, Paul?"

"Oh, Mother, may I go down to Kyleses' for half an hour, when we've finished here?" Megan asked.

"Of course, Megan."

Megan looked at Paul, who was standing at the door.

"Paul, would you care to come across with me? They'd love to meet you and I think you'd like the walk—wouldn't he, Mother?"

As her mother looked inquiringly at Paul, Megan thought swiftly, Damn! Why did I suggest that? Now Julian won't bring me home. But there was nothing to be done about it, now.

Mary Carmichael was saying, "If you're feeling too tired, Paul . . ."

"No," he said eagerly. "No, I'm not tired. Yes, Megan, I'll come. I'd love to come."

He held the door open and then followed Mary across the hall to the living room.

II

James was alone when they entered the living room, and he laid aside his book and smiled at them as they came to sit near him. He sat in a high, straight-backed chair, a dark brown rug across his knees. Beside him, on a white mat in front of the fire, lay a long, lean ginger cat, blinking amber eyes at the firelight. The fireplace was cream, as were the walls, and blue floor-to-ceiling curtains hung at the windows. It was a very long room, covered completely with blue carpet and, at one end, a shoulder-high bookcase ran from wall to wall. Several easy chairs and a long settee, all covered in flowered linen, completed the lightness and gaiety of the room.

21

"Come in, come in," said James. "Jenkins and I are bored with each other."

Only the slightest slurring of his words betrayed the fact that there had been a time when one side of his mouth was so distorted that he had hidden himself from his daughters for two long months. His wife seated herself at one end of the settee and Paul sat beside her; Megan had come in behind them with the coffeecups, and now she knelt beside Jenkins on the white mat.

"He's not bored with me," she said. "Jenkins is a highly intellectual cat and tires easily of commonplace conversation, don't you, darling?"

Jenkins cast her a look of cold contempt, stood up and licked his fur where her hand had touched it, and moved pointedly to the other end of the white mat.

"Well," said Megan, "did you ever?"

They were all delighted at her discomfiture; she wriggled over on her knees and sat beside her father's chair, and he stroked her thick, brown hair with his sound hand.

"No creature on earth can be so gracefully insulting as a cat, Paul," said James. "It's because they so frankly don't care a hang for anyone on earth but themselves—and because they're spirited and beautiful and can, therefore, never be inelegantly rude."

Honor came in, carefully carrying the coffee jug, which she set down beside the cups on the low round table that Megan had placed in front of her mother.

"Guess what?" she said in an amazed tone. "Joady said I needn't help her wash up, and when I insisted she simply threw me out."

All the Carmichaels looked surprised.

"You're an honoured guest, Paul," James said, smiling his faintly crooked smile at him. "That's the first time I can remember Joady's relaxing a rule—eh, Mary?"

His wife laughed and nodded as she handed Paul his coffee.

"Well," said Megan gloomily, "I bet she'll tighten up tomorrow, just to show she's not getting soft. I'm on duty all day—I suppose she'll make me scrub the kitchen."

Honor sat in a chair opposite her father and leant her head

22

back. "It's just that she's realized that I'm getting frail," she said dreamily. "You know, I think I'm outgrowing my strength, or something."

"Never mind, dear," said her mother gently. "Your physical strength will always outlast your mental powers; we can be sure of that."

"Just to avoid an ugly family row, Paul," Honor said, suddenly jumping to her feet, "I'll sing to you. Shall I, Mother?"

"Yes. Sing two songs: Paul should be able to endure just two, even if he objects to singing."

"No," he said, sitting back happily. "I love singing."

Honor opened the piano and began to sing "Where e'er You Walk" in an easy, sweetly high voice. The light from a cream-shaded lamp on a ledge beside the gleaming, dark piano, shone on her straight, shoulder-length hair, turning its pale honey colour to a deeper shade; she did indeed look frail, Mary thought, as she gazed at the delicately textured skin, the faintly upturned nose, the large, deeply blue eyes. But she wasn't; she was thoroughly healthy, and, therefore, this ethereal appearance would only be an asset as she grew up. For Honor was going to be beautiful; she was really beautiful now, in an unfinished way, but when the richness of maturity came to her she would be startling. What are her thoughts, her central, most abiding thoughts? Mary wondered. But one never knew that about anyone but oneself.

James smoked his pipe, holding it for practice in the hand that was so gloriously recovering from its uselessness. A rush of delight always came to him when he managed to manipulate something successfully with that hand; it seemed as if the happiness of returning strength would never grow less. He turned his head to look at Paul; he was leaning forward, his hands clasped between his knees, his eyes unclouded and serene with pleasure as he gazed intently at Honor. I suppose he has no idea, James thought, of how violently he has made us all feel today. His coming had stirred up anguish that had been overcome, had made cruel longing strong within them, had twisted remembrance as a knife into wounds that were healing. But Paul was quite unaware, James knew; there was obviously some

23

mental disturbance there, he thought, and it was just something they could do for Adrian's memory if they helped to ease it and calm it a little while he was with them. Suddenly his attempts at detached reasoning broke down as he had, briefly, a vision of Adrian sitting there. If only he were there beside this lad! Dear, beloved boy—Adrian. How could he be gone, nowhere, not in the world? His lips trembled, and he transferred the pipe to the other hand, giving up the struggle temporarily.

Paul sat listening to the lovely notes, absorbing the gentle melody into his mind; an unusually beautiful voice she had, and she sang with artistry far beyond her years. Oh, these people were soothing. He had been so right to come here—he thought exultantly of how right he had been. Though he had only spoken to him once, he felt that Adrian was near all the time, had been near ever since he had come; and he knew that tonight they both would rest, that there would be no dream. And he had only to carry out his part of the bargain and this happiness, this heavenly freedom, would continue always. Not that he didn't want Adrian at night; but that was a different Adrian. In the daytime, or whenever Paul was awake, Adrian was always alive and gay and a good companion; but the Adrian that came at night was—dead. No! . . . Had he said it aloud? He looked at the others, but they were listening quietly; with the relief came the tears, and he grimaced in order to fight them back.

Honor let her hands lie in her lap for a moment when she had finished, her head slightly bent. Gosh! she's a showman, Megan thought admiringly. What a complicated creature she is; nothing obvious or easily recognizable about her. As Honor began to sing Megan turned her head to look at her mother. How—how civilized she is, she thought. In fact, we're all pretty highly cultivated, or we wouldn't be behaving as well as this. She hadn't yet recovered completely from the shock of meeting Paul and of realizing almost at once that, despite his pleasant and fairly unremarkable appearance, he was odd and strange; she wondered if the others knew—but of course they must. And he was nice; he was very likeable, his helplessness, his unvoiced appeal for gentleness and kindly forbearance making one yearn

24

over him, as it were. Yes, she decided, she liked him tremendously. Suddenly he grimaced furiously and turned his head away. Megan looked away, too, her heart beating heavily for a moment.

Honor was singing in the world where one day she would sing, to a magnificent audience, to royalty, to the great ones of music, as, carried away by their wild appreciation, they rose and called her name, their gleaming satins and velvets rippling in the darkened theatre. Dame Honor Carmichael. . . .

Her hands lay for a moment in her lap, and then she spun merrily round on the piano stool. She came and stood in front of Paul, who gazed up at her seriously.

"Did I sing well? Did you enjoy it?" she asked.

"Beautifully," he said. "I would like to hear you sing often; very, very often."

Pleased, she pirouetted to the big chair and lay back once more, looking into the flames.

"It's half-past seven, Mother," Megan said, rising. "I think Paul and I will go now, so that we can be back when Anthea comes. She won't get here till about nine, will she?"

As they were moving to the door, Honor sprang up and ran to Paul, grasping both his hands as she looked up at him.

"Tell me, Paul," she said, tensely earnest, "are you the kind of person who can't bear to recall awful things that have happened to you, or do you not mind if we ask you things? You see, we're all wanting to know about Adrian and the things that happened to him—all the things, the good things and the horrible, dreadful things. Will you tell us some time, or would you rather we didn't ask?"

Where angels fear to tread, James thought, smoking quietly. Mary was looking aghast. Paul looked down at Honor.

"No," he said, in a surprised tone. "I don't mind. I didn't want to make you sad. But I'll tell you anything you ask—I don't mind. There's only one thing I don't like to think of . . ." He looked away from her quickly.

"Then don't think of it," she said, and laid her hand over his eyes. "I'm so glad you've come, Paul. Don't go away for a long while. . . ." She was gone, her footsteps echoing in the

25

little silence she had left behind her, as she raced towards the kitchen and Joady. After a moment Megan rose.

"Thank goodness we've got one well-brought-up daughter in the family," she said resignedly. "That girl just gets worse, Mother. Come on, Paul, or we'll never be back. Bye-bye, Father —we won't be long, Mother."

They stepped out together into the moonlit mist of the night.

III

They sat listening to the sounds of the footsteps and voices until they could no longer hear them; then, after a moment, they looked at each other, both realizing suddenly that each was strained and tense. Mary stood up, put some wood on the fire, and then sat in the chair Honor had occupied. James sat opposite her and they both looked soberly at the flames.

Mary Carmichael felt relaxed and spent, but burdened with a deadening heaviness; she realized how gloriously simple it would be to stop trying to behave well, to scream and sob, to curse one's misfortunes—and how fruitless. That was the real bitterness, to face the fact that there was nothing to do but endure. It had been like that for both of them ever since Adrian had gone into the silence, which had begun with his capture and from which he had never emerged until this night, when the young stranger had walked up the path and spoken his name. And one was spared nothing; every remote dread she had conjured up had eventuated. At first she had not dared to hope, but when he had come through the Middle East campaign, the possibility of his returning had awaked in her mind and she had begun to long and hope for it. And then, even though he was thousands of miles away, she had developed an unreasoning dread that he would be involved in the war in the Pacific, for she feared the Japanese more than any other enemy. And it had happened in just that way: Adrian had been with those who had landed in Java, and, after his capture, the long silence had closed over him.

26

The terror of his ill-treatment in Japanese hands had filled her mind for months, while kind people had tried to assure her that there were rules of warfare, that the Japanese, for their own sakes, would never dare . . . But then came the night when the whole nation was requested to listen at nine o'clock to an important news session, and, as she listened to the stories told by the survivors from a torpedoed Japanese prison ship, she heard everything she had dreaded being confirmed and horrors being recounted that were more frightful than anything she had been able to imagine; and, at that time, the certainty of his dying, slowly and in agony, had come to her. Again they had reminded her that many thousands had survived and would return; could be nursed back to health; but she had turned away from their comforting words. She knew—and had no hope. And then finality had come, with the telegram—"died of illness." That meant dysentery, probably: beastly, frightful, unnecessary disease, the result of dirt and starvation, of all the things that should never, in all his life, have touched him; and she had seen him, a skeleton still living, creeping slowly to a filthy death —him, her bright, her vivid Adrian. And she knew that this boy, Paul, when he began to talk and to tell them of Adrian, would confirm all the hatefulness she had imagined of his dying. Yet she must listen, must know; for this boy was the last of Adrian. After he had told them his story, Adrian would cease for ever; and yet, though it would have been less pain not to have to listen, she was thankful to be forced to endure it, thankful that he had come. It prolonged, just temporarily, the final parting; it was like seeing again, briefly, someone to whom she had said a heartbreaking goodbye, an agonizing reliving of agony for which one was yet thankful.

"James—oh, James." Her eyes were dazed as she held her hand towards him.

He moved his chair until it was beside her, and he looked down into her face anxiously. She looked broken, her lips loose, her strength gone. He braced himself to help her, suddenly mindful of the long time during which she had had to endure his illness as well as her thoughts of Adrian. This might well be too much for her.

"Mary," he said quietly, "shall I get rid of him pleasantly? If it's going to be too much for you, I will, you know."

She roused herself and looked at him as if he had shocked her.

"James, no!" she cried, straightening herself in the chair to face him. "Good heavens, no! That would be dreadful. I'm all right, really; just a momentary lapse. It was rather a strain at dinner. . . but oh, no, he's a nice lad; I feel quite fond of him, already. But he's in a state about something; there's something on his mind, I think. I'd like him to stay awhile. I shan't put on any more fancy turns, I promise you."

She lifted her head and smiled at him, and then turned back to look into the fire.

"You know," James said thoughtfully, "Adrian might have come back like this, with secret horrors and torments in his mind. I watched the lad carefully, and I'd say that, now and then, he was on the verge of hysteria. Perhaps being here with us, with Adrian's family, may smooth something away. We'd be glad if someone had done the same sort of thing for Adrian, I suppose. By the way, he let slip the fact that he's just out of hospital, though physically he seems quite well; he's thin, of course, but he's full of vitality. Too much, I think. He's strung to a very high pitch."

"Well," she said, her voice calm and firm once more, "it will be interesting to see whether he improves here. Anyway, I hope he'll stay. Goodness knows where he's come from or where his home is, but I think we'd better not ask questions just yet; tomorrow, perhaps, do you think?"

"Yes," said James, "perhaps tomorrow." She's over it, he thought, she's better. He felt deeply relieved. Mary was very strong, always quietly strong, and it had frightened him badly to see her so close to breaking point.

Thankfully she leant her head against his arm, and they sat silently for a moment.

"Anthea will be here soon," she said. "Thank God for Anthea."

"Thank God for Anthea, indeed," James said.

IV

Once they had stooped to pass under the low-hanging branches of the monkey puzzle tree, the world of people was lost to them; the house might have been miles away. Outside the gate they passed through the little thicket of young wattles, and then Megan turned left and they walked across a square paddock, along a narrow track that passed under trees here and there— a tall coolabah, then farther on a group of she-oaks. Young gums stood very straight on either side, and the moon shone on their leaves, turning their trunks to an artificial whiteness. The outline of anything more than twenty yards away was softly blurred with mist, and the air was sharp with autumn.

> *"Dear God! how sweet are all things here!*
> *How beautiful the fields appear. . . .*

Do you know who wrote that?" Paul asked suddenly.

"No." Megan was surprised. "No, I can't remember his name. But I know he was one of the early Romantic Revival people."

"Yes," he said, chuckling, and he jumped to break a twig from an overhanging bough. "Yes, I've been thinking of those lines ever since I got off the train. Wish we knew his name."

"I'll ask Julian," said Megan. Always it was a blessing to say his name.

"Who is he?"

"He's the man we're going to see tonight."

"But who is he? What's his other name? What does he do for a living? How old is he? Tell me all the things about him."

This was heaven-sent. Excitement raced through her as she began to tell him about Julian.

"Well, he's—oh, I don't know how old he is. But that's not important. But Alec's twenty-two, so he must be about . . . oh, what does age matter, anyway? He's an artist, a terribly good artist. And he has a horrid job, teaching art at the Technical College. He's so much too good for it." Her voice lost its careful

29

nonchalance. "It's a wicked shame. But he's going to be famous one day."

"Well," said Paul reasonably, "he's leaving it a bit late, isn't he?"

Megan was painfully shocked.

"Why," she said indignantly, "lots of artists begin late. Look at Van Gogh."

"Yes, but he *was* Van Gogh. One in a hundred might do it. Anyway, what about the others? He's got a son, you said. What does he do?"

Her mind steadied from its angry hurt and she said, "Well, Alec has never really been able to do anything. He paints, too, and I think he's very good, and his work has been praised in the city. But he's hardly ever able to paint. He's more or less an invalid."

"What's wrong with him?"

"Oh, no one knows, much. He's just sort of ill. He had rheumatic fever about five years ago, but even before that he was always ill, ever since they came here about ten years ago."

They walked in silence for a few moments.

"There's something unusual about his illness, isn't there?" Paul asked at length.

There was a pause before Megan answered, and there was an uncomfortable note in her voice when she spoke. After all, he was a stranger, and although one could tell strangers—some strangers, nice ones like Paul—about oneself, there was a hesitancy in her mind as she began to tell him about the Kyles family. But she was so eager to talk about Julian, and the others as they affected Julian that she began to tell him the whole story about Alec and his mother, about her appalling possessiveness and her leech-like grip on both the men.

"We've talked about it for years at home," she said, "but there's never been anything we could do. Alec was always a charming creature, and clever, too. He has Julian's talent, and his painting has always shown promise; but his mother somehow took possession of him, I think. Of course, she's been wonderful; he used to take these bad colds, and that's why they came here from the city. But instead of helping him to overcome whatever this

30

weakness was, she seemed to foster it; people said she coddled him, but it was more than that. She took away his confidence, made him feel he was different from other boys; and finally she seemed to isolate him from everyone. She found a doctor who said that he mustn't play games; and then it was decided that he must leave school—and since then she's had him properly. When he was about seventeen there was some kind of upheaval and Alec left. He went to the city and began to work in some store, as a salesman; he was sharing a studio with a friend and he studied hard at his painting. He might have made a success of it then, but he had the rottenest luck. He fell ill—rheumatic fever—and the friend sent for his people—and so he came home. He was dreadfully ill, and his heart was affected in some way. Mrs. Kyles was wonderful. She nursed him and made him well in the most devoted way. But then she set about keeping him a semi-invalid—and now he's hers, body and soul. He feels that he will only bring suffering on her if he rebels against any of her injunctions, and so he obeys her in everything. She kept him in bed for almost a year, and now, when he does go out at all, she always goes with him. He goes up in the hills, painting, a good deal, but she drives him everywhere and stays with him while he works and brings him back. I very seldom speak to Alec alone. . . ."

As her voice trailed off Paul said, "What about the father? What part does he play in all this?"

"Oh, Julian. Well, what can he do? And he's an artist, and terribly sensitive. And she's such a dreadful woman—so formidable. His life would be made unbearable with scenes and ugliness. No, he could do nothing."

"Strikes me," Paul said, looking at her closely, "that he could do a great deal, if he tried."

As he saw the angry, indignant expression on her face, he went on quickly, "And why are we going there tonight?"

"Well," said Megan, "this is a secret. I'm not telling the family tonight, but I wanted Julian to know. . . . I've won a scholarship to Oxford—a two years' scholarship."

"That's wonderful," said Paul happily. "You must be very clever. Congratulations, Megan."

31

"Thanks," said Megan. "But, you see, Paul, I'm not going."

"Oh. Why?"

"Well, there are things which keep me here—things I'd rather have than that."

"Are you sure you'll still want them more in another twelve months?" he asked slowly, turning to look at her.

"Yes," she said. "Yes, I'll always want them, all my life."

They had come to the barred fence that skirted the road, and Paul leant his back against it, resting his elbows on the top bar. Megan stood in front of him, her head lifted, her face and hair dusted with moonlight, her hands clasped in front of her. She was exalted with renunciation; an ecstasy of sacrifice shone from her.

"There are things," he said slowly, "for which you'd give your life at one time, which can become valueless to you in twelve months' time."

"Oh, no," she said vehemently. "No, Paul, not this. This is for ever."

They looked at each other for a moment. It was impossible that they were strangers, Megan thought.

Then, "Maybe," he said. "Time will tell. Are you going over or through?"

Happiness swept back to her.

"Over, of course," she said. "D'you think I'm a sissy?"

But she stumbled on the other side of the fence and had to lurch for four or five staggering steps before she could recover herself. And Paul laughed—a hearty, strong laugh. She thought, with surprise, I believe I'm good for him—and quickly she threw a clod of earth at him and ran. He caught her up in a few paces and took her arm happily. They swung into step down the middle of the road.

"Now," he said, briskly, "point out the landmarks to me; tell me where everything is and where everyone lives."

Obediently, she told him who lived in the houses whose lights shone here and there among the trees. Ahead of them the rounded hills rose into the night, and here again Megan identified the houses by the lights seen distantly from the valley road. Over to the right a tiny gleam of moonlight on an iron roof betrayed the presence of the military camp, which stretched away down the other side of the hill, towards Mitcham. They passed a little white house, nestling among spreading camphor laurels.

"And there's poor Mrs. Croft's light," said Megan.

"Is she poor?—or only poor Mrs. Croft?" he asked.

"Oh, it's pitiful about her. She's a dear thing; gentle, sensitive —always looks as if she needs protection."

"And has she no protector?"

"No. Her husband's not yet back—he's been in New Guinea —but he'll be home any day."

"Well, then, there's a happy ending."

"No," said Megan. "It's not going to be as easy as that. You see, she's got a dreadful child; I think he's deranged; he really needs analysis and treatment of some sort, I'm sure."

"Symptoms?" Paul asked.

"Well, he's madly cruel and mischievous. He's been sadistic since he was able to walk and talk; he's thirteen now. She's had to take him from a couple of schools for unmentionable things. And she's so proud—and frightened; everybody knows about him, but she pretends there's nothing wrong. And Paul, he actually hurts her; I've seen bruises on her face—once her eye was cut; and she's beginning to look frantic and distraught at times, now. No children in the village are allowed to play with him and, but for her constant efforts and because people like her and pity her, he'd have been in a reform school by now, for things he's done to children and animals. She adores her husband, but he's a hard man, really, and what will happen when he gets home and discovers all this, goodness only knows; and the little brute's so cunning and intelligent . . . handsome, too. But there's a madness in him somewhere. If only she'd admit it and face the situation, perhaps something could be done, but she pretends so bravely. . . ."

"Perhaps the husband will be a changed man when he comes back."

"Perhaps, but I don't know. . . ." She turned and began to point out other places as they walked down the road; there, a tiny glowing pin-point in a fold of the hill, was Laing's dairy, and farther to the right, though its lights were hidden, was Cedar Hill, where Anthea lived.

At first his head turned obediently as she pointed, but gradually she felt the different quality in the clasp of his hand on her arm—a slackening, a withdrawing. Soon she realized that he hadn't been listening for some little while. His hand dropped to his side and he lowered his head, completely absorbed. Megan fell silent and they walked on much more slowly.

His mind was a pitiful confusion of panic and guilt. He'd forgotten! For a few moments he'd quite forgotten why he had come. God! God! Don't let me forget. Supposing it went right out of his thoughts and he left with his promise unfulfilled, returned to an endless succession of nights with Adrian. . . . And he might never get the chance again. He recalled the violent shock he'd felt at dinner when he'd misunderstood Mrs. Carmichael, when he'd thought that the children wouldn't be there. But they would be here tomorrow. Suddenly he realized that he could do nothing before tomorrow, that he was free tonight, that he could relax and think of other things tonight. Relief came to the turmoil of his thoughts. Yes, but still . . . he mustn't forget entirely, as he had done just now; that was dangerous, for things did go quite away from him sometimes, things that he could never recall clearly again. He must do something that would keep it in his mind. . . . But what? What? Then he glanced down at his wrist and joy came to him. Of course, of course—and such a simple thing.

Megan's heart turned over as he suddenly unstrapped his watch from his wrist, laid it on the ground, and smashed the glass with his heel.

"Paul!" Her voice was shaking with the shock of experiencing the inexplicable. "Paul, why did you do that?"

Quite composed, and smiling now, he strapped the watch back on his wrist.

"Why? Oh, I—I had to," he said. "Never mind about that. Where on earth do these people live?"

They walked on, but this time he talked and Megan tried to calm herself to face the Kyles family.

34

They turned from the road and went through a dilapidated double gateway. It was a sad house, weary and dejected under the burden of two engulfing black pine trees, which lay on either side of it. Even the gay moonlight was unavailing against its darkness and the meanness of its appearance. An uncompromising front door, flanked on either side by rooms with narrow french windows, showed a faint light through the fanlight. Megan rang, and brisk footsteps approached; the door was opened violently and an unwelcoming voice said, "Whoever . . . ? Oh, Megan. But why the front—oh!"

"Mrs. Kyles," Megan said nervously, "I've brought a friend to see you—a friend of Adrian's—Paul Quentin."

"Well, this is unexpected. . . ."

As she stood aside for them to stumble past her into the narrow hallway, she conveyed clearly to them that she was not pleased. They emerged from the dark hall into a room lit so dimly that Paul found himself narrowing his eyes. A dark-eyed man rose from a chair near the empty fireplace, an orange-painted wooden chair with a green canvas seat, which leered in a ghastly attempt at cheerfulness in the grim light.

Megan presented Paul to Julian in an uncertain voice, and they were shaking hands when suddenly Paul jumped, as an alarmed voice screamed behind him, "Alec, don't get up—lie back, now. Megan and—her friend will understand."

A pale-faced lad, who had been in the act of raising himself from a day bed covered with an obviously home-dyed hessian coverlet, now leant back on his cushions—of the same material, but of a striking shade of yellow—and his mother hastily drew up the rug he had flung back, and covered his chest with it.

"This is my son, Alec." Julian Kyles's voice was deep and tranquil.

Paul went over to the divan and took the thin hand in his. The young man looked up at him with a shrug and a grin. My God, Paul thought, I've seen hundreds like him. Prisoners—

starved, desperate prisoners. Something very wrong here, without a doubt.

"It's nice to see you," Alec Kyles said, in a subdued, pleasant voice. "We don't see many people here—only the faithful Megan."

His eyes followed her gently as she went across to a table in the opposite corner of the room. Mrs. Kyles's piercing voice rattled on, making conversation difficult for the men. She was showing Megan some new material, which she had been covering with stencilled design, and her description seemed as maddeningly incoherent as the design itself appeared to be, on the sickly mauve background.

Julian stood at the end of the day bed, stuffing tobacco into his pipe and looking down at his son morosely. Then, raising his voice above the din, he said, "Oh—won't you sit down?" He brought a chair up to the end of the bed, where Paul could sit facing Alec, his back to the purplish horror that Mrs. Kyles was brandishing at Megan. Julian resumed his seat by the fireplace and at once became inconspicuous, a figure in the background.

Paul's eyes ranged over the room. Everywhere there was evidence of Mrs. Kyles's interest in arts and crafts; the window, innocent of any frippery lace curtains, was draped starkly with dull-red, dyed hessian, hanging stiffly and with an extremely rough-dry appearance; across the lower end, a succession of jade-green stencilled beasts of some kind walked menacingly. They could be panthers—or camels. No, they didn't look sufficiently good-natured for camels. On the mantel and on the two bamboo tables were examples of her interest in modelling: a white, clay-modelled, nude, female figure, very sagging as to the pelvic region, very indeterminate as to features, slumped beside a slightly crooked horse, which was lurching uncertainly across the little table beside Julian's chair.

The shattering voice ran on.

"You see, I'll have black dots, half-crown size, running in diagonal rows this way—you see what I mean? And then these shilling-sized ones will cross them, running transversely this way. You see? Then, I thought, to vary it . . ."

Paul forced his attention back to Alec. God in heaven, these people would drive him crazy; he felt a trembling beginning in him somewhere.

Suddenly she deserted Megan and swooped on the three men.

"Now, let us get to know each other—just quickly, for you mustn't stay long, you know. Alec must be in bed by eight-thirty. He hasn't been at all well this week, but he's greatly improved today and we don't want to overdo things. My good-ness!"—the high-pitched voice rose to a shriek—"It's ten minutes past the time. Oh; Dr. Seddon will be angry with me."

She rushed out of the room, and came back with a glass and two white tablets that she handed to Alec, saying angrily, "It's just what happens when people come unexpectedly. Really, Julian, I don't know why you couldn't think of it. You do noth-ing to help when people come. I always have the burden of entertaining them left on my hands. Surely it's not too much . . ."

His head sank lower as she spoke, and he gazed steadily at the handmade felt rug at his feet.

As she went out with the tumbler, Alec managed to ask, "Were you a prisoner—with Adrian?"

"Yes," said Paul.

"And you're quite fit again?"

"And—oh, yes. I'm very well."

"When did they take you? After Singapore?"

But she was back again. "Now, now, no horrors, please," she said sharply. "Alec must not be made miserable; I endeavour always to keep Alec's mind on happy things. Dr. Seddon says that I'm the ideal nurse, because I'm so consistently cheerful—so, young man, if you don't mind, no reminiscences while you're here."

No, Paul decided, he couldn't endure much more of this.

With a swirl of movement, she rose. "Now talk about pleasant things while I fill Alec's hot water bottles. But I'll only be a few moments."

They relaxed perceptibly when she had gone, though Julian Kyles still seemed nervously uneasy; he fingered his pipe with one hand, and with the other he tapped on the arm of the chair. He said nothing, but now and again he glanced quickly across at the three of them and then down at the tapping fingers.

37

"Of course, you haven't been here long enough, I suppose," Alec said, pushing back the rug and rolling on his side to speak to Paul, "but how do you like this part of the world?"

"Very much," Paul said. "It's good country—beautiful, too."

"Isn't it?" The tired eyes shone with sudden eagerness in the pale face. "I've painted it for a good many years—not very well, I'm afraid. Conditions aren't ideal. . . ."

"You'd like the countryside where I come from," Paul said. "The Dorrigo district. Grand country."

"Yes, I've seen pictures. Yes, I'd like to see some other places. What do they know of England, you know. I'd paint Ambara much better if I'd seen Brittany and the Black Forest."

"Well, it's a good way from the Black Forest," Paul said, "but perhaps one day you'll come to Grassmere. Let's hope so, anyway."

"You're very kind." Alec's face was flushed with pleasure. "Somehow I feel that that's going to happen; I don't quite know how it could, but still—"

"Most things can be made to happen, I suppose," Paul said off-handedly.

Megan listened delightedly. He's a lovely person, she thought; he's kind and cultivated, and he has poise and assurance, though he's very young. Though she had been willing herself not to do it, she contrived to glance at Julian. His dejection, the look of crushed sadness about the drooping figure, made her uneasily miserable. If only he were happy, as happy as she had seen him when they had been briefly together; she felt sad to have to witness his sadness, to have to be conscious of it all the while, when she wanted to be listening to the talk of the two young men.

Then Mrs. Kyle was back, a tempest of upheaval and disquietude sweeping into the room with her coming.

"Off you go now, visitors," she said, with devastating mock-gaiety. "Alec, you're looking excited and upset. Now I suppose I'll have another sleepless night; not so late with your visits, another time, Megan."

Paul rose abruptly and held out his hand to Alec.

"Good-bye, old chap," he said, his voice filled with a quiet

38

tenderness. "We've a lot in common: you're a prisoner, too, but you'll have to fight harder than we did to escape; and if you're caught trying, you'll be brought back and tortured, just as we were—only in a more refined way, of course. But if I had the choice, give me the Japs any time; I'm not so sure now, that they are the most ruthless people in the world."

As he stood at the door leading to the hall, he said, "I'll wait for you, Megan. Don't hurry. . . ." and he was gone.

There was silence. Alec lay back on his yellow cushions, a thoughtful line between his brows. Julian looked up uneasily at his wife, and quickly returned his gaze to the felt rug. Megan sat still, horrified; and yet, behind the awful embarrassment, she felt exhilarated, for somehow the room seemed healthier, the air less oppressive. Desperately she swallowed a laugh.

Veronica Kyles was dumbfounded, utterly silenced by the fact that something had happened here, in this room, in her house, which she had neither willed nor desired. It was quite beyond her understanding, it was without explanation, and yet it had shaken her. She rallied suddenly.

"That young man is mad," she said to Megan accusingly. "Where's your common sense, Megan? To bring a man like that into my house at this time of night, to upset Alec before he goes to bed! You should have more consideration."

"I'm awfully sorry, Mrs. Kyles. You see, he's still suffering from some nervous strain, I think."

"Nervous strain? Rubbish! These young men trade too much on their experiences. He's perfectly healthy. It's just a pose to draw attention to themselves, that's what it is. Heavens above! If he had to endure all I have to, he'd know what nervous strain is, I can tell you. Just rudeness—but he must be insane. What did he mean? Do you know what he meant, Julian?"

He looked up at the face drawn into angry lines, at the eyes flashing bad temper, at the hands gripping the arms of her chair, knuckles white with suppressed rage. For a moment he continued to gaze at her.

Oh, Julian, tell her, tell her, Megan's mind willed him; tell her she's a cruel fiend, that she's set about making Alec ill since he was a boy, so that she could always have him to dominate; tell

39

her that she's robbing him of youth and strength, of friends and love. Oh, Julian, fight against her, for your own sake.

But in a moment, with a strengthless gesture of his hand, he looked away, almost furtively, and said, in his deep, quiet, toneless voice, "No, Veronica, I don't know what he meant. He was talking most erratically."

"I should think so," she said, wriggling her hard-set hair in a gratified manner. "I'm sure no one could understand such nonsense. And I tell you, Megan—"

Megan was standing now, only anxious to get away, the reason for her coming seeming of infinitesimal importance.

As she began to excuse herself, Alec suddenly said, "I do."

They all looked at him. He was lying with his hands locked behind his head, gazing at the ceiling, a smile on his lips. He rolled over and raised himself on his right elbow, looking at them with a bright, eager expression that Megan had seldom seen on his face.

"Yes, by Jove," he said. "I understand the fellow."

He swung himself off the bed.

"And now," he said, "I'm going to bed."

He looked very frail and ill as he stood before them. Putting a finger under Megan's chin, he tilted her head and kissed her on the lips, lightly.

"Good night, Megan," he said. Then, his voice edged with bitterness, he went on, "Don't worry—no germs. What I'm suffering from isn't catching."

As he walked towards the door, his mother rose with a wail of horror, and rushed after him; a moment later they heard his door slam, and the wailing grew louder as she called his name and begged him to let her in . . . his hot milk and brandy, his nasal drops.

Julian had risen and was standing dejectedly, fingering his pipe.

"Julian—oh, Julian." Megan's heart yearned with compassion for him. He looked at her oddly, an almost inimical expression in his eyes.

"I think perhaps you'd better go," he said.

40

His wife caught the last words as she whirled back into the room.

"Yes," she stormed, hysteria, rage, and fear in the hissing word. "Yes, go, you've done enough damage. I think everyone has gone mad."

Megan backed to the door, murmuring apologies half-heart-edly. Paul had left the door open, and she pulled it shut after her and ran down to the gate, where he was waiting for her. He was whistling the tune that Honor had sung, softly, as if remembering her singing it, and he seemed quite unconcerned. As he pulled the gate shut behind her, he took her arm companionably and started towards the roadway, but Megan drew back and faced him.

"Don't you think—?" But his surprised glance at her outraged expression bewildered her. "Aren't you even going to say you're sorry?"

"I wasn't," he said; "but I will if you like, if you're angry with me."

"If I'm angry! You come calmly into a house, to people you don't know, to friends of mine, and you create an awful situation and leave me to face it alone. And then you say 'if I'm angry'!"

"Would you rather I'd said nothing?"

"Would I rather! Of course." She looked at him, for the moment astonishingly uncertain of her anger; he was looking at her face, washed clear of colour by the moon, watching its changing expressions. She noticed how calm he looked; he seemed master of himself, as if he had escaped from his anxious mental tangle for a while. Suddenly she glimpsed the strength in him. If he had not had to suffer as he had done, if he were able to fight free of the bonds which, she knew, still shackled his mind, what a complete man he would be. She felt a nobility in him, and it made her less sure of herself than ever.

"You see, Megan"—his voice was kind, and he took her arm again as they stepped on to the road—"what I said tonight can't do any harm, and—you never know—it may do some good. Of course, the poor old boy—the husband—he's done for. He lost the struggle long ago; there's defeat all over him. But there's hope for the young chap, and if I'd not spoken I'd have felt

41

exactly as I would if I'd refused to help a fellow in the camp; you always got it in the neck for a bit, but you went on doing what seemed the decent thing."

"Paul, don't talk any more. Let me think about it." Her voice was blurred, and she held back the tears she was determined not to shed. They walked on slowly, in silence.

Megan felt sick and dazed with the suddenness of the change that had overtaken things so familiar to her. Words and images, tiny flashing memories, rushed through her mind. "The poor old boy—the husband." Was this her glorious Julian, whose glance, whose touch had made her wildly happy? "He's done for . . . he lost the struggle long ago." For a moment rage flared up, and she turned to Paul, longing to cry at him, "I love him— Julian! He's not old, he's not done for. He's everything in the world I long for!" But it wouldn't do. Something honest in her knew that she fought too strongly for her love-dream of Julian, and her image of him seemed to shrink. If only he had spoken when he should have—but he hadn't; he had miserably and meanly flattered the dreadful woman by saying what she expected of him. Rushing upon this came a comparison with the admirable way Paul had spoken. Not rudely. No, he hadn't been rude, but he'd made the whole situation devastatingly clear. In a few moments she had seen what had been there for her to see for years. And Alec had seen it, too. All at once she realized that Julian had always seen it, but had never had the strength to cope with it, and tonight he had felt angry only because he had been made to face his own inadequacy, had been made to acknowledge it before her, Megan. She remembered the almost ugly look in his eyes as he had advised her to go. Oh, Julian, Julian! Her mind clouded with sadness. How absurd she was, how unstable! After leaping into this mad, intoxicating love for Julian, after spending two months in feverish fancy, in ecstatic longing and imagining, now, faced for the first time with the need to defend the picture she had built up of the man she loved, she was too weak, too lacking in conviction, to maintain her faith in him. But it would come back, her dream of him; this was only an incident. Tomorrow she would have recovered from it—she must, she must. Her world could not revolve without

Julian. But even as she struggled with it, she knew that she had lost. There was no remedy for disillusionment; whatever remained of it all, rapture had gone. Her eyes filled and she sobbed. She turned to Paul, and he held her face against his jacket and soothed her; he was a stranger and yet he was the only person on earth she could bear to turn to now, in this misery of loss and confusion, and, though he had been responsible for it all, she no longer felt any anger towards him. He was good and fine, and she was deeply grateful to him, and when she could speak without making awful gulping noises, she said, "Paul, I'm glad you did it. It was important to, I think." And as he wiped her wet face and pushed back her dark hair, she told him what Alec had done after Paul had left.

"Good chap!" he said happily. "That's great news. She can put that in her clay pot and model it." And they both managed to laugh.

"Come on, we must hurry. Anthea will be there, and I'll have to creep in and wash my face. Oh, Paul"—Megan turned to look once more at him as they walked hastily across the paddock in front of Thornfield—"you're hardly restful, but you're awfully nice."

He laughed, looked quickly at his smashed watch, and then laughed again, quite heartily. Hurriedly they threaded their way through the wattles, stooped under the monkey puzzle and ran up the steps to the veranda.

VI

It was nearly nine when Anthea drove down the side road past Thornfield. If you wanted to drive into Thornfield you had to go in by the back road, through the double-barred gate, for there was no drive in the front. Anthea liked to come this way, for then she saw the place with the hills behind it, and on a night like this it would be lovely. When she had closed the gate behind her, she drove a little way across the paddock, and then stopped the engine. Numbed by the sudden silence, she stood

43

beside the car for a moment and looked towards the house. There were tall gums scattered here and there across the paddock, casting deep shadows. Still, unbelievably still. Over to the left she could hear Johnny snuffling gently at the grass, and far away there was a train. She began to walk towards the house, past two weather-beaten sheds, silvered splendidly tonight. Outside the white-railed fence, which marked off the kitchen garden from the paddock, a tall heap of neatly cut red wood stood as high as her shoulder; she stood there, remembering the day when Joady had disturbed a snake in the laundry. In a flash it had slithered out into the wood pile, and Adrian and James had spent all day moving the logs, one by one, in the dazzling January heat, while the women watched, neglecting duties urgently needing to be done. And then, at sunset, they'd found him. He had writhed out from under the last two logs, and Adrian had swung an axe, glinting sharply in the sunset rays, and the snake was vanquished. Joady had had lemonade and biscuits ready for everyone, and there had been great rejoicing, for a snake that had disappeared is a constant dread until he is found.

Iago bounded round the side of the house; he had been dozing in the abandoned fish pond, under the wistaria, but he didn't want that to become known, so he pretended to sniff suspiciously, as if he were on the alert for burglars, for he was most anxious to achieve a reputation as a good watchdog. Then he fussed round Anthea, making the amiable and ingratiating noises that sometimes gained him admission to the fire on very cold nights. He knew that this was not a very cold night, but there was no harm in trying. To his joy it worked, and he walked most decorously behind Anthea, into the kitchen; then, as she appeared preoccupied with Joady, he sidled past her and went very slowly and sedately up the hall to the living room, rather more than nervous of his reception there. To his surprise, no one noticed him, so, bowing and scraping, he crept forward to the white mat, where he seated himself and prepared to listen to the conversation. He knew that at suppertime someone would remember his biscuits. He was a contented dog.

Anthea found Joady cutting a cake into slices on the white-scrubbed kitchen table, beside a tray laden with supper things.

44

Before she had time to alter it, Anthea noticed the unusually troubled expression on Joady's face. Anxiety raced through her mind.

"Hullo, Joady dear."

Joady's quick smile did little to ease her mind. There was something; she was going to have to face something.

"Hullo, Anthea. Came in the back gate, did you?"

"Yes—just wanted to smell the paddock. I met Jenkins out there. He's a silver cat tonight."

"He's a devil any night," said Joady. "Go on in, dear. I'll be in later."

Everything was as usual, of course. Silly, jumpy little worries were always eating at her now. But Joady had been quiet. Anthea went up the hall, warm and welcoming with its rose-pink light, and entered the living room. They were sitting side by side, and the delight in their eyes overwhelmed her, as they looked up. Oh! If she ever lost them, this place. . . .

"Here she is," James said gladly. "Lord, you look lovely tonight. Doesn't she, Mary?"

"Anthea is beautiful." Mary gazed at her lovingly.

She stood smiling down at them. She wore a white woollen frock, square-necked, short-sleeved, with colours worked brightly at the neck and the slit-pockets of the skirt, gathered softly at the waist. Her shoes were scarlet, flat-heeled, her short-sleeved cardigan dark green. Her dark hair was drawn softly above small ears and coiled at the back of her head; grey eyes looked steadily, almost sternly, from beneath long, dark brows. The face was thin, a little too pale, and the lips were perhaps too firmly set. But Anthea was beautiful.

"What's the matter here tonight?" she asked them gently.

Mary Carmichael put out her hand and pulled Anthea towards her.

"Sit down here with me, dear," she said, and Anthea sank on to the sofa, sitting stiffly on the edge, still smiling, but watchfully now, very tense.

"We've had a visitor, Anthea," James's voice was a little more blurred than usual. "A young man who was with Adrian. He seems to have been a very close friend of Adrian's."

45

His face wavered before her in a way that made her feel sick; she closed her eyes momentarily, and the sick thudding of her heart grew heavier. I knew I couldn't escape, she thought. He'll know—perhaps he's even read the letter. How silly all the struggle had been. One never escapes. I don't deserve to escape—but I love them all and they'll suffer again, everyone will suffer because of me.

"We should have rung you," said Mary, stroking her hand remorsefully, "but it seemed better to wait until you came. Oh, Anthea, dear—"

"No, darling—no, Mary." The effort of speaking helped her to come back to them. "It's nothing. What is his name? And what is he like?" Anything, so that they would talk while she pulled her mind round to face the situation.

"His name's Paul Quentin, and he's a very nice thing—a good deal younger than Adrian, we think." Mary continued to clasp Anthea's hand in hers while she spoke. "He hasn't had a great deal to say. He's in a very nervous state, I imagine, and he seems to have something that's troubling his mind. For a long time he's quite cheerful and pleasant; and then some little thing seems to upset him and he'll begin to tremble. And sometimes I've seen tears in his eyes. But there's something rather fine about him— the girls seem quite taken with him; Megan has taken him over to the Kyleses' place. They should be back any moment."

Anthea leant back and looked at them, and then down at Iago, who half rose and bowed apologetically, hoping that she wasn't going to take exception to him. Then Anthea, the cool, efficient one, Anthea, who had never wept before them or showed her feelings—Anthea leant forward and grasped James's hand and said, in a ragged, broken, pleading voice, "Darlings—Mary, James—you do love me, don't you?"

Mary was shocked; a sudden moment of realization made her aware of a strangeness in her home tonight, and she felt lost and uneasy. She felt that it was all connected with the coming of this boy—but in what way? There was nothing very unusual in his visit. In her confusion of mind she sat silent, gazing with troubled concern at Anthea.

46

James pulled Anthea to him with his sound hand, so strongly that she sank to her knees at his feet.

"We love you most dearly, Anthea. You've been son and daughter to us, and we're grateful just because you exist—and because you're among us."

And Mary murmured, "Dear Anthea—dear little Anthea."

For a moment she stayed, gazing from one to the other, and then she sprang to her feet as voices sounded, footsteps running up the steps and across the veranda. When Paul came in from the hall she was standing composedly in front of the fireplace, nudging Iago gently with one foot.

VII

Wonderful, Paul thought, as James introduced them and he shook hands with her, how unmoved he was at the sight of her. It was most fortunate that the whole thing affected him so little; he expected that he would feel just as impersonal about the children when he saw them. There was no warmth at all in his thoughts of them; they seemed less real in his mind than the others; Megan, for example, or little, lovely Honor. It was as if Anthea and her children were beings removed from him, set aside behind a veil of some substance impermeable to feeling, and he realized now how much more difficult it would have been if he hadn't been protected by this indifference. He was pleased with Anthea's beauty and her gracious presence, but he felt no enthusiasm, no feelings of revenge or pity. He seated himself, at Mary's bidding, beside her on the sofa, and Anthea continued to stand, looking down at them from the fireplace.

He has a beautiful head, she thought, and his face is finely formed, sensitive, clever. The expression in his eyes was unfathomable; they didn't come to an increased animation when his lips smiled. It would be difficult to find out what he knew, but somehow she must do it; but warily, carefully. She must get him away from them—and soon. Tonight. The feeling came to her strongly that this was no casual, friendly visit; he was here

47

with some definite purpose, for he was not the type of person to pay unimportant calls. She had a sense of urgency, that time was short, that she must be quick.

Joady came in carrying the supper tray. Paul stood up and took the tray from her while she went back to the kitchen for the coffee. When she returned Mary said, "The girls should be helping. Where's Megan, Paul?"

"She went straight up to her room," he said.

They could hear her running down the stairs and up the hall, and when she came in she was flushed and inclined to talk too readily to everyone. Silently, Honor drifted in from the hallway, a long mauve chiffon scarf draped, sari-fashion, about her head and shoulders. Everyone stared, and Anthea said, abruptly, "Why?"

"Oh, it expresses my mood," said Honor, beginning to sink back languidly into a chair.

"No you don't, my lady," Joady said firmly. "You get up and do some handing round, and mind you don't fall and break your neck with that dingle-dongle thing."

There was a burst of laughter, some of it a little hysterical; but Paul's laugh was loud and hearty. Honor was far above bearing malice, and she lost none of her effect as she waited on them, gently swirling her draped veil as she handed buttered scones and cups of coffee. Then she pulled up a low stool and sat, leaning her head against her father's knee, remote from them all. Soon they became silent. After a moment James spoke, as he began to fill his pipe.

"Will you tell us what you can about Adrian, Paul?" he asked quietly.

"What do you know already?" Paul's voice had changed; it was deeper, the lightness gone from it; but there was no sign of uneasiness or reluctance.

"Only that he died of illness," James replied. "Is there anything else to know?"

"Yes," Paul said thoughtfully. "Yes, there's plenty. You'll hear more about it later, I should think. Adrian will certainly get a posthumous award."

48

They all looked at him. Honor untied her sari and rolled full-length on the carpet, her chin supported on her hands.

"Why?" she said.

"Because Adrian was a brave man. If he hadn't been, he might have saved his own life—though I don't know. You see . . . I'd better start right back, I think."

For more than an hour they listened to him, while his voice went on evenly, telling of suffering so terrible that it seemed impossible that the frail, delicate mechanism of a man's body could endure it. He told them of the first trip in the Japanese ship that took them to Moulmein, of the filth and the dysentery, the thirst and the heat; of the trip by cattle truck to Utakiang, and then the march deep into the jungle to the railway camp, the first of many such marches, deeper and deeper into the jungle. In a calmly unmoved voice he told them of the settling down to starvation, illness, persecution, and death. He seemed almost exhilarated by the memory of it, by the recalling of incidents of careless heroism, of men, doomed to die, who could laugh and help others who were farther along the road to death. It was at Utakiang that he had formed his firm friendship with Adrian, who was fighting a mad, desperate fight to maintain a hospital, which consisted of squalid huts, insanely crowded with dying men, lying on bamboo slats, tortured by swirling red dust, sick men without the solace of bedding or bandages, antiseptics or food.

"I was sent down to this so-called 'base hospital' because of the festering sores which were spreading all over my legs, and for four months I was there. Adrian worked like a madman. . . ."

Pictures of Adrian came to them as they listened; Adrian refusing to allow dying men to be taken from their beds to build the accursed railway; Adrian protesting, demanding, defying; Adrian lying in mud and his own blood, smashed by the rifle butt of a comically conceited little Japanese camp commander; Adrian, half-delirious with malaria, climbing weakly from his bed to tend those who would never leave their beds again.

"Apart from the sores and a bout of dengue, I wasn't too bad, and I helped him as much as I could. I was always afraid for him, for he was recklessly fearless. Then I went back to the jungle, and we didn't meet again until July 1943, when Adrian came up to the camp hospital where I was. We were nearing the end of our tether by then, and the men were dying like flies; I was down with dysentery when he arrived. He was very good to me, the thing they called a hospital was only a filthy death house, but Adrian set to work just as he had done before. . . .

"For some months he had kept up his fight, but there was a drink-maddened little camp commander there, whose brutalities were on such a gigantic scale that, for the first time, I met men who were glad to die, who were willing to risk the torture and death that inevitably followed on the slightest suspicion of attempting to escape. One night the camp commander, rolling and crazed with drink, lurched into the hospital hut while Adrian was there, and shrieked for the men to stand to attention and salute him. Two men, delirious and dying, were too far gone from this world even to understand that he was there, and he ordered the guards to force them up. They were kicked and bashed and held up to attention, their heads lolling forward, jaws dropping, eyes rolling; then the little Jap smashed his rifle butt into the mouth of one of them, breaking his jaw and shattering the bones of his face. Something must have broken in Adrian, for he leapt at the camp commander and brought him down. . . ."

Paul's voice trailed off and he stopped speaking.

"Go on," said Mary Carmichael, in a whisper.

"There was only one answer to that," he said slowly. "They tortured him till he died—he lived for nine days—until the twentieth of November 1943."

They sat still for a time, almost oblivious of each other. Mary Carmichael felt the memory of Adrian surging into her mind, bracing her, strengthening her. Strange that the knowledge of his supreme suffering should have the power to do this; now she was able to face the fact of his death, now she wouldn't shrink when his name was mentioned. She realized that, in some vague way, she had been trying to keep him alive in her mind; she had refused to contemplate his dying, and so she had hidden from it. But there was something invigorating about the

50

manner of his death; it was not the mere passive sinking into nothingness that "death from illness" had conveyed to her. He had died in a last vigorous fight against the unbearable, and, from beyond death, he had been able, through this lad, to lift that sickening blankness from her memory of him. It was the lively, fiery Adrian she had always known that she'd seen again tonight, and she felt that now she could let him go, she could say good-bye to him tranquilly.

Anthea's mind fluttered with thoughts like beating wings. But how did they torture him? I must find out, I must know. Ah, Adrian, your face and body were so beautiful! Were you hideous, bloodstained and pain-maddened when you died? Oh, God forgive me, did you get the letter? Because, if you did, you knew worse torture than ever those brutes could devise for you. And I, who loved you, who love you so sadly and wildly now— I had the power to make you suffer as no one else could. If only . . . But this man, this Paul, would know. She must find out from him, find out about the letter. What madness had made her write it? What insane, childhood-instilled strain of honesty had driven her hand to the pen? I must have wanted to hurt him, in my heart, she thought. But no, I didn't, I didn't. I was merely selfish. I wanted to exorcise my own devil, so that I might live at peace with myself, and I didn't try to spare his pain. I could betray Adrian with Howard, but I couldn't deceive him. That seemed the ultimate crime against him, then; but now I know that undeceiving him was the greatest wrong I could have done him.

In that fantastic riot of feeling, her judgments had gone astray, values had toppled, and everything about her had become unfamiliar and unrecognizable; and when the mists had cleared and things had come grimly and bleakly back into perspective, it was too late: the letter had been sent and, as she had feared for four dreadful years, had probably been received. Since then, silence and the solitary dread in her own heart, a fear she could communicate to no one. But this thing could still rise from beyond the grave and strike her down, rob her of the love and respect that surrounded her at Thornfield and make her scorned by these people who meant everything in the world to her and to whom she was so important. She shivered at the thought of their changed expressions if they knew—knew that she had tortured Adrian for two years, whereas the Japs had only done so for nine days. There were only two people she had to fear: Howard, and this Paul Quentin. Howard would have to wait; if there was any solution to that problem but the unthinkable one he suggested, then it hadn't come to her yet. But she would fight; she wasn't going to give in without a struggle, and she would start tonight by making sure of this Paul.

Honor stroked Iago's soft ear with one hand, leaning on one elbow on the white rug, her hair screening her face. Most of the children in a family are children at the same time, she thought; but Adrian was sixteen when I was born; he was always grown-up, too old to be brother, too young to be parent. He was something between, something splendid and handsome and exciting. I've never felt very young, she thought; children always seemed young to me. I was always closer to Adrian's world than, say, Megan's. There had been an inspiration in him; he had always satisfied a longing in her for the colourful, the heroic in the people she knew; he had possessed the same qualities of strength and fineness as she had found in Hester Laing, and even in the manner of his dying he had left something vivid and unforgettable to her, something that would help her to urge herself forward in emulation of the standards he had set himself.

And Joady saw a little solemn-eyed fellow, staggering on bowed legs, saying "Joady." He gave me the only name I've known for thirty years, she thought. And as he stepped into the car that night when he went away, elegant and impressive in his khaki, he'd looked at her and said "Joady," and the years had rushed together, telescoped. She bent her head.

Megan saw her world anew. Things seemed absurdly small, trivially unimportant; her all-absorbing adoration of Julian was negligible, her little triumph in winning her scholarship pitiable. A sickening scorn for herself filled her mind.

James lit his pipe expertly with his twisted hand. I've become too self-centred, he thought, too careful; I can struggle much harder than this. If he could struggle like that, for months and

52

months, against hopeless and appalling difficulties, amidst filth and brutality and disease, surely I can do better than this, surrounded by loving attention and expert medical care. I'll be back at my job in a month, he vowed to himself; I'll relieve Anthea of this burden she's been bearing for me. I'll give her back to her children, Adrian's children, and I'll train someone to take my place this time, so that when the next stroke comes she won't feel obliged to go back. I can at least do this for Adrian.

And Paul was finishing the story in his mind. They dragged Adrian out and tied him to a tree, and in the hut the men could hear the blows; then Adrian shouted to them, to him, Paul, not to come near him, not to try to help him—and all the next day he was tied there, lolling across the ropes that held him to the tree. Then they had dug a hole, right in front of the hut door, and they'd half-filled it with water; and there Adrian had stayed until he died. The little rats had given him just enough food and water to keep him alive, so that the others might learn to the full the lesson of the punishment that awaited any who dared to lay hands on one of the exalted race. He remembered the nights, when he used to crawl from the hut and lie flat on the ground beside Adrian, stroking the poor battered head, whispering to him, moistening the swollen lips; and he remembered Adrian telling him, in the sullen silence of the last night when he was able to speak coherently, of the children, his children, of how he had longed to live, so that he might return and take them away from the man Anthea had chosen instead of him. Adrian had told him the story long ago, when they had been at Utakiang, and Paul had marvelled then that a woman could reject the strength and the beauty, the wit and the grace of Adrian, and give herself to a man so much less important, so crude and cheap as this Howard seemed to be. And on that last night, Adrian had whispered:

"I tell you, Paul, I'd rather kill them, strangle them with my own hands, than let them grow up with that swine as their father."

The next night his mind had been wandering, and he'd sometimes shout and sometimes mutter unintelligibly; and the guards were active, so Paul had crept back into the hut. In the

53

morning Adrian was in a coma, just an unrecognizable thing; eyes sightless, jaw gaping; mud-spattered, filthy. Some time during the night he had died, and his body had just been thrown away. Sick men had wept that day, for Adrian, and the gloom had never quite lifted from the camp.

It was strange, though, that he had not realized then what he had to do for Adrian; the endless toil and misery of days and weeks and years had gone on and Paul had continued to endure, had even learnt to laugh again. Then the air raids by Allied planes had begun, and early in 1945 he was at Chantagong, when it had been smashed by Liberators. There was a bomb dump inside the camp, which would have blown them all to pieces if it had caught fire, so he had got together a few of the men and they'd fought the fire round the dump, and it was just as they were feeling safe that something had exploded. He hadn't been badly hurt, but there had been an enormous flash, he remembered, and the world had burst asunder beneath him as he was flung into the air.

After that things had been different; after that Adrian had come back and had been almost always with him. It was a great pleasure to be with him again and they had had long talks; it was then that he had promised Adrian that he would come back and strangle the children for him, and Adrian had been pleased. He hadn't been too clearly aware of his surroundings after the bombing, because most of his time had been taken up in talking to Adrian, and he'd found it hard to understand other people for a time; but the war seemed to end very quickly, and soon he was home again with his loving family and kindly friends, who bewildered him because they seemed to live in another world and he could hardly make them understand him. The awful thing was that Adrian had left him as soon as he had returned home to the quiet station homestead, and he had felt terribly alone; then Adrian had come back—but at night, when Paul was asleep. (Though his mind revolted sickly from the contemplation of it, he forced his thought on.) But this Adrian was dead, always; he was always staring out at Paul from a thickly massed wall of jungle undergrowth, and the heavy, hot smell was there; and the trees and the vines were moving and alive, and the tendrils would come writhing towards Paul, into his head, deeply into his brain. Adrian's eyes were glassy, and he looked just as he had looked on that last day. And as soon as Paul went to sleep Adrian would be there and Paul would wake, shouting and raving and screaming in terror, for this vision of Adrian almost reminded him of something, something which, if he ever remembered it, would destroy him utterly. Though he did not know what it was, he knew that the memory of it was lying quietly, somewhere in his mind, and he knew, with a horrifying certainty, that once he recognized it, it would rise and strike him down, rob him of his sanity and his grip on life. And every night when Adrian came thus, the danger was increased; so far he had managed always to wake himself in time, but every time the memory came closer and the dread in his mind increased.

His days came to be spent in longing for Adrian to come and in dreading that he would come at night; so he began to work out little ways of walking and tapping his fingers and arranging things in patterns, which he was convinced were a help. Then, one day, realization came to him, and he knew why Adrian was doing this. He had been riding across a paddock at the time, and, immediately he had swung his horse round and had ridden back to the house; he had gone in to pack, so that he could come to Ambara at once and carry out the promise he'd made to Adrian. He remembered running joyfully down the stairs to tell his mother that he must go away. She had agreed without any argument, and she and his father had said they would drive him in to the station. There had been a strange man, a serious-looking fellow, in the back of the car with him, but he was so happy that he hadn't minded that. But they hadn't taken him to the station; they'd driven him to Sydney, to some sort of hospital or sanatorium, and he'd been watched and forced to stay there. The cruelty of it—the treachery! And Adrian had come that night.

Then they began to give him treatment—shock treatment, they called it—and it had terrified him more than anything, for it made him forget, for a long time, what he had to do. He was always terribly anxious, even while he couldn't remember, for

55

he knew there was something he should have been remembering, and at these times they said he was improving and everyone was delighted; then, after a while, he would remember, and Adrian would come again when he was asleep and they'd say he'd had a relapse and they'd give him more treatment. At last they had let him go home, and things were different again. Adrian didn't come at all then, but Paul knew that that was because Adrian was such an understanding chap and he realized that Paul just couldn't get away at once. However, he'd been better, as they called it, for so long this time that they'd granted his wish, and so he had got away at last; but he knew that this week end was his very last chance. If he didn't succeed now, then Adrian would come back to his dreams and they'd say he was worse again and he'd never get another opportunity. They'd lock him up for good this time.

But today everything had turned out well; as soon as he had arrived Adrian had come back to him. He felt aware of Adrian's gay, friendly presence everywhere, and he was tremendously happy to be here. He wished that he could tell them all—tell Megan, anyway—about what he had to do for Adrian; it would have been a heavenly relief, but he knew that they coudn't see things his way and they might try to stop him. And whatever happened, nothing must stop him. Nothing. But these people were wonderful; he liked them all, and the end of the whole dreadful business was in sight. He sighed happily and smiled round at them.

Joady rose from her chair and hurried outside, and the spell of their thoughts, which had kept them sitting there, was broken. Mary Carmichael stood up.

"Good night, Paul," she said, her eyes smiling gently up at him as he stood, his hand caught in hers. "Thank you for telling us. It's been a strain for you, we all know that—and we'll always be grateful to you."

She went to James and began to help him to his feet, and Megan ran to open the door and called down the hall to Joady. James's face was bright and he looked at Paul with a considering eye. By Jove!—he'd do. This lad would do splendidly, if only he had no other plans. How he'd love to have the young chap with him! It would be a good thing for Paul, too, in the years to come; it was a splendid business, and it hadn't lost anything since Anthea had been running it.

"Good night, lad; I'll see you in the morning. There's something I'd like to talk over with you. Oh, Anthea"—she roused herself and made an effort to smile at him—"can you come down tomorrow, Anthea? We can't talk now, but there are some very important things."

"Yes, James," she said, but her voice was vague. "Yes. I'll ring tomorrow. I'll let you know. Good night, now. . . ."

In a moment they had dispersed; Megan said good night soberly, but Honor suddenly sprang up, and, running across the room, threw her arms round Paul and held him tightly, then as suddenly she was gone, and they were alone. Anthea said, in a stiff aloof voice, "Everybody seems to want to talk to you about something, but—"

The wide grey eyes looked up to his and there was a wild distress in them. He looked at her in silence, waiting.

"Well"—she looked down at her watch as she spoke—"It's only just after eleven. . . ." Suddenly he looked at his wrist and she saw that his watch was broken; he glanced at it in a pleased way and then swung his attention back to her, as she went on. "Would you care to drive up to Cedar Hill with me for a drink? I'll run you back later on. I must talk to you."

"Of course," he said. "Yes, I'll come; but how about here?"

"Thornfield's never locked—you can come in any time."

"Well," he said, "I'll just have to get some things before they go to bed."

"I'll wait for you out at the car." She walked quickly from the room.

He went up the stairs to his room. The light beside the bed shone softly on the green quilt, the down-turned sheets; there was a gown lying across the bed, pyjamas lay neatly folded on the pillow; slippers, toothbrush, shaving tackle, a book, water in a glass jug winking in the light—everything was there, even to the trim riding clothes for the morning. Joady knew what a man needed in order to feel comfortable and at home. He switched off the light. White muslin curtains, frilling at the

57

edge, hung gently at the window, and, outside, the quiet autumn night enfolded Ambara; the hills rose above the pale mistiness, folding and billowing with huge shadowy patches, under the moon. Paul went out, closing the door quietly behind him, and hurried down the stairs and out through the kitchen to the paddock and to Anthea, waiting beside the car.

VIII

He stood under the great white-stemmed paperbark tree, holding the gate open, as Anthea swung the car through; and then, closing the gate, he climbed in beside her and she drove slowly along the little back road. When they turned into the made road she drove swiftly and they made no attempt at conversation.

There was scarcely a light in Ambara at that late hour; they seemed to be committing an error of form in being abroad, in not yet having completed their day, and the noise of the car was an intrusion on the stillness. Peaceful folk, with quiet minds, can go early to bed, Anthea thought, and it was testimony to the wild confusion that had entered her own life that she should be in this situation, driving a stranger through this silent place in a vain effort to bring herself some comfort. For it would be vain, she felt sure. This man had no peace to offer her.

Far off to the left a light shone through the mist. That would be Croft's place. There was another poor woman with a frantic mind, her wretched problem insoluble; and perhaps these houses, softly hidden behind their trees, held many people who lay watchfully, striving in their minds to deal with things beyond their capabilities. At the level-crossing she stopped, and, before she could ask him, Paul jumped out and opened the gates. Now they raced along between smooth paddocks, tree-dotted; the planks of the white bridge, with its almost equally white gums overarching it, rattled under the wheels, and they began to climb into the hills, winding up to the right, to the main road. Anthea pulled the car sharply across the road, and they drove slowly down the steep little drive to the open door, through which light beamed on the porch.

Anthea closed the porch door and led the way in to the sitting room. She switched on two shaded table lamps, one on a ledge near a cushioned window seat, the other on a low table just inside the door into the hall; then she went to the cabinet by the wall near the window and took out some glasses.

"Do sit down," she said. "What will you drink? Sherry?"

"Yes, thank you," Paul answered.

She brought the tray across, and set it down on the table he pulled forward for her. Then she sat before him on the window seat.

"This is a nice room," he said; "but it doesn't look as if any-one lives in it much."

"No," she answered. "There's no time to stay long in one place. And besides, it's not very pleasant, anyway, if one's thoughts are unrestful."

As she leant forward to offer him a cigarette from the little enamelled box, she said, "You know, don't you? Adrian told you . . . about me."

In the moment's pause while he drew on his cigarette, she prayed wildly: let him be puzzled, bewildered, God; let him think I'm mad; let him ask me what on earth I mean. . . . But, quite calmly, he said, "Yes—yes, he told me," and coldness swept over her. She sat still, her eyes lowered.

"Then . . . he did get the letter?"

"Yes."

She looked up and met his eyes.

"When—when did he get it?"

"About a year after you'd sent it. Several of the men had letters while we were in the various railway camps."

"Did he ever get any more—any other letters from me?"

"No. Some of the chaps did—it was better in some camps—but we never got any more."

She swung round and leant her arm on the window ledge, her head resting on her hand; she pushed her hair back wearily from her forehead.

"Was it . . . did it make him suffer?"

59

"Yes," Paul said, as if the matter held little interest for him. "I think it made things very hard for him."

Her control broke and she jumped up, her hands clenched.

"Don't sit there saying the things I dread to hear." She managed to keep her agonized voice low-pitched. "Haven't you any feeling about it—about him—about Adrian?"

"Yes." He seemed surprised at her outburst. "Yes, of course I have."

"I'm sorry." She sank back and leant against the cushion. "Will you listen while I tell you? There's never been anyone to tell it to. Will you let me tell you about it?"

As she began, rapidly at first and then more falteringly, it sounded quite unfamiliar to her, this unlikely story. It seemed as if it were some other woman she was describing, some inexplicable creature, whose actions and emotions were without coherence or reason; not the capable, the reserved, the aloof Anthea Carmichael, respected wife of a rising young medico. And indeed the whole thing had always been like that; she had never been able to explain any of it to herself.

"He was, and is, an utterly worthless person. I knew very soon, but a craziness came over me. I had to be with him. I didn't love him. I've loved Adrian since I was a girl and I still love him. All my interests were with him, all my pride was in him and my children. And yet I had to be with him, with Howard. . . ."

Each time she had left him she had felt sick with distaste; but she had only to be an hour away from him and every feeling left her save the mad desire to see him again.

"Adrian had been away for more than a year when I first met him. He's a singer; I went with the McGilvrays, one night, to a recital he gave at the Conservatorium. He was good—that's the one worth-while thing about him, his music. They knew him, and we went round afterwards and then on to supper. Since that night I've never known peace of any kind—that was in September—September 1941. He never really cared for me, I know, but he pretended that he did. I've plenty of money of my own, you know, and he soon found that out and I began to pour it out on him. It was the only thing which interested him; I quite literally bought my way in. . . ."

Her face was white with disgust, and she pressed her clenched fists to her eyes for a moment, leaning her elbows on her knees and rocking a little, to and fro, as she recollected details and incidents. But it had made no difference to her feeling, to this insane longing to see him and to be with him.

"I don't know yet what attracted me to him; he's nothing that I've ever admired, physically or mentally, and I suffered cruelly with disgust for myself. Always I felt disgraced and a bit unclean; I wouldn't touch the children, or kiss them. Cassie was wonderful; she did everything for them and for me. She used to wait up for me; sometimes I wouldn't get home till daylight, sometimes I didn't come at all. And Cassie lied for me to the people at Thornfield and to the children, and never asked me a question. And when I came home, exhausted and wretched—and already longing to go back to him—she'd soothe me and get me to bed. I managed to keep up appearances somehow with the people I knew—did some war work, helped to organize money-making functions in the village here—but my whole life was swallowed up in the longing to be with him."

There had never been any happiness in it for her; they had always quarrelled and he had used his hold over her to humiliate her in a hundred ways. It was three months of utter and complete wretchedness—and over it all was the bitter guilt in her heart because of Adrian. If only he had been there, if only he had been able to get leave.

Then had come the news that his unit was to be transferred from the Middle East to another battle zone. She had convinced herself that he was coming home, and she had wavered between the wildest joy and despair. She had nerved herself to tell him, to beg his understanding and his mercy, to implore his help to cure herself of the madness that was destroying her. Finally, distraught with guilt and dread, unable to bear the waiting, she had written it all to him, told him everything, transferred the burden to him. And he had not come home; he had been sent to Java. Singapore had fallen and silence had closed over Adrian. For four years she had fretted and mourned over that letter; the

61

writing of it had been quite unnecessary, for almost at once she had begun to come to her senses; the shock of realizing the bitter harm she had done to Adrian seemed to restore her balance—or perhaps it was simply the fact that Adrian knew that had helped her to fight her way back. She didn't know. Then she had begun to hope that perhaps he had never received the letter, that it had been lost, with thousands of other letters; she had pursued every line of inquiry, but no one could tell her for certain about the chaotic mail deliveries. She had written to the wives and mothers of other prisoners, but they also had had nothing to tell her.

She had broken entirely with Howard, had come back to Ambara and had taken up her life again. She had assumed once more the quiet dignity of Anthea Carmichael, the young widow of Major Adrian Carmichael, and no one, except Cassie, had ever known of that evil time when she had been lost and desolate in an alien world where no one respected her and where, finally, she had lost respect for herself. When James Carmichael had been paralysed by a stroke she had thankfully taken over the managing of the large and prosperous bookshop and, guided and tutored by James, had slaved day and night to make a success of it. In this way she had almost won her way back to peace. Never completely, however, for the hideous blunder of writing the letter was always there in her mind, and to be alone was torture to her. And now, tonight, she knew that everything she had dreaded for so long had happened. . . . She stopped speaking and gazed dully at Paul, looking pitifully defenceless as she waited for him to speak.

"This man," he said suddenly. "Do you ever see him now?"

She continued to look at him as if the physical effort of shaping words with her lips was almost beyond her; then she sighed—a sigh in which there was a shudder somewhere, a terrible sigh that ended in a moan.

"No," she said, "but I'll have to soon. He's threatening me now."

"Threatening? How?"

"He's had a long series of misfortunes. He fell ill while he was on tour in New Zealand—some throat infection—and he

62

couldn't fulfil a number of engagements. Things have been going very badly for him for a long while, and now he's looking for some security; a month ago he rang me and told me—he told me—" Her voice faltered and she went on almost in a whisper, "He said I must marry him. He wants to come to live here—here, at Cedar Hill, Adrian's home, with my lovely children. And he says that if I refuse he'll tell them at Thornfield; he says he'll disgrace me and the children."

Her eyes were large and filled with terror as she finished. There was a pause, and for a moment Paul frowned down at his hands; then he looked up and she was astounded to see a smile on his face, an easy, confident smile: he seemed like a person much older than she was, though he must be years younger.

"That sort of talk is easy to deal with, surely," he said.

"I can see no way of dealing with it," Anthea said. "What can I say?"

"Lord!" He laughed aloud. "Blackmailers are the simplest people in the world to outbluff. Just tell him to go straight ahead, and that you have placed the matter in the hands of your lawyer, who is going to take legal action immediately. Tell him to expect the police at any minute. It's all a bluff, of course, but he'd fall for it. Anyway, you might ask your lawyer's advice, if you have a helpful one; he'll certainly advise you about it. But the main thing is to take the aggressive line."

Some kind of heaviness lifted from her mind as she listened. If this were true—but it couldn't be. She deserved her punishment and she would be forced to endure it; but oh, if only it were possible!

"Will you promise to do that?"

"Yes," she said, urgently, "if you think it would be of any use. Yes, I'll ring tomorrow and make an appointment to see him on Monday. Would I—would it be necessary"—the words came with difficulty—"I wouldn't have to see him, Howard, would I?"

"Perhaps. I don't know. You'd have to leave the details to your lawyer. Why particularly don't you want to see him?"

"Just distaste, and embarrassment." There was a pause while

63

she sat, with her head lowered, and then she forced her gaze up to meet his.

"No, that's not true—or it's not all the truth," she said stiffly. "Really, I'm frightened to meet him. I'm terrified that it might happen again and that, while I was with him, I might give in, I might be like I was before with him. When we parted, you see, he didn't want me, he had no reason to try to keep me with him; I'd put him on his feet, financially, for the time being, and he never plans far ahead. But now, he's in desperate need and he'll do everything. I hate him now; I've hated us both ever since; but supposing I began to feel like that again? I can't imagine that it could ever happen again—but it might; after all, I could never have imagined the original situation. I might agree to his plans and then he'd be here, here in my home—and my children . . ." Her hands twisted round her handkerchief and she begged him with her eyes for reassurance.

Paul glanced at his broken watch, and when, after a moment, he spoke, his voice was quite calm. "I don't know about that," he said, looking away from her. "You'd have to put it strongly to the lawyer chap. I imagine those fellows know how to arrange things. I'd better go now, I think."

They stood up, and for a moment things were unsteady before her eyes. At the door he turned. "Can I come up and see the children tomorrow?" he asked abruptly.

"Of course. Come about eleven."

"Will you need the car before then?"

"No," she said. "No, I won't need it. Why?"

"I'll drive myself down in it, then, and bring it back in the morning, shall I? That's if you don't mind? You can get to bed. It's well after one o'clock, I should think."

"Yes." They were on the porch now, and Anthea stood looking up at him. "Thank you."

"Don't," he said, and there was only indifference in his voice. "Please don't."

He swung into the car and slammed the door. In a moment he was gone, the sound of the car echoing and vibrating on the silence of the night. Anthea went in and closed the door, and a moment later the porch light went off.

3

SATURDAY MORNING

∼৵৵৹৵৲৺৲∽

I

THE days began early at Thornfield. Paul had been lying awake
for some minutes, his hands clasped under his head, wondering
what the time could be, when he heard the chime of the hall
clock and then six brisk, cheerful strokes. He looked at his
watch affectionately; it was no use just now for telling him the
time, but it could tell him much more than the most efficient
watch. It had taken a great weight from his mind, and he felt
that he could relax much more because of it. Instead of always
having to keep his mind concentrated on one thing for fear
he should forget, he was able to think freely of a hundred
things, to rejoice in his happiness, to contemplate all the people
he had met here and meditate about them; and then a glance
at the smashed glass reminded him easily and without giving
him any unpleasant shock.

The curtains blew gently into the room, and the scent of
citrus blossom came to him. The orchard would look lovely at
this early hour. He was on the point of getting up to look from
the window, when there was a knock at his door, and when he
called, "Come in," Honor walked in and sat on the end of his
bed.

"Come for a ride and a swim?" she asked.

He gazed up at her. Her hair was smoothly combed, pale-
gold and gleaming; her white silk pyjamas were covered by a
wrap of navy-blue satin, mannish, trim, and sophisticated; her
hands were rammed deep in the pockets, and she wiggled one

foot in a heel-less scarlet slipper; her face was gently flushed, the pale skin almost blue at the temples and beneath her eyes.

"You're very beautiful this morning," Paul said.

Composedly, she answered, "Yes, I am good-looking; I seem to get better looking each year. You look nice yourself this morning—not so grim." She twisted her face into a hideous, frowning grimace. "Not like yesterday."

"Did I look like that?" he said.

"Practically," she said indulgently. "But I didn't mind; I think it suits your lean, hawklike type to appear grim."

"Of course," Paul said, rolling over on his side and gazing out through the curtains, "that's why I do it: to attract and fascinate snow maidens like you. It's a wonderful morning."

She came to the window.

"See over there," she said, pointing across the orchard to a thick little forest of young wattles away across the paddock.

"M'mm," he said.

"That's part of Trent's place. Ted and Maurice Trent bought that place and Ted brought his wife there, before the war. They started a flower farm. It was a lovely place. They did it awfully thoroughly—developed the ground, had a sprinkler system—everything; and they were doing very well. Then both men went to the war, and the wattles moved in and took possession of the beautiful soil and the comfortably cultivated beds. I'm sure no wattles have ever lived in such luxury, and in the early spring it's a glory; it's one mass of gold and everybody admires it. People who don't know come and compliment poor Marcia Trent on her lovely wattles, not knowing she hates them; they've devoured her flower farm."

"Are they—the men—coming back to it?" Paul asked.

"Ted's not coming back," said Honor shortly, "and there'll be no flower farm for Maurice. He lost a leg and an arm."

Silently they contemplated the deceptively beautiful little grove of young wattles for a moment. Then Paul said slowly, "That's rather a terrible little story."

"Isn't it?" Honor said. "If I let myself I could brood about it and do something crazy, like burning them to the ground. But that's just one thing the war's done which doesn't bear

66

thinking about. Come on," she went on, moving towards the door. "You're only trying to keep me talking because you want to laze in bed all day."

"Me!" he exclaimed indignantly. "You come into my room and delay me, swanking about your exquisite beauty—"

"You!" she said icily. "Why, you're not even ugly; you're simply commonplace." And she was gone.

There was no one about when he came hurrying downstairs; he went out through the kitchen, and there, at the white-railed fence, Honor was standing with Johnny and a little brown mare with pale-gold mane and tail.

"This is Xanthippe," she said. "She's mine, Johnny's everybody's pony."

They mounted, and walked the ponies across the paddock, under the tall gums, to the gate; but when they came out on to the road, they let them canter. They were going away from the hills, and the road ran between gently sloping paddocks; here and there groups of cows stared woodenly at them from under a patch of gums round a little dam; the road turned a corner and, over on their right, the hills stretched to the horizon, blue-tinted with distance, patched with ploughed fields, dark with lines of heavily foliaged trees where the creeks ran. Paul slowed Johnny to a walk while he gazed over his shoulder, and Honor turned to look at him.

"Come on," she shouted. "We've not much time. You'll see it ahead of you all the way home."

Reluctantly he urged Johnny forward, half-turning in his saddle. The gloriously wide sweep of it, lying quietly there before him! What would it be like with the sun setting behind it! He must ask Honor to let him come and see it. He raced Johnny after her and caught her up. They left the road now and turned on to a grassy track through a little forest of tall gums, and then they came to a broad open space occupied by a number of indignant, gobbling turkeys, who abused them roundly for their intrusion and spread their tails furiously, their bell-like gobbles echoing away to the other side of the gorge.

"Aren't they like High Court judges?" Honor said.

67

They dismounted and tethered the horses, and Honor led the way down a rough track to the river.

"It'll be icy," she warned him, "but it's beautiful just now—now and when the full moon rises. Will you come one night with me and watch the full moon rise?"

He said nothing, and she looked at him in surprise. He was looking at her uncertainly, almost with suspicion, and, as she watched him, his lips twitched a little. Honor turned away.

"Back in a minute," she called, and disappeared below the rock they were standing on.

He was sitting on the edge of the rock, waiting for her, when she reappeared, in a pale blue and white figured suit, her body a deeper honey colour than her hair. Below them the river lay unstirred by wind, reflecting its banks with minute exactitude. The sides of the gorge rose steeply, and trees growing out of the red earth bent widely out over the water. The sun was touching the edges of the gums now, turning them to a deep lime colour, startling against the redness of the bank and the clear blue mirror of the water.

"Why is it," Paul said, "that Nature's colours don't clash? She can put things together that would be vile in a man-made version."

"Except poinsettias," said Honor. "They were a bad mistake."

She ran to the edge of the boulder. He felt himself gasp at the beauty of her, poised against the foliage and the water, the sun just catching her pale brown body as she swung her arms above her head to dive, a slim-formed, vital, gallant little creature. She dived, a beautifully timed dive, sideways into the water; as she came to the surface, shaking her clinging hair from her face, he was about to follow her, when suddenly she shouted, "Don't!" He stopped, standing still on the edge of the rock as she swam towards him. Gasping, she said, "Your watch, Paul; you forgot to take off your watch."

He felt a spasm of fear; no one must try to take his watch from him; no one. He was lost if it went, and his new happiness and freedom would give place to that hideously anxious concentration. She was looking up at his strained face, noticing the

68

muscles near the mouth quivering. What is the matter with him? she wondered.

"Well," she said, "aren't you going to—" and she was startled as he dived over her head.

The icy water shocked him horribly at first, but he felt better as he swam towards the opposite bank; when he turned she was poised to dive again, and this time it was a swallow dive, effortless, leisurely. He swam across to her and called, "You dive beautifully."

She laughed and floated on her back.

"I'm awfully good," she said dreamily. "I've got rhythm and grace. . . ."

"Yes—and you've got the most thundering conceit I've ever come across," he said.

"Maybe I have," she answered indifferently. "Why not? Have you ever known anyone as outstanding as me before?"

He was still laughing when they climbed up from the water. They rubbed vigorously for a few moments, and then Honor disappeared to dress. When she returned they sat on the rock, looking at the river, both of them glowing and warm and exhilarated. After a moment she turned and looked down at him.

"Why did you want to keep your watch on, Paul?" she asked abruptly.

A choking, black panic seized him. He felt trapped; they knew, and they would try to stop him. But they shouldn't—by God, they shouldn't! Then he looked up at her, and the graciousness, the gentleness of her glance soothed away his fear and the tension that had gripped him.

"Do you mind if I don't tell you, Honor?" he said. "I could tell you some silly lie, but I don't want to—I'd hate lying to you."

She was silent for a moment and then she said idly, leaning over to look in the mirror of the water, "That's rather a nice thing to say. I'm sorry to have been curious—Mother says it's the ultimate impertinence."

After a pause she said, nonchalantly irrelevant, "Have you ever liked anyone very much, Paul?"

He looked up at her as she sat there, clean-washed by cold

water; exquisitely delicate, a purity in every line of her, every movement.

"Oh, I've had my moments," he said; "but no, I don't think I have properly, I've always been too busy. But if you stay in that pose much longer, you never know—"

"I shouldn't wonder," she said. "But save your enthusiasm; it'd be a shame to throw it away on me."

"What!" he exclaimed. "If I were suddenly to throw myself at your feet and vow I couldn't live without you, you would be unmoved?"

"Quite," she said, and as she turned to look down at him, her face was changed utterly. The self-possession, the aloofness had vanished, her eyes smiled softly at him; she was momentarily quite without her armour. "No, but seriously; there's someone I like very much." Then she leant back against the rock, hands clasped behind her head, her eyes dreamily following a hawk as it circled silently in the clear sky.

"Do you?" Paul's surprise came into his voice. "Who?"

"Someone called Hester," she said, still dreaming.

"Oh, I see." Paul rested back on his elbow.

"You don't at all." The sing-song voice was almost toneless. "You only think you do. You'd have to see her and talk to her before you could appreciate her goodness."

"What's she like, then?" he asked politely.

"Oh, she's not remarkable to look at," Honor said. "But she's tremendously clever and she's witty and she's kind. She's awfully good to me—she lends me books and she's helped me a lot with my German and my Spanish. Oh, she's just wonderful—but . . ." Her voice trailed off uncertainly.

"What's the but?" he asked.

"Oh, the family don't like her," Honor said unhappily. "Nobody does—here, I mean, in Ambara. She's got very advanced views on politics and things and she got a bit notorious for them, once during the war; but she doesn't talk to me about them. She's just kind and good and clever—but she's lonely, I know, and I'm not much company for her, but I'm the only friend she has here and I can't give up going to see her. And yet I hate disobeying Mother. . . ."

70

"M-m," Paul said reflectively. "Bit of a poser, isn't it? Still, if you try to do what you think is best, things can't go so far wrong, can they?"

"Oh, Paul," she said, and she jumped up and pulled him to his feet, "you're the most satisfactory person I've ever met; one day I shall probably marry you."

"And then Heaven help me," he said, as they began to climb up the rocks.

When they had mounted she suddenly swung Xanthippe round and said, imploringly, not at all sure of herself for a moment, "Will you come and see her?—today, some time? Hester, I mean."

"If you'd like it."

She turned the little mare back and set her at a gallop. In a moment the trees hid them from Paul's view, though he could hear Honor calling "Yoicks! Yoicks, lass!" long after she was out of sight.

II

Megan's bed was made. She had just finished smoothing the far side of the counterpane, carefully kneeling very lightly on the foot of the bed where she was less likely to leave a dint in the smoothness, when she had heard Paul going downstairs, and she had gone to the window on the landing and watched them ride away down the back road. What a self-possessed creature Honor was! Megan would have liked to have gone, but she would never think of rousing a strange man from his bed and forcing him to accompany her like that. And yet, nothing Honor did ever seemed out of place. Anyway, she couldn't have gone, she reflected, as she went back to her room, because she was on duty with Joady this morning. She looked at the little tortoise-shell clock on her desk and saw that she had three-quarters of an hour before she need go down. She took her nail file from her dressing table and climbed on the foot of the bed, where she faced the mirror and the window. She looked about the room to see that everything was neat, and then began to file her nails. The pale sunlight was just beginning to light up the colours of the books on the six rows of shelves beside the desk, and she eyed them with peaceful pleasure. There was no decoration needed in a room that held many books; they were colour and warmth and interest in themselves, and they gave life and richness to their surroundings. Her life had been filled with books and talk about books, and often she tried to imagine how people filled their lives, their minds, their conversation without books. It had always seemed an impossibility. I suppose a musician would feel the same about music, she thought, and an artist about pictures. Her mind balked at the association; and to divert it she turned to consider herself in the mirror, which hung in its dark oval frame between two twisted arms, its base resting on the narrow, kidney-shaped table of the same wood. Here, on a white linen runner, Megan's silver-backed brush, comb, and mirror lay in precise arrangement.

She looked plump and shapeless in her blue woolly gown. I'm an unremarkable person, she thought. Compared with Honor, I look ordinary, earthy; I've none of that exquisiteness she possesses—no one would pick me out of any group I was in. Just completely ordinary—brown hair, brown eyes, complexion quite good, mouth just well shaped, nose a bit turned-up, but not enough to be charmingly *retroussé*. She picked up her hand mirror and twisted her head to see her profile. Not much better. Her neck was too short, and she'd probably be fat later on. No, the best one could say was "pleasant—and no freckles." It was better than plainness, but it only added up—unremarkable. If I was found drowned and unidentified, the police description would help no one. But she wouldn't be found drowned. Too unusual.

She put the mirror down and turned her attention to her nails; still, after all, certain remarkable things would happen to her, things that didn't come to every girl of her age. Not every girl, for instance, left her country at twenty. . . . Suddenly she stopped filing, and let her hands lie in her lap. So she had made up her mind; before she had fallen asleep last night, she had tried to disentangle her feelings, but she had gone to sleep before anything was clear. This morning it all seemed to be taken for granted; she knew that she would go to Oxford, now. She tried to recapture the state of mind she had been in last night, when she'd walked up the bush track from the station, but it would not come; then she had felt so completely fortified by her thoughts of Julian that she had felt able to withstand anything: the difficulties of lying to the family and misleading them, the temptation of two years at Oxford, of seeing a strange land and knowing people and places that would ever afterwards enrich her life, the flatness of taking up some mediocre work like teaching—all these had seemed easy things to endure last night, because only Julian mattered in all the world. And then Julian had become tragically less important. It had all been trivial, that incident last night, and, probably, if she had possessed greater depth, more strength of character, she would have been able to dismiss it from her mind; but this morning, when her only feeling about Julian was that she didn't want to think of him, the difficulties of renouncing the scholarship seemed insuperable and the arduousness of attempting to surmount them without purpose, for she no longer felt the stimulus that had previously urged her forward. What a pitiable, mean spirit she had! It would be a long time before she trusted any of her enthusiasms again.

Perhaps it was fortunate, she thought sadly, that things had happened as they had last night, for what a horrible situation it would have been if she had first made the renunciation, and this change had suddenly swept over her afterwards.

She began to contemplate the work she would do. She must get some definite information about the curriculum and the methods of working at Oxford. There would be a thousand things to do before August, but old Professor Hemsley would certainly help her. He had done a great deal for her already; it was through him that her love of drama had awakened. She remembered the pleasure, the excitement, of listening to his lectures. He was one of the world's great actors lost to the stage, and the small honours class had sat entranced, in the late afternoon lectures, while they listened to him. His ordinarily deep voice had a dozen different tones, it was completely malleable.

73

It was the voice of a callow youth, a desperation-maddened Macbeth, a simpering fop, a nobly tragic woman; it brought out every finest shade of wit, points felt only by the dramatist, little sly ironies, the most delicate pathos. Yes, there would be no one at Oxford like Hemsley. How incredibly fortunate she was to have been able to take his lectures—he was retiring at the end of this year. It had been just touch and go.

Suddenly she realized that remarkable things had already begun to happen to her. Knowing Hemsley, winning her scholarship—these might be the beginning of other and more wonderful things. Her spirits lifted; she leant her chin on her hands, as they lay folded on the end of the square, wooden bedpost, and the realization came to her of the richness of this stage of her life. It could lead anywhere; everything now depended on her, and she felt confident of her ability to endeavour and to persevere, and there was a measure of tranquillity in the feeling, for she had been without this ability to strive ever since she had devoted herself to Julian. At least she was recognizable once more; she was again reliable, capable Megan Carmichael. After all, rapture and ecstasy were ill-suited to her, she decided, whereas hard work and achievement in the field of literature were part of her. Yes, last night had been a blessing, no doubt —heavily disguised, but a blessing. Abstractedly, she licked the bedpost, which was quite bereft of paint, for Megan had acquired this habit early in childhood; her mind was filled with the pictures she had seen, the poems she had read, of Oxford and its dreaming spires.

III

Mary Carmichael lay still, not wanting to wake James before it was necessary, for it was only a quarter-past six and James usually didn't stir until seven. She heard movements overhead and then light footfalls running down the stairs. The girls were always up early.

She raised her head a little to look at the day through the long french windows, which opened on the side veranda. A beautiful morning. She could see the orchard through the wistaria, the early sun shining, weakly as yet, on leaves still gleaming with last night's mist, and, beyond the orchard, the wall of wattles that marked Trent's place. She lay back, not trying to organize her thought, letting half-remembered scenes and events race through her mind. I've a mother's memories, she thought; the mind of a woman who had spent so many years in bringing up children must be essentially different in character from that of a woman who had lived in the world as an individual. After so many years of motherhood you weren't a separate, single person, she thought; you were extended, as it were, into other people, you projected yourself into them, so that you experienced something of their feelings as well as your own. Possibly it was a bad thing; you ceased to be very important to yourself, you ceased to be a whole person, you were dispersed. Perhaps mothers of this generation, mothers who continued with their professions and careers, would escape this feeling of division. It didn't bring a great deal of happiness with it; if you were striving for things for yourself there was a satisfying feeling of being master of your destiny, of reaping as you sowed; but you couldn't feel like that when you were striving for the goals of others. No, she thought, mothers like me, old-fashioned mothers who are nothing in life but mothers, are completely dependent on others for their satisfaction; they must hope for love and kindness from their children, but they can't command it and they are lost without it. It was much the same if you were a wife; a wife can fulfil her hopes and dreams and ambitions through her husband, a mother through her children . . . an entirely negative position to hold in society. And yet the solace and the sweetness that compensated one! She had been fortunate. All her life she had had the reassuring warmth of love in her home, and she had had her fill of vicariously fulfilled ambition; James's business had always thrived, he had always worked hard in it and looked to the future for all of them; Adrian had been a brilliant student, a successful young doctor; Megan had undoubted literary ability and had pursued a straight path to success as a student; Honor was an unknown

75

quantity at present, but her voice was lovely, she was beautiful and clever. Yes, and through it all she, the mother, had been the centre of all their activities; they had turned to her confidently, had consulted her, lavished affection on her. What if she herself were unimportant, as a person, her activities negligible? Had she not contributed much to the world's productive work through the achievements of her family? Supposing she had remained single, had pursued some personal objective, had developed some talent to the full? Could she be said to have contributed as much? For there would be her children's children, and all that they would produce. Perhaps that really is woman's greatest role in society, she thought: the replenisher, the figure in the background, seeing that her menfolk, her children, were so armed against difficulty, so developed, that they could achieve the highest that was in them. A vexing problem—a situation that seemed always to leave women with a faint sense of grievance, no matter how happy their lives, how fortunate their circumstances. This led, too, no doubt, to the ambitious mother, feverishly urging her children forward to achievements for which they had no capacity; it led to elocution lessons and to fine, silky hair being tortured into permanent waves; and to many similar horrors.

She thought about Adrian. Why was it that she felt so differently this morning about Adrian? The situation was no better than it had been yesterday; really it was worse, for Adrian was in no way restored to her, and the manner of his death was, in point of actual suffering, more dreadful than she had previously imagined. Could it be simply because she had had still another vicarious triumph, his final gift to her? He was a hero, his memory would be honoured. Surely, surely I can't be as bad as that, she thought—happy to know my son died in torture because I can be proud of him, for the last time, proud of the bravery and the self-sacrifice which brought about his death. Supposing he had come back safely and I knew that he was safe only because he had acted in a cowardly and selfish manner, would I be content? Is it my son I want, or is it something to be proud of?

Why do I bother with these thoughts? she wondered wretchedly. There's no use in it, for when I reach a stage where I must acknowledge ignoble motives, I'll deceive myself, I'll never admit them. She sat up in bed, seized her wrap, and said, though it was still too early, she knew, "Are you awake, James dear?"

James had been lying still for some minutes, anxious not to wake Mary until it was time; quietly he had been exercising the fingers of his right hand, clenching his fist tightly and then slowly, one by one, forcing his fingers back until his hand was spread as widely as possible. After ten times he paused and worked the muscles in his face, pursing his lips as tightly as he could and then extending them in a wide smile. Ten times of this and then back to his fingers; he'd have to leave the arm and leg until later, or the movement might rouse Mary.

He felt excited as he lay there, a jumble of thoughts and plans and memories streaming through his mind. He wondered if anybody had ever known how much he had loved Adrian. He used to feel self-conscious about it when Adrian was a little chap, and he had always striven to conceal it. He had been afraid, too, of its consequences for the boy, for everyone knew what happened to children with overfond parents: they became little horrors, failures in later life, and their parents became objects of derision. But he needn't have worried; the boy had been a perfectly normal boy, though in James's eyes he had always been nearly perfect. He had delighted in Adrian, adored him, admired him; and somehow he had managed always to preserve a semblance of a not overintense interest and affection; he remembered having to force himself to leave the house, when all he wanted to do was to stay and delight in his son, and he remembered the gaiety and excitement of coming home to him at night.

Though he had grown calmer as the boy grew up, his love and admiration for Adrian had never wavered and had never suffered a setback, for the boy had caused him no sorrow and no anxiety; he had miraculously fulfilled every hope James had had for him. His path had been so straightforward that, even when the widening of his activities had removed him from the small home circle, there had been no weakening of the tie between them. When Adrian had gone to school James had not felt a chafing loneliness; rather he had had an increased

77

excitement and delight from his son's more complex life; and it had been the same with his university career and his marriage: everything seemed only to increase his love for and interest in Adrian. Even when he had left for the war, though for the first time dread had come to James, pride and delight were still there and they had helped him to overcome his fears; and it was only when the certainty of Adrian's death had come to them that James's world had crashed to pieces.

He had sometimes felt qualms lest he was neglecting the others, Mary and the girls, but he had never had any evidence that this was so. Of course, he knew that his passionate love for Mary had changed, with the years, into a quiet, deep, satisfied affection for her as Adrian's mother; but that, he had argued with himself, was natural. Passion was temporary, unsuitable as the basis for a life-long association; but an affectionate, kindly love was enduring. And the girls had had all that they needed of him, never-failing interest, thoughtful affection, but the pivot of his world was his son, rather than his wife or his daughters. The readjustment, after illness, had been cruelly hard, but he had always prided himself that no one had ever been able to guess the depth of his devotion to Adrian, and he had redoubled his efforts, as he slowly came back to living, to see that they should never know.

And now, this morning, he felt again the delight that had always come to him when he was doing something for Adrian; he had felt it when he helped Adrian to mend his bike, or when he took him for a day's fishing, or, even earlier, when he had bought him a big, golden teddy bear. Now he was still able to help Adrian and Adrian's children—at least, he would be able to if he persevered steadily with these exercises; just give him a month and he would be back at work. And this boy, Paul. Adrian would be pleased if he could know that Paul had benefited at his father's hands; he would talk to Paul today, offer to teach him the business, then a partnership, perhaps. If only the lad's inclinations lay that way, it would be a happy arrangement for them all. Excitement and joy overwhelmed him, and he was just about to risk exercising his leg when he heard Mary moving. And then she said, "Are you awake, James dear?"

78

"Yes, Mary." His voice was eager as he turned his head to her. "Mary," he went on, in an offhanded manner, "I—would you care to help me this morning? I think I'm getting over this —this self-consciousness or whatever it is, and I've been a perfect pest to Joady lately. I think I'll soon be able to manage things better by myself, but would you just help me a bit?"

"Yes, of course." Mary took up her brush and began to brush her hair swiftly, so that he couldn't see her face. At last, at last he's coming back to me. Thank God—and you, Adrian. It's you who have done this for me. . . . But James wouldn't want effusiveness. She managed to speak in an ordinary tone.

"I'm awfully glad, James. Will you come to breakfast this morning?"

"I'd like to try it," he said uncertainly. "You don't think— with the lad here—the girls wouldn't be embarrassed, do you think?"

"I'm perfectly certain they wouldn't be," she answered calmly. "It's been a bit lonely without you at mealtimes, you know."

"Yes," he said, and his voice was anxious. "But, Mary, you have understood about it, haven't you? About Joady doing things for me, and so on. . . ."

She put down her brush and came to the side of the bed, and as she stooped and kissed him the deep solace of knowing her love for him calmed his mind at once.

IV

Joady tied the end of a long white plait with a tiny piece of tape, and then rapidly twisted both plaits at the back of her head until they formed a tidy mound of shining, disciplined hair on her neck. Her plain grey frock, with its white collar, threw up the bright colour in her cheeks and the gay blue of her eyes. She slipped her grey-stockinged feet into flat-heeled, well-polished black shoes and began lacing them carefully. Her face was troubled and thoughtful, and she felt none of the brisk

79

delight in starting a new day that usually sent her singing down to the kitchen, especially on such a perfect morning as this.

There's trouble, she thought, as she laced the other shoe; there's trouble and none of them can see it. It's not that I don't like him, he's a nice lad; but there's something awful hidden in him. They'd say I'd grown imaginative in my old age, if they knew I'm thinking this; Megan would say, "That's what comes of reading all these fancy books of Father's." And they'd laugh. But still—she'd always known when trouble was looming; even when some one of them had been getting sick, she had always known before any symptoms appeared; and that time when Megan had pitched over the handlebars of her bike and had broken her ankle, she had known. Megan hadn't been home at teatime, and ordinarily none of them would have worried, but she had made them ring up, had made them take the car and look for Megan. And there she'd been, poor mite, crying and moaning in the dust on a lonely back road. And this boy—as soon as he'd entered the house she'd felt sick with fright, and she still felt sick. And she couldn't tell anybody. Wait—what about Anthea? She had her head screwed on, had Anthea, and a more sympathetic girl you couldn't imagine. Strong, too. Well, if she could get Anthea alone a minute today. . . . She straightened the doily on her dressing table, and was just about to pick up her white apron when there was a knock at the door and Mary's voice said, "May I come in, Joady?"

Joady opened the door quickly, in alarm, and Mary's face, bright with her news, calmed her sudden fear. Mary spoke softly.

"Joady, James seems such a lot stronger this morning. He's coming in to breakfast and he's asked me to help him. He says he's run you off your legs lately, and he's sorry. Oh, Joady"—she took her hand—"isn't it wonderful?"

"I'll say it's wonderful, Mrs. Car." A swift little feeling of pain came to her as she realized how much she'd miss the quiet hours she spent with James, helping him to eat, guiding his clumsy hand, talking, talking, talking. Selfish pig, she said to herself, perhaps you'd like to see him worse, instead of better, just so you can be big and important. She smiled broadly.

"My word, it's just in time, if you ask me. You know what?

He was going to start on modern poetic drama next week, and I had a look at this T. S. Eliot—and honestly, Mrs. Car, I think he'd have been the death of me. But really and truly, I'm glad."

"But you've made him better, Joady. You've given him confidence and helped him when the rest of us were powerless. Joady, darling, bless you—we've so much to thank you for."

They walked along the landing to the head of the stairs, Mary's arm round Joady's plump shoulders. Then Mary stopped and looked at her.

"Do you know what has completed the cure, Joady? I think it's this boy, Paul. James seem filled with eagerness to get to grips with things again—I think he feels that in some way he has a part of Adrian back again, now that Paul is here. And I feel different this morning, Joady; I feel tranquil about Adrian, as if I've almost contentedly said good-bye to him at last. I feel satisfied about him."

Joady tried to smile at her, but a desperate weight of foreboding swept over her and she lowered her eyes. She must say something, she thought; she must not dim this new brightness in Mary's eyes. Surely she's suffered enough, without me acting like Old Moore's Almanac, she told herself.

"He's—he seems a nice young chap."

"Joady." Mary turned Joady's face up to her own. Joady's cheerful blue eyes were strained, her mouth set in an unconvincing smile. "What's the matter, Joady? Aren't you happy? Did it upset you last night to hear about Adrian?"

"Yes," Joady lied uneasily. "Yes, that was it, Mrs. Car; but I'm all right now, really." She slipped away from Mary's arm and turned briskly to Megan's door. "I'll just inform certain people that they should have been on duty five minutes ago."

She thumped on Megan's door.

"You lazy so-and-so," she called to Megan. "Five minutes late already, you are."

Megan opened the door and Joady looked into the room.

"Room left like the pig's breakfast, I suppose."

Mary smiled and went downstairs to James; she could hear Megan protesting loudly, averring that the room was perfect, inviting Joady in to inspect and see if she could find one thing out of place. Really, Joady had been more than half responsible for the pleasure the Carmichael children had always taken in orderliness and for the disciplined way they had managed their possessions, right from the days of dolls and teddy bears; for nothing escaped Joady—no good to push unmended stockings into a drawer, to run a mop over a floor that needed polishing; dusty shoes meant banishment from the breakfast table, untidy fingernails meant two days washing-up instead of one; and even though these offences lay remotely in the past, Joady still kept to the view that their natural inclinations were towards the pig-sty, and she acted accordingly. As Mary went into the bedroom she heard the two of them hurrying down the stairs and out to the kitchen.

V

Anthea lay and wondered at the mood in which she had awak-ened. She felt extraordinarily relaxed; as always, her mind was aware of anxiety, but this morning it could be pushed into the background, it was not so naggingly close to her that she must jump out of bed and become feverishly active. It was not happi-ness, this feeling: that was something she was never likely to feel completely any more. No, it was a negative state of mind, she decided; an emotional limbo, a blessed absence of acute sen-sation; it would not last, but she grasped it to her momentarily, revelling in the unusualness of being able to lie still in silence. Later in the day she would have to banish this passiveness, would have to start grappling with the new situation, telephone her lawyer, make her plans; but not now. The telling of her story to Paul last night had done this wonderful thing for her; it was as if she had undergone some purifying process, as if, by revealing her rottenness, she had begun to cleanse and heal it. The fact that someone else knew the story seemed to release her, and the realization that she could, by her own efforts, do some-thing to better the situation had given her the healthy feeling that comes with activity. It was like the stories Paul had told last night, stories that had made her wince, of Adrian's gouging

82

out the sores on the men's limbs and bodies—sickeningly painful, unbearably revolting process, and yet, in the circumstances, the only possible way back to health.

She felt that if he had shown sympathy, an indulgent under-standing, she would not have experienced this emotional relief; it was the dispassionate way in which her folly had been openly examined, her guilty feelings brought out of their hiddenness, that had seemed so salutary. There had been so much subter-fuge, so many desperate attempts to preserve the illusion of the exquisite Anthea Carmichael, devoted wife, paragon of mother-hood, that to have faced the real Anthea Carmichael, not very good quality and a little shabby at the edges, shoddy, second-rate, was like taking off elegant but too-small shoes. Once the lost illusion was admitted, the resulting comfort was very re-freshing.

She turned over on her side and lay facing the windows. Usually, if she lingered in bed for ten minutes, her head would throb and pound with the distressed pulsing of her blood, but this morning she could lie here and let peace flow through her. She watched the muslin curtains gently moving in the almost still air. Soon she would get up, but not because wild thoughts drove her, and she would ride down to the station, leading the children's ponies—they seemed to think time was wasted if it was not spent with some of their animals, and they always in-sisted on riding home. Then, Paul was coming at eleven. She must ring Mannering, the lawyer; and James wanted to see her today. This evening there was the "Welcome Home" social for some of Ambara's returned men, at the Progress Hall, and she had promised to help with the supper. She'd take the children down to the little carnival that had set itself up in Barnett's pad-dock, behind the polocrosse field, and let them ride on the merry-go-round, and then she'd drive them home and go back to the Progress Hall.

A busy day, filled with pleasant, uneventful duties—except, of course, telephoning Mannering, but she felt quietly confident of her ability to deal with this matter, now. She would place herself entirely in his hands, the telling of the story a second time held few fears for her now. Then, when all the unpleasant business was finished, she would really be free, free of Howard; she would only have to bear, for the rest of her life, the memory of what she had done to Adrian, and since that could bring unhappiness to no one but herself, she would be glad to endure it, she would take pains always to remind herself of it, for it was the just punishment of the evil she had brought about. It was the dread of others—the people at Thornfield and John and Libby—having to share in her punishment, her disgrace, that made the thought of it unbearable.

Or is this all too high-minded? she wondered cynically. Perhaps I can bear my lonely remorse because it is a safe way to atone and no one will think the less of me. Adrian is dead, and there's nothing to fear from him but sadness, sadness which, in time, will inevitably be assuaged by the good will and kindness of those I love, those whom I want to respect me. It is losing that respect, not being able to save my face, that I fear. No doubt I'd be willing to sacrifice others quite cheerfully if I could only be sure that the smooth surface of my life wouldn't crack, revealing ugliness, selfishness, and mad folly for the world to gaze at. In fact, I'm a hypocrite as well as everything else, she reflected.

On the thought, she swung out of bed and, seizing her wrap, went quickly through to the bathroom.

VI

As soon as she rose from her bed Madeleine Croft knelt down beside it and prayed. She did this every morning now, instead of only at night, and sometimes during the day she would come up to her quiet little bedroom and pray for Martin. She felt inexpressibly comforted when she had talked to God, and though Martin showed no improvement yet surely, as her fervour increased in intensity, if she became truly worthy of God's indulgence, surely then He would help her with Martin; but He would have to answer her prayers quickly. If Martin was no better when George came home, then she knew there was no escape for any of them. Disaster would engulf them swiftly, for George was hard with the boy, had been even when he was tiny, and George despised her methods of managing Martin. Whatever would happen if George whipped Martin? She forced her mind back to her prayers.

"He's only a little child, God dear," she said earnestly. "Give me the strength and the understanding to help him, God, so that he will become kind and gentle to me and to all your other creatures. And especially, God," she added hurriedly and more fervently, "please, please let him have forgotten about the knife, when I go in to wake him—please, please."

. As she thought, with dread, about the knife, she heard herself saying, "Please, please," over and over again, and she forced herself to end the prayer somewhat hurriedly.

She tried not to get her left hand wet under the shower, for fear the adhesive tape would peel off, but it was hard to manage. It was a deep cut and it still hurt; it was throbbing now that she had begun to use her hand, but she didn't mind the pain; it was the fear of what she had to face today that troubled her most. Still, she had been wonderfully firm, last night, and today she would persevere, she would not give Martin the knife again— great, ugly thing that it was.

As she dried herself with difficulty, she remembered, shudderingly, the look on his face when she had refused to give it to him. She had hidden it, locked it in a drawer and hidden the key under the paper in her dressing table, and when she had told him that he couldn't have it back, he had just looked at her silently and had not looked at all like a child for the moment. How much easier it had been when he had had tantrums! She had worried terribly then, but now it was much worse, for he never showed any of the usual childish signs of temper; he was just cold and silent, and then he would do some dreadful thing, suddenly and stealthily.

That was how he had cut her with the knife. She had been sewing, listening to some music on the radio, when, soundlessly, he had appeared beside her chair and gashed her hand with the knife. She had screamed and seized the knife, and she recalled, with a sick feeling, the horrid, scrambling run to the bedroom,

85

slamming shut the door on him, hiding the knife and then the key, blood pouring from her hand. Of course, she knew why he had done it—because she had taken the little kitten back to Mrs. Watts. Martin had brought it home yesterday and had hidden it behind the old boxes in the garage, but it had mewed so loudly that she had found it. This sort of thing had happened several times. Martin was always bringing animals home, but of course, she couldn't let him keep them, because he did terrible, horrible things to them and she knew it was bad for him to have them. So she had taken the kitten back to Mrs. Watts— fortunately she'd guessed where it had come from—and Mrs. Watts had been very grateful and had not asked her any questions. She was always so afraid that people would know or guess about Martin, would talk about him and exaggerate his weakness—for, of course, he would grow out of it; all small boys had this strain of cruelty in them, and it was only because Martin had had no father to guide him and she was not a very wise person that he was a little worse than the others. But she had been a little afraid to tell him what she had done, and she'd pretended gaily that the kitten must have strayed out of the garage. He had said nothing at the time, had shown little interest in the matter, but then, when she was sitting there quietly, thinking he was in bed, he'd done this dreadful thing to her.

It was the worst thing he had ever done to her, and she had felt really frightened of him. That was where she was so silly —to be frightened of her own little boy, a child of thirteen. She had wrapped her hand carelessly in one of George's big handkerchiefs and had gone back to him; he was sitting in a corner of the settee, indifferently looking at a magazine, and she had sat beside and talked gently to him, tried to make him see what a dreadful thing he had done. She had talked and talked, and when she stopped, he said, "Where's my knife?"

"I'm not going to give it to you, Martin. It's dangerous for you—you might hurt yourself. And you've been naughty, cruel to your mother. . . ."

"If you don't give it back to me"—his almost black eyes stared at her, making her tremble more violently—"I'll do something worse to you, much worse. When you're not expecting it."

"Now, Martin darling, you mustn't talk like that. I will not give you the knife. Daddy would be furious if I did. Now, come and hop into bed and we'll pretend that none of this nasty thing has happened, shall we?"

When she had bent over him to kiss him good night, he had said, lying on his side in his bed, "I want that knife tomorrow."

It had been after three o'clock when she had fallen asleep, and this morning her eyes were red and swollen from the hours of helpless weeping. She'd have to bathe them in warm water and wych-hazel, because she would have to go down to the village this morning and people were always so eager to gossip; and though she didn't care, for her own sake, what they said, she was always afraid that some busybody or other would, in some way, interfere and get Martin into some serious trouble. There had been a few difficult situations. There had been an awful scene with that loathsome Scott man and his slatternly wife; the pair of them had come to her door one night and had shouted at her, threatened her with the Children's Court, said that Martin was an uncontrollable child and that they'd have him put in a reformatory, all because of some story one of their dirty, sore-covered little boys had told them of things Martin had said and done to him while they were playing in the creek. Oh, they had said the most unmentionable things—and she'd just said quietly, "Please remember that Martin is just a little boy, not an evil, grown-up man, and he knows nothing of such things; and I refuse to listen to such filthy, lying talk."

"Little boy be damned," the man had shouted. "That boy's a devil, and if he ever comes near my kids again I'll flay the hide off him." It had been a dreadful scene and she had been in a nervous tremble for days after it, and she knew the wretched creature had spread his wicked lies about Martin.

And there had been other things, too. She hadn't been able to be friends with Major Anstey since the time when someone had cut up some little lovebirds, which were his wife's pets, and he'd insisted that Martin had done it. Of course she knew that he hadn't, but she did not like to go to Anstey's again, though Margaret Anstey had been a good friend to her. In fact, she had withdrawn more and more from the people she had known,

87

during these last two years. She had even told Mrs. King, who used to come for a few hours each day in the house, that she wouldn't need her any more, and since the lies had spread more widely about Martin she had kept him away from the children round about, so that now they lived very much to themselves.

Martin had not been to school since the trouble at the prep school at Christmas, but after Easter she must make arrangements for another school. George would be angry about his having missed nearly a term, but he didn't understand how sensitive Martin was, and he wouldn't realize how much the unsympathetic treatment Martin had received at the school had upset him and how much he had needed this little rest at home with her, though it hadn't been as successful, yet, as she'd hoped it would be. Perhaps she should have taken the headmaster's advice and consulted a psychiatrist; but she was afraid of these people, for they were always so much inclined to suspect abnormalities and insanity. That was how they'd driven Mother . . . but that was the thing she never thought of, the thing she'd never told George, the thing she was always afraid he'd discover. They had said that Mother was melancholy—and she was only worn out with grief after Father's death. Melancholy—and they'd called it a "rest home," when really it was an asylum and Mother had died there of a broken heart. But she had known that it was not insanity and she'd never told George; she was an only child and was not close to any of her relatives, so she had told George that her mother had died of heart trouble, and there was very little likelihood of his finding out. And it *was* heart trouble—a broken heart.

But she didn't want them to do the same thing to Martin, and so she had tried to cure him herself, by rest and quietness and understanding; but she sometimes felt uneasily that he was growing away from her, becoming more secretive. Of course, she realized that Martin needed care, that he did have this weakness, this strain of cruelty; but he was a dear good boy underneath, and if they would give her time she would help him to grow out of it. If only he wouldn't go wandering away for such long periods. He would go away after breakfast, and sometimes she wouldn't see him again until teatime, and then he'd come

88

in, pale, hungry, and excited, nervous. It wasn't good for him. And she would go hunting for him, spend hours walking along dusty roads in the heat, not liking to ask people directly whether they had seen him, knowing that they were talking about her after she'd left them. And he was often, she knew, up at the soldiers' camp on the main road—ugly, bare place. Twice she'd found him there and had brought him home.

He always came quietly with her. Indeed, he was becoming quieter and quieter, more withdrawn into himself, stealthy even; silly, but she'd developed the habit of listening to see where he was in the house, jerking her head suddenly, in fear, to see if he was behind her. He'd begun to do that, lately; only, of course, to tease her, but she felt frightened when she would turn suddenly and find him behind her chair, standing still and watching her so intently. She'd always been afraid that something like last night's incident would happen, but she still couldn't believe that it had really taken place. He had hurt her at other times, of course, but that had been when they'd been struggling about something, or when she had tried to give him a little slapping, that had been only accidental, really, but this was so deliberate, so terribly premeditated.

She wiped the bath carefully with the bath cloth and then knelt on the bath mat to wipe the splashes from the tiled floor; the attitude reminded her of God, so she put her hands together on the side of the bath, closed her eyes, and said another little extra prayer, so that Martin would not think about the knife this morning. At last she rose and unlocked the door; she was getting so silly that she really only felt safe in a room whose door was locked. She crept past Martin's door again and returned to her fluffy, frilly little bedroom, sweetly fresh in the morning air. She opened the cupboard and took out a pink gingham frock, which tied with a bow in the middle of her back, thinking that she must make herself pretty this morning, because all the articles on child psychology said that children responded better to pretty clothes and gay colours. Looking at her pale face in the mirror, she decided to wear a little rouge this morning, though she seldom used it except under artificial light. As she dressed, she knew that every task completed, every hook fastened, brought nearer the moment when she must go to his door and pop her head round it, gaily calling, "Awake, sonny boy? Got a kiss for Mummy this morning?" And something sour and sick and heavy seemed to make her stomach turn over.

VII

Alec Kyles could hear his mother moving about in her bedroom across the hall, and Betty Wilkins, who came five days in the week to help Mrs. Kyles until midday, was lighting the kitchen fire, the subdued noise indicating that she was being mindful of his mother's very thorough instructions that Alec must on no account be roused or disturbed before seven. He congratulated himself on the simple but effective strategy that he had devised to give himself this quiet hour in the morning. For many months now, since he had first suggested that he would benefit by sleeping later, he had been able to enjoy this peaceful prelude to his days, for invariably he was awake before six, and, by remaining quite still, he postponed the rush of assiduous attention that persisted throughout the rest of the day. At first she had had the habit of stealing into the room to see if he were awake, and he had had to feign unconsciousness; but he had settled that by several times awaking with a start and saying that the shock of finding her staring at him had made his heart pound. So now the early morning was his own, as were the hours between bedtime and midnight or, sometimes, long afterwards, as he lay staring into the darkness. It would have been pleasant to read at night, when he was wakeful, but she seemed to sense the light in his room, even if she were in bed, and she would come crashing in, dramatically demanding whether he wanted to kill her as well as himself, as her nerves would not stand another bout of his illness—and so on.

He was particularly glad of his little scheme this morning. He felt interested in life, he decided; the dull feeling of waking to a day that would be exactly similar to all the years of days which had gone before it was absent, for last night he had made

90

his decision finally, and this morning he must begin on his plans for putting it into operation. He leant on one arm and gazed round the room. It was a good room, large and well lighted, with a bareness, an emptiness that pleased him. As he looked at his canvasses lying untidily against the walls, at the long wooden bench covered with his painting equipment, at the wall of thickly stacked bookshelves, he admitted to himself that here she left him alone. But then, she never quibbled over non-essentials: let him potter away to his heart's content while he was innocuously painting in his studio. She was certain that he could come to no harm there, that there was nothing to threaten her dominion in the large, quiet room. But that was where she was wrong, he reflected; like all cunning people, she was extremely stupid in some ways, and she did not realize that here, in this room, was lodged her most powerful foe—and his own strongest protector. Yes, he thought, yes; to do the job properly she should have stifled my urged to paint. If I had lost that I would have lost the fight. But each month and each year it had been giving him back his strength.

He gazed at the great pile of beautifully arranged and illustrated books on the lives and works of the great ones in the world of art. She had never spared any expense in providing him with these books, for to her it seemed just a further means of keeping him contentedly out of the world. But, as he had studied them—and he had worked hard to become thoroughly self-taught—something had been gradually coming to him from these men, these famous ones; they had stretched their hands to him across the deep gulf of time and he had become stronger, he had reached the stage when his spirit was among them and he was struggling to stand erect with them. During the last eighteen months his work had matured and developed, he felt sure; but he had kept very quiet about it and she was glad not to have him talking too much about his painting. She liked to come in and appraise a canvas, talking confidently about line and composition and feeling; but if he had attempted to send any of his work away for criticism, if he had dared to ask some of the artists he knew in the city to come and discuss things with him, she would have pounced.

91

Of course, there was his father—and Julian's work was good; at least, it had been good once and probably could be again, though Julian had painted very little in the last five years and there was a weariness about his work now, the feeling that it was the product of a mind not fully alive. It was a damned pity, but Julian was no help to Alec now, except in the matter of his earlier paintings, which were well worth anyone's study and which had first awakened in Alec the desire to show, on canvas, that he, too, knew beauty in colour and line and that he could give evidence of that knowledge by painting. He could, of course, have learnt a great deal from Julian, just by talking to him, but this his mother would never allow; he had heard Julian being warned and threatened not to encourage him, on the grounds that it would overstimulate and excite him and that his physical frailty made it impossible for him to engage in any activity in a thorough and laborious manner, though it was quite healthy for him to have painting as a gentle hobby that would keep him harmlessly occupied, like a child daubing with a box of paints on a wet afternoon, safe from the rain and out of the way of the adults.

He turned his thoughts to last night's scene. That had been just what he needed; it had provided the impetus to send him forward now. He wondered whether that chap (Paul? Yes, Paul) had meant what he had said about Alec's visiting his home. Though it had been put obliquely, he felt sure that it had been intended as an invitation. Yes, but he was in no position to accept such an offer, for he had no money at all. Save for that brief period, five years ago now, he had never had any money; when he needed anything it was bought for him, but he hadn't even the money for his fare. The stark fact was that he must get some work to do at once, when he left here. How he was to leave he couldn't yet decide, but he must at once seek work. Perhaps he could do some advertising illustrations; Digby would know about that—if Digby was still in Sydney. He decided not to bother about that; first he must plan to get away. Suddenly he knew what he must do. Megan would help him, he felt sure.

As he thought of Megan, of the way she had looked at Julian last night, he felt sick with desolation. It was this, he knew, that was really driving him away. He couldn't remember when he had begun to love Megan, when the deep and intense feeling he now had for her had replaced his affectionate friendliness, but it had flared into flame when the knowledge had first come to him that she was fascinated by Julian. He had known months ago, and since then his position had become intolerable. He still desperately hoped that it was only a passing feeling with her, a romantic infatuation for someone who didn't exist outside her imagination, for otherwise it would be hell for her. The whole situation had aroused in him an unbearable mortification. He had stopped drifting and had faced his own position. In other circumstances, if he were living a normal life, if he were an ordinarily healthy, strong man, he would have risked trying to intervene; but when he turned his gaze upon himself he beheld such a pitiable figure that he saw his only hope in escape, in flight, for he could not stay here any longer and watch this hateful situation develop. He realized bitterly that he was a weakling in everyone's eyes—and deservedly so; physically, he was devoid of strength, and spiritually he was a craven. But, poor thing as he himself appeared, how much meaner and more culpable was Julian. Julian knew Megan's feeling for him—he must know, Alec felt sure; but, instead of killing it, ending the impossible, tragic farce, Julian had done everything to foster it, deriving some wretched and despairing consolation from her blind admiration. To think of little, brown, chubby Megan, bright, strong, clever little Megan—to think of her squandering her brilliance on a spent force like Julian, a man who could never have possessed a man's strength, to have crumbled, as he had done, in the grip of a hard and cruel woman! And if it went on, the consequences for Megan would be deplorable. Supposing his mother even suspected Megan's feeling for Julian! Why, the whole place would ring with her derisive, contemptuous rage.

Suddenly he realized that, even if he were going away from it, he must try to do something about it before he left. What he

93

could do, God only knew, but he must at least strike a blow at this thing which threatened his little, beloved Megan.

Cautiously, he climbed out of bed, and, putting on his dressing gown, went to the window. It was a beautiful morning; he knew how the light would look on the hills about three o'clock this afternoon—he had painted it one day and it had been a success. He turned to look at his canvases, wondering about them. There were a lot of them, and she would certainly destroy them if he left them here. Perhaps the Carmichaels would keep them at Thornfield for him. He had enough to exhibit, really—enough good ones, too. He began to look through them, mentally rejecting those he felt to be unworthy, but they commenced to slide across the floor and he was afraid of bringing her in, so he started across the room to his bed. He passed the mirror and paused to gaze wonderingly at himself. Why am I so damned thin and gaunt? he thought. His cheeks were hollow and he was very pale, the bones in his face easily discernible; he held up long, bony hands, well-shaped, delicate; brown hair hung straight and lank over his forehead, but the eyes were bright, eager; straight nose, crooked, intelligent mouth. You know, he thought, if I could pull myself together I might build something out of myself. He felt a sudden, overwhelming thankfulness for his ability to paint. But for that I'd be doomed, he thought. But my work's good, as Julian's once was, and mine is going to be known, not only here, but in other countries, and I'm going to get to those other countries to paint them. I've only to get away from here—from her; she's the only thing that ails me, really, though it's taken me about half a lifetime to realize it. And if I get myself strong physically I won't be behind other people of my age—in fact, I'll be ahead of them, because I will have accomplished something good. And then, if I can come back and if Megan is here . . .

He turned slowly as the door swung back, and he did not answer when his mother screamed, "Alec! Standing there in the cold! Now get back to bed at once and I'll turn on the radiator. It seems to me sometimes that you like to give me anxiety. . . ."

He lay in bed and smiled at the ceiling as the stream flowed over him. Another day, but there wouldn't be many more of them now; he could afford to be patient. He began to plan his moves so that he could get a few minutes alone at the telephone to ring Megan.

VIII

Honor and Paul dropped the saddles in the corner of the back veranda and came into the kitchen. Joady was cooking bacon, briskly and efficiently, standing sturdily in front of the big fuel stove. Megan was about to carry a pile of plates into the dining room, and she put them down for a moment and sat up on the end of the kitchen table.

"Well," she said, looking at them admiringly, "you do look out-of-doors and wholesome. Like a Health Week poster, or a scene from *The Squatter's Daughter*."

"Either is an attractive effect, just what we've been striving after," said Honor, as she went through into the hall.

Paul stood smiling in the doorway, his hair untidy and his eyes bright, alive, as they hadn't been last night. My word, Megan thought complacently, we're working a cure here; a few more days of this and he won't have any more nerves.

"We had a great time," he said, his voice quick and enthusiastic. "Jove, Megan, I'd like to watch the sunset from that high, flat road—you know, looking over to those hills beyond Borrowdale. Do you think we could go this evening?"

"Of course we can. That is—do you think I can get away this evening, Joady?"

Joady turned from the stove.

"As far as I can see," she said, "you'll still be sitting on that table by this evening, and I'll be waiting to serve breakfast."

"Oh, Joady, you're a wet blanket."

Megan slid off the table. Paul picked up the plates and carried them in to the dining room. As he put them on the dresser, Megan said, "I think we can go. If Joady doesn't say 'no' straight off, it's generally all right." And she hurried back to the kitchen.

Paul ran lightly up the stairs and swung round the post at the head of the staircase, to his room. As he closed the door

95

behind him, he was overjoyed to see Adrian there, standing by the window; he greeted him, happily and sat down on the bed to have a good talk with him.

The curious thing about these talks with Adrian was that, since he had come home, he'd always had to do the talking. Sometimes, indeed, he couldn't really see Adrian, though he knew he was there, of course. After the bombing, in the jungle, it had always been Adrian who had done the talking and Paul who had listened. However, it didn't matter; if the old boy didn't want to talk, why should he? He always smiled and nodded and showed he was listening—and this morning he was quite clear, quite close and plainly to be seen. Paul began to tell him all that had happened since yesterday, how much he loved the Ambara countryside and Adrian's family. The words tumbled out incoherently, as he tried to describe everything at once, for he knew that soon they would call him to breakfast and he'd have to go. As he told Adrian about Honor and some of her quaint ways, he shouted with laughter and slapped his knee with enjoyment. Just at that moment there was a knock at the door and Honor's voice said, "Breakfast! Didn't you hear the bell?"

He sprang across from the bed and opened the door just a little way, because he didn't want her to see Adrian. She looked past him into the room, and swiftly he looked over his shoulder; but Adrian was gone, so he opened the door wide. Honor gazed at him in surprise.

"Who've you got in there? I heard you laughing your head off."

"I was talking to—" He paused and looked at her uncertainly.

"Well, who?"

"Nothing and nobody," he said happily, coming out and shutting the door behind him.

As they came to the top of the stairs Honor stopped and, one hand on the stairpost, looked up at him.

"Man of mystery, aren't you?" she said, and her voice was not mocking. Then she turned and bounded down the stairs.

James was sitting at the head of the table as they came in, and he welcomed Paul warmly. Mary was seated at the opposite

96

end of the table, and the others slipped quickly into their places. James began to eat his porridge carefully, and Honor told them about their early ride.

"And Mother," Megan broke in, "not only has your younger daughter no manners, but even her sense of decorum is rather dim. She was in Paul's room at some dreadfully early hour, enticing him to go riding with her."

"He'll have to marry me now, won't he, Father dear? Or will you drive him down the front steps with a riding whip?"

"If a riding whip is to be used," James said judicially, pushing his plate towards Megan, who took it to the dresser, "it can be put to much better purpose, my dear. It's a nice idea, though I think my razorstrop would hurt more; it has that metal buckle at the end, you know."

Mary turned to Paul.

"Poor Paul," she said. "No doubt you didn't expect to find yourself in this wild, bohemian atmosphere, with young females roaming in and out of your bedroom."

"Well," he said, "they don't usually end up by making you ride ten miles and then plunging you into an icy river."

"Practically the only literature read in this house is the penny novelette," said Honor. "You can easily tell that from their conversation."

"Seems to me," Joady said, "as if some people don't know what to do with their time if they're not on breakfast duty. Oh, well, there's always a remedy for that, eh, Mrs. Car?"

"Good for you, Joady," said Megan gleefully, as she handed James his scrambled eggs and bacon. "Then the serious-minded, studious people in the family could devote their mornings to the pursuit of the things of the mind."

"The things of the mind would be in little danger from such a pursuit in this house," her mother said calmly. "Where are these studious people lurking, that we've never observed their presence?"

James managed the third forkful of scrambled egg quite easily, his eyes twinkling with pleasure.

"Oh, indeed!" Megan laid down her fork dramatically. "Now that's just where you're wrong, Mrs. Carmichael, my love; that's just where you can't see beyond your nose. Here is a serious student"—she stabbed her chest with her knife—"at least, the English Department seems to think so."

They stopped eating and looked at her.

"How come?" Honor said curtly.

Paul beamed with delight. So she was going to tell them, she must have decided to accept it. Good show, good show!

Honor's sharp eyes missed nothing, before Megan could reply, she said, "Paul seems to know the answer to this one."

Megan looked disconcerted for a moment.

"Yes," she said, a little uncomfortably, "I happened to tell him last night. But, listen, I've won the Proctor."

There was silence for a moment, then Honor pushed back her chair and rushed round to hug Megan.

"Oh, you adorable thing!" she cried. "I'm madly proud of you."

There was a general stir. James put his sound hand on Megan's and smiled at her, forgetting to control the crooked side of his mouth; Mary left her seat to kiss her; and Joady sat staring ahead of her, stupefied with delight. Jenkins came padding in from the hall and Honor seized him and whirled him aloft, his yellow eyes blazing, as she sat him down, he spat at her contemptuously, having no time at all for vulgar displays of enthusiasm, and he ran across and sprang on to the window ledge, where it took him quite five minutes to calm his nerves.

They resettled themselves in some disorder. Mary's table napkin lay on the floor; Honor had brought her chair round to sit beside Megan, her feet on the side rungs of Megan's chair, while she gazed into her sister's face and gloated over her; Joady had managed to say, "Well, I'm damned," and was now sitting in a happy daze. Nobody bothered to eat any more, but, in a few minutes, Honor began to pour out coffee. Megan brought a box of cigarettes to the table and they sat on, talking and admiring and planning. Seldom had a meal at Thornfield ended in such disorder.

In the midst of her delight, Megan remembered guiltily that, last night, she had been going to deprive them of all this joy. The thought was incredible; she could not conjure up a mental

98

image of what this scene would have been like in reverse. She looked round at their eager faces, all smiling with happiness because of her success. They were good and generous people, and she didn't deserve their praise. Thank heaven she'd gone to the Kyleses' last night, and thank heaven for Paul. She turned and smiled at him affectionately, and his glance told her that he was following her thoughts. She looked at her mother, and suddenly realized that she was going to leave her, to leave them all, and that they'd suffer through it, but would say nothing of it lest they should mar her happiness.

They began to discuss details: when she would be leaving, how long she would stay, what degree she would get from Oxford, how much money the scholarship would carry with it, what the chances of booking a passage would be.

"Two-fifty pounds for two years," James said. "Well, that won't be enough for you in postwar England, I'm afraid; prices will be certain to soar now. There you are, Mary, she's only going to be an increased burden, I can see; there's never a rose without a thorn where our family is concerned."

No, Mary thought, there's always the choice to be made: the present joy of having them safely with you, mediocre, their ambitions unfulfilled, or the ultimate triumph of pride in their happiness and their achievements. Here was another one going, another empty place in the house; but it was the cycle of life, inevitable, heartbreaking process. Every stage in their lives meant a parting, when children grew up. Suddenly she saw clearly the time when she would be alone in this house, perhaps with Joady. The end of my life is facing me, she thought—the lonely, closing years. She smiled at James and said, "There'll be stacks of clothes, of course, James—I hope you're allowing for that—and nobody's coupons will be sacred. She'll leave us all without a stitch to our backs, I've no doubt."

"And with precious little money left to buy food, I suppose," James said gloomily. "And of course," he went on, turning to Honor, "your career will have to be sacrificed to that of your brilliant sister. That always happens to the youngest in any family. I think we'll take her away from school at once, Mary, before she gets any fancy notions about herself. They're crying

99

out for young women in industry, and, limited as she is, I should think some of the more unpleasant types of factory work—say, a canning works—would have her."

"Can I work somewhere where you get 'stench money'?" Honor said dreamily, her head on Megan's shoulder. "It must be wonderful to get extra money just for smelling something. Of course, all work smells, to me, but they only pay you for literal smells."

"Since you've brought it up, I'll tell you something," Joady put in energetically. "Megan's off duty today and you're on, my proud beauty—and no stench money, either."

"I don't care," Honor said, "I don't care about anything today. I'll work my poor fingers to the bone for her—"

"No," said Megan, protestingly, "I'm going to work, Joady."

"You'll do as you're told, my girl," Joady said firmly, pushing back her chair. "And it's time someone started some sort of work. Bless you, chick," she added, and she kissed Megan as she went past her chair.

No one had asked her, Megan suddenly realized, why she had kept her news secret until this morning; no doubt they credited her with tact and delicacy, thinking that she had seen that it would have been in poor taste to have intruded on last night, which was Adrian's. And immediately she saw that that was so, that even if she had not been undecided she would surely have had the sense not to have taken the edge off their pleasure by, at the same time, taking the edge off their sorrow, and she felt less guilty as she stood up and began to help Honor to clear the table. This had been the right and fitting time to tell them; it would help them today to have something to contemplate that was sheer happiness to them all. Contentedly she went out to the kitchen for a tray.

As Mary went to help James to rise from his chair, Paul came to himself and stood up. He had been thinking, with a pang of regret, that they would not be as happy as this tomorrow; no doubt they would be very sad. He wished again that he could make them understand, could make them see that he was doing something that would make Adrian happy, as nothing else could; but he knew it was hopeless, that the situation was beyond

100

their understanding, that, unless they had been with Adrian, unless they had lain beside him on those last awful nights and had heard his almost incoherent words, unless they had talked with him all these months since his death, they would never appreciate Paul's point of view. It was a pity, but it could not be helped; but it grieved him to know that they would misunderstand his motives, would think him ungrateful—mad, perhaps. Still, it was part of the sacrifice he must make for Adrian, and, fortunately, he was so sure in his own mind that there was nothing but good in what he was doing, that, though he desired their good opinion of him, the fear of losing it would in no way deter him. The whole thing was so right and sensible that he felt almost indifferent about it; it was just the fact that they were going to hurt themselves that made him a little sad.

He handed James the stick that hung on the back of his chair.

"Paul will help me, Mary," James said. "I want to have a talk with him. Is there anything you want to do just now, lad, or can you come into the study for a while?"

"Yes," Paul said. "I've nothing to do now. I'm to go to the village with Megan, later, but there's a while yet, I think."

"All right, James," Mary said. "I'll go and help Joady to write out the shopping list."

She stood aside at the doorway to let them pass, and she watched delightedly as James walked confidently down the hall, one arm through Paul's, one hand lightly holding his stick, and then she turned back into the room. She felt the excitement of unaccustomed happiness flowing through her mind, and for a moment, to steady herself, she went to the window seat and sat down beside Jenkins, who was gazing out into the orchard, watching Iago foolishly racing round after rabbits that weren't there, snuffling and bounding and barking, dissipating energy which Jenkins kept carefully in reserve, so that when Jenkins crouched to spring at a bird, that bird would never escape.

Idly, as she looked out over the sunlit orchard, and contemplated some of the work she would do there this afternoon, Mary reflected that dogs were masculine creatures, whereas cats, regardless of their sex, were always feminine; dogs were open-hearted, clumsy, strong, and a little obtuse—they could be very easily outwitted by a cat's sharp mind; beside them, cats were frail and delicate, fastidious, withdrawn, secretive. Dogs ran hither and thither, amiably aimless, but a cat always seemed to have a particular destination, it was always coming from somewhere and proceeding to somewhere else; otherwise it slept tranquilly, so that, in its very old age, it was still graceful and beautiful, whereas an old dog was often a sloberry, tattered, ragged thing. . . . A blue butterfly fluttered uncertainly across the persimmon tree, vivid with autumn, and Iago barked and blundered and generously warned the butterfly of its danger, whereas Jenkins would have waited, muscles working under silky fur, and a swift, cruel paw would have smashed the frail fabric of the blue wings. She stroked, very lightly, the extreme tip of Jenkin's nose, and he purred, a small dynamo of pleasure starting up somewhere in his inside. She felt drugged with pleasant contemplation, adrift from things around her, tasks to be done, plans to be made. . . .

Joady came briskly into the room with the shopping pad, pencil poised, brow thoughtful, her mind preoccupied with the problem of food. She sat down beside Mary and they began to compile the grocery list.

IX

James Carmichael's study was a large, uncluttered room, with wide windows opening on to the side paddock. Paul helped James to the chair behind the wide, square desk in the centre of the room, and he lowered himself slowly into it, hanging the stick over the arm. Then Paul went to a low, leather-covered chair by the window, and sat down. They both filled their pipes, and Paul looked about him with pleasure. Bookshelves were on three sides, their contents neatly stacked with an eye to economy of space; there were pictures of sailing ships on the walls, and on the mantelshelf over the dark-red, brick fireplace there was an incredibly delicate and intricate model of a three-masted ship;

102

the middle of the floor was covered by a wide, square rug, in a deep shade of maroon. This was surrounded by darkly shining floor boards, and long, maroon-coloured curtains hung at the windows. A quiet room, a room used for hard work.

James watched the boy's eyes as they examined the room; he had a fine face—clever, quick, observant. And so much more tranquil than it had been yesterday. The desire to know him, to place him against some background, grew strongly in James's mind.

"We haven't bothered you with questions, Paul," he began. "If you were just to be a casual guest, just with us for a few days, I probably wouldn't bother; but I'd like to know something about you—your interests, your people, your background, if it doesn't worry you to talk of them. It's not mere idle curiosity—I've a definite reason."

"Why, of course." Paul smiled at him, removing his pipe from his mouth. "No, it doesn't worry me. It's not very interesting, though."

"What did you do before the war?"

"Well, I hadn't much time to do anything. The family— my mother and father, that is; I'm an only child—have a property in the Dorrigo district. It's thriving and prosperous, and when I left school I was to have gone there to help manage the place; but instead I went straight into camp—that was in 1940. I was eighteen then."

"I see," James said slowly, disappointment in his voice. So he was a country lad. Probably he had no interest in business at all. "And was that what you wanted to do most?"

"I wasn't quite sure what I wanted, but it woudn't have been the land, I think. I was brought up to it, and somehow I reacted by preferring the city. I'd thought a bit about law, or perhaps getting a business job and doing a B.Ec.; but even before we left school none of us was bothering much about the future—most of us were only waiting to get into the Army."

James's eyes brightened.

"Well," he said, slowly, "what do you plan now? Any preferences?"

He noticed the sudden disturbed unease in Paul's expression.

103

Perhaps he was blundering like a fool into the boy's mind; after all, Paul was still convalescent, he was not prepared, perhaps, to face any kind of effort just yet. James hurried on.

"I don't want to make you feel that there's any urgency about this, but I've a plan in my mind and I'm so excited about it that I feel I must tell you. Shall I go on?"

"Yes." Paul's voice was quite calm; he was staring down at his hands. "Yes, go on, please."

"I wondered if you would care to come into my business, in some capacity. As you know, Anthea has been carrying the burden of it for a long while now, but I'd like to relieve her of it. She wants to have the children home with her, I know, and besides, she's fagged out with it all—she's been looking far from well lately. Now, I'm going to pull myself round and get back to it myself, but I know I won't have long; a stroke is always followed by another one, you know, and that may come at any time. If you were agreeable I could teach you the business, and I'd be very happy to make you my partner. You could do your economics course at the same time, and then, when I have to retire permanently, you would be in a position to carry on."

He paused. Paul sat without a movement, staring up at the model of the ship.

"Well, how does it strike you?"

Still he sat there, and now James could see that he was trembling. He cursed himself: this boy was ill.

"I'm sorry, Paul. Forget all about it; you're not fit yet."

"Yes." Paul's voice was high-pitched. "Yes, I'm quite fit. Only, you see . . ." His voice trailed off, he sank back in the chair and lowered his head, his pipe held in one slack hand, which lay limply over the arm of the chair, the fingers of the other hand tapping out a series of little rhythmical, patterned sounds on the arm rest.

"You see,"—as he looked up at James, his eyes were clouded, straining with the effort to convey his meaning—"there's only today, isn't there?"

James regarded him in bewilderment.

"And tomorrow, perhaps," Paul went on, hysteria in his voice now; "but no longer. There mustn't be more than tomorrow. I can't bear it if it should . . . I can't talk about my days after tomorrow, because that's when it all ends. It must!—nothing must stop it! Nobody must try to stop me! Don't talk about afterwards, don't! There's no afterwards. . . ." Tears filled his eyes, and ugly sobbing sounds came from his throat. His eyes were fixed piteously on James's face, looking for understanding and reassurance that could never be there. A mad terror came to his mind that perhaps they knew and were plotting together to prevent him. He rose to his feet and stood swaying, shaken with sobs, distraught. Perhaps they had guessed and had hidden the children, perhaps they wouldn't be there when he went up to see Anthea this morning—how else would they be able to talk calmly about things like business pursuing their normal way? And he knew he only had until tomorrow night, for tomorrow night, if he had failed, Adrian would come back, and this time the horrifying, mind-destroying remembrance would come. He knew this with terrible certainty.

"No!" he shouted, and spun round to face James. "No, I tell you." His pipe clattered to the floor, and he fell back into the chair, spent and shaken.

James couldn't believe that it was happening. He managed to struggle from his chair, and, leaning on the stick, one hand on the desk, he made his way slowly across to Paul. He wouldn't call the women unless he must; it would only embarrass the boy and perhaps lead to further upset. This was his doing and he must make what amends he could. Curse it, curse it! Just when Paul was so much improved, so tranquil and happy. He bent over the limp form and touched Paul's shoulder.

"Paul," he said softly, "I'm sorry—I'm terribly sorry. Try to calm yourself; forget everything I've said. . . ."

Still he lay shuddering, his eyes closed, his body inert. Inspiration came to James. "I know that there's only tomorrow," he said quickly, and was pleased to see a change in the boy's face; his eyes opened and the trembling sobs grew quieter.

James went on, "It would be foolish to make any plans. I must have been crazy. Now forget it all—how about a brandy and soda?"

Painfully he went to the cupboard, and poured the drink.

When he turned again to Paul, he noticed that his eyes were clearer, that the panic had gone, and that he seemed to be aware of his surroundings again. Paul drained the glass quickly and sat up, wiping his face and eyes with his handkerchief, warmth and reassurance flowing through him, for it seemed almost as if Adrian's father was in sympathy with his point of view; this was better than anything he had hoped for, and distress faded quickly from him. Indeed, he was rapidly forgetting what exactly had upset him: some fear that they were all plotting against him. But they weren't; he was convinced of that. Why, Mr. Carmichael had seemed to understand wonderfully how he felt. Suddenly he was very happy as he had been when he came in here—happier even, for now he sensed that he had a real friend and sympathizer. Should he tell Mr. Carmichael of his plans? No, better not, perhaps; better not, he thought regretfully. Something might go wrong. He would be better to work on his own.

"You've been awfully good," he said cheerfully. "I felt rotten for a moment, but I'm quite all right now. I hope I didn't give you a scare."

"You certainly did, my boy," James said ruefully, as he made his way back to his chair. "Pour me a drink like a good fellow, will you?—I'm all in; that is, if you feel able, of course."

Paul took the drink to him.

"I'm quite fit again, now," he said.

"You'd better rest awhile, though," James said. "You've had a nasty turn, and it'll make you tired later, if you don't rest. Like to stay in here, or would you sooner go upstairs?"

"I'll stay here," Paul said, sitting back in his chair. "That is, if you really think I should." He lay back, and in a few moments, as James watched him, he was asleep.

James's heart throbbed heavily, and a weight of pitying sadness oppressed him. He felt that he, too, could easily let go and weep for this boy; not only for him, but for all the young men like him, coming back to a world they couldn't manage, thinking thoughts incomprehensible to ordinary people, plagued by visions and memories that would never let them be quite normal again. And what of those without money, with people depending on them, a pension between them and starvation? And so soon people would forget, forget the dark days when the posters of the anthropoid Jap, fingers spread over Australia, shouted at one from every billboard, "He's coming south!" And as they forgot, so would they forget these men, these men who were broken in mind and heart, even while their bodies mended.

With immense effort, James raised himself from the chair and hobbled to the door; he couldn't stay there another minute gazing on the ruin his well-intentioned obtuseness had brought about. Quietly he closed the door and walked down the hall to the living room.

X

Honor was stacking plates along the shelves of the blue and white dresser in the kitchen, and Megan was wiping down the table when, suddenly, they both stopped at the sound of a shout from the study. Paul's voice! Raised, hysterical. Honor put away the last two saucers very quietly and went on thoughtfully hanging up the cups and jugs on their hooks. Megan went to the sink and, after wringing out the cloth under the tap, spread it to dry over the upturned washing-up basin. They both turned at once to face each other's solemn expression, and they both smiled uneasily. Honor sat up on the table and swung her legs, gazing out on the paddock; Megan stood by the window, looking out to the tree where the possum slept, his long tail hanging down, as he lay in a fork of the branches. Honor spoke at last, soberly.

"Have you noticed him doing queer things?"

"Yes," Megan said, without looking at her.

"What, for instance?"

"Well, he gave me an awful shock last night," she said, and she told Honor the story about the watch. She had forgotten, since last night, just how much it had shocked her, but all the inexplicable strangeness of it came back to her now. Joady had come in quietly and was transferring three dozen eggs from a basket to the egg box, carefully placing the delicately coloured

107

eggs in the rows of holes, counting them as she did so. She appeared not to be listening.

"M'm," Honor said thoughtfully. "He's certainly got a thing about that watch; he wouldn't take it off to swim, this morning, and he looked like murder when I tried to make him."

Joady went into the pantry with the egg box and the basket; then she walked quietly through the kitchen and out into the hall, where, her face pale, her hands clasped tightly together in front of her, she leant against the wall, horrified, her heart thumping.

In the kitchen the girls went on talking quietly.

"I don't suppose it's anything, really," Megan said. "He's got a neurosis of some sort, no doubt; after all, when you think of the things he told us last night—and there must have been dozens he didn't tell us about."

"Yes," Honor agreed. "For instance, he didn't tell us how Adrian died. Nobody asked him either. Why do you suppose we didn't?"

"Because we didn't want to upset him, and because we couldn't bear to hear. I don't want to know."

"No, we don't want to know," Honor said. "We don't want to know because we're cowards; we want to know that he died heroically, we want to worship his bravery; but we're too yellow to endure to the end with him. We only want to go so far and then, when it gets too revolting, we want to leave him to it."

Megan looked at her in astonishment. Where on earth did she get her insight? She was little more than a child, she had known Adrian less than any of them, yet she had discovered this thing that, no doubt, they were all anxious to conceal from themselves. But Honor's mind did not linger on things, and while Megan, her thoughts troubled and confused, was trying to answer the charge she had made against them all, Honor went on, "But he's nice. Golly! I like him, don't you?"

"I like him tremendously," said Megan, thankfully escaping from her disquieting thoughts. "He's not at all like a stranger; I feel really fond of him, as if he's the sort of person you couldn't bear to lose, once you've met him."

"Oh, yes, yes." Honor stretched her hands above her head.

"I adore him—and he's madly good-looking. Well," she went on, "on with the toil. I don't know why Joady's letting us sit here comfortably like this; she seems to be losing her grip since Paul came. You taking him down to the village?"

"Yes." Megan looked at the clock. "My hat, look at the time. It's nearly nine o'clock, and Paul's got to be up at Anthea's at eleven. He wants to see the children."

"Funny," Honor said. "You don't expect a young man to be so mad about kids."

"Well, no doubt Adrian spent a lot of time talking about them, so naturally Paul would be anxious to see them. It's nice to think they're such lovely kids—they won't disgrace us." And Megan hurried out of the kitchen and ran up the stairs to her room.

Honor sat for a moment longer; she stretched her legs out stiffly in front of her and frowned intently at her feet. At last she said aloud. "Maybe. But it's queer, all the same," and then swung herself down from the table.

The telephone was ringing when Megan, dressed for the village in a short, straight-cut, tweed skirt and round-necked, grey pullover, came running down the stairs. She swung round the stairpost to the recess under the stairs, which housed the little telephone table and a stool, picked up the receiver and said, "Hullo . . . oh, Alec," in a voice which was ordinarily cheerful at first, but which ended on a lame note, as last night's scene rushed confusedly through her mind. Anxiously she concentrated on gauging his mood, and his friendly, easy voice brought her own confidence back.

"Listen, Megan," he said, "I can't talk much now, but I'd like to see you today."

"Would it be all right—I mean—" She paused, thinking of his mother's fury, of Julian's anxiety for her to leave, last night. "Do you think I should come there?"

"Perhaps not," he said. "No, but could you drive down this afternoon and pick me up? I'd like you to drive me somewhere where we could talk; I've some plans to make."

"But, Alec, do you think you're well enough?" Megan's voice was dismayed; it was ages since Alec had been out of the house,

109

and Mrs. Kyles wouldn't thank Megan for driving her sick son about in an open car, catching cold, perhaps.

"Yes, yes." His voice was mildly exasperated. "I've got a bit of a cold this week, that's all. Forget it. You will come, won't you, Megan? Promise?"

"Yes," she said. "Of course, Alec—I'll be there about two. Will that do?"

"Do fine, blessed little Megan. Bye-bye."

She sat for a moment, on the stool, after she had replaced the receiver. So he had meant it, last night: he was going to try to break the bonds that had held him for so long. Well, it wouldn't be easy, because, even if he wasn't actually ill, Alec was not well, either; he was debilitated, weak from never having attempted to develop his strength; he would need help, and he obviously looked to her for it. She was really frightened of Mrs. Kyles, had been for years, but suddenly she was pleased that she was to have an opportunity to struggle against her, even if in the indirect way of supporting Alec's escape. And it was a good thing to help anyone as gifted as Alec. Perhaps, if he left that place, he'd have a chance to show some of the beautiful stuff he'd been doing during the last couple of years; if he did, Megan felt sure that he'd soon become known. He's bound to succeed, she thought, and she felt a delighted rush of affection for him; they'd been friends for many years and had always respected each other's work—he'd be glad to hear of her scholarship, too. As she stood up from the stool she thought that it was odd that she should be telling her news to Alec before Julian heard it and that it no longer seemed outrageous to do so.

She had reached the foot of the stairs when Paul came out of the study, looking a little white and with a vagueness about his movements.

"I wondered where you were, Paul," she said. "I'll be ready in a minute. I've just got to get the list from mother."

From the living room her father's voice called her name sharply. Megan said, "Oh, just a moment, Paul," and went quickly up the hall.

James was standing by the window, leaning heavily on his stick, and she thought, with a pang of compassion, that he

110

looked very weary; perhaps he's been indulging in an energetic bout of his exercises, she thought. But there was something more. She glanced at his face, noted the expression, set firmly into a pattern of self-control, and said, "Yes, Father?"

"It's Paul," he said abruptly. "Make sure he's quite fit to go before you take him walking. He had a nasty turn while he was in the study with me." His voice sank into self-accusation.

"What kind of a turn, darling?" Megan knelt nonchalantly on the end of the settee. When people wore such an expression as she saw on James's face, you didn't make a fuss about things, or become emphatic—that is, if you were a Carmichael.

"I don't know. Yes, I do. I was clumsy—it seems to upset him to talk of the future; he has some idea that time doesn't extend beyond tomorrow—a *carpe diem* outlook run riot. However, he's over it, and it may do him good to go with you; but be careful: don't make the mistake I did. Don't talk to him about anything that affects him beyond tomorrow."

"No, Father. Now, darling," she said gently, "won't you come and sit down? You've upset yourself." He let her lead him to a chair, and he was glad to lie back while she brought his books and papers, his tobacco and his spectacles.

When she had gone out he closed his eyes and gave himself up to dejection. All the gladness, the hopefulness, had gone out of him, and he gazed at his life across the distant years. What had he done with it, this precious span of living? What was there left to him of any worth? He felt himself alone, solitary among them all, apart from them. That girl who had just left him—what did they know of each other? Nothing. They were an ideally happy family; every one of them knew it, and strangers were quick to perceive and acknowledge it; there were few disputes; he could hardly remember any real quarrels. The unfortunate bungling of Honor's defence of Hester Laing was the only outstanding discord in their harmonious lives together; but there was a feeling among them of dwelling apart from each other. Perhaps that was why they were able to be happy together—because they were aloof people and, for the most part, they respected each other's aloofness; they were polite to each other, for Mary and he had always insisted on courtesy

111

in their home. Oh, yes, there was always a stream of abuse, but it was persiflage, a safety valve; it occurred to him that all this had probably followed from his own attitude. He had cut himself off from the others, even from Mary; he had not wanted to acknowledge to himself, or to allow her to guess, that his worship of his son far surpassed his love for her, and perhaps she had guessed, had wrapped herself, for protection, in this cloak of pleasant calmness; and, he thought unhappily, if she had known, so, probably, had the girls; they had, no doubt, realized that, though they had their father's kindly good will, they were unimportant to him. Yes, perhaps they had known all these years, while he had been feeling so confidently that he was keeping his secret from them all; and now Adrian was gone and he was terribly, terribly alone. He had not realized, until his hopes for Paul had collapsed, that his relations with the others so lacked warmth.

A feeling of panic seized him and made him turn his head restlessly from side to side. He did not want kindliness and forbearance; he wanted warm love, unrestrained affection. Suppose he called to Mary to come to him, now, desolate as he was; supposing he said to her, "Mary, caress me, reassure and comfort me, by showing me I am everything in the world to you." She would be alarmed, afraid that he was ill, because, of course, he was not everything to her, he was one among several people who were important to her. He himself had made conditions in his home that denied him the right to demand such a thing.

No, he decided, such a thing as a happy family was an illusion, but perhaps they were unhappy less often than many families, simply because they were cultivated people, among whom open strife was considered bad form and absence of open enthusiasm for one another the usual thing. In any case, he felt responsible for the existence of such an attitude among them all, and perhaps, he reflected, there was a good deal to be said for it, at least from the children's point of view; they were all able to live together with a certain dignity, and the children were able to develop whatever talents they possessed, with a minimum of intrusion into and interference with their affairs

112

and emotions, by others—and their attempts to interfere with Honor had been convincing proof, for them, that it was a bad method. Perhaps, then, he had not done badly for the children; but for himself—and for Mary?

He tried to think back, to trace exactly the time when he had begun to relegate Mary to a different position in his mind, when he had come to regard her as Adrian's mother rather than as his beloved, the adored girl he had married. Suddenly despair rushed through his whole being, and he sobbed with regret and with a bitter sense of loss, of mistakes made blindly; the infinitely pathetic realization of himself, an old man in an easy chair, negligible and tiresome, came to his mind, and he covered his eyes with his hand and sobbed. And nobody came to him. He could hear Mary's voice giving final instructions to Megan, then Paul's voice saying good-bye. Their young, light steps went along the hall and down the steps, careless voices growing fainter. He could hear Joady scolding Honor and Honor's light laugh in reply: all, all on the surface, none of them saying the things that were in the hearts of all of them, the dark, sad things that no one must hear but the self. Oh, Adrian—Mary—I have lost you, lost you both. I am myself alone and unable to hide. . . .

XI

The hills lay, sun-bright and shadowless, before them, as they stooped under the boughs of the lemon tree and walked down to the gate. Excitement rose in Megan's mind, the stirring of feeling, without a specific cause, that such a morning could bring to her. Some days, in every season, hold the essence of that season in their hours—and this was more than an autumn day. It was autumn. It said, "Here is autumn in Ambara. Gaze on it, for you may not see it all at once again; one morning you may see a perfect, dew-jewelled web between the young wattles; one morning you may see the smiling green hills, bright in the sun, as they are now; one morning you may smell that delicate

113

soil smell, damp with the ground mist; but you'll never again see and feel them all at once. Here is autumn spread before you—gaze on it." Things were transfigured in this perfection; the shopping expedition was a privilege to be fought for, the walk to the village a delight, the ordinary process of breathing was exquisite, stirring.

"Oh, Paul, I'm happy, I'm gay, I'm delighted," she said, skipping now and again, as they walked through the small, tree-dotted paddock, along the same track they had followed last night. Could that have been she, Megan Carmichael? If it had been, then it was not the same as this morning's Megan Carmichael.

"Yes, so am I," Paul answered happily, swinging the shopping basket he was carrying for her.

"Hey, don't do that—mind the jam."

"Why?" he asked blandly, "are we carrying coals to Newcastle? Or do you shop in kind, in this primitive place? Does one jar of jam equal four chops?—and then we swap two chops for a bar of soap, perhaps."

"Ass," Megan said. "We're taking the jam to Mrs. Croft. Didn't you hear Mother tell me?"

"And why are we taking jam to Mrs. Croft? Has she insufficient means, or can't she read her recipe book, or has she no sugar coupons?"

"It's an old Ambara custom," Megan explained patiently. "Nobody ever makes jam without distributing jars of it around; the result is that everyone always eats everyone else's jam, for you never have any of your own left. And so one man, in his time, eats many jams, and some of them are decidedly odd. Still, it broadens one's outlook; one sees how the other half lives—and, also, what a lot of it probably dies from. Paul, what an awful lot of rot you talk!"

"You're not so bad yourself," he said admiringly, and they climbed through the fence and began to walk in the middle of the road.

Paul's mind was untroubled by recollection as they walked briskly along, talking only intermittently, and he gave himself up to the tranquillity through which he walked. Roads and

114

tracks branched off to the right, and as they came abreast of them he gazed eagerly down their length for the tiny, tree-framed vista they each afforded, every one ending in the slow swoop of the road-patterned hills. At length they turned into a narrow road, bordered thickly with ranks of foliage—in front the young blue-green gums, then wattles, straight and soldier-like, then paperbarks and the tall gums, every gap filled by the eager, crowding blackthorn. At the end of the road rose a smooth, unfoliaged hill, yellow-green in the sunlight, and another away beyond it, velvet-surfaced, obscured momentarily by a snowy wisp of smoke, flung across it from the engine of a train; and still farther away, the perfection of perspective, a tiny rim of blue hills, underlining distance, emphasizing its own far removal from them. Paul raised his eyes; the sky was a confusion of cloud, helter-skelter, erratic, yet each line and rippling spray correct, unerringly placed in the design.

"You'll never see anything more beautiful than this in your travels, Megan," he said.

"No," she said slowly, "there'll be plenty of places as beautiful, in different ways, I suppose, but nothing could be lovelier than Ambara."

She turned from the road, on to the grassy sidewalk.

"This is Croft's," she said.

Tall camphor laurels, red-splashed, hung low over a white-barred fence. They opened the double gate and walked up a path between smooth lawns and neat gardens. The house, white, two-storeyed, stood on a little hill, overlooking the garden, a daintiness about its windows matching the tidy, colourful garden.

"Mrs. Croft does all this herself," Megan told him, as they approached the front porch. "She's an awfully energetic little thing. Oh, there she is."

She left Paul and crossed the sloping lawn, calling to the little figure in the bottom corner of the garden. Mrs. Croft stood up, looking startled, then pleased, and then hurried to meet Megan. They stood talking a moment, and Paul looked appreciatively about him; the doll's-house atmosphere of the place was in keeping with this diminutive woman, in her fresh pink frock, her fair hair clouding childishly round her head. A pretty

115

place, a place where a woman had lived for years without a man. Suddenly he noticed the discordant note struck by the state of the long, white windowbox, running across the front of the house, below the wide windows, with their flower-sprigged curtains. It was ragged with unturned soil; nasturtiums, which should have trailed prettily over the side, were broken, the smashed, velvet petals ground into the soil, earth straggling across the sills. Perplexed, he gazed at the damage, then turned as the two women came up to him, Mrs. Croft talking breathlessly, nervously to Megan.

"This is Mr. Paul Quentin, Mrs. Croft. He is a friend of Adrian's, and he's staying with us for a little while."

"How do you do?" She proffered her hand shyly, realized that she still wore a grubby gardening glove, pulled it off, dropped it, and thanked Paul prettily when he picked it up. "You—then you must have been—a—a prisoner? Or perhaps I shouldn't speak of it—oh!"

She looked at Megan with large brown eyes, conscience-stricken, her fingers at her lips.

"Paul doesn't mind." Megan smiled at her reassuringly. "He talked to us for hours last night about his experiences—do you, Paul?"

"No," he answered, smiling too. He liked this timid little creature; everybody must want to comfort and reassure her, he thought. "No, of course I don't mind, Mrs. Croft."

"You're very brave," she murmured, still worried. "You mean —oh, Megan, men are wonderfully brave and strong, aren't they?"

Megan patted her shoulder and nodded. They both smiled down at her.

"Oh, but you'll come in? Do stay for a moment . . . some coffee. And I'd like you to see Martin. . . ."

"How is Martin?" Megan asked, as they turned towards the front door.

"Oh, Martin . . ." She looked at them, appealing for their approval, begging them to like Martin. "He's very well—and he's been a very good boy indeed."

She led the way across the tiny hall, talking to them over

116

her shoulder as she ushered them into the sitting room. They both stopped inside the door, blocking her view of it for a moment, and then Paul stepped aside for her and she saw.

She said, "Oh," and the break of despair in her voice made Megan's heart sick with pity for her. Soil and broken flowers were everywhere; trailing vines of nasturtium hung over the back of a chair; drooping petunias, uprooted savagely, hung from the white mantel over the fireplace; the long settee, covered with a blue-patterned linen, was stained and ugly with soil, trampled in by a boy's sturdy shoe; and the delicate blue carpet was a ruin of smashed petals, broken stems, and trodden earth.

"Martin!" The word was a thread of sound, tiny, thin, gasping; her face was white, and a hundred fears showed in her eyes, fears she dared tell no one, but which needed no telling.

He sat nonchalantly on the window seat; after one swift glance from dark eyes under lowered lids, he turned his back on them, unmoved by their presence. Paul looked down at his mother; her hands were clasped in front of her, her face scarlet now with shame and helplessness; tears filled her eyes and she looked from one to the other.

"I had to—I punished him a little last night," she said, her voice dull, apathetic. "I took his knife, and I hid it, and he was cross with me."

Paul noticed the injured hand, and as he looked at it she quickly covered it with the other hand. He could stand no more of this, he felt, and he walked quickly over to Martin.

"Did you do this?" he said sharply.

Martin looked at him expressionlessly, and then turned back to the window. Paul seized him by the shoulders and swung him round, and Megan felt a sudden shock at the expression on the boy's face, a look of astounded loathing; then she took Mrs. Croft's arm and hurried her out into the hall.

"Oh, don't—let me go to him—he mustn't touch Martin."

"Don't, Mrs. Croft." Megan forced her to sit on the chair beside the telephone table. "Paul won't hurt him, but he needs a lesson and you're not strong enough to give it to him."

An angry scream came from the sitting room, and then the

117

sound of solid, heavy slapping. Mrs. Croft covered her face and leant forward in the chair, weeping hopelessly. Megan, her face wrinkled with worry and distaste for the sounds coming from behind the closed door, smoothed her hair and murmured to her.

"Oh, he shouldn't have touched him—I never beat him. Martin will do something awful now—I know it, I know it. I've been afraid for George to come back, because I knew he'd beat Martin and then Martin would do something—oh, what shall I do? Oh, God, dear—dear, dear God, help me. What shall I do?"

"Come and make us all some coffee, Mrs. Croft," Megan said, putting an arm round her and leading her down the hall. Somehow she managed to get her to the kitchen; wringing a handkerchief under the tap, she bathed the streaming eyes and the scarlet, distressed face, and gradually the sobs quietened.

"Now sit still and tell me where everything is, and when you're feeling better you can take over." Briskly Megan began making coffee, talking cheerfully as she put cups and saucers, sugar and cream, on a tray.

"There's really nothing to be distressed about, Mrs. Croft. Martin needs a man to show him that he mustn't do these destructive things, and it will be very good for him, no doubt. Of course, Paul shouldn't interfere, I suppose, but I'm glad he did. It'll make things easier for you, you'll see."

As she talked on, some of the agony of tension eased from the childlike face; the brown eyes, fixed on Megan's face, ceased to fill with tears; and, after a while, Mrs. Croft began to talk, to tell Megan of the misery and the hopeless fight. She showed her the cut hand, always excusing Martin, blaming herself, or the school, or the unkind people of Ambara. The relief of it all, of having someone who was really interested, in a kindly way, filled her with a new hope, which she realized was empty, but which momentarily soothed her and made her feel stronger, as if reinforcements had arrived when the struggle was proving too much for her. But always there was the thought that they would go; they would leave her to face such a Martin as she had never known before, and the terror of tonight, tonight, when she would be alone with him, came to her mind. She

118

stood up quickly and began to finish the arrangements for the coffee; together they carried the coffee things out to the little crazy-stone piazza that ran across the full width of the back of the house.

After the first scream of unbelieving fury, the boy lay quietly while Paul thrashed him, thoroughly and dispassionately, with the leather belt he had unbuckled from his waist; after a while a sick disgust, a feeling of the uselessness of this as an argument, made Paul stop, and he stood up. Martin lay huddled on the floor by the settee while Paul buckled on his belt. Then Paul stooped and pulled him to his feet.

"Now," he said, a little breathlessly, "start cleaning up."

The boy looked at him for a moment, and Paul threateningly lifted his hand again. Silently, Martin twisted out of his grip and bent to pick up the flowers from the carpet. Paul sat on the settee and lit a cigarette as he watched.

"Pick up all the plants and put them in the wastepaper basket," he said. "Then go and get a dustpan and broom and start on the soil; when you've got as much as you can off the carpet and things, start on the windowbox—your mother will have to finish in here. You've got to replant that windowbox perfectly, refill it and plant new flowers in it. Understand?"

The boy nodded, his head averted.

"And then you're to come out and apologize to your mother —and don't be long about it."

Paul stood up and left the room, closing the door behind him; uncertain where to go, he paused in the little white hallway and then followed the sound of their voices to the piazza. Mrs. Croft looked timidly at him as he emerged into the sunlight, and Megan, her face troubled, managed to smile at him.

"I'm sorry, Mrs. Croft," Paul said. "I suppose you're cursing me, but I had to give that fellow a hiding. He's a man's job, you know."

"Yes," she said, sadly. "Yes—I know you're kind, and I do hope you're right; but I've always been afraid to beat him. . . ." She broke off and the tears welled up.

"Do sit down," she went on, wiping the tears away and beginning to pour the coffee. Resolutely she began to talk about other

119

things, her voice still trembling and her hands fluttering uncertainly among the cups. After a moment Megan told her about the scholarship, and she managed to express her delight and her congratulations. They went on to women's talk about clothes and how Megan's absence would affect her family, and in a little while the tension eased.

Paul sat back in the cane chair, lethargic, saturated with sunshine and the peace of the garden, idly noting the touches of beauty this little woman had created about her: Virginia creeper, hanging over a lattice, as absurdly overdone and unreal, in its autumn colouring, as a picture on a glossy-papered calendar; a pomegranate tree, decked stiffly with pinkly shining toffee apples. She was meant for such gentle, colourful harmony; she could produce it around her and become it with the sweetness of her own presence; and she had to live in a black hell of dread and anxiety, with this boy. He looked at her hand and wondered how she'd received that long cut; no doubt it should have stitches in it, but she'd be too ashamed and fearful to go to a doctor with it. A feeling of deep affection for her filled his mind, as he watched her and noted her eyes, distressed behind her smile. Then steps sounded from inside and Martin came out.

"Why, Martin, darling." Her voice was a flurry. She half rose, pleading with her eyes to him.

"Have you cleaned it all up?" Paul said quietly.

"Yes."

"Well, finish the job now. What else did you have to do?"

The dark eyes looked blankly at Paul, for a moment, and then he turned to his mother.

"I apologize."

"Oh, Martin, darling—oh, Mr. Quentin, Martin is a good boy, really he is. You mustn't think . . ." She pulled Martin to her, her arm round his waist, and pressed her face against him. Martin gazed steadily at Paul; he looked unperturbed, even pleased, Megan thought, but it was not comfortable to watch, all the same. She rose suddenly.

"Mrs. Croft, would you think badly of us if we go now? I'll be awfully late with Mother's shopping."

120

"No, of course, Megan." They all rose, and Mrs. Croft led them through the hall to the front porch.

"You've a very pretty garden, Mrs. Croft," Paul said, as they stood looking down to the camphor laurels.

"Paul is very much taken with Ambara," Megan said. "Honor took him out as far as the river before breakfast, and tonight, on our way home, we're going to walk up to Raikes's meadow to see Ambara by moonlight."

"You'll love that, Mr. Quentin." Her arm round Martin's shoulders, she stood looking eagerly up at Paul, her composure completely restored. "It's so perfect from there on a moonlit night. The moon's on the wane, though, Megan."

"It was full only last night," Megan said, "so it'll just be right between eleven and twelve; we're going after the Welcome Home, so if we leave there soon after eleven we should be in time. Are you coming down to the hall, Mrs. Croft?"

"Oh, well . . ." She paused, as if the thought of the pleasure of mixing with her neighbours tempted her strongly, then she wavered and said, "No, I hadn't planned—I don't generally go out at night. It would be nice . . . no, Megan, dear, I shouldn't think so."

"Well," said Paul, to end her uneasy hesitation, "may we call again tomorrow morning, Mrs. Croft? Martin is going to replant the windowbox for you and I'd like to see that he's done a good job. Could I come about the same time?"

"Oh, yes, Mr. Quentin." Her delight and pride in Martin's reform sounded in her voice. "You are so very kind. I'm sure he will do it beautifully, won't you, Martin?"

He said nothing, but the expression of pleasure deepened in his unwavering gaze as he looked at Paul.

"Good-bye, Mrs. Croft." Megan pressed her arm and kissed her cheek.

"Good-bye, Megan dear—and Mr. Quentin, good-bye."

They moved down the path to the white gate and she called after them, "I'll see you tomorrow, Mr. Quentin—tomorrow morning."

"No, you won't." The words came slowly and quietly from the boy beside her. "No, you bloody well won't."

121

She turned to look at him, a hard lump of fear welling up in her throat; he was watching Paul as he latched the gate and waved, before he disappeared from view. Martin was smiling; as she stared at him, he began to laugh silently, hysterically, clasping both his arms round his waist, swaying in a paroxysm of laughter. She put her hand out to touch him, but suddenly, with a shrill, screaming laugh, he twisted away from her and ran round to the back of the house. She sat down on the step and pressed her hands to her head, rocking miserably to and fro, her false confidence, her illusion of happiness gone. Now what had she to face, what dreadful thing, more dreadful than anything she had known so far?

"Our Father, who art in heaven . . ." she murmured desperately. After a few moments she felt calmer, and she was suddenly convinced that her prayers would be answered, and this terrible, unbearable burden had been lifted by loving, strong hands from her weak shoulders. How her problem could be solved she did not know, but for the present she was content in her conviction that the solution had already been arrived at by the One who could see that it was beyond her powers.

XII

"Well!" Megan exclaimed, as Paul jumped the grassy ditch and began to walk down the road beside her. "Well!" she repeated, half-amused exasperation in her tone.

"Yes?" He looked at her attentively, inquiringly.

"You're certainly the ideal caller. Do you always produce upheavals out of your hat when you meet people for the first time?"

"You're angry?"

"No—and that's the infuriating thing about you; you go and do the thing or say the thing that really needs doing or saying, and you make one realize one's own cowardliness. That boy needed his whipping, just as much as Alec needed his jolt last night—and yet you leave the onlookers appalled. . . . Oh, I don't know what I feel about you. The things you do are outrageous, and yet they need so much to be done; at the time they seem to be the one thing one wishes to avoid above all others, but afterwards they seem perfectly right."

He felt a wave of heart-warming pleasure; perhaps they'd feel the same about the children, so that, in time, he'd be able to make them see things his way. Recollection startled him with a stunning shock and he halted suddenly, staring at Megan, pale and shaken.

"What's wrong?" She stopped, a couple of paces ahead of him, puzzled, then uneasy, at his staring immobility.

"Megan"—the words came dragging from his lips—"what's the time?"

"It's—it's just half-past ten," she said, still half turning, ready to walk on.

He put a hand to his forehead, his head moving slowly from side to side. Megan came back and stood in front of him.

"What is it, Paul? Aren't you feeling well?"

"I almost forgot." There was anguish in his voice. "I mustn't forget, I must think. Now, now. . . ." His knuckles beat against his forehead violently, then his tenseness eased and he turned to her eagerly.

"Megan, would you mind—would you think me an awful swine if I didn't come with you?"

"No—no, Paul, of course." She was still puzzled, but she forced herself not to ask questions. "I'll be quite all right."

"Look," he said, "leave any heavy parcels. Leave them—oh, somewhere—and I'll bring them back with me. Will you?"

"Yes, I'll leave them at the station, then."

"Thanks, Megan—thanks awfully. Good-bye."

He handed her the basket and began to walk violently, stumblingly, back along the road. She stood watching him, and soon she saw him beginning to run. She turned and continued her walk to the village. Lord, she thought, this is a week end and no mistake—one thing after another. Now whatever could have made him behave like that? As she turned into the red gravel road that ran beside the railway line, she remembered suddenly that he was to be at Anthea's at eleven. So that was it! But why all the alarm and fuss?

She walked along the grassy edge of the road and then stopped for a moment while she thought about it, leaning on the top bar of the railway fence; there, away to the right, Cedar Hill rested gently in its hill-fold, peacefully white among its massed green trees. Perhaps, she thought, he was like this over any appointment, perhaps it was part of the anxiety in his mind to worry about keeping appointments. She turned back to the roadway, feeling a little weary of all these unusual disturbances. She was awfully late with the shopping, and this afternoon there would be Alec; and somewhere at the back of her mind there was an unpleasant, niggling little distaste about Julian. Also, there was a great deal of thinking to be done about Adrian. And then there was this inexplicable Paul. Oh, heavens, things had suddenly become complicated. Depression settled on her, and her steps grew slower as she neared the village.

XIII

Joseph's workbench stood underneath the big cedar that grew outside the two-storeyed barn at Cedar Hill; the top storey of the barn, which was built up to the level of the drive, was the garage, and the bottom floor was Joseph's workroom and the storing house for all the fascinating odds and ends he needed for the garden. Here he kept his tools, and every Saturday morning he brought them out to the wide, brick-paved kitchen terrace and sharpened them at his workbench; and for years the children had sat there with him, while he put gleaming, razor-sharp edges on axes and knives, while he mended harnesses or soldered intricate pieces of mechanism. On wet Saturdays they sat inside in the workroom, but, whatever the weather, the Saturday morning ritual never varied.

Libby was sitting, now, at one end of the huge bench, and John sat on a weather-beaten, unturned cask; they were silent and intent, for at this time every week Joseph told them the

124

story of a film that he had seen many years ago, in the days of the silent pictures, when he had been a rabid film-goer. When sound came to films, Joseph had been bitterly offended; the gentle quietness, broken only by the subdued playing of the pianist, had been very precious to Joseph and had given his imagination full scope. These people, rolling their r's and talking as if they all had tonsillitis, displeased him greatly, and so he had turned his back on the film industry. But he held the stories of all the pictures he had seen in his memory, and the three of them could go through a long cycle of Saturdays without ever having recourse to an already told tale, and, even so, the children welcomed an old story perhaps more than a new one, and they were swiftly critical of any alterations Joseph might introduce.

On Thursday and Friday Joseph would ponder over the story, making sure of the exact sequence of events, and on Saturday morning he recounted it, in a wealth of detail, to Libby and John. There had been a time when it was all well over Libby's head, but she had never admitted it, and gradually, with the years, the situations and the characters had become so familiar that now she was seldom lost, for it was surprising how similar all the stories were, no matter how different the subject matter purported to be. Joseph was in some sort responsible for this, for it had quickly become obvious that not all the matters treated of in the films were suitable for his audience, so when this happened—and it happened frequently—he simply substituted his own characters and situations, so that the godly were rewarded and the evil-doers were subjected to a catastrophic series of misfortunes.

Joseph believed in the technique of audience participation, and from time to time he would pause and ask, "An' whadd'yer think she done then?"

In turn they would give their suggestions, one answering one question and the other the next, and nearly always they were right; after all, it took only a little mental agility on Joseph's part, and no harm was done to the story.

This morning they had hurried down to the terrace as soon as they had arrived, for it was later than usual and Joseph had already started sharpening. As soon as they were seated, after he had listened to a résumé of the news of the week and had inspected the large cavity which was all that was left of one of Libby's milk teeth, he began. They sat alertly, watching his face as he talked; they were both correctly attired in riding clothes, Libby's apple-green shirt vividly showing up her shining red curls, her soft, brown eyes gazing solemnly at Joseph's face, her mouth slightly open. Her skin was delicately pale, and, so far, she had few of the freckles which Anthea feared would one day prevent her from being beautiful. John was dark-haired, brown-skinned, quick and cheerful in his manner and expression, another Adrian already. Joseph often had to chide him for asking questions, for Joseph very wisely allowed no interruptions other than those he made himself. A general discussion and questioning period was allowed at the end of the story, during which time Joseph underlined the moral issues heavily, so that sometimes Libby was oppressed by a sense of sin for quite a long time afterwards; but Joseph had early realized that no story would ever be finished if he were to let himself be led astray by questions. Not that Libby was inclined to interrupt; she was a stolid, good child, "beautiful but dumb," Anthea said. This morning, however, she would have been glad to talk as much as possible, because her speech was characterized by a pleasant whistling sound, owing to the extensive gap left by the departed tooth; but they were both well aware that silence was Joseph's golden rule, so she must be content to wait. He had reached a strongly gripping point in the story, and she leant forward, her mouth gaping more and more widely; even John was sitting more quietly than usual, instead of indulging in the twisting and fidgeting that sometimes caused Joseph to pause maddeningly in the narrative, to say, grimly, "Now, look 'ere, is yer name St. Vitus, or is it John Carmichael?"

He would not continue until John, much out of countenance, averred that it was John Carmichael.

"Well"—Joseph's crushing reply was always the same, but somehow lost nothing by reiteration—"then don't act like St. Vitus."

The story, this morning, was about the unhappy plight of a

young man, beloved by two women, one a shining example to all her sex, womanly, sweet-natured, fair and long-suffering, the other possessed of practically all the failings and weaknesses known to woman. By some vile stratagem, the second woman had convinced the man that the noble example was dead, and on the eve of his marriage to her, his former love suddenly returned to claim him.

"Well," said Joseph, "there 'e was—all of a muck and a sweat what to do. 'E 'ears that 'is sheila's not dead, but 'e don't dare show up, because 'e's gone to the dogs, as yer might say; 'e don't think of nothing but the bottle, now, and 'e spends all 'is time in them gambling dens with this vamp, see. But this other one 'ears it all through the old parson—real saintly old gent, 'e was, silver 'air done long and curlin' up at the ends—and she's real cut up: 'owls something cruel when the old reverend tells 'er. And she says, 'Take me to 'im,' she says. 'Not on yer sweet life,' says the parson. 'Them places 'e 'angs round ain't fit fer yer little feet to tread in,' 'e says. 'What's the odds?' she says, flingin' 'er arms around. 'I can take it,' she says. Well, after a lot of argy-bargy, the kind old parson takes 'er down to the gamblin' den one night, but the girl's bloke ain't there—and she's that nice-lookin' that all the gamblers stop gamblin' and look at 'er, and one bloke that's just goin' to swig off a big mugful of whisky, 'e 'urls 'is glass to the floor and reforms that very minute. But one party, a nasty-lookin' bit o' work that's 'alf-blotto, 'e comes staggerin' up to 'er and 'e says, 'Ullo, sweet'eart, 'ow about a little kiss?' And she give 'im a look! That's all she done—she just give 'im a look. But she's got such a way about 'er that 'e breaks down and cries, and 'e kneels on the floor and kisses the 'em of 'er skirt. So then this 'ere vamp comes up to them—she's got on a tight, black satin frock, split up the sides, and 'igh-'eeled shoes and a lot o' muck on 'er face—and she's got a glass o' beer in one 'and and a fag in the other. And she sneers at this 'ere nice dame, see; and she calls 'er a milk-and-water type and says that Dennis don't want 'er no more and she tells 'er to scram. But the other one says, very 'aughty, she says, 'Out o' me way,' she says. 'I besmirch meself by maggin' to yer,' she says. Then she turns to all the gamblers

127

—they're all 'uddled shame-faced against the walls—and she says, 'Ain't there no one, won't no one take me to Dennis?' Well, the bloke that smashed 'is whisky glass, 'e says 'e'll take 'em both, and so they go upstairs, and there they find this 'ere Dennis; 'e's laying across the table, and 'e's so tight that 'e's knocked over the candle 'e's got stuck in a bottle, and the flames 'ave caught the curtains and 'e's just set 'imself alight, when she rushes in. She tears off 'er shawl and wraps it round 'im, and she starts stampin' all the flames out. The others all come crowdin' in then, and by this Dennis is stone-cold sober. When 'e sees 'er, 'e says, 'Gloria! Gloria, me love, yer've saved me life; 'ow can I ever repay yer?' 'e says.

" 'By signin' the pledge,' she says. So 'e says okay, and then, after a while, yer see 'em in their little 'ome; they've got a couple o' nippers and 'e's got a good job and there they are, 'appy ever after."

There was never any embarrassing uncertainty as to when one of Joseph's stories was finished, because it always ended with the same formula.

They sat in silence for a moment, thinking about the story. Joseph pulled out his pouch and slowly filled his pipe. His face, as always, expressed a deeply resigned dejection, though his calmly uneventful life had given him very little occasion for any kind of unhappiness; his forehead was wrinkled into sad furrows and his mouth was a semicircle of hopeless melancholy, the corners drawn down almost to his chin; his faded blue eyes stared pathetically ahead of him, and his shoulders drooped despairingly. To the children he was a source of continuous delight and excitement, their most exhilarating companion, a constant stimulus to their imaginations.

"Why did the bad lady have her thkirt thplit up the thides? Wath the a fat lady? Jotheph, doethn't my tooth whithle?" Libby asked happily.

"You be careful, or you'll blow the 'ole lot out," Joseph said darkly; "then you'll 'ave to live on slops. Well," he went on reflectively, "these fast sheilas, they always seem to 'ave their skirts split; they think it's classy."

"Could you thee her panth, Jotheph?"

"No, yer couldn't," said Joseph shortly, "and you be careful, my girl. Refined girls—real little ladies, as yer might say—don't never mention their pants; nor any of their other underwear, neither, come to that."

Libby was not abashed; after a moment she said, anxiously, "What-th thloph?"

"Porridge," Joseph said.

She was silent, appalled by the thought of a diet of porridge slops; it made her think of the well of treacle in *Alice*, which had always made her feel a bit sick, anyway.

"Gee, the feller must have been a dope, Joseph. Fancy knocking the candle over! You know what I'd have done, if I'd been a fireman and they'd rung up for the brigade, Joseph. . . ." They sat and watched while John jumped out of bed, dressed, slid down the pole, and drove the engine to the scene of the outbreak, providing sounds of the siren realistically, from somewhere behind his nose; when he was carrying the helpless victim down the ladder, Libby effectively shattered him by saying, soberly, "John'th thowing off, ithn't he, Jotheph?"

"I'm not, am I, Joseph?" he asked defiantly, and half-heartedly he finished the scene; but he was miserable, and the last sequences were agony to him, because he knew now that he was John Carmichael, whereas, before she had spoken, there had been no doubt whatever that he was fearless Joe Hawkins, the famous fire chief. Girls couldn't play games properly, he thought wretchedly, as he sat down again, and he felt that he would be out of sorts for some time.

Joseph was smoking thoughtfully while he arranged in his mind the lessons to be learnt from the story about the evils of drink and gambling and inconstancy; but, before he could get them neatly rounded off, Anthea came round the corner of the front drive with a young man, and they began to descend the stone steps to the kitchen terrace. She was simply dressed in a brown tweed skirt and a fawn sweater, brown suede shoes on her feet, her hair smoothly shining. She was talking quickly and nervously, over her shoulder, to the tall, thin, dark young man.

They all stood up and Libby rushed to throw herself worshipfully upon her mother.

129

"Hullo, chicks," Anthea said. "I hope we're not interrupting, Joseph, are we?" When he shook his head dolefully, she turned back to Paul. "This is Mr. Quentin, Joseph. He's come to see the children. Come here, John. . . ." She stood in front of him, holding a child by either hand. They looked an adorable trio as they all stood looking up at him, and he smiled happily at them.

"I think they'd better call you Paul," she said, more sure of herself in the protection of her children; they were a testimonial for her, they were living evidence that she was a good mother, whose happy, healthy children loved her and rejoiced in her affection. "I hate this artificial 'Uncle' business," she went on, "and 'Mister' removes you somewhat, I think. Now, this is Libby and this is John." She gave Libby a little push, and she came to him, her hand politely outstretched.

"Hullo," she said gravely. "My tooth whithles becauthe of the hole—thee?"

"Yes." Paul examined the gap, which she revealed in a hideous grimace. "Yes, so it does."

"And I thpit a bit when I talk," she went on eagerly, carried away by his genuine concern.

"M'm," Anthea said reflectively. "You never fail to grasp things here through being given insufficient data. John. . . ."

John shook hands delightedly; he felt cheerful and relieved because this pleasant interruption had solved his difficulty about getting over the unhappy fire chief incident; also, he liked Paul at once.

"Paul was in the jungle with daddy," Anthea said, deliberately offhand. "If you don't plague him, he might tell you things. You don't mind, Paul?"

"No," Paul said easily. "There are one or two things John would be interested in, I know."

"He'd like to hear about the jungle hospital, I think. He's quite sure he's going to be a doctor."

"Gee, yes," John said excitedly. "Did Dad have a hospital all of his own? Was he the head man?"

"Did Daddy pull the tholdiers' teeth out?" Libby generally pursued one line at a time with overwhelming thoroughness.

130

"Well, look," Anthea interrupted, "I think I'd better go in. I've a ton of things to see to. John, take Paul down to the lower terrace—there's a seat there, under the lemon tree—and don't forget to show him Patch and Bucephalus. Will you stay to lunch, Paul?"

Paul thought quickly. No, he decided, it would be better to wait until tomorrow, he'd make his plans with the children now, but there were too many people about this morning and he must have no risk of interruption. Besides, somehow he felt bound to go back tomorrow morning, to see that windowbox of Mrs. Croft's; and there was Honor: he'd promised to go with her to see this friend of hers; and Megan and Honor were going to take him to see the sunset this evening, and they were all going to the Welcome Home and then up to Raikes's meadow tonight. . . . Oh, there were a dozen things to think of, but first of all he must have a watertight plan about the children. He turned to Anthea.

"No, thank you," he said. "I've to take home some parcels for Megan from the village; no, I'll come again tomorrow, if I may."

"Well, I'll ring them at Thornfield and arrange to go there for lunch; I have to go some time today, so I might as well drive you down—it's a long walk, you know."

"Yes, it is—well thank you."

As she turned and hurried up the steps, John said, "Come on, come on. Don't let's waste time."

They went down the steps to the lower terrace, this was a broad, rectangular lawn, and from it the hill sloped gently down to the line of thick trees that marked the course of the creek. As he sat down on the seat, under the branches of the lemon tree, he saw Joseph gazing suspiciously at him, over the top of the steep grassy bank that stretched downwards from the kitchen terrace; that fellow would probably be a menace, Paul thought. Idly he gazed at the long, white, glass-filled façade of the house, two-storeyed at the back; Cassie was leaning from a window, shaking a duster—no doubt she always had an eye on the children, too. H'm, he thought, it's not going to be too easy; I'll have to get them away from this place, at all events. Still, he felt delighted to think that he was actually beginning his task—

131

after all these endless months of contemplating the thing he had to do from afar off, it was an exquisite relief to be getting to grips with it at last. He felt a triumphant sense of accomplishment, and he knew that Adrian would be more than pleased with the progress he was making. He smiled down at the children, who were sitting on the grass in front of him.

"What shall I tell you about first?"

"About Daddy and the hospital," John said.

"Well, suppose I start about where we were taken prisoner, and then I'll tell you how I first met your dad, eh?"

As he talked on, simplifying things, highlighting incidents connected with Adrian, telling them details about the animals and the birds in the jungle, he formulated his plan. Gradually he began to tell them about the men who had built radios and secreted them from the Japs, about desperate escape measures, concentrating always on the secret life the prisoners lived and the devices they employed to hoodwink their captors. John was enthralled, and even Libby succeeded in grasping the main essentials of the stories; her mouth fell open and her eyes grew wide with fear and delightful suspense. After a while Paul paused to light a cigarette.

"Jings!" John said softly. "Jings, they were brave. Didn't the Japs ever catch them getting out of the camp?"

"Hardly ever," said Paul. "But you get very good at it after a while; you learn how to wait until they're sure to be doing something, and then you creep out, and once you're in among the trees you're pretty safe."

"I'd be too thcared," Libby said longingly, "I'd cry."

"No, you wouldn't. Look," he said, smoking reflectively, "I'll bet you two could do it. Now, suppose we try tomorrow morning. I'll bet you could get out of the house and down to the creek without anyone seeing you—and I'll be the Jap guard. I'll come along looking for you and I'll bet I won't find you."

Their eyes glowed with a fearful delight; they looked at each other and then John said disgustedly, "I could—but Libby's hopeless; she'd sneeze or something."

"Wouldn't!" Libby was a plump fury of indignation. "I'm

better than you; you're clumthy on your feet—Mother thayth tho."

"And she can't keep a secret," John went on. "When Mother hears her say her prayers tonight, she'll go and blab all about it."

"Beatht! Beatht!" Libby's eyes filled with tears; she jumped up and flung herself on Paul. "Let me, let me," she said despairingly. "I'm better than John—I won't thay anything."

"Well—" Paul looked at her consideringly and then, helplessly, as man to man, at John—"we've all got to learn, you know, John; and somehow I think she could manage it. After all, Libby looks intelligent."

"She's not, then," John said, glumly. "She'll be sure to muck it."

Libby had been looking hopefully from one to the other, but now she burst out. "You muthn't thay muck, it'th a bad word. And if you don't let me, I'll tell Mother you thaid muck. I'll tell her . . ."

"Oh, all right," John grinned at Paul. "And if she mu . . . if she makes a mess of it, I'll wring her neck."

Libby beamed, the fury and anxiety melting in one of her rare, dazzling smiles. She burrowed into Paul's side, and he kept his arm round her while they made their plans. They were to be down at the creek by eleven o'clock, and they were to hide between the white bridge and the paddock below the dairy, a distance of about fifty yards. If Paul failed to find them within an hour they were to get a shilling each.

They finished just in time, for Cassie was coming down the steps with a tray, with cups and glasses on it, and Paul could see Anthea on the drive, obviously coming to join them when she had finished speaking to Joseph. Paul stood up and took the tray from Cassie.

John said, with an air, "Cassie, this is our new friend, Mr. Paul Quentin."

As they shook hands, Libby said shrilly, "Oh, Cathie, he'th lovely. We've been having a wonderful talk"—her voice died away as she caught the malevolent glare John was casting on her—". . . about thingth," she finished triumphantly.

133

Paul felt reassured; yes, the little one would be all right, he was certain; the last shade of uneasiness faded from his mind and he gave himself up to the pleasure of gazing out over the valley at Ambara, lying peacefully before him. Anthea came hurrying down the path and began pouring coffee for him, and he could have wept with the bliss of his relief, at the glorious absence of tension. . . .

Suddenly, as Anthea was talking to the children about their luncheon procedure, he fell asleep, under the lemon tree, and they were all startled. Anthea sent the children away and then sat down quietly to wait until he should awaken, for she guessed that he would not sleep long. As she watched him, his arms folded across his chest, his head bent, she thought, He looks very delicate, very fine-drawn. God knows what hell a sensitive creature like him will have suffered—and how much he is still suffering, unknown to any of us, absorbed as we are with our ordinary little affairs. There's no nobility in our unhappiness, she thought, for most of it is self-caused, through envy or indulgence or jealousy; but his ordeal was forced upon him, through no fault of his own, and his endurance is, in some way, admirable.

His eyes opened and he smiled quietly at her. I really believe he thinks none of the ordinary thoughts about me, she thought; where another person would feel disgust or anger or perhaps compassion, he just doesn't bother, he has other things to think of.

"Rested?" she asked gently.

He sat up and stretched his arms above his head, then clasped his hands at the back of his neck.

"Wonderfully," he said. "You'd hardly believe that this is the first time since it happened that I've felt really peaceful—or almost. Tomorrow I shan't have a care in the world."

"Since what happened?" she asked, surprise in her voice.

"Why," he replied, as if equally surprised, "the bombing, of course." He stood up. "Are you ready? Shall we go?"

She was still puzzling a little about it as they ascended the steps to the drive. The children were waiting at the car, and they were relieved to see him so obviously normal, for in their experience people—grown-up people, anyway—didn't fall asleep sitting up, and Libby had been tearfully of the opinion that he was dead, and though this melodramatic nonsense had brought down John's scorn on her head, he, too, had been a little uneasy.

The children farewelled them vociferously, and then, as the car swung out of view, they raced down to the back terrace to watch its progress, for, from Cedar Hill, you could watch a car go all the way to Thornfield. Cassie called to them, most irritatingly, before the car was even at the railway crossing, and regretfully they left it to continue on its way without their scrutiny —and all because Cassie was so peculiar about washing. Resignedly they climbed the steps and surrendered themselves to Cassie's thorough methods with soap and water.

XIV

Megan came back to Thornfield the long way, along the back road and into the paddock by the big white gate. She felt heavily depressed; not one of her disturbing problems had resolved itself, and in addition, she'd made a bad job of the shopping. Joady would be cross because the meat had cost too much and because, even to Megan's eye, it was obvious that a considerably longer time had elapsed since it had been lamb than Mr. Dwyer would have had her believe; and the only biscuits at Paget's had been very grim and she hadn't bought them, so that would turn out to be wrong, too, no doubt, and the bread wasn't ready, which meant that someone would have to ride down for it later. She was worried, too, in case that erratic Paul forgot to pick up the parcels at the station; and that, too, would need explaining to Joady, who would, no doubt, wax extremely acid about people who had been accustomed to carrying their own parcels, until a handsome young man appeared on the scene. Oh, dear! And how to explain to Joady that it was only to ease Paul's mind that she had given him this task to do? She couldn't tell Joady about his sudden, inexplicable desertion. . . . When she had looped the rope over the gatepost, she walked

135

slowly over to a flat-topped tree stump and sat down, lowering her string bag to the ground beside her. She just wanted to stay here for a while and stave off the awkward things waiting for her at the house. She felt hot with walking, and she slipped off her brown jacket and hung it round her shoulders.

It was beautifully still. This was her favourite view of Thornfield, lying against the hills, the house nestling cosily, redly, against its side-covering of wistaria, the benevolent cedar leaning across the upper storey; nearer to her, and over to the left, were two weathered sheds, unpretentiously harmonious, one with a tiled roof, orange-red—an unnamable colour—and wall of weather-greyed boards; the other leaning against it, sway-backed, hiding its age with a shawl of green creeper, flung careless-wise over one shoulder. Beyond the house lay the hills, blue-misted from here, rising above massed treetops, too distant to be more than a hint, yet giving, by their semicircular solidity, a comfortable complacency to Ambara. . . . "Here we are, the edge and limit of your world; stay here, within our circle, and things will be perpetually as you now see them, ageless, still, and undisturbed. Venture farther, and the ugliness, strife, and violence of men's relationships will engulf you. Here is peace, here tranquillity; accept them, their limitations, and happiness is yours." Happiness, Megan wondered, or merely absence of struggle, stagnation? The thought, and the urgent "hurry, hurry" call of a peewit, made her swing herself to the ground. Picking up her parcels, she walked soberly across the paddock, planning ways of dealing with Joady's righteous indignation. If only she hadn't left the cheese at the station for Paul to bring—she'd completely forgotten that Joady had especially wanted it to make the spaghetti for lunch, and the horrid recollection had only come to her when she was almost home. As she shut the white gate that led into the kitchen garden, she heard Honor calling her name from somewhere in the orchard. She put up her hand to shield her eyes, while she looked for her sister.

"Here—" a hand rustled the leaves of an orange tree—"come over here when you've finished."

"All right," she called, but she thought of the extra trip to the village; it would be some time before she had made up for

136

the mistakes of the morning. She turned and walked briskly into the kitchen. To her relief Joady seemed pleased, if a little preoccupied. As she put the parcels on the kitchen table, she was about to confess all her shortcomings, when Joady forestalled her, and she was delighted with her good fortune as one after another of her difficulties was solved for her.

"Anthea's coming to lunch," Joady said, above the whirr of the egg beater. "She's driving Paul down, so they should be here soon. I told her to call in for the bread, in case you were too early, and Cassie's sending a huge batch of biscuits. Thank goodness for that; I haven't time today, and we don't want to give them Paget's variety."

She stopped and looked at Megan.

"You're looking washed out," she said. "Anything the matter?"

"No," said Megan. "It was a bit hot, that's all; and there were a lot of things, Joady, so Paul said he'd bring some of them."

"All right." Joady seemed to be giving much less than her usual attention to the unloading of the goods. "Put the meat in the fridge and make out the account, and then get yourself a glass of milk—I won't want you here. Go and have a rest."

"Joady, you're wonderful and beautiful and passing fair." Megan put her arms round Joady and bunny-hugged her.

"Get out before I make you clean the egg beater," Joady said.

Megan drank her glass of cold milk and walked thankfully out into the sun, round the side of the house and through the inextricable, orderly tangle of the bush house to the white gate that opened into the orchard.

"Hullo," she said, and lay down on her stomach, on one side of the groundsheet that Honor had spread between the orange tree and the wistaria, beneath the outer branches of the cedar, bare now except for their little, Oriental, bamboo-coloured seed pods and a few feathery sprays of leaves here and there.

"What's the time?" Honor asked.

"About twelve, I think."

They were silent. Honor was drugged with sunshine, removed from the world beyond the orchard by the blaze of light and greenness around her. She had been here since half-past ten, and for an hour and a half she had worked energetically; a de-

137

tailed, neat date list of the history of Germany after 1815 lay beside her, the edges of the paper beginning to curl slightly in the warmth, and now she had abandoned herself to dreams and lotus-eating and the stupor of autumn sunshine in an orchard. Like the bees, she thought—I'm drunk with sweetness and warmth, and I can afford to be because I've done my work well. She wondered how people could enjoy idleness, who knew nothing else; she liked to work hard, with intensity and fury, and then to give herself up to the ecstasy of relaxation. I'll always work hard, hard, she thought, and then I'll loaf and loll. Looking down at her straight, slender body, stretched out before her on the grass, she thought, One day I'll be fat—I'll have to be. All great singers are deep-bosomed, and when I start my training next year I'll begin to get fat, I suppose. But I shan't mind —thousands of people can be slim and unimportant, but few women can sing as I will. She almost stirred herself to take up the book of German vocabulary she always kept near at hand, but she realized that this was her relaxation time—she must not spoil it. Drowsily she leant back, her clasped hands beneath her head, her face lightly dappled by the slight shadows cast by the cedar.

Megan rolled on her back and gazed down the long slope of the orchard; the orchard surrounded them, engulfed them, and they became part of it, aware of its growing things as its inhabitants, as the things that lived their lives here, in their own place —the wooden-posed orange tree, laden with little green oranges, untouched as yet by their own bright colour; placid-leafed pumpkins, spreading, comfortably uncorseted, over the earth; the persimmon, down by the fence, hysterically autumnal with its orange and tangerine leaves; the almond trees, spiking with coming foliage. Beyond, a row of tall gums hid the closest hills from their view, but over to the right they lay in a long, sweeping line, their colours and objects as delicate as those of a Chinese colour print, their lines picked out with a microscopically fine brush. Faintly, to the far right, the line of army huts crouched just over the hill top—ugliness distance-dimmed; from behind the orange trees came the "fit fit!" of a small bird, a violin string plucked by a skilled finger, melodiously without

138

melody, a rhythmic beat underlying some music she couldn't hear.

The orchard was orderly, cared for well, as was everything else at Thornfield; amazing how some people were able to maintain a high standard in every phase of their lives, Megan thought; their mother had an excellence about her that she communicated to things and people around her, so that anything shoddy, either of a material or spiritual nature, stood out conspicuously at Thornfield. Mary had laboured in her vineyard, and she'd made them labour, too; and now, twice a week, Joseph came down from Cedar Hill and the two of them worked all day together in the orchard. Nothing had been allowed to fall into decay at Thornfield; war and illness and sorrow were not considered good enough excuses for slackness. Megan knew that she would never be like that. No, she thought, I'd get wretched, like I did this morning, just because a few things went wrong, and I'd lie down beside it all and let the clutter engulf me. She sighed deeply and sat up, her hands clasped around her knees.

"Wha's ser matter?"—from under Honor's hat, down-tipped over her face.

"That Paul."

"Wha's 'e up to now?"

"Oh—unusual and disturbing things."

"Such as what?"

Her hat fell off, and Honor slowly struggled up and sat, cross-legged, chewing grass.

"Well, for one thing, we paid a duty visit to Mrs. Croft, and he gave Martin a horrible hiding."

"Great news," said Honor. "I like that Paul."

"Yes, but it's very awkward when you're there; I didn't tell you, either, what he did to Mrs. Kyles, last night."

Painfully, she forced herself to go over the incident, and it hurt more than she had thought it would; the recounting of it showed her, the more clearly, the role Julian played in that household, and yet it brought anguish with it, a longing for the Julian whose image she had been living with so happily in her mind these last few months, and a misery because she saw the

139

silliness and the futility and the wickedness of her devotion to him.

Honor rocked to and fro with delight.

"Marvellous!" she gloated. "Gosh, what wonderful things people can do when they're not blocked by politeness or good manners—or whatever it is that makes us all such hypocrites. That Paul—oh, he's a gem."

They were silent for a few moments; from above their heads, in the cedar, came the hoarse, pleading, agonized scream of a magpie, rising to its hopeless, thrilling crescendo, sinking to despair. That's what I feel like, Megan thought; if I could make a noise to show what I feel, that's the noise I'd make. Somehow the thought raised her spirits.

Honor was looking at her sharply.

"What's wrong with you?" she asked.

"Oh, this week end's just a bit much, I think—things happening everywhere. I like a vegetable existence."

"Paul been up to any of his antics again?"

"Only one thing: he nearly threw a fit on me when we left Croft's, but that was because he'd almost forgotten that he had to be up at Cedar Hill by eleven."

"Yes," said Honor. "You should have seen him come racing round the house and throw himself into the car. I rode down to the gate on the running board to open and shut for him, and he drove off, pursued by devils."

"Oh, well," Megan said, "that's nothing much. People in a nervous state often go crazy about appointments. That didn't really worry me much; but it's just everything—and Adrian and everything."

"It seems to me"—Honor gave her a slow, searching glance—"that the 'and everything' is the most important part of all that."

"Yes," Megan said, curtly, "you're right there, it is." She rolled over and, supporting herself on her elbows, began to pull up stems of grass in an earnestly careless fashion.

All right, let her be, Honor told herself; don't pry, don't fuss —the fundamental rules of Carmichael behaviour. She sat silently, and Megan felt a deep sense of gratitude, because there was no need to say more; how beastly it would be to live in a family where nothing was sacred, where you had to talk about things that mattered to you, because then they never mattered quite so much. And things had to be important, vivid—and they could only be so in the mind; once they were dragged out and exhibited, the strong light of day destroyed their rich colours; and yet how awful, too, to have to endure a too obvious concern for one's state of mind, the dreadful exaggerated whispering and tiptoeing among one's feelings—that would make you equally self-conscious, make you want to deny the existence of any complex emotions. Lord, I want an awful lot from people, she thought, and suddenly she realized that here, in her home, she received just the treatment she had always needed; here was the delicate balance between indifference and interference which her mind demanded, which any ordinary mind needed if it was not to be damaged by shame and fear and guilt. Still, even in her own family there were limits, of course; she couldn't imagine that her violent feelings about Julian would have been treated very delicately, if she had revealed them. Still, no one tried to find out things about you, no one pried or spied on you —that was the important thing. Yes, I'm fortunate, she thought, and so are we all; a deep feeling of love for Honor and appreciation of the reasons for her silence just at this moment, made her lean on one elbow and smile up at her sister, who grimaced broadly at her in reply. The moment was interrupted by the sound of the arrival of the car, in the back paddock, and Honor jumped up and waved.

"Come on," she said, pulling the groundsheet from underneath Megan. "Action stations."

Still a little stunned by the brightness of the orchard, they went through the white gate and round to the back of the house. Anthea and Paul were carrying the parcels in from the car; Paul was talking cheerfully, and Anthea looked radiant as she greeted them. They all trooped into the kitchen, completely disorganizing what Adrian had called Joady's pre-prandial calm, for the kitchen was a place of tranquil orderliness before the serving of a meal at Thornfield; Joady would have no fuss and confusion during the last tense minutes before the food was carried in to the dining room. Today, however, she welcomed them heartily, stored away the groceries, complimented Anthea on her new hand-knitted gloves, told Paul that he was putting on weight, and then hurried them off to wash and prepare themselves for luncheon. As the girls went through into the hall, she laid her hand on Anthea's sleeve and pulled it sharply. Surprised, Anthea turned to look at her; behind her smile Joady's face was tense, and Anthea said lightly, "You go on up, Paul; I'm clean, really. I'll just stay and help Joady."

"Right," he said, and walked inside; they could hear him humming as he ran up the stairs.

"Yes, Joady dear?" Anthea said.

"Anthea . . ." Joady's voice was hesitant, lacking its usual firm decidedness.

"What's wrong, Joady?"

"Look, Anthea—I don't know. I don't know if there is anything wrong, but listen: make an excuse to come up to my room after lunch, will you? I don't want to worry them but . . . anyway, I'll tell you later."

"All right, Joady, I'll come up as soon as things are tidy."

"Good." A desperate relief sounded in Joady's voice, and some of the tenseness left her expression. "Run along in now, or they'll think it's funny."

Anthea smiled at her, but as she went through the hall and knocked on the door of James's study she felt a sad uneasiness somewhere in her mind, a certainty that it would be no ordinary little trifle which would cause this unheard-of weakness in Joady, the rock on which the house of Carmichael had rested securely for so many years.

4

SATURDAY AFTERNOON

I

In the general coming in and sitting down and handing round of food, it was not noticeable, but when the meal had commenced Mary Carmichael became aware of a disturbance among them all. Or is it only in myself? she wondered. She glanced round the table and listened to the light conversation; it seemed quite as usual, but . . . no, there were differences, the faint discordances, the very occasional wrong notes such as a finely trained ear would detect in an orchestra that might seem flawless to the general audience. Only long acquaintance with the score could produce this skill, and this particular score she had known by heart for most of her life. She listened carefully. Joady was talking when it was not necessary to do so; Megan sometimes failed to reply when it was necessary; and Anthea's serene quietness was marred by a recurring little frown. She glanced now and again from one person to another, as if she could discover something she must know, from observing the faces of those about her. Honor seemed, as usual, in command of herself and the situation in which she found herself, but Paul—something about Paul was different; she watched him, as he talked happily about the things he had seen during the morning. Then James began telling him of the various routes to be followed in walking among the hills, and he listened intently. Yes, but too intently; he was held on a leash, too ready to spring forward; his eyes were bright and his face alive with animation and a delighted interest. There should be nothing disturbing about that; indeed, she should rejoice to see him so changed, so free from the uncertainty and uneasiness of last night. . . . I know, she thought, I know what it is; there's something larger than life about him. He seems to be filled with more joy and excitement than is suitable for one person. Hysteria is too crude a word for it, but his emotional pitch is higher than one can watch, comfortably. She looked along to James. James, my darling, my darling. . . . She almost murmured the endearment aloud.

She saw that he was talking carefully, eating carefully, guarding his expression, so that no one would know the state of his mind, no one would guess that, little more than an hour ago she, Mary, had held him in her arms, while he sobbed wildly, in a deep desolation; even though her mind ached with the pain of remembering it, she felt the exultation that had come to her when he had told her, his eyes bewildered with despairing pleading, of his sudden, overwhelming need for the reassurance of her love for him. It was a reliving of a period of her life so long past that it was almost forgotten; the placidness and contentment of their comfortable attachment to each other was shattered, and the painful and passionate need of one for the other, which had belonged to the time when they were only two, before absorption with children had blunted the keen edge of their love, was momentarily restored. She realized that they had forgotten excitement, that it had dropped out of their lives and had given place to anxiousness or comfortableness, or to the hundred other unimportant sensations that inevitably come to overlie the major emotions when passion kills itself with its own fulfilment. Perhaps that was why she felt so keenly aware of things—things like these undercurrents of feeling about her at this moment— for excitement sharpens one's mind and makes it more sensitive. She felt that this was a good thing to have happened to them, even if it was distressing; the joy that had come to her as she had soothed James's anguish was sweet to remember, for she felt that she had been able to do it completely; she had not comforted or patted him or tried to minimize the sadness in his heart, but she had met his wild longing with an equal intensity of love, she had turned aside his self-accusation about his absorption in Adrian by averring that she, too, had drifted from her total con-

144

centration in him, her husband. And now, for the little while that remained to them, she felt that they would be alone together again, as they had been long ago. It was an important thing that had happened to them, a rare thing, for two people at this time in their lives, so close to the end, when the sun had been quietly setting on them; it was as if a ray of light had shone through the clouds, so that the twilight would hold the afterglow, until darkness finally came.

"Mary," James was saying, "you remember that path along the back line of the hills—the one that crosses the water race. Doesn't that lead you round to the magnificent view above Borrowdale?"

As she replied and joined in the argument, which necessitated drawing lines on the tablecloth with forks, and arranging the salt shakers as landmarks, she remembered the water race and the days when they had toiled over the smooth hills to the magnet of the swiftly flowing, clear water; she remembered the glorious feeling of plunging a tin mug into the cold stream and drinking deeply, lying on one's stomach, draining the mug and filling it again; and then the leisurely stroll to the flat across the bridge, where she-oaks bent over a stagnant little stream, choked with water plants; and frying chops, the scent of wood smoke painfully sweet in the air; and then a long afternoon in the shade, lying on the grass, talking, smoking, reading, and, finally, descent into the valley, amethyst and grey-blue with smoke.

"Remember the 'Burke and Wills' day?" James's eyes smiled at her, Mary nodded, and as he told them briefly about it she leant back and felt it, felt strongly the scent of bushfire in the summer morning, a morning far too hot for them to have gone, a morning when the sun was not merely light cast on the earth, but a pale, moonlike ball in a heat-hazed sky; she felt the throbbing clang of pain in her head as they climbed upward, having come too far to return, the water race their goal, the only end of their existence, the only thing in the world worth attaining. She had had to give in, and she lay panting in the unbreathable air, while James toiled on to the water race and then came back with water; the taste of the water, sweet to a parched tongue, came to her mouth now. That was youth: the self-imposition of avoidable difficulties; with age came the wisdom of seeking ways to lighten one's burden, the calculated avoidance of strain, the careful conservation of energy. As she listened to their plans for the afternoon, she had to resist the temptation to warn them against overtiring themselves, and especially the desire to counsel Paul to rest, not to overstrain his increasing strength. All too soon they'll begin to do these things for themselves, she thought; they'll husband their physical resources and they won't see their doing so as a signpost, pointing to middle-age. After all, she reflected, that was how she and James had come to buy Thornfield, because they were young and strong, and nothing seemed a trouble to them. Everyone had said that they were mad to bury themselves out in the bush, thirty miles from Sydney, that the travelling would kill James and the loneliness would kill Mary. But they had seen Ambara once and loved it for ever, and nothing was too much trouble for them if they might live there. And they had been right—she felt sure of that; for, although their friends had had more sleep and more company and more comfort, she and James had had beauty with them always, and their children had grown up with the love of beautiful things. . . . She was suddenly surprised to hear Megan asking for the car. The Carmichaels had always preferred walking to driving.

"Yes, you may," James replied. "Nobody will be using it."

Having given his consent, he did not, of course, go on to ask where she was going, but his voice was faintly surprised and there was a perceptible curiosity among the others, and Megan felt constrained to give some explanation.

"I'm not going far," she said. "I mean, I don't want much petrol; but Alec rang this morning and asked me to bring the car and drive him somewhere."

"Anywhere particular?" Anthea asked.

"No—just somewhere. He said he wants to talk."

But it still sounded inadequate, and there was a brief silence. Megan sighed in a gasping way. "Oh," she said, "it's all very complicated. It's really Paul at the bottom of it."

Like most things here today, Mary thought; if you could discover the cause of this slightly offkey emotional atmosphere,

146

you'd probably find that Paul's presence was the common factor present.

Paul sat undisturbed throughout Megan's account of the story; he seemed pleasantly preoccupied with other things, and he had completed a complicated little pattern of rectangles with the crumbs on his plate, manipulated with the tip of his knife, by the time Megan had finished telling them about it.

The general approval that followed encouraged Megan to say, "But that's not all. Do you want to hear how he did Martin Croft over this morning?"

As Megan told them, Mary watched him; he was changing the pattern, and now he was fashioning a clock face with the crumbs, the hands pointing to eleven o'clock; with a rapid movement he turned the hands of his shattered wrist watch to the same time, and then he sat contemplating it, his face pleased, excited, and yet content. He's grown wise in his suffering, Mary thought; he can see the essentials of existence and he's not held back by the superficialities that bind us, by the feeling that it's bad form to interfere or gauche to proffer unsought advice; he sees a thing that needs doing and he does it. But, she reflected, there must be a certain ruthlessness going along with this attitude, and, to the extent that we are not ruthless, we are, perhaps, civilized. She felt suddenly his foreignness among them all; he and they understood each other's language, but their thoughts belonged to different realms.

The talk ranged widely now, and she forced herself back into it; it was little more than desultory gossip, and finally it died away and she stood up and went to James's chair. He glanced up at her happily and slowly raised himself; he stood, one hand on Mary's arm and one on his stick, as he turned to Anthea.

"Did you bring all the stuff down, Anthea?"

"Yes, James—my case is in the study?"

"Well, shall we start straight away?"

"Wouldn't you like a rest, first? I'll come up in half an hour; I'm just going to let Joady take the pattern for those new gloves of mine."

"Yes—all right, Anthea. In half an hour. . . ." He walked slowly out of the room with Mary.

147

Honor and Megan had been swooping in and out with trays, and by now the table was almost cleared. Honor had set Paul to work in the kitchen, scraping plates and rinsing cups; Joady closed the doors of the dresser on the folded tablecloth, and came out into the hall.

"Come on up," she said, and led the way upstairs to her room.

What perfect taste she has, Anthea thought, as she seated herself in a low-slung cedar armchair, upholstered in dull-blue, brocaded satin; it faced the window, which looked over the back paddock, and between the frilled, white muslin curtains Anthea could see the gleam of Johnny's brown coat, rippling and shining with movement, as he cropped the yellowing grass; the boughs of the cedar bent over the window, which was on a level with the thickly leafed trees limiting the view beyond the white gate at the bottom of the paddock. Anthea turned as Joady sat down opposite her, in the other armchair, which was cedar, too, its dull yellow velvet padding mellow with age and care.

"I sometimes think this is the prettiest room I ever was in," Anthea said.

"I love it," Joady said curtly.

The shining floor was the colour of claret; three oval, maize-coloured rugs, velvety in texture, threw up its richness with their sharply contrasting colours; Joady's divan bed was concealed by a correctly tailored, deeply green, velvet coverlet, knife-pleated and stiffly corded, and four velvet cushions, cream and brown, were piled on it. A low, fat chest stood against one wall, and above it hung an oval mirror in a dark frame, a little gate-legged table stood across the room, covered with a stiffly starched, embroidered cloth, and on it a squat little jar, startlingly blue, held a bunch of yellow chrysanthemums. The harmony of comfort and beauty, Anthea thought, as she took a cigarette from the silver box Joady offered her.

When they had both lit their cigarettes, Anthea said, "Now. . . ."

Joady gazed out the window; her expression was stern, but there was uncertainty in her eyes.

"Look," she said suddenly, "you'll probably think I'm crazy, but . . ."

148

Anthea said nothing; Joady stood up and went to the window. Then she turned and looked down at Anthea.

"I've always had feelings about things that happen here," she said. "I've been right so often that I'm scared when I get another of them. And I've got another of them." She paused and drew on her cigarette. "Right now," she went on, "I'm scared right into my spinal column."

"Why?" Anthea asked. "And, incidentally, Joady dear, why choose me to tell it to?"

"Well,"—Joady came back and sat down on the edge of her chair—"I'm telling you because you're level-headed; you don't lose your block about things; you know the sensible thing to do and you do it."

My God, thought Anthea, here's irony, if you like. If you only saw the broken reed you're leaning on, Joady, you'd really be scared.

"Thanks," she said. "But go on, Joady; I don't get it all yet."

"No, and I don't suppose you ever will." Joady's voice was suddenly tired, and she leant back in her chair for a moment, her arms hanging listlessly along the arms of the chair; then she sat erect again and her voice was vigorous with alarm.

"Look," she said urgently, "it's that Paul; there's something queer about him—I know there is. I've been watching him, and I tell you he's not right in the head."

"No, I suppose he's not quite, Joady; but I think we all realize that—and we don't expect him to be. No one could live through his experiences and be back to normal immediately; but he's been ill, Joady, and he's still ill. . . ."

"Yes, yes, yes," Joady broke in nervously. "But it's more than that. I can feel something about him—he's a menace or a threat —or something."

Anthea looked at her; Joady's face was twisted into seldom-seen lines, its calm serenity vanished.

"And what would you suggest could be done?"

"Get rid of him," Joady said flatly. "Get him away somehow. He's come here for something, I know he has, and it's something that's going to injure someone here—or perhaps everyone."

149

Anthea felt shock run through her; she stared at Joady blankly.

"Oh, don't look at me like that," Joady said miserably. "I suppose you think I'm hard."

"Hard!" Anthea's voice was unsteady with anger. "Do you mean to say you'd turn him out, just because he's not quite like us—not quite normal?"

"No, but . . ." Joady's voice trailed into deeper wretchedness.

"And why are we so beautifully, delightfully normal? Tell me that! Well, I'll save you the bother—I'll tell you." Anthea stood up and took another cigarette. "Because people like Adrian gave their lives and people like Paul lost their grip on normality, or almost lost it. If we had been living under Japanese occupation now, I don't suppose we'd be going about in such a noticeably sane manner; I should think we'd be doing more than tapping with our fingers and acting a little hysterically; we'd probably be stark mad, and there'd be no one to help us."

Joady's hands were clenched, tightly, in her lap; her lips were set in a firm line, but the wide, youthful blue eyes, which looked steadily out the window, were filling with tears. Compassion came swiftly to drown Anthea's anger; she threw her cigarette out the window, and kneeling down beside her, took Joady's hands in hers.

"I'm sorry, Joady dear, but I think you're wrong, and, because you love us all so much, you're being blind and selfish on our behalf."

Joady said nothing, but two tears rolled down from her eyes.

"You heard him talking about Adrian last night," Anthea went on. "You could read between the lines, Joady; you could tell how devoted he was to Adrian, how much he must have done to repay him, risking death and torture to do it. We can't repay him for that—we can only do the little things he seems to want; he wants to stay here, just to spend a few days among Adrian's people, to see his children. It's so little to do for him, and it's apparently satisfying some urge in him that he's only partly aware of."

Joady's expression hadn't altered; Anthea knelt there, gazing

150

up at her. After a moment she reseated herself in the chair opposite Joady.

"I'm not convincing you, am I," she said quietly.

"No," said Joady, her voice thick and blurred, "and I'm not convincing you."

"No, you're not—and you never will. And you won't convince anyone else here, either." Anthea's voice was harsh, now. "I'm frankly disgusted with you, Joady; I can't understand what's come over you. But simple gratitude and kindness to people who are in need of it have always been the rule at Thornfield— at least, they have been since I've been here—and you'll get nowhere with your suggestion that you turn Paul out—get rid of him, as you put it."

She stood up.

"I'm going now," she said. "I've got a lot to do, and I don't want to waste any more time on this nonsense."

"Go, then." Joady's words came more firmly now. "You've been cruel and hard and blind; but, if you've got one ha'p'orth of the sense in your head that I've always thought you had, keep those children of Adrian's away from that man."

Anthea stopped, her hand outstretched to open the door; a chilled feeling ran through her, a fierce tremble of fear; then she remembered the scene on the lower terrace this morning, with Libby burrowing into Paul's arms, John sitting cross-legged at his feet, the three of them eagerly happy in each other's company. She came back into the room, and taking Joady's hands, she pulled her gently to her feet.

"I'm sorry, Joady; I've been quarrelsome and sharp. But you're wrong, dear, terribly wrong. Paul and the children were playing happily together this morning, for a long while; they're friends already, and you can see he loves them, because they remind him of Adrian. Oh, Joady, dear, get these horrible thoughts out of your mind—they'll eat into you and harm you."

Desperately, Joady gazed into Anthea's eyes and saw that it was hopeless; there was nothing there but a kindly anxiety for her, Joady. She thought, frantically, of some means of convincing Anthea.

"Well, look," she said finally, "it won't hurt you to do this—

151

and it won't hurt him. Will you promise me to see that they're not left alone with him? Will you see that Joseph or Cassie or someone is always with them? You can easily do that, Anthea. . . ."

Anthea's eyes hardened again, but finally she laughed and put her arms round Joady's waist.

"All right, you dear, crazy thing," she said. "I'll trail them wherever they go. Now, for God's sake, Joady, cheer up, if this household got wind of the fact that you'd been crying, they'd be sure that there was nothing left to live for. Now I've really got to go."

Joady took her to the door and kissed her; then she closed the door and came back into the room. She stood still in the middle of the floor, her hands held tightly in front of her. Waves of fear swept over her, the more dreadful because she didn't know what to fear. She sat down on the divan; after a moment she relaxed and began to weep bitterly and silently, a crumpled, lifeless figure on the wide, velvet couch, her tears staining the deep cream of the cushions, irreparably.

II

Anthea ran down the last few stairs, and placed her hand on the round, placid, shining newel post, preparatory to swinging round into the hall, on her way to James's study. A sudden thought made her pause, and she stood a moment, listening. She looked at her watch: still ten minutes of her half-hour to run, before she was due to see James. This was how she had come to parcel out her days now, days overburdened with diverse duties. Well, ten minutes could be put to good purpose. No sound came from the front of the house, but there was a murmur of conversation from the kitchen. As she moved down the hall, towards the back of the house, Anthea told herself that, in justice to Joady, she must see as much of Paul as possible, must observe him, must try to understand him. So far, she had considered him solely as playing a part in her affairs; he was

152

nothing, in her eyes, but a link with Adrian. Now she was determined to try to account for Joady's hysterical outburst, to see if there was really anything more unusual about him than could be attributed to the effects of his bitter experiences.

He was the first to see her as she entered the kitchen, and after a moment he stood up; but there was indifference in his smile, in his very movements. The girls were both sitting on the table, facing him as he stood, now, with his back to the window, and Anthea could tell that the three of them had been deeply absorbed in their conversation. Megan was still talking, but when Paul stood up the two girls looked over their shoulders, inquiringly, towards the door. Honor extended an arm, backwards, towards Anthea, and as she approached, Honor clasped her round the waist.

"Come to us, sweet," she said, "and tell us words of wisdom. Paul is trying, somewhat, to pull us out of the mess he's got us into—or rather, the one he's got Megan into, though of course me heart beats heavily wif concern for me little sister."

Anthea leant against the small table under the window, and faced the two girls; Paul had reseated himself and was tranquilly smoking his pipe.

"What's the poor backward girl mean, Megan?" Anthea asked.

"Oh, just a thing, Anthea." Megan's voice was heavy with a resigned exasperation. "It mightn't be anything, really—but you heard at lunch; I've got to go and meet Alec this afternoon, and —you know—you heard about the business there last night. . . ."

"You know—Paul doing his version of how not to pay a social call. He does it everywhere; it's getting quite well known," Honor interpolated.

"Well, what happens, now?" Anthea asked.

"That's just it. I don't know. I might be worrying unnecessarily, but I think Alec's going to do something about it—something immediate and active."

"Only cause for worrying would be if he weren't," Paul said curtly.

"Maybe," said Anthea, "but I still don't see what's the matter. How are you involved, Megan?"

"Oh, I suppose I'm not, really, not in any direct way; but I've

153

got to go and talk to him, and I won't know what to say. That's what we're doing now—trying to make up my mind."

They were silent for a moment; Megan still looked dejected and uneasy, Honor appeared to be considering other and pleasanter things, and Paul smoked peacefully.

"Well," Anthea said briskly, "let's be business-like. Now, what are the problems? First, he's probably planning to get away from that she-cat, isn't he?"

"Sure to be," Honor said lightly. "That's if he's really come to his senses."

"And he's got no money, has he?" Anthea went on.

"None," said Megan. "She's got all the money in that family, and no one will get any of it unless they're doing what she wants."

"Is he really ill?" Anthea asked. "I haven't seen him for years."

"No, but he's got no strength—or something," Megan said uncertainly.

"Looks as if he's grown up under a stone," Paul said.

"M'm . . ." Anthea paused, and there was silence again.

"Well," she continued, after a moment, "he'll need to be built up, first, to some kind of strength, that's certain; but he'll have to earn some money at the same time. Now, what sort of work would enable him to do that sort of thing?"

"Why is it"—Honor's voice came from far away—"that sick or disabled people have to drive elevators? Riding in one, even once in a while, is a bit more than most strong people can stand; and yet you see poor, sick, frail things everywhere, driving them. No one should operate an elevator for others; anyone who's too stupid to press the right button in an elevator should have to climb the stairs. There should be only automatic elevators. . . ."

"Tell you what—" Paul stood up and knocked his pipe sharply against the side of the ash pan, under the stove—"how about six months at our place?"

"Where's your place—and what, exactly, is it?" Anthea asked.

"My family have a property at Dorrigo," he replied. "I mentioned it to Alec last night, but I put it in the form of a painting holiday; it's artists' country—healthy, too. But if he needs a light

154

job, out of doors, my people would be delighted to give him one; they'd pay him well, too—they're glad of any help, these days."

"Angel!" Honor swooped on him, in a long leap from the table. "Megan, isn't he marvellous? There's one thing: if he breaks your head, he gives you a nice thick plaster for it."

Megan's eyes were bright with pleased contemplation.

"Oh, Paul," she said, "do you think they would?"

"I'll write straight away," he said. "But I can promise now; I know it'll be all right."

"It seems ideal," Anthea said slowly. What an amazing part he's playing in the lives of people here, she thought; people he's never seen before will feel—for ever, perhaps—the effects of knowing him.

"Yes," she went on, "I can't see anything wrong with it."

"And look," Paul continued, "supposing he doesn't want to be a farmer, when he's strong again. I was thinking of your father: he seems to need someone as badly as my dad does—he might find a place for him."

"I know," Honor broke in eagerly. "Why couldn't Alec take over the Art Department—the prints and the gallery?"

"That would be just the thing," Anthea said thoughtfully; "from our point of view, anyhow. We've just been carrying that department lately, since young Davidson went, and we could do with someone who knew about paintings, my word we could. It'd be a great weight off my mind, anyway."

"And it would be awfully good for Alec," Megan said enthusiastically. "He'd be right in the midst of the artists there; Carmichael's shows are good—at least, they used to be." She turned to Paul. "Do you think Father would agree, Paul?"

"I'm sure of it. As a matter of fact, he was offering me a place with him, but . . . I don't think I'll be available."

It was said casually enough, but his whole manner had changed. He frowned down at his pipe, as he filled it, and his forefinger beat out a little pattern of movement while he patted the tobacco into the bowl. Anthea watched: one, two—one, *two*, three, *four*. As they watched him in silent conjecture, he grew more uneasy; his face flushed and his lips moved jerkily; then, to their surprise, he suddenly rushed from the kitchen, stumbling

155

at the corner of the table and crashing into the lintel of the door.

The violence of his movements had startled them all, and Megan jumped from the table and made a movement to follow him, but Honor caught her by the hand.

"Don't," she said, gently. "Let him be, the poor dear; he's pursued by something we're not able to see."

"But what upset him? He was quite happy and interested, talking about Alec's plans."

They stood there for a moment, puzzling over the conversation they had just had, trying to see at what stage he had broken away from them and had begun to follow the twisted paths along which his mind led him. So this is what Joady means, Anthea reflected; this is being queer in the head. Well, what of it? It was just as she had said to Joady: he was a prey to fears and anxieties that he couldn't put into words, and therefore he was the more deserving of their sympathy and understanding. A deep feeling of sadness for him came to her mind, the more so because the turmoil of his thoughts must inevitably earn for him, among the undiscerning, the reputation of insanity. Yes, I'm a snob, she thought, but it is typical of people of Joady's class to fear what they cannot understand, to regard as dangerous any departure from the familiar paths of their own limited experience. And in her mind she dismissed Joady's fears in a completely final manner.

"I know what it was," Megan said, pulling abstractedly at the cord of the kitchen window blind. "Father told me this morning to be careful not to mention anything about the future. How stupid and clumsy I am! Don't you see?" She turned to the others, self-accusingly. "While we were discussing Alec's future, he was interested and happy; but then we touched on his own plans, and he simply couldn't stand it."

"Maybe so," Honor said; "but why, I wonder?"

"Father says he's got some idea that time doesn't extend beyond tomorrow, and you can see that's true; we mention something about what he's doing after that and he goes to pieces."

"Good thing we know, anyhow." Anthea looked at her watch. "Lordy, I'm late—James will be waiting."

When she had left them, Honor said, comfortingly, to Megan,

156

"Anyway, this is one of the ills which time will definitely heal. He'll come an awful thud when he finds it's Monday."

"Hope so," Megan said. "Gosh, I'll have to go—it's twenty past two. Do I need to change?"

"No, sweet," Honor replied. "There's no special dress prescribed for assisting young men to leave home. You're either the type that can or else you're not. Anyway," she added, "no one will ever believe you're a clever woman if you're well dressed; if you're really to achieve a reputation as a scholar, you must look like a ragbag—otherwise they'll say you got your scholarship by sitting on old Hemsley's knee after hours, working back."

"Come down to the car with me." There was a pleading note in Megan's words.

"Sorry, sweet, but no; I've got to go and rootle Paul out of whatever funk hole he's crept into. And besides, don't try to comfort yourself by holding your little sister's hand until the very last minute. Go on, now, and don't worry your distinguished head too much, my beautiful Proctor Travelling Scholar. . . ." And Honor kissed Megan loudly on the cheek.

"Where are you going?" Megan asked, suspiciously certain that, wherever it was, it would be a pleasanter place than the front seat of the Hillman.

"This'll slay you," Honor said, her colour heightened, her eyes suddenly unfriendly, "I'm taking Paul up to the dairy to meet Hester."

"Oh." Megan was elaborately indifferent.

"Exactly," Honor replied, defiantly unyielding.

"Well, have him home by about half-past four, then. I want to take him round to High Flat, to see the sunset. Want to come? Joady said we could get away."

"I may," Honor said flatly, "and I may not." She went quickly out of the room.

Megan crossed the paddock to the shed that housed the car, and while she backed the Hillman out and closed the shed door she reflected, unhappily, on the little scene with Honor. This was the one abiding cause of disagreement in the family: Honor's tenacious and defiant defence of Hester Laing. It was the only thing that had ever caused the intelligent understanding of

Mary and James to falter and had led them to interfere, seriously, with the affairs of one of their children. As she climbed back into the car and drove off, after shutting the paddock gate, Megan recalled the time when, three years ago, Honor had first developed her absorbed interest in Hester Laing; she had been sent to the dairy, one afternoon, to buy some cream for visitors coming unexpectedly, and she had not returned until after sunset, and though nothing had been said at the time, beyond Joady's irate rebuke for the late arrival of the cream, Megan could still remember the disapproval of her parents' expressions when, later, Honor had begun to enthuse about Hester Laing. They had managed it all badly, and had only succeeded in rousing in her a fierce feeling of protection for Hester Laing.

For Hester Laing was no ordinary person. At forty-two, she had achieved an international reputation as a journalist and playwright; had taken a first in history at Oxford, and had written three plays, two of which had had phenomenal runs in New York and London. Her brilliant career had come to an abrupt end when Russia had been acknowledged as an ally of Britain, for she had always been a bitter opponent of communism; and when the great *volte-face* had taken place, when radio stations hurriedly played the Internationale and newspapers proudly displayed pictures of Stalin, "our gallant ally," she had continued to denounce the Soviet. She had finally disgraced herself when, at an important Loan Rally speech in London, she had declared that Britain's better policy would be to throw in her lot with Hitler in his attack on Stalingrad and wipe the evil menace of Russian communism from the face of the earth. She was declared disloyal, a traitor, an agent of Hitler; her plays were withdrawn, she was shouted at and abused in the streets of London and New York, she was universally reviled. Abruptly she disappeared, and there had been widespread astonishment when she had suddenly appeared, on her father's death, at the dairy at Peppercorns, which had always been his pride and delight. For nearly five years she had managed the prize Jersey herd, and had devoted herself to the successful running of one of the finest dairies in the district. She lived alone in the stone house on the summit of the hill, on whose gentle slopes the dairy was situated, and she was firmly shunned by the right-thinking people of Ambara, who would have been glad to have been able to do the shunning more actively, for she was seldom seen in the village and appeared quite unaware of her isolation. However, Laing's dairy had supplied Ambara with milk for more than forty years, and no change had occurred when this outlandish woman had taken over its management. In fact, Hester Laing had completely sunk into obscurity in Ambara, and this in itself was somewhat disappointing to the population, whose tongues had wagged excitedly and indignantly when she had returned from America. She had no contact at all with the village, other than that provided by her name on the bill heads of its milk accounts; none, that is, but her continued friendship with Honor Carmichael.

Since that time, three years ago, the matter had been ignored at Thornfield, but Honor had always visited Peppercorns as she wished, prepared to fight furiously if she were prevented, in any way, from seeing Hester. No disaster had followed, and to Megan it seemed as if Honor's development had been accelerated in every way in these last three years, for she had had access to more books and music and a wider view of the world than she would ever have gained in her own environment. But there had been no contact between Hester Laing and the rest of the family, for Honor resented their early disfavour; Hester Laing was a self-elected recluse, and the Carmichaels, scholarly and enlightened people though they were, could feel no sympathy for unorthodoxy as strongly expressed as were Hester Laing's views. Megan realized, however, that Honor was now, at sixteen, years ahead of her own standard at the same age; perhaps she was deplorably older in mind than her years, but if she were to cultivate her voice, if she were to become known in the world of music, there was little benefit to be derived from her remaining a child. Yes, Megan reflected, this was one instance in which the family had been proved wrong; and yet, unhappily, the breach had never quite healed, for Megan had righteously adopted the family's attitude, as had Anthea and Joady, and Honor had withdrawn from them accordingly. Still, she thought, as she turned into the road which led to the Kyleses'

159

house, no doubt every family had these cleavages, and there was no need to lament unduly, for Honor genuinely loved her family.

Megan drew level with the Kyleses' house, and as Alec rose from a deck chair on the veranda and walked slowly towards her, she wrenched her thoughts round to the problem that she knew she must face now. She opened the door and smiled at him as he seated himself beside her.

"Good," he said. "Now get going, Megan; let's go down to the creek behind Barrett's farm."

"Does your mother know you're out?" she asked anxiously, as she started the car again.

His pale face lit up in a smile that twisted his lips a little.

"I don't suppose you meant that to sound like a music-hall song," he said; "but you hit the nail on the head, all right. No, I'm nearly twenty-three and my mother doesn't know I'm out at three o'clock in the afternoon. Isn't it shocking?"

Megan's face flushed with confusion; she said nothing, but drove faster.

"No need to look as if you could bite your tongue out, as it is sometimes so crudely put," he said lightly; "nor need you drive like blazes; she's not hotfooting it after us, you know."

Slowing down as she rounded the bend into the road that ran beside the railway line, she glanced at him uneasily, and, seeing the good-humoured expression on his face, one eyebrow raised at her discomfiture, she laughed aloud and at once felt happier.

"Oh, Alec, you're a nice fool," she said; "but aren't things messy?"

"That's no reason for taking oneself too seriously," he replied, and they drove on in silence. As they crossed the railway line, the good smell of newly baked bread came from Tillet's little bakery, and the scent lingered in Megan's nostrils as she turned into the road, which swept in a wide curve, past Barrett's farm, to the creek. It's wholesome, she thought; that's why Ambara's so delightful—like the smell of that new bread. There are only plain and simple things here, the luxury and pother of urban existence hasn't touched us yet, hasn't complicated living; you

160

only smell primary smells here, like earth and hay and rotting leaves, and colours are simple and the shapes of things are not fanciful; the perfection of that little stone silo on Barrett's farm comes from the fact that it was constructed merely to serve its purpose well, to be solid and useful and not to give itself airs. The whole of the Sydney Botanic Gardens, she reflected, with all their rare shrubs and their orchid houses, their carefully cultivated trees and their rose gardens, couldn't achieve the effortless beauty of these paddocks, almost white with seeding grass, dotted here and there with white-stemmed paperbarks and the rusty trunks of red gums, lying against the towering line of dark-green shrubs and tall trees that marked the course of the creek.

As they came to the bridge, Megan pulled the car off the road and stopped it on the grassy edge; they left the road, and walked slowly across the paddock to the green, gently sloping bank that led down to the creek bed. Here they sat down and for a moment they gazed silently up and down the creek. Trees, Megan thought; thank God there are thousands of trees everywhere in England. Across from them, on the opposite bank, a sturdy, rugged coolabah, its dark branches showing up abruptly against yellow-green grass, stood, carefully posed, against the little round hill that rose sharply behind the creek; in front of it a dancing cluster of gossamer-leafed she-oaks looked almost black, above the green riot of blackthorn, crowding at the creek's edge; on their left a willow spilled its trailing branches into the water in an abandonment of grief; above them swallows were gathering, mere black movement in the sky, now and again swirling over their heads, the strangely exciting sound of their flustering fuss of feathers beating and throbbing through the air.

"Well," Alec said, "I'm clearing out."

"Yes, I thought it would be that."

"Disapprove?"

"No—oh, no, Alec; I think you need to—I want you to. . . ."

"But . . ." he said. "That's what you mean, isn't it? But!"

"In a way."

"I've done a lot of thinking," he said. "You mustn't think it

161

only began last night; that chap just put the cap on things, I guess, but I've been thinking about this for a long time, getting ready for it. Megan—" he turned to her urgently—"you saw me grow up; you were there—how did this happen to me? How did I let myself get like this?"

"Well—" her words came slowly, hesitantly—"you were never very strong, I think; you used to get bad colds—we never thought you were properly fed—and then there was this doctor and that one, and your mother began to buy patent medicines and pills. Oh, I don't know—I suppose its effect was cumulative."

"Yes," he agreed, "it was, too; and after a while, when you've somewhat lost the desire to play football, when, finally, you've got no companions to play with, it's so much easier just to stay in a house and be looked after; and you get scared to take any risks, because if they don't come off you know that it won't only be you who'll suffer the consequences, but your poor mother, who's devoting her whole life to making you well. The last time I did take a risk—when I was seventeen—it didn't come off, and it just about finished me. You see, if you never leave your house you've hardly any decisions to make—that's very tempting, too; and if you're prepared to grant the initial premise, that you have no mind of your own, there's no conflict at home. Oh, yes, it's all been very tempting: the fact that all of you doesn't add up to one whole man seems of very little importance, until suddenly something makes you see. Well, that's what happened to me, and I've known for some time that I've got to do something painful and difficult and sudden about it—and I never again want to be comfortable or safe. If any woman ever tries to look after me, throughout the rest of my life, let her beware."

"And what are you going to do, Alec? You know, for one reason or another, you're not very—you're not really strong, are you?" Megan spoke a little timidly, aware that no man likes to recognize the fact that he's not strong.

"No," he said, "I'm not; but I'm going to get out—that's the first step. If I don't succeed in getting something to do I'll probably die, but I'd prefer that, any day."

"Alec,"—she was still uneasily hesitant—"would you think we

162

were looking after you? You see, Paul and Honor and I were talking about this, and it was Paul's suggestion. . . ."

As she outlined the plan they had made she saw his expression lighten, and he turned to her eagerly.

"Megan, little Megan—why, it's just the chance I need. I'm madly lucky. If that Paul hadn't come last night . . . listen, when can I go to this place? And to have charge of the gallery—Megan, it's a wonderful chance. But I could do it; I'll make a good job of it, I swear I will."

They sat on, talking and planning; he had only to wait for word from the Quentins, they decided, and then he could leave secretly. Megan would drive him to the station, and he determined to pocket his pride and ask for a week's wages in advance; Paul would understand, and he'd work himself to exhaustion to give value for it. . . . At last they fell silent. Alec lay on his back, hands clasped behind his head, his eyes large and excited in his pale, thin face; Megan sat cross-legged, pixy-fashion, more at peace with the world than she had been for many weeks, for it really did seem as if things were disentangling themselves to some extent, and reluctantly she admitted to herself that she was a little glad that everything that was happening was not hopelessly complicated by her love for Julian. Yes, she thought, I'm glad I'm enduring the pain of not being in love with him, rather than the joy of loving him to the point of infatuation.

Alec said softly, "Megan."

"M'm?" she asked, absently.

"Remember I said that something had made me wake up and see things clearly?"

"M'm," she nodded.

"Want to know what that was?"

"Yes," she said, curiously, "I wanted to ask, but I thought perhaps you'd rather not say."

"No, I want to tell you," he replied. He lay staring into the sky, and Megan, looking into his eyes, could see the reflection of trees and cloud. "You see," he went on, in a calm, expressionless tone, "it was you; I fell in love with you, I mean."

She stared down at him; she had felt a sudden startled shock spreading over her as she heard his words, and for a moment

163

she thought confusedly, and Julian and Alec became inextricably mixed in her mind. She said nothing, but looked in alarmed puzzlement at him.

"Oh, don't bother about it," he said easily. "It's not your fault—you're not supposed to do anything about it. I'm just explaining what happened to rouse me from my torpor."

Megan moistened her lips and looked away; then she turned to him again.

"When—how long ago was this?"

"Oh, not so long; just as soon as I realized that you imagined yourself in love with Julian."

Would the shocks never cease! This time she trembled with the unexpectedness of the attack; her face was white as she looked at him and she felt suddenly sick. Then Alec pulled himself up and sat beside her.

"I'm sorry, Megan," he said, gently. "I'm being rottenly cruel —just trying to work off my spite and jealousy and misery on you, that's all."

"How—did you know about it?"

"Just knew."

"Did the others—did everyone know?"

"No," he said. "They're all too eaten up with themselves; but when you do nothing as energetically as I've done it for twenty-odd years, you become acute in some ways: sensitive to impressions, aware of nuances in people's tones and looks. Oh, yes, I knew all right—and it's pretty nearly driven me mad."

"I'm not, now; not any more, Alec."

He looked at her steadily; then, in an incredulous tone, he said, "No more you are—I really believe you're not." After a pause, while he continued to gaze at her, he said, "I'm very glad. Are you quite sure?"

Tears in her eyes, she stared up at him and nodded her head.

"Don't think too much about what I've said," Alec went on. "I suppose I shouldn't have told you—beastly selfish, as usual— but I couldn't help myself; and, after all, I'm going away soon. . . ."

She interrupted him.

164

"I'm going away, too," she said sadly, and told him about her plans.

"I'm glad, Megan," he said warmly, "I'm terribly glad; it's the best thing that ever happened. You need to get clear of all these things for a while, away from your home and everything connected with this place. You can live your own life, instead of half a dozen other people's. And Megan—" he put his finger under her chin and forced her to look at him—"when you come back I'll have done something with myself, and maybe then we'll see; I wouldn't presume to offer myself, as I am, to anyone, much less to you. Kiss me?"—and he bent his head and kissed her lips lightly.

"Now, that's the last word about that," he said, getting to his feet. "Drive me home now, Megan?"

Slowly they walked back across the paddock to the car, the swallows gathering, calling and whirling above their heads in the sunlight, which was mellowing now to a deeper gold.

III

When he was certain that she had gone upstairs to lie down, Martin Croft went quietly out through the back of the house, across the piazza and up the stone steps, to the old toolshed under the camphor laurels, at the end of the garden. When he had closed the door behind him it was very dark, but he could find his way easily enough to the old petrol drum in the far corner. As his hands groped about in the dimness, they finally closed on a small, heavy object, and he gave a quiet, exultant laugh. Holding it carefully, he left the shed and walked quickly round to the back of it, glancing up casually to see whether she was watching him from her window; but the curtains hung quite still in the calm air, and he couldn't see any movement behind them. Now, behind the shed, he put the precious object on the ground, very gently, and then knelt down beside it. Not that he was afraid it would go off; oh, no, he knew too much about them for that. Ever since he'd found it, up on the hillside near the camp, he'd been discovering everything he could about them; he'd even gone to the School of Arts at Mitcham and looked up the encyclopaedia there, the volume which had grenades in it, and one of his books, *Wonders of Modern Warfare*, had had drawings and diagrams of one, and the various soldiers he'd met from the camp had helped him, amused by his passion for detail. At any rate, he knew now how they worked, that was the main thing, and the trouble he had taken to find out was well worth it. He had always known that he'd need to be able to use it, at some stage, and he'd been looking forward to the time; but he had never imagined that such an excellent opportunity as this would occur, and he felt immensely glad that he hadn't wasted it on her, because, though it would be nice to see all the mess and blood, it would be ever so much nicer when it was someone you hated as much as he hated this man. You couldn't hate her, she was just silly and annoying; in fact, he hadn't had the pleasure of hating anyone in earnest since she'd taken him from that school; there were a few there he'd like to have wiped out with this, but no one had ever filled him with such an excitement of hate as this man, and joy ran fiercely through him as he thought of the ecstasy of doing this tonight. Now he must do everything properly. He tried to arrange his plans neatly, in his mind, but wild gusts of hate and delight kept surging through him, making his hands and forehead wet, and his mouth full of saliva. He swallowed, wiped his hands, and tried to think.

Yes, he'd go to bed at the usual time, and then he'd slip out. She wouldn't hear him because she went to bed early, about nine, and that girl said they wouldn't leave the hall till eleven. Still, he'd get there about ten, just in case; better to wait an hour than to miss him. If they turned off in the usual direction for Raikes's meadow—and there was no reason why they shouldn't—the track would give him plenty of shelter until they were away from the village (he'd better go down there later, and walk through the bushes behind the track, just to spy out the land); but he'd have to throw it before they came out of the bush, to cross the railway line, so he wouldn't really have very long—perhaps half a mile. Still, that should give him plenty of

166

time. It would be good if he could somehow make him stop; perhaps he could make a sound in the bushes and the man would stop to listen—and then he'd let him have it. And he'd blow up into a thousand bloody little bits, lying here, there and everywhere, and clothes and flesh and dust would be all mixed up together, and bits of hair and teeth and bloody fingernails scattered in the bushes. . . .

His eyes set in a glassy stare with his excitement, and his jaw dropped foolishly. Suddenly his ecstasy was too much for him and he was violently sick; he lay gasping on the ground for a moment, and then he began to feel better. He stood up and went over to the garden tap. When he had washed his hands and face he went back, picked up his grenade carefully, and carried it into the shed. By the time he had closed the door again he felt quite recovered, though he was pale and his hands trembled a little. He quite often had these sick fits lately, when anything happened which he particularly enjoyed; he'd been the same yesterday, when he'd got that bird. . . . But that had been when he had had his penknife; he had to have that knife and he meant to get it, but it would be better to get this other thing done first. He stopped suddenly as a splendid thought struck him; he sat down on the top step, overlooking the piazza, while he made his plans, and as the full joy of it came to him, he rocked to and fro with delight, his hands clasped round his knees. It was so simple, and yet it meant that he'd never have any more trouble with her; he'd just come straight home, wake her up and tell her what he'd done, and she'd be so scared that anyone would find out that all he would have to do in future would be to say he'd tell what he had done, and then she'd let him do anything he liked. He laughed hysterically as he thought of his good fortune. Everything was wonderful today, though it had begun so badly; in fact, he felt sure it was going to be the happiest day of his life. His mother, calling him from the kitchen at that moment, was delighted when he gaily answered, "Coming!" and bounded down the steps, instead of silently appearing round the door, as he usually did, watching, watching until she began to drop and spill things in her nervousness.

When they had crossed the railway line and had turned into the road that faced the hills, Honor and Paul let the horses walk. Iago loped delightedly along in the tall grass beside the road, his head raised like a swimmer keeping his chin out of the water; the rest of him was invisible, merely a long rippling movement in the grass. Over to the left the sound of thudding hooves came from the polo field, where impeccably clad men and women, wearing topis, raced their horses madly after a ball. Honor looked across at them and grunted.

"They make me sick," she said.

"Do they? Why?" Paul asked.

"The horses hate that beastly game," she said angrily. "Lord! We give animals a rotten time, and yet we thank God we're not savages like the bear-baiters of the Middle Ages. Look at those lovely animals—their mouths pulled and twisted, their nerves in rags with strain and excitement. If those fools want to chase a stupid ball around, why don't they get down and run around on their own legs? It's about all they're fit for—there's nothing in their heads."

"Well, you tell me; why don't they?"

"Oh, because it's stylish to play polo; you see, common, ordinary people can play football and tennis; but you've got to have money to play polo, because you've got to have at least two good ponies. I'd wipe it all out, if I could—and dog racing, and horse racing, especially those insane steeplechasing things."

"You'd change a lot of things if you could, wouldn't you?"

"Yes, and when I'm famous I'll use all my power to change them; instead of pictures of Dame Honor Carmichael using someone's hair tonic or eye lotion, there'll be interviews with me, condemning all the things I object to in the world."

"Only popular people carry weight, and you won't be popular for long at that rate."

"Oh, yes, I will. I'll wait until I'm in an unassailable position, and then I'll use it for all I'm worth; by then I'll be so good that they won't be able to come back at me."

He looked at her, smiling.

"You're very sure, aren't you?"

"Of course I'm sure. I'm going to be known and revered in every country in the world."

They rode on in silence, the horses' hooves alone breaking the stillness around them. From far away to the south they could hear the gradually quickening *shur-shur* of a train leaving a station, the increasing tempo hurrying to a broad, continuous roar that died away out of earshot; the polo players were a mere prickle of sound behind them, and they two alone seemed to be abroad in the world. As they approached the white, gum-shaded bridge at the foot of the red hill road, they passed a small paddock of brown-eared wheat, on which a flock of sparrows had descended; they were gently and gracefully swinging up and down on the stems, which bent beneath the weight of the tiny bodies, the whole paddock a mass of slow, rhythmic movement. Paul was fascinated by the little creatures, and they halted for a few moments to watch. A white goat came down to the gate and looked at them with palely staring, inquiring eyes.

When they had crossed the bridge, Honor said, "It must be nearly three o'clock," and pointed upwards.

"Why?" he asked, looking to where she pointed.

"See—the first of the Jerseys coming up from the paddock for milking."

A little line of red dust marked the track of the slowly moving Jersey herd.

"My word, they're beauties," Paul said admiringly.

"Aren't they? Before the war they used to carry off all the prizes at the Easter Show, and they're even better since Hester's had them; she works as hard with the dairy as she does with anything she's interested in."

"Tell me about her," Paul said. "You know, I've heard nothing about her, except that you're very fond of her."

"I am, I'm very fond of her."

"Then why do you sound so sad when you say it?"

Honor paused and looked up to the house on the hill.

169

"I've had a lot of trouble about it," she said, "and it's made me a little sad, I think; you see, she's Hester Laing—the famous one, I mean."

"Oh, yes," he said. "Of course I've heard of her. So that's who your friend is."

"Yes," she said. "That would have been enough to damn her; any woman who holds her views on things must be bad, people like my family think.

"Oh, Paul, what is it about you that brings you so close to the hearts of people? I've never been able to tell a soul about these things, and yet I want to tell you."

She pulled Xanthippe to a halt, and turned sideways in her saddle to talk to him, as he halted too; her troubled, deeply blue eyes searched his face.

"There are things in your own mind that you would do well to let me know, Paul; can't you tell me?"

For a wild moment fear rose in him and she saw it in his face; then he relaxed, for he could tell she knew nothing, and he managed to smile at her.

"No, Honor, there's nothing I can tell you."

"But there's something keeping you all the time preoccupied, isn't there? I can feel you beginning to relax sometimes, to enjoy our company, and then you seem to recall something and you stiffen and look haunted. Paul, it's something to do with that watch, isn't it?"

She was a little aghast at the change that came over his face; his lips tightened to a hard line, and his eyes suddenly glittered with suspicion and fear.

"I'm not afraid of you, Paul," she said, regarding him steadily. "I know that even if you were suddenly to set upon me and murder me, it would not be through rage or spite or cruelty, but simply because you'd consider it necessary, according to your lights. You can't be afraid of a person who thinks like that."

Suddenly he laughed, and, leaning over, kissed her cheek.

"Honor," he said, "you're the most unusual, unexpected, charming, and interesting woman I've ever met: that's the astonishing thing—more than half the time you're a woman,

170

grown and wise, and then you're a funny child again. Oh, I'm so glad I've known you!"

She smiled back at him, and they set their horses forward once again, coming into the cloud of red dust left by the endless line of Jerseys.

"We won't follow their dust," Honor said. "We'll cross the road and go down into the valley; then we can come up to the dairy from the back way, and I'll show you the most beautiful piece of roadway you've ever seen."

They topped the rise and, descending into a shallow valley, turned left into a wide road, grass-covered, lying between sloping paddocks and ending in the hillside where the dairy buildings stood among the trees.

"There!" said Honor.

Tall gums bent across the road, and lantana hedges covered the fences; green, in every shade, was here, and at the end of the road the dark mass of brown earth, across which the gently coloured Jerseys filed slowly up to the milking shed; the trees above their heads were filled with the gaudy, flashing colours of a flock of rosellas; and two starkly white horses stood watching them stonily from the left-hand paddock.

"It's perfect," Paul said, drawing in a breath. "It's everything the Australian artists have ever tried to put on canvas."

Honor nodded silently, and they rode forward. At the foot of the hill they turned to the right and climbed a steep slope to the road fronting a white, two-storeyed house, which was Hester Laing's home.

"She'll be in the dairy just now," Honor said, and she dismounted. They tethered the horses at the double gates that opened on a winding drive leading down to the sheds, and left Iago on guard, to his considerable disappointment, for the dairy was filled with creatures he would have liked to chase and there were other dogs there and innumerable exciting smells. When they closed the gate he put his nose wistfully through the bars and made sad little noises in his throat, but human beings, he had early come to recognize, had hearts of stone, and so he was left to guard two great useless ponies, who were well able to

171

look after themselves. He settled himself down gloomily to wait, a disappointed and disgusted dog.

"Why all the cars outside?" Paul asked.

"Cream time," Honor replied. "People come from everywhere, with jars and bottles, when they're separating; it's heavenly cream."

She led the way into a narrow passage at the end of one of the sheds, and then into the room where the separator was. A white-haired, ruddy-faced man was standing by the machine, and a little group of people, clasping bottles and jars, stood patiently waiting; there was swift movement everywhere, for the milking sheds opened out of this room and the noise of the clanking machines made talking difficult.

"Hullo, Mr. Cliff," Honor shouted.

He waved to her and smiled, his bright blue eyes alertly watching his machine.

"Miss Laing's outside," he boomed, waving towards the milking shed.

"Wait here, Paul," Honor said, and went out swiftly to the broad, veranda-like structure, at the back of which the milking machines were situated.

Paul turned to the window and gazed down from it. Why, the place was perched on the very side of the hill; how on earth did the cows get up? And yet they kept coming; a lad in gum boots, leaning against one gate, opened it every now and again to let in a clumsily lurching cow, and at a gate at the other end of the shed a plump-faced girl in blue overalls was sending them out again. It was perfectly rhythmic, timed, so often rehearsed that all the cast, including the cows, knew their parts perfectly. Paul craned his neck. He could see them coming up now; they climbed the steep hill in a long, slowly moving queue, a sluggish line of gently obedient animals, the dark brown earth beneath their hooves and the dim, green leaves of the gums towering above them, the perfect foils for the delicately understated colours of their silky coats.

The place is actually in the treetops, Paul thought; whoever would think of balancing a dairy like a bird's nest, of making it a thing of beauty? He went to the end window and stared

172

out across the whole valley and plain of Ambara, seen through the branches of the gums, to its farthest horizon, its green pencil-grey with distance, the faint smear of a red roof here, the heavy blue-green of a lucerne field there, the minute pocket handkerchief of a dark, ploughed field far away to the south. Heavens, he thought, no wonder Honor loves this place! Across to the left and perched on a higher hill, he could make out the white line of the house at Cedar Hill, and then he could faintly see the terrace where he had sat that morning with the children. Was that merely a matter of hours ago? he wondered; it seemed months and years in the past. And was it only a few hours before he would be going that way again? He lowered his gaze to the dark line of the creek; yes, that was where he was to be. In how many hours? About twenty hours. He caught his breath with excitement. In twenty hours he would be free from fear. . . . He turned as Honor touched his arm.

"Come on," she shouted. "Hester's waiting outside."

She came quickly from the other end of the shed, as they emerged into the quiet warmth of the afternoon sunlight, and he was at once struck with the strength and vitality of her movements, the eagerness and animation of her expression. She was small, a trim figure in a dark-red wind jacket over a brightly white shirt; she wore grey jodhpurs, and her flat shoes shone richly with many polishings; her hair had been very dark, but was deeply streaked with grey now, and she wore it short, the ends curling lightly; her face was thin and brown, laughter-wrinkled at the mouth and the corners of the widely set brown eyes. She extended a firm, brown little hand to him and said, "I'm very glad you came; I have no visitors here but Honor, so I've rather got out of the habit of donning a filmy house gown in the afternoons, to await callers."

"Are we interrupting your work?" Paul asked.

"No," she replied. "They can carry on quite well; even if they couldn't, I shouldn't bother. Come up to the house and let me make you some coffee."

As they climbed the stone steps that led up to the lawn at the back of the house, she said, over her shoulder, to him, "It's a new experience for me to meet a returned prisoner; I hope

173

you're not still feeling it too acutely, because I'd like to hear you talk for hours—not today, of course, because Honor says you must be back by half-past four, but I hope you'll come and see me again."

She held back a wire door, and they entered a kitchen in which everything was white, except the red-checked window-curtains and tablecloth, and a row of bright green pots, filled with scarlet geraniums that stood along one window ledge.

"The coffee's made and I've only to heat it; it'll be ready in one minute. Will you set up the tray, Honor, and then we'll take it through to the sitting room."

Paul thought he had never seen anyone capable of such rapid movement; without any apparent haste, with a complete economy of effort, she moved from cupboard to stove, to the table and back to the stove, and before, seemingly, she had properly commenced, the tray was ready and he was carrying it, complete with scones and some little homemade biscuits, honey, jam, and cream, through the doors she held open for him.

He carried it the length of the long sitting room to a little table that she pulled forward into the centre of the wide, semi-circular bow window, the seat of which was thickly padded in deep red velvet. They seated themselves here, and she poured the coffee and talked to Honor, in her quick, soft voice, about her work. Paul looked down the room; there were hundreds probably thousands of books, making the room vivid with colours, the cedar shelves dark and glowing above the russet-green carpet.

"You've a wonderful library, Miss Laing," he said.

"Yes," she replied; "my only self-indulgence, now."

"And does your work here give you time to read them?"

"Yes," she said firmly. "Otherwise I should give up the work. But I'm very fortunate; I have people to help me to such an extent that, though the work is strenuous, I have regular hours, and I ask nothing more from life than hard work in the day, which yet leaves me plenty of energy to read at night."

"And what about your writing? Have you abandoned that?"

She gave a shrug and a wry smile.

"In one sense, yes; that is, I've abandoned the kind of writing

174

which made me notorious—there's too much ballyhoo associated with that, now; people will produce my plays, in America, simply because they coin money, though they themselves are opposed to everything I believe, and others will act in them and they'll all fall over themselves to have some little part in their production, because they're money-makers—and that seemed to me to be a bad thing. And no one bothers, any longer, to ask whether my work is good; it's just that it bears my name, and that's sufficient to make the money roll in."

"And so you've given it up?"

"No, I've just changed the nature of my work; I'm writing a history of the recent world war, which is taking me years to prepare and which will probably mean very little financially for me; but I'm discovering how utterly ignorant I am—and that is worth more than riches, I think."

Honor sat gazing at her, storing up memories of her face and her voice and her quick, lively movements. How many of the people she knew would give up the chance of continually making money, because they thought the means of making it were bad? And yet they condemned Hester Laing and said she was a bad influence; she felt that she had learnt more of real goodness from Hester than from anyone she had ever known, more of real courage. . . . Oh, Hester, Hester.

"Come and look at my books"—Hester jumped to her feet—"and then I suppose you must go. I could keep you here all night, talking, but I know you have an appointment to keep."

While they were looking at the books and talking, Honor knelt on the window seat and gazed down into the valley. The shadows were lengthening down the sides of the hill slopes now, and there was a solemnity and a hush in the folds at the base of the hills; soon the smoke would begin to drift upwards from the hearth fires, and the aching melancholy of the autumn evening would rise into the air with it. And soon she must part from Hester again. . . .

It was nearly a quarter-past four when Hester waved good-bye to them from the gate and then walked lightly back into the house; they let the ponies canter down the dusty red road, but

175

when they had crossed the bridge and were back on the flat, Honor slowed Xanthippe to a walk and turned to Paul.

"Well?" she asked.

"I think she's fine; she's a woman in a million. You're very lucky to know her so well."

"Yes, I am—oh, I know it." Honor's voice was melancholy.

"But I think it's about time you changed your feelings towards her."

Instantly she was angry, defiant, and she flashed a contemptuous glance at him.

"You, too?"

"No, not me, too," he said agreeably, jogging easily along on Johnny's broad back.

"Well, explain what you mean."

"Every time you mention her you're saddened, you seem to be yearning, dissatisfied."

"I'm not, I'm not," she said hotly.

"Anyway, that's the impression I get, and I think it's a true impression, too, no matter what you say."

She was silent, her expression mutinous.

"I think," he went on, slowly, "it's time you stopped trying to defend her and began just to like her; the way you're going, you'll end up by hating her and she'll be bored to tears with you."

"Oh, you're hateful—you're impudent!"

"Oh, no I'm not, and you know I'm not; but I'm telling you something you don't like to hear, that's all. That woman has so much to give you—and she's perfectly willing to pour it all out on you, too, you lucky little wretch—that you should be continually thankful that you know her; but you're asking more of her than she can possibly give; it's not in her nature to act the rôle you've assigned to her and, inevitably, if it continues, you'll become angry with her and she'll find you a nuisance. Now take the goodness she's offering you and look elsewhere for something to protect; otherwise you'll lose someone who'll be more valuable to you than anyone you're ever likely to know."

Honor kicked her heels into Xanthippe's sides and sent her

176

bounding forward; over her shoulder she shouted fiercely, "I hate you—I hate the very sight of you."

Dust hid her from sight. Paul jogged on thoughtfully, peaceably, checking Johnny's attempt to race after Xanthippe. At the end of the road Honor was waiting for him, her face dusty and tear-stained, and, leaning across, he held his folded handkerchief to her lips.

"Lick," he said briefly, and meekly she moistened the handkerchief with her tongue. He scrubbed energetically at her face and removed most of the damage, while she sat looking up at him, unusually defenceless, queerly uncertain of herself, not at all the cool and immaculate Honor the family were accustomed to seeing.

"Paul," she said at last, in an unwilling tone.

"Yes, darling?" he asked gently.

Her eyes widened in surprise.

"Why do you call me that?"

"Why? Well, I don't really know. It just occurred to me what a dear, worth-while little thing you are—and I felt a very great affection for you."

She gazed earnestly at him, her eyes searching his deeply.

"I've behaved badly and stupidly," she said, "and you've been sweet. I'm going to spend a long time thinking it all out. I've known you always, Paul, I think, and I'll know you for ever, now, even if you're never where I am—and I feel a great affection for you, too."

She put her hand on his, for a moment, and then they turned the horses and cantered briskly along to the railway crossing.

5

SATURDAY EVENING

I

MEGAN felt a sense of comforting relief as she came into the kitchen and saw Joady rolling flour on the pastry board. Home is a lovely place, she thought exultantly; it's warm and reassuring and familiar and undramatic. She knew just how Joady would look at her and what she would say.

"Hullo," Joady said noncommittally, looking up briefly from her rolling pin.

Megan went round the table, and putting her arms round Joady's comfortable middle, she hugged it, her chin on Joady's shoulder.

"You said it—and just the right way, Joady."

"Said what?"

"Said 'Hullo' to me," Megan explained.

"You're wandering in your head," Joady said amiably. "And stop squeezing my stomach—you'll give me indigestion."

"I love you, Joady," Megan said pensively.

"Cupboard love," said Joady curtly. "I've been told people love me more times than enough, when I'm making pastry. And if you really love me, you'll please—stop—squeezing—my middle."

Megan swung herself up on the end of the table.

"You're a disillusioned old thing. Were you ever seriously in love, Joady?"

"Maybe," Joady replied. "A lot of chance I had, anyway, with you three always tagging after me."

"Did you always love us, Joady?"

178

"Love you! I'd have given you to the trashcart man often enough, only your mother always had some maudlin sentiment about you."

Did I love them! she thought bitterly. A hundred images of Adrian came crowding into her mind; she could see him in every corner of the kitchen, a chubby toddler, a Boy Scout with heavy responsibilities, a gay youth—and then, in his khaki.

"You loved Adrian best, didn't you?" Megan asked.

"I hated the sight of the lot of you," Joady said testily, "and every time one was born I was for drowning it in the bucket."

Megan gave a shocked giggle.

"You're awful, Joady; can I have a tartlet?"

"There you are!" Joady exclaimed triumphantly. "Whenever they come in with this lovey-dovey stuff, I know it won't be long before the cadging starts."

They heard steps on the veranda and the sound of saddles being dumped in the corner.

"Here's more of them," Joady said grimly, as Paul and Honor came in.

"Tarts, Joady! Oh, Joady, can Paul and I have some?"

"No," said Joady.

"Oh, Joady, and you're letting that fat pig of a Megan stuff herself full of them, and you know I'm outgrowing my strength —and Paul needs building up. And we're going up to High Flat."

"You're not going anywhere before that poor boy has a rest," Joady replied, menacingly. "You've been dragging him round since dawn—and him just out of a hospital." She was pouring milk into a glass; she put two little tarts on a plate and said to Paul, "Now, take those up to your room and eat them, and then lie down for half an hour; you're very tired and you know it. And if these two devils try to disturb you before half an hour, I'll box their ears."

She pushed him out the door, while they all begged and protested, and when he had gone she faced the two girls.

"Now," she said, "since you're both so abounding in energy, do some work. You get in there and get the dining room ready, Megan, and you stay here and do the kitchen-maiding, my world-famous prima donna."

179

When Megan had disappeared, Honor began washing cake pans resignedly, and then began to peel potatoes.

"Where's everyone, Joady?" she asked, after a while.

"Your mother's resting, your dad's writing letters in his study, and Anthea's gone. She and your dad had a long talk; there's some talk of your dad taking that young Alec into the business."

"Yes. What did Father think of it?"

"Seemed real pleased," Joady answered, carefully filling tart shapes with lemon-cheese. "Appears he wanted to give that young Paul a job, but he wasn't having any."

"Yes—pity, isn't it?"

"Why wouldn't he take it on?"

"Oh, I don't quite know, Joady. He's got some thing about the future; thinks everything stops tomorrow—can't seem to think beyond that—but he'll be all right on Monday."

Joady pressed her lips together and went on working in silence, the tears of fright hidden as she bent her head to open the oven.

At last Honor said, "I've finished, Joady; there's not another thing to be done here, unless you'd like me to holystone the deck?"

"None of your lip," Joady said. "All right, go in and see what that good-for-nothing Megan is doing, and then you can all go star gazing, if you like."

As Honor skipped out the door, Joady called after her, "Don't you be a minute later than a quarter-past six, mind."

When she entered the dining room, Honor gave a shocked exclamation, for Megan was sitting in the window seat, her feet on the cushion, with Jenkins lying beside her in an agony of pleasure while she scratched his heavy jowls.

"Well," Honor said, indignantly, "and I've peeled half a hundredweight of potatoes and washed all that claggy goo off fifty pie dishes!"

"Shut up," said Megan, rubbing Jenkins' soft stomach, his purring rising to a shriller, almost hysterical note of ecstasy. "I did everything in ten minutes, but you know what Joady is; besides, I'm the Proctor Travelling Scholar and it's beneath me dignity to soil me fingers."

180

Honor came across and helped with the scratching.

"You make a fool of that cat," she said, as Jenkins, abandoning feline dignity, forgetful of the position he had to maintain in the household, rolled on his back, his four paws lolling helplessly.

"So do you, but we all like it, and as long as we keep it in the family and don't let the world know our cat is a voluptuary, what of it?"

They continued to stroke for a moment, then Honor said, "Think I'll go and get Paul."

"Right," said Megan. "I'll meet you at the front gate."

When they joined her, a few minutes later, she said, "We'll have to go like smoke—the sun's nearly setting."

"How long will it take us to get there?" Paul asked.

"A quarter of an hour, if we're smart. Let's see, it's five past five; the sun sets at half-past, so we should just be in time."

They walked at breathless speed, saying little, keeping their breath for extra speed, and soon they had left houses behind. They began to ascend to smooth, flat country with few trees, and those mostly in clusters round the tiny dams where the cattle drank. They were walking away from the hills, purpling now in the shadows, but soon they turned, following a white road leading to a farther rise, at the top of which paddocks stretched widely on both sides and ahead of them, to the very foot of the hills. This was farm country, the only houses the infrequent farm dwellings, nestling beneath their trees. When they came to a paddock, rising slightly to their left, they stopped and climbed halfway up its slope, where they sat down to watch the day change into night.

On one side of them, in the west, was a startling bright, hard, clear, yellow sky, lying vividly between the blackness of the earth's rim and the blue-grey mass of cloud that hovered thickly above, the silhouetted trees dancing giddily before it, an undisciplined ballet, pointing to the sunset, jibing, "Here is sunshine, here light; you're deprived, you're left behind back there, and for twelve hours you must make do with the moon." The light lingered, loitering in an afterglow, to spoil the moon's subtle entrance; now they turned and the moon was there, gleaming silver

181

resting stilly on amethyst, above a line of turquoise, and before it all a dead gum raised lamenting, accusing limbs to the sky, cursing man, the slaughterer. Paul looked down, over the darkening paddocks; this was not merely the fading of light from the world, but the coming of a delicate, powdery darkness, filling in the deeper hollows first, then gradually rising until it reached the slope where they were sitting. Far up in the hills he could hear the low hum of a motor, and, far away, someone slammed a window shut; from some hidden place came the metallic, dull monotony of a radio, and everywhere there was a trilling of insects, a muted sound.

They waited until the indiscriminate light deepened into moonlight, and then they commenced to walk back. Honor was walking slightly ahead, and suddenly she crowed with delight and bent over a puddle in the road.

"Look!" she cried. "Look—it's caught the moon! Remember the little boy in the First Reader?"

The muddy puddle, drab and insignificant by day, was now a gleaming silver mirror, the moon caught and held in its inconsiderableness, all heaven blazing up below its exquisitely clear surface; devout in their moon-worship, they knelt down and exclaimed.

As they turned into the long road that led back to Thornfield, Honor began to sing, softly, *"Au Clair de la Lune,"* and their exhilaration mounted; some pieces of glass lay along the road and, moon-touched, made their way a royal progress for a few yards, a carpet strewn with jewels in Oriental lavishness. Here's beauty, Megan thought; everything is pure and good tonight, and in all my life I shall not know many nights as perfect. They passed the whitened ghost of a gate, in the centre of a plump and living hedge. Why did it die? Megan wondered. Perhaps that fat hedge had overwhelmed it and sucked its life away. . . . She felt sad for the gate.

Adrian knew I should love this place, Paul thought, and so I do—every inch of it. And these two girls are the sweetest women I have known or shall ever know. Honor—little delicate thing; look at her sweet, grave face and listen to those glorious notes of hers. I'm happy—I think I shall never be anything else, now.

182

Honor finished the little song, and strode along with her hands in the pockets of her tweed riding jacket. Heavens! How used I've grown to having him here, she thought, and how quickly it's all happened. Whatever shall I do when he goes? And when will he go, I wonder; I believe we should be able to cure him completely if he'd only stay a little while longer—he's almost normal now, though I wish he'd throw that poor mangled watch away. And he's so fine looking; when he turns his head and looks back over his shoulder like that, he looks glorious. How slim and supple his hands are, too, brown and strong; and his lips are strong and firm, they felt cool and hard against my face when he kissed me this afternoon: it was . . . pleasant, a new feeling. I feel happier tonight than I've felt for years.

"Lord!" Megan exclaimed. "It's quarter-past six! Come on."

They raced across the paddock to the front gate, and in a moment they were rushing down the hall, shouting, "We're not late, Joady. Look at us, we're not late."

II

While the children were having an early tea in their playroom, Anthea dressed quietly and at leisure. Her dark hair hung softly, almost to her waist, as she brushed it. She was tired, but, for the first time in months, pleasantly so, not in a nervously exhausted, frayed fashion. It had been a busy day, but in a good, manageable way. She had rung Mannering when she returned from Thornfield, and had arranged to see him on Monday morning; without revealing the nature of her business, she had made him aware of its importance to her. In his cool, impersonal fashion he had been reassuring, congratulating her on her good sense in throwing her burdens on him, and when she had told him doubtfully that it was by no means an ordinary legal matter, but something intensely personal, which he might find himself reluctant to deal with, or incapable of handling, he had soothed her by saying that there were few matters in which legal advice could not be of some value. She had been comforted by the feeling that he would regard her despicable behaviour in much the same way as a doctor would regard a disease, and that she would be less likely to lose his respect, because she had probably never had it, because to him she was, and had always been, merely a case. The fear that he might lose faith in her was of no importance, compared with the fact that she no longer had faith in herself; even now she could not be certain that that madness would not overcome her once more, if and when she was confronted with Howard, and there was no way of knowing save by seeing him and testing herself directly—and this she feared to do. Still, it must be done; but not tonight; at least she could shelve it for the time being and enjoy this measure of rare tranquillity.

When she had twisted her hair smoothly at the base of her neck, she went to her wardrobe. She needed something which would be suitable for the merry-go-round in Barrett's paddock and which would not necessitate her changing again for the Welcome Home. . . . Not so easy, she decided. Finally, she chose a leaf-green, light woollen frock, high in the neck, with a little white collar; she could wear flat-heeled shoes and slip into her more elaborate brown suede ones, with the buckles, when she returned. Now, her water-mole coat, soft, green suede gloves, brown bag. She was almost ready when Cassie's knock came.

When Anthea opened the door, Cassie said breathlessly, "Yer'll just 'ave to come, lovey; I've done me best, but Libby's got the chews."

"Oh, dear," Anthea said anxiously, "whatever's the matter with her?" Throwing her bag, coat, and gloves on the bed, she left the room hurriedly, listening to Cassie's worried explanation as they hastened down the hall. The long, glassed-in veranda that they now entered was the children's playroom, and living room, at the far end of which, overlooking the valley, was their bedroom, divided from the rest of the room by glass partitions. When they came in, John was standing at one of the windows, dejectedly pulling at the blind cord, and he raised his eyebrows at his mother in a helpless, exasperated fashion, at the same time gesturing towards Libby, who, red-faced and tearful, was sitting at the table, chewing desperately, her face bewildered with anxiety, which merely deepened when Anthea sat down on the little bench.

"Hullo, chick," Anthea said tenderly. "Got the old chews?"

Libby nodded miserably and went on chewing, her mouth filled with a horrid, choking ball of food.

"Spit it out for Mummy, darling," Anthea coaxed.

Libby shook her head fiercely and chewed for dear life. Anthea looked up at Cassie.

"You and John go and listen to the radio, eh, Cassie?"

Cassie nodded, and she and John went outside, as Libby looked after them despairingly, the tears rolling down her cheeks. Anthea went to the door.

"Send Joseph, Cassie," she whispered, and Cassie nodded and went on down the hall.

While she waited, Anthea sat beside Libby and sang little snatches of songs, in a low voice. It was a long time since Libby had had one of these fits, which had made her babyhood a nightmare; she must be very excited about something—surely it couldn't be the merry-go-round, Anthea thought worriedly. It was going to be awful if this happened whenever she was to have a little treat of any kind; she would just have to take her to a psychiatrist if it was going to recur like this, though it seemed a pity to give it undue prominence if it could clear itself up, as it seemed to have been doing during the last two years.

Just now, Anthea was pinning her hopes on Joseph; the last few times he seemed to have been able to work wonders, by what means she did not know; even he seemed vague as to the methods he used. The trouble was, of course, that they were never able to detect the beginning of these attacks. Libby was always a slow and solemn eater, chewing her food laboriously before swallowing it, and it was only when she began to show signs of distress that they realized that she had been taking mouthful after mouthful, retaining it in her mouth and rolling it into an unswallowable ball, a ball that she refused to relinquish one way or another. Then they would coax and scold, bribe and threaten, but still Libby would chew, and if they tried force she would grow scarlet and purple with near-asphyxiation. There had been some horrid scenes about it, and John was always in

185

a state of dread that it would happen again; for some time the children had had to have separate meal tables, until Libby had shown signs of recovery. Sometimes it was possible to detect the cause of the anxiety behind it, but more often it was inexplicable. It seemed to be associated with excitement, fear, and guilt, for once a dreaded visit to the doctor had caused it and once it had happened when Libby had been playing with a precious fan of Anthea's, and having broken some of the delicate ivory spokes, had hidden the remains under her mattress. But it could have a thousand different causes, and one could not anticipate its occurrence. So much goes on in a child's complicated mind, Anthea thought worriedly, that adults have forgotten all about and can never recall. . . .

Joseph knocked, and came shuffling in gloomily, and Anthea, hugging Libby tightly to her for a moment, stood up and went out. Joseph sat down on the bench on the opposite side of the table and began to clean out his pipe, Libby's eyes fixed on him imploringly.

After a few moments, he said, "Got yer new tooth yet?"

Tearfully, she shook her head.

"Bet you 'ave," said Joseph. "Show us."

She paused for a moment, and then chewed on.

"Garn! Yer scared to show us," Joseph said challengingly.

She chewed more slowly and shook her head indignantly.

"Well," said Joseph, "go on, show us, then."

After eyeing him for a while, mistrustfully, she slightly opened her mouth and Joseph peered in.

"There y'are," he said triumphantly. "It's growed right up as 'igh as the others."

She looked amazedly at him.

"Want a look?" he asked.

She nodded, her jaws still. Joseph took the little blue-backed mirror from the dressing table and held it in front of her, at the same time reaching for the glass float bowl that was standing, empty, on the window sill. Libby gazed into the mirror, saw the repulsive mass of food, and was at once very sick into the bowl, which Joseph obligingly held for her. When it was over he took the bowl to the bathroom, which opened off the

186

children's bedroom, and there was the sound of much water flowing. She was still sitting at the table, looking dazed, but now delightfully relieved, when he returned, and she flashed a brilliant smile on him.

"You told a th-tory," she said gleefully.

"Yes," he replied, sternly, "I did—and it's your fault. And when I goes up to the pearly gates of 'eaven and the angel looks up me sins in 'is golden book, all studded with diamonds and jaspers, it'll be your fault when I gets knocked back, see?"

She rocked happily on her chair.

"And then you'll go down to hell, won't you, Jotheph darling?"

"I s'pose that's where I'll end up," he said sourly.

"And I'll be a lovely, bright angel with huge wide wings, won't I, Jotheph?"

"You won't never be no angel," grunted Joseph. "You 'aven't got it in yer; more like you'll be down below, stokin' up the fires."

"Yeth, I will," she said, smugly. "I'm going to be a lovely angel. Will you have a long tail with a pointy thing on it, Jotheph?"

"I prob'ly will, and I'll know 'oo to blame, too—makin' me tell lies. I'm goin' to 'ave me tea now, and don't you let me 'ear no more of these antics, me girl—they upsets me stummick."

"No, Jotheph," she agreed obligingly. Then as he tramped morosely to the door, she said, as an afterthought, "I love you, Jotheph."

"Maybe," said Joseph darkly, his hand on the doorknob. She was still looking at herself in the mirror.

"Am I pretty without my tooth, Jotheph?" she asked anxiously.

"Yes," said Joseph, with unwilling honesty, "you'd still be pretty if you never 'ad no teeth at all, nor yet no 'air; but, let me tell you, my fine miss—" he wagged his finger menacingly— "let me tell you, 'andsome is as 'andsome does."

"Yeth, Jotheph," she replied, absently. "It th-till whithles nithe, doethn't it?"

Joseph closed the door with a disgusted snort.

They were all sitting by the radio when Joseph came down the hall and poked his head in.

"She's okay," he said, glumly.

They relaxed; Anthea jumped up and came over to him.

"Oh, thank you, Joseph; it's wonderful how you handle her. How did you manage it?"

"Dunno," he said, dubiously. "Just magged a bit. She's a young so-and-so—wants 'er be'ind dusted, if yer don't mind me sayin' so."

"And I can see you performing if I tried to dust it." Anthea smiled at him. "What should I do with her, Joseph? Would it be better to put her to bed?"

"No," he said. "She's forgotten all about it by now. Take 'er down to the show. Least said, soonest mended."

"Yes," Anthea said, "you're right—you're a wonderful child psychologist, Joseph."

"Thank Gawd I never 'ad no kids of me own," he said, as she walked down the hall with him. "Drive yer barmy, they would."

"Joseph, you're an awful fraud," Anthea said, affectionately. "You adore them as much as they love you."

"Oh, they're not such bad kids," he replied, offhandedly. "As nippers go, they ain't so bad."

Back in the sitting room, John was congratulating himself on a near escape.

"My word, Cassie," he said, thankfully, "that was a close thing; I thought she'd mucked the whole night."

"Don't you dare use that word," Cassie replied, severely. Then she added, "Poor lamb, I wonder what made 'er do it; what's she got on 'er mind now, I wonder?"

John hid his guilty face as he bent to adjust the wireless.

"Oh, I expect it's nothing, Cassie," he said, in a small voice, for he knew that, even if he wasn't telling a lie, he wasn't exactly telling the truth, either. The silly little goat, he thought; I knew we shouldn't have let her in on it. He and Paul could have had a wonderful time together. . . . But he knew she'd let it out somehow, though he hadn't anticipated a fit of the chews. He felt vaguely sorry for her, and a little ashamed of himself for not protecting her from herself, for she must have got into an awful state to get the chews again—it was nearly two years since she'd had them. He resolved to talk to her firmly when they went to

188

bed tonight and to persuade her to stay home tomorrow morning.

Anthea and Libby appeared in the doorway, Libby looking adorable in a white woolly coat and beret, her eyes alight with happy anticipation. John's guilty mind was eased by her obvious equanimity, and joyfully he said good-bye to Cassie and raced out to start the car up for his mother.

6

SATURDAY NIGHT

~~~

I

Mary and James were sitting in the living room when the three of them came in to say good night, and Mary was moved to delight by the accumulated effect of their youth and good looks, their vitality, their shining eyes and hair, their smiling faces, their vigorous, graceful movements.

"You're an attractive trio." James voiced her thought.

"Aren't we?" said Honor. "You'll find, though, that I always lend a quiet distinction to any group I'm with; I'm well known for it."

"And for a number of less creditable qualities," James replied composedly.

"Paul, you're a different person," Mary said, smiling up at him. "I can scarcely remember you from last night."

"No," he answered, happily. "You people agree with me—and it's very beautiful here. Besides, everything's worked out so splendidly. . . ." His face eager, confiding, he seemed to be on the point of telling her something more, but, after a pause, he gave a nervous little laugh, and taking out his cigarette case, he began to tap a cigarette on its surface.

The two girls had seated themselves on the settee, and Megan began to talk to James about Alec. Mary pointed to the chair beside her, and as Paul sank into it, drawing quickly on his cigarette, she said, in a low voice, "Paul, I hope I'm not being a nuisance, but I was wondering if you'd let me write a line to your mother."

He drew a couple of times on his cigarette before he replied; he seemed to be thinking absorbedly. Then he said, "Yes—yes, that would be very kind of you. I'm sure she'd be glad to hear. You see, I—I didn't let them know where I was going."

"Why not?" she asked calmly, keeping surprise from her voice with an effort.

"I thought," he said vaguely, his eyes roving round the room, "I thought they might try to stop me."

"Why should they do that?"

"Well," he said, in a doubtful tone, "they did before—they played a cruel trick on me. I was coming here a long while ago —I can't remember exactly when—but they said they'd bring me here and they didn't; they took me somewhere else."

"Where was that?"

"It was a big place"—his voice was still vague—"with trees and a lot of lawns; it was a nice place, but it wasn't where I wanted to go."

The others had stopped talking now, and they were all listening. Iago appeared quietly at the door, smiled humbly, his tongue hanging ingratiatingly, and took advantage of their pre-occupation to slide gently round the back of the settee. He came to rest within distance of the fireplace and judged it better to remain here for a time, rather than to focus attention on himself by advancing directly to the fire, for there would be opportunities later to get to within the range he liked best, where the firelight played on his coat and made it singe just very slightly. He put his nose on his paws and blinked contentedly at the winking flames, a patient dog biding his time.

"That was a private hospital, I suppose," Mary said offhandedly, bending to replace a piece of wood that had rolled on to the hearthstone.

"I suppose it was," he said. "Anyway, they thought they'd cured me there and they were all very pleased; but I knew they hadn't—I knew that the only thing that would cure me would be to come here."

They were silent, astonished; then James said, gently, "What gave you that idea, lad?"

"Well, it was so obvious. . . ." He stopped and looked round

191

at them, and now his eyes were tense. How he longed to be able to tell them, to tell these kind and friendly people, these people who loved Adrian. If only their love was strong enough—but it wasn't, no, he acknowledged to himself sadly, it wasn't; it wasn't strong enough.

They felt awkward and embarrassed in the face of something which was incomprehensible to them, but which was so clear to him that he could call it obvious, and Mary sensed that further questioning was useless, that it might even spoil his evening's enjoyment.

"Anyway," she said lightly, and the others relaxed, as she dismissed, as of no importance, something that they felt to be momentous, "I shall just write and tell your mother how much it has meant to us to have you here—and I shall tell her how much improved you are, shall I? I suppose you couldn't stay?" She felt James's watchful eye upon her and remembered that any mention of the days beyond tomorrow was dangerous. "Perhaps you'd care to add a little note yourself, Paul, and I'll slip it in with my letter."

"Yes," he said, consideringly, "I suppose I ought to; she'd like to have had a note from me, I suppose. They were—very attached to me," he finished, a little shyly, glancing round at their smiling, encouraging faces.

Curious tenses he uses, James thought, but it was too difficult on the spur of the moment to work out the significance he knew to be there. Mary thought, compassionately, Of course they are, and they must have suffered heartbreak since he returned, for no doubt things were very black at first. Probably he had been recovering steadily ever since he had come, but they must have had to endure courageously for a long time.

Megan stood up.

"It's eight o'clock," she said; "after eight, a bit, so perhaps we'd better go. Good night, darlings, you'll be asleep when we get back."

After they had gone Mary and James sat quietly talking. Iago edged gently forward until the flames stung his nose a little, and then he slowly turned on his side. Ideal—no position could have been more perfect. He dozed off until biscuit time.

Joady came in, bringing the darning basket, and they prepared to pass the evening with all the richness of half a lifetime's association as a background for their quiet conversation, listening to the music they all liked, reading, sewing, or thinking. And if James and Mary noticed, from time to time, that Joady was a little preoccupied, her speech a trifle heavy-hearted, they felt that she was thinking of Adrian, as they were themselves, and, respectfully, they made no mention of it.

II

The Welcome Home was having a rare measure of success. Anthea was dancing gaily with Herb Pierce, the son of William Pierce, who owned Ambara's thriving wood and coal delivery service, and Megan was being carefully steered round the room by Sid Beck, whom she had been congratulating on his recent meteoric rise in the railways, but who seemed dazed to a state of semi-coma by finding his arm encircling Megan's waist; she was chatting brightly to him now, feeling, as she did so, that he was hardly pulling his weight in the conversation, his contributions, so far, being limited to a refined "Pardon?" which he had now said eight times, and a glazed smile of uneasy joy. She couldn't know, of course, the high degree of anxiety existing in his mind as to whether the smell of the petrol that his mother had used to clean his navy-blue suit was as strongly obvious to Megan's nostrils as it was to his own hypercritical sensitivity. He had had words about it with his mother, earlier in the night, and he was now resolved to establish his manhood properly on his return home. His sister's comment, "My, Sid, you do stink!" uttered when he had unwillingly but dutifully danced the first dance with her, had done nothing to ease his mind, nor was he mollified by her hastily added, "But it's a nice clean smell." He held Megan as far away from him as possible, hoping that the new verbena-scented hair oil he was wearing for the first time would offset his aggressive cleanliness.

Honor was being expertly wafted through the dancers by

193

Eric Harding, the son of Dr. Harding, from Borrowdale. He was splendid in his squadron leader's uniform, and as sophisticated as Honor herself. They appeared to be quietly amused with each other, their cool, extremely cutting, mutually unflattering remarks uttered aloofly and tersely, though occasionally the gravity of the one was slightly shaken by the wit of the other.

Paul was sitting out at the far end of the hall, wedged between Mrs. Travers, the postmistress, round and jolly in blush-pink rayon, and Mrs. Paget, in dusty black, tall and thin and hawk-nosed, who disliked Mrs. Travers and thought her among the common element who always forced their way into these functions. Mrs. Travers was trying to interest him by pointing out the merits of the various girls who were dancing before them, enumerating their excellences of character, behaviour and physical attribute, while Mrs. Paget was trying to describe to him, in some detail, the difficulties set in the path of Mr. Paget, who was at this time attempting to arrange for the opening of a new branch grocery store at Borrowdale. A man, Mrs. Paget knew from experience, was interested in nothing so much as business matters, and she thought it in very poor taste for Mrs. Travers to be appealing to the worst in any man by flaunting the charms of the opposite sex before his eyes. Paul was quite happy between the two of them, and they were both pleased with him, he having been able, by some means, to convince each of them that the other was boring him to tears.

"There's Marie Fisher." Mrs. Travers beamed after the somewhat broad back view of a girl in blue. "Now that girl's been a saint to her mother: arthritis, you know, and various ulcers. Marie works in the laundry at Mitcham, and she keeps that home like a new pin—oh, and that's Lorraine Field. There's a pretty girl—a bit plump, but that's how you men like them." She paused to give him a roguish smile and a dig in the ribs. "I know you—you're all the same."

As Paul smilingly acknowledged this weakness, common to all his sex, Mrs. Paget leant across and said, "As I was saying, Mr. Quentin, it's not the lack of material or labour, it's the red tape. Mr. Paget has met everywhere with the same thing, he said to me tonight, as we were having dinner"—she glared at

Mrs. Travers, who was well known to refer to the evening meal by the vulgar name of tea—"he said, 'This country is being strangled by red tape.' Rather neatly put, don't you think, Mr. Quentin? Strangled, you know, by red tape."

"Yes," said Paul, with deep interest, "yes, indeed."

"Don't the girls do their hair pretty, Mr. Quentin?" Mrs. Travers said, admiringly. "All curls. I do like a bit of a curl in the hair, whether it's put there by Mother Nature, or by the hairdresser."

"I think," Mrs. Paget put in, cuttingly, "that the natural way one's hair grows suits the face better than any artificial device."

"That's true, dear," replied Mrs. Travers, with a burst of jolly laughter, "but when you look at the faces, you think, 'Well, even if she can't do anything about her dial, at least she needn't keep her hair like that.' No, I'm all for a bit of a curl myself."

There were items and speeches as the night wore on. Squadron Leader Harding thanked the residents of Ambara, on behalf of the returned servicemen, for their kindly gesture of welcome. He looked amiable and self-possessed, as he stood carelessly beside the piano at the end of the hall, one hand in his pocket; but there was a little tremor of warmth, quite unexpected to himself, when he remarked casually that there were several people whose presence was felt here tonight much more strongly than that of those who were actually and visibly taking part, and that, though it was a frightfully good show and tremendously jolly, it was, like any such function, not completely an occasion for gaiety, because the roll call at these do's was never complete. At this stage, shocked to find himself in such a welter of sentiment, he went very red and ended his speech abruptly and a little incoherently.

The dancing recommenced as soon as he had finished, and Miss Grace Kale, the youngest, at forty-two, of the three daughters of the late Colonel Kale, who had successfully, during his lifetime, prevented his daughters from doing anything that they were incautious enough to let him know they were anxious to do, almost wrecked the old piano as she pounded out a series of old-time waltzes. While she crashed her way through "After the Ball," she dutifully reminded herself of how lovely it would

195

have been if Father could have been here tonight, but an uneasy certainty that, in that event, none of his daughters would have been present, interfered a little with her regret for his absence.

Mr. Dwyer, who had modestly agreed to act as M.C., and whose wife had lain awake for several nights racked with anxiety for fear he would not be asked but would be passed over in favour of Mr. Paget, then announced that they were to have a rare artistic treat, in that Miss Beverly Cameron was to perform for them the Dance of the Dying Swan, and Miss Grace Kale struck up the music in a bad temper, because her eldest sister, Miss Frances Kale, had stolen some of her thunder by obligingly turning over for her; there was no need to turn over, and she knew that Frances just wanted to pose beside the piano in her new navy-blue, expressing her appreciation and wide understanding of the music by much facial movement, closing of the eyes and raising and lowering of the brows, as well as by an unrhythmic swaying of the body, which distracted Miss Grace in a quite intolerable fashion. Really, Frances is getting ludicrous, she thought, as the swan bounded heartily on to the little stage.

The swan died dramatically, to applause which was heartfelt for one reason or another, although, as Dr. Harding remarked in a low voice to Anthea, its days were numbered anyhow, the end, he maintained, being merely a matter of time, as it would have succumbed inevitably to the Parkinson's Disease from which it was obviously suffering, its tremblings and shakings on its somewhat unreliable toeshoes being pitiable to behold. Mrs. James, who did not like its mother, Mrs. Cameron, was careful to speak very clearly when she said that its skirt was many inches too short, and the neck of its bodice too skimpy, as it was very well developed for its age and needed more control, its present appearance, she averred, being simply sloppy and thus highly unsuitable for the noticeably appreciative gaze of her second-youngest son, now at the critical age of fifteen years and six months. It was obvious to many, however, that her envy was interfering seriously with her judgment, and the swan was a tremendous success.

After supper the dancing continued until, at eleven, Mr.

Dwyer approached Honor and requested, a little nervously, that she sing "Home, Sweet Home" for them, before the playing of the National Anthem. Honor smiled pleasantly at his perspiring face, and walked up to Miss Kale. Then, standing by the piano, her hands in the pockets of her gathered peasant skirt, she began quietly to sing, without any announcement and while people were still talking animatedly. Gradually the conversations died away and people stood still, in the poses in which her magic caught them, some with their backs to her, some outside the door; wherever they were they remained, and the softly swelling voice strengthened in the silence.

Anthea thought, She's exquisite, and this is a beautiful and unforgettable thing. Through the window, behind Honor's white-clad figure, the moonlight glinted on the leaves of trees, and the soft stillness of the night outside, forgotten in the noise of people's rejoicing, formed a gentle background for the lovely notes.

That's a song you can't hackney, Eric Harding thought. And that girl—what glorious possibilities she's got! That delicate face, the honey-coloured, silky hair. . . .

He felt suddenly impatient with the gathering of people about him, and as the last tender phrase fell softly among people who were more deeply stirred than many of them had been for years, he walked abruptly away and outside, where he lit a cigarette and smoked in a rapid way for a few minutes, trying to make up his mind to go in and say good night to her, perhaps get her to let him drive her home. He felt unusually restless and ill at ease, and he kept thinking unaccountably of old Johnnie Hall and wondering what had become of him. Best navigator he'd ever had—but why should he be thinking of old Johnnie, anyway?

There was no applause, from inside, and after a moment the National Anthem was played and Squadron Leader Eric Harding, stubbing out his cigarette with the toe of his boot, stood automatically to attention, by himself, underneath the camphor laurel that grew in front of the Progress Hall, and, as the moon went behind a thick pile of white cloud, he felt confused and a bit lonely, but unwilling to go back to the hall, for he was back in a world where those people had no place, whose language they did not know.

<h1 style="text-align:center">III</h1>

When they had left the hall, Honor and Megan and Paul lingered for a while by Anthea's car, engaged in a gentle argument as to whether Anthea would drive them home to Thornfield, or to Cedar Hill, for drinks, or to Raikes's meadow; the last she considered to be the worst choice of the three, and she held firmly to the views that they were crazy, that Paul would collapse from exhaustion before they were done with him, and, her most potent argument, that they had seen the last of the clear sky for tonight, for rank upon rank of white, feathery clouds were marching across the moon by now. By the time they had convinced her that they intended to go to Raikes's meadow and that they preferred to walk, most of the gathering had dispersed into the night and only Mr. Dwyer and the Pagets were left in the hall.

"All right," Anthea said, climbing into the car, "so you're crazy and no one can do anything about you." She slammed the door shut and then touched Honor's hand, as it rested on the edge of the car. "Good night, you," she added, tersely. "Thank you for the song; it was one of those important things that don't happen to me often." She turned to the others. "Good night," she said. "This has been a good day for all of us, and I've been happier than I ever deserved to be again."

They watched her turn the corner into the road to the station, and then they walked in the opposite direction.

"I'm inclined to think she's right, you know," Megan said, looking at the sky. "There's a ton of cloud up there; it's amazing how quickly it can clear away, of course, but I'm not so sanguine tonight; looks a bit as if the weather might be changing."

"Well, there's nothing much at stake," Paul said tranquilly. "I don't know about you people, but I feel like a bit of quiet walking after all the hubbub. After all, you haven't spent most of the evening between Mrs. Travers and Mrs. Paget."

He described some of the conversation to them, and their laughter sounded very loudly in the stillness. After a while they walked on in silence, until Honor said, with a little shiver, "My word, I'm glad you two are here; this half-moonlight in the bush scares me into the trembles. While the moon's clear I never feel it, but there's something livid and ghastly about it when it comes through cloud."

"M'm," Megan said reflectively. "No, I don't feel scared, but it makes me feel forlorn and lost; all the things you know so well—trees and things, and bushes—seem changed and strange, the way you see a place you know well in a sad and lonely dream."

"Oh, well, there's only about another ten minutes of it and then we'll be in the open," Honor said, comforting herself. "It's only the bush that does it—it's not the same in the paddocks or on the hills."

For some minutes Paul had been turning his head from side to side, and now they both noticed that he seemed to be listening intently. At last Honor burst out, "For heaven's sake, Paul, are you trying to create atmosphere or something? I'm quite susceptible enough without your building the thing up for me, you know."

He didn't reply for a moment, and then he said quietly, "I'm awfully sorry; I don't want to frighten you, but I'm afraid there's something—or someone—behind those trees."

They both felt a cold shock of alarm. Suddenly Honor was filled with a wild certainty of disaster, of inescapable tragedy. She clenched her teeth and forced herself to walk on, though her steps were stumbling and erratic now. Megan said, in an uncertain voice, "Go on, Paul—it can't be anything. Rabbits, perhaps." Then, in a surer tone, she went on, "You've been too long in the jungle."

"I've been too long in the jungle," he replied, in an undertone, "not to know when someone's following me. After another few paces we'll stop, and then you'll be convinced. It's coming from over there, to the right."

199

When they stopped, breath held, eyes and ears straining, they distinctly heard the sound of movement over to their right, movement that ceased a moment after they had stopped. Honor's heart was thumping, and she began to breathe noisily and jerkily; Megan was trembling and her knees were aching with weakness; Paul stood very still, tense and straining. Then he began to walk again, and somehow they kept up with him.

"Now do as I say." His voice was calm and gentle. "When I stop again you go on and try to talk; I'm going to wait for a break in the trees, and then I'm going to try and get in behind whoever it is. Talk to me as if I were with you, and if anything unexpected happens, run. Promise?"

They promised, and Megan began to talk, in a voice pitched a good deal higher than her ordinary tones, about Miss Frances Kale and her all too obvious appreciation of music; it was amusing, and once Honor laughed hysterically and then stopped. The track lay straight ahead of them, but there was a bend about a hundred yards away, a bend that would lead them out to the road by the railway line. Something's going to happen before we get there, Honor thought wildly, something frightful and hideous is going to happen: God in heaven, stop it, stop it!

Megan's eyes searched the sky: yes, there was a clear patch coming, but the moon would not appear for five minutes. On either side of them the bush hedged them in—young gums and wattles close to the edge of the track, and beyond them the tall trees and undergrowth; everything was washed clear of colour, and dimness lay over earth and sky. They could hear the sounds from among the bushes quite clearly now, for there seemed to be less attempt at concealment, or perhaps the path was proving more difficult for the follower to negotiate. As they came to a slight break in the line of trees, Megan talked more quickly and loudly, and Honor managed a reply or two, Paul had turned off the track and was making his way beside them, in among the trees, penetrating more and more deeply, until at length he was gone from them.

And Martin Croft saw him coming towards him. He was plunging wildly over ground which had seemed to afford quite easy walking when he had traversed it in the clear light of the afternoon, but which was now a mass of pitfalls, for thorny bushes had torn at his clothes and scraped painfully down his face, and ruts and holes in the ground had made him stagger and almost fall, so that by now he was so distressed, so breathless and beside himself with fear, that he had lost all his grip on his plans, and all he could remember was that this was something he must go on doing; he must keep those figures within sight, he must not lose the sound of those voices. And then he saw the dark figure coming towards him, about twenty yards away, and terror closed over his thoughts. But when he heard a voice saying, "Come here! I want to talk to you," the haze of dread cleared, and like a flash he remembered the time when he had heard those words before. His father had come into the doorway of the garage, where he had had a puppy, a puppy that was whining and choking as he twisted the piece of wire more tightly around its throat. And his father had said, "Come here! I want to talk to you," and he had seized Martin and punched him; then he had dragged him to his feet and had beaten him with a heavy stick, beaten him till he had fallen again, a half-fainting mass of sick pain and hatred. . . . But this time it couldn't happen that way, for his protection lay grasped in his hand. He had taken the pin out earlier, keeping his thumb carefully pressed on the lever, and now he raised his hand and took a stumbling run forward. But before he could throw it, he fell heavily and it spun out of his hand. Frantically, for he knew there were only five seconds, he groped for it, but his fingers grasped only earth and stones and the stems of plants. He struggled to his knees and crawled forward, and, all at once, just before the roar of the explosion, he knew a brief, agonizing moment of longing for his mother, and he had just time to call to her before the end came. . . .

When he heard the explosion, Paul flung himself on the ground, thinking swiftly, The one you can hear never kills you. Then something struck him heavily on the temple, and for the second time in Paul Quentin's life the bomb dump in the camp blew up, just when he and his men felt sure that they were safe, and as he lost consciousness it flashed into his mind that something right at the edge of the dump must have caught fire—and then his mind settled down to blackness.

Honor and Megan had almost reached the bend in the track when they heard Paul calling loudly, "Come here! I want to talk to you."

In the silence that followed they walked forward a few paces; then they stopped, and Megan put a trembling arm round Honor's shoulders. There was a sudden crashing in the bushes and another shout from Paul, but they couldn't distinguish any words. . . . Suddenly the quiet bush was filled with a fearful roar of sound, and Honor fell to the ground. Megan stood still, incredulous, completely incapable of moving, and it seemed to her that she had been standing there, motionless, for a long while, listening to the reverberations of the unbelievable volume of sound through the silent bush, when she finally sank to her knees and bent over Honor, who was only partly conscious. When Megan touched her she began to moan and gasp, and then the dust from the track made her cough; when she managed to sit up she was very sick, and she sat for a few minutes with her head between her knees. Megan said jerkily, "I'm all right; there's nothing—wrong with me; I'm going—back to find Paul—you stay here. . . ."

"No." Honor's voice was a whisper. "I'll come—I'm coming with you."

Megan's arm round her waist, she lurched back down the track.

"Someone will come," Megan kept on saying to her. "They'll have heard the noise. Someone will come and help us. Mr. Eames—he's not far away, he'll come—someone's sure to come."

But when they reached the place where Paul had left them, there was only silence, and they breathed choking dust and some kind of sickly, chemical smell. They stopped, and Megan said, at last, "No, Honor, we can't do anything; we'll go on to Eames's place. They'll have lanterns. . . ."

Slowly they went on down the track, and now they could hear a horse's hooves. They screamed and tried to run, and someone shouted to them, encouragingly. At last Derek Eames saw them and jumped from his horse, a lantern swinging in his hand. They tried to tell him, their lips stiff and their voices broken and ragged, but he stopped them, quickly aware of the extent of their shock.

"Come and show me where," he said briefly, and they clung to his arms, grateful for the solid, quiet strength of him and for his kindly, reassuring words.

"Good," he said, when once more they came to the place where Paul had disappeared. "Now, you two poor kids go on back to my place; you'll meet June—she's coming after me. Tell her to take you back to the house, and then ring some people and tell them to come here—and tell her to ring Dr. Harding at once."

While he was speaking, someone shouted, down at the other end of the track, and in a few minutes Mr. Styles, the station master, came running heavily towards them, his torch flashing brightly.

"Here we are," Derek Eames shouted. "Oh, it's you, Mr. Styles—good! Now go on, you two, there's nothing you can do."

The moon was shining brilliantly, in a clear sky, as they turned to go; behind them they could hear Mr. Styles, heavily puffing, saying, "What the hell's going on here?" And Derek Eames replied, grimly, "That's what we've got to find out—and I don't think it's going to be too pretty, somehow."

Before they had gone fifty yards someone came hurrying round the bend towards them. Megan gave June Eames her husband's message, and she, talking soothingly to them, though she was completely bewildered and intensely curious, turned back with them, in the direction of her house.

IV

Although it was after one o'clock, Anthea was still sitting before the well-banked fire in the sitting room. She was sleepy, but there was not a great deal to do tomorrow, and it was a pleasant indulgence to sit idly here in the quietness. It was a tribute to her altered state of mind, she thought, that the wireless was silent, for tonight she could face her thoughts, and she welcomed the stillness that allowed her to pursue them without interruption. She was, for a moment, completely incredulous when the telephone bell screamed through the silence, and then she sprang up and ran across the room to it. Joady's voice was almost unrecognizable, she was talking too quickly, her words tumbling out, and it was a moment before Anthea could pin her down to the main essentials of what she had to say.

"Oh, can't you hear me?" Joady asked desperately. "I've only got a minute, Anthea. They're bringing Paul up here—there's been some sort of accident, an explosion or something—and they're bringing him here. Mrs. Car and I have to stay here—the girls are still down at Eames's place—Honor's pretty done up with the shock. And Mrs. Car wants you to come down—someone ought to go to Mrs. Croft."

Anthea broke in abruptly.

"Now stop, Joady, and answer questions. Of course I'll come at once; but tell me, who's been hurt?"

"Paul—he's unconscious. He's got a bang on the head; he was near the explosion. And Martin Croft's dead."

"Dead! How, Joady?"

"I don't know—it was the explosion. . . ."

Anthea decided that she need know no more, and reassuring Joady that she would come immediately, she hung up the receiver.

Cassie was standing there when she turned from the telephone, standing quietly, aware of bad tidings, awaiting instructions.

"I can't tell what's happened exactly, Cassie, but there's been some sort of accident, an explosion. Martin Croft is dead, and Paul Quentin is somehow injured as a result of it. I'm going now and I don't know when I'll be back. Tell the children some tale if I'm not here by breakfast time, Cassie—but I'll ring you, anyway."

"All right, lovey," Cassie said soberly. "Look after yourself. That poor woman—she's suffered hell with that boy. And now he's dead. . . ."

Anthea left the car at the front gate of Thornfield, behind

204

Dr. Harding's car, and ran up the path to the veranda steps. The house was filled with movement, and lights were on everywhere. As she came into the hall Dr. Harding came out of the living room and, nodding to her, went up the stairs with Joady, who pointed towards the living room. Anthea went in and found Mary sitting in front of the fire, her face very pale against the dark red of her dressing gown, her eyes anxious. She looked up thankfully as Anthea came in.

"I'm glad you've come, Anthea," she said, as Anthea put an arm about her waist.

"What do you want me to do?" Anthea asked.

"Well," Mary said hesitantly, "first, I think, you should go down to Mrs. Croft. She may not need you—there may be other people there by now—but I can't go myself just now, and some one should be there, I think—someone from here, I mean. Just see if there is anything we can do. She might like to come here or to go up to Cedar Hill. And then come back here, dear; if the girls aren't back, you could drive down to Eames's and get them. I must stay with Paul and James and wait for the girls."

She stood up, looking stronger and more alert.

"I don't know how it happened," she went on. "I can't understand such an appalling, outlandish thing happening at all, and I dread the effect it may have on Paul. I've got to ring his mother—I'll put the call through as soon as Dr. Harding has finished examining him—and that's an awful task. However, Mrs. Croft is the one who has most to bear, so go now, Anthea."

On her way to the door Anthea paused and said, over her shoulder, "I wouldn't, you know—not yet."

As Mary stared at her uncomprehendingly, she continued, "Ring his mother, I mean; only if Dr. Harding advises it—he'll tell you soon enough if you should."

"But," Mary said, "she'd want to know."

"God knows what anxiety that woman's had to bear," Anthea said. "She's probably dreading that something's happened to him. If he's not in a dangerous state, let it wait awhile; you'll be glad later on, if you've spared her a journey like that, every minute fearful of what she may find when she gets here. No,

205

if it were me, I'd wait till the morning—or at least ask the doctor's advice first."

After a pause, Mary said, "Yes—yes, Anthea; you're wise and cool-headed—I'll wait."

Anthea kissed her and ran down the hall and out to the car. This is a hell of an assignment, she thought grimly, as she swung the car round into the road that led to Croft's; I scarcely know the woman. I didn't know the child, except by hearsay, and she'll probably think I'm an interfering humbug. Never mind, she told herself, just do the task that's close at hand.

She was shaking with nervous distaste as she rang the doorbell. She had seen a light in the front room, but otherwise the house was dark. The door opened, and a small, childlike figure, in a little pink dressing gown trimmed with white swansdown, stood before her. Anthea began to speak rapidly.

"I'm Anthea Carmichael, Mrs. Croft," she said. "Mrs. Carmichael is very worried about you and we—I wanted to know . . ."

"Please come in." The voice was low, but firmly under control.

Mrs. Croft closed the door and they went into the sitting room. Anthea tried not to observe the traces of Martin's activities with the windowbox, but the earth stains were very plainly visible. She sat on the settee, and Mrs. Croft seated herself in a dainty little rocking chair with a frilly chintz cushion; she rocked gently to and fro, her eyes expressionless, looking past Anthea to the undrawn curtains at the window. Desperately Anthea began to talk.

"Mrs. Croft," she said, "I haven't come merely to intrude on you or to worry you by talking, if you'd prefer to be quiet. If you can think of any way in which I can help you, any little messages or chores you'd like done, please tell me. And if you'd prefer not to stay here tonight, will you come to Cedar Hill with me—or to Thornfield? Please tell me what I can do—or, if you'd rather, tell me to go away."

"You're very kind." She turned dry, tranquil eyes to Anthea. "No, I don't think I'd like anything . . . Yes, just one thing: on your way back, would you call in and ask Mrs. Anstey if she

206

would come and see me? We used to be great friends—once—and I was very fond of her, and perhaps she might care to come and see me now. . . ." The voice trailed off and she was silent again.

Anthea went on, "I know nothing of what's happened, Mrs. Croft, and I don't know what you've been told or who has told you. How did you hear and what did you hear?"

"I heard," she said quietly, "that Martin was dead. Some men came—and Dr. Harding—but I sent them away, though they said they'd send other people; but I don't want other people—only Margaret Anstey, if she will come." She looked timidly at Anthea and added, "I don't mean that I want you to go. I wouldn't have asked you to come, but now that you're here I like you and I'd be glad if you'd stay for a little while. But there's no need to feel embarrassed or to think that you'll upset me by talking about it or by asking questions. You see," she went on, pleating the skirt of her dressing gown carefully, "I'm not a bit surprised by any of it, and I'm awfully glad it's happened."

Anthea looked her surprise.

"Oh, of course I didn't realize what exactly would happen, but I knew Martin was planning something: I knew that this morning. Martin would never stand being beaten, and after Mr. Quentin left this morning Martin said something which should have made me realize that it was no ordinary thing he was planning in revenge. He had been threatening me, too, you see. After he cut me with the knife—" she held out the bandaged hand—"I took it away and hid it, and he threatened then that he would do something much worse to me. And as Mr. Quentin was leaving, he said he'd be back tomorrow and when he had gone Martin said, 'No, you bloody well won't,' and he laughed in an hysterical way—so I think I see exactly what happened. Martin knew when Mr. Quentin would leave the hall tonight, because he and Megan were talking about the time the moon would rise, and Martin knew they were going to Raikes's meadow. I think that he had had this explosive for some time; whatever it was I don't know, but he was several times warned about going too close to certain places up at the camp, and he was very friendly with the soldiers. He must have picked this

207

thing up somewhere—perhaps someone was careless. I've read of four or five cases, during the war, where children have found these things—grenades, or something like that—and have killed or injured themselves and their companions. I think Martin has been waiting his chance to use it, and I know that he must have hated Mr. Quentin as he had hated no one else before—except, perhaps, his father—and so I believe he lay in wait for him. But probably at the last moment he lost his nerve or bungled it in some way, and so he killed himself—he was only a little boy, after all, though in some ways he was as old as a grown man. That's how I think it happened, but I shall not say anything of this to anyone, and I shall bind you to a solemn promise not to repeat what I have said." She stopped and looked questioningly at Anthea.

"Yes, I promise you," Anthea said quietly. "Tell me, why do you say you're glad it's happened as it has?"

"Oh, surely you can see that," she said, in surprise. "Supposing he had succeeded, supposing he had killed or seriously injured Mr. Quentin or those lovely girls: what would we have had to face?—something one could barely live through. And for the rest of his life he would have been shut away from me, either as a criminal or as a maniac. Or supposing Mr. Quentin had never come here: then the same thing would have happened as soon as his father returned—George would have beaten Martin and he would have tried to kill his father. He might have succeeded, too. No, there was no future for Martin; he would have been hated and feared by everyone all his days—because, Mrs. Carmichael, he was mad, you know." She said the words calmly, pityingly, looking wistfully at Anthea.

Now, what can one say to that? Anthea thought. Somehow she kept her voice matter-of-fact.

"I find that difficult to believe, Mrs. Croft," she said. "Are you speaking literally?"

"Oh, yes." Her voice was very sad and weary now. "I've known for a long time, really, though I've tried so hard to conceal it from myself and everyone else, and I think I loved him the more for it, as one does with any child who has a weakness, you know. Of course, I was afraid of him and for him, but he needed someone so terribly and I always tried to pretend to myself that it was just that he was sensitive and highly strung. Perhaps I should have had him to a doctor, but I couldn't bear them to shut him away, so I just looked after him, though it was becoming very hard. You see, he loved to see pain, the poor boy—he loved it. And lately he had come to hurting me, and I'm such a weak creature, I was really growing very frightened of him. It couldn't have gone on much longer, and the end could have been so much worse than this. So you see Mrs. Carmichael, it's all been very fortunate."

"Yes," Anthea said. "Yes, I can see something of what you mean."

"It will always be a mystery now, some inexplicable accident that no one will ever understand, and George won't have it all to face when he comes home, and I can really welcome him. And people will begin to think kindly of Martin, now that he's dead. Oh, yes, it's ever so much better this way. There's only one thing that can possibly turn out badly: he may have injured Mr. Quentin—the shock may do him great harm."

"Don't think of that now, Mrs. Croft." Anthea rose and stroked her bright hair, hanging in its long, childlike plait over the thin little shoulder. "He's in good hands and everything will be done for him."

"I shall pray," Mrs. Croft said earnestly. "You know—George laughs at me—but I'm a great believer in God; all this is His doing, you know. He could see how bad things were; I was telling Him only this morning that I was coming to the end of my tether and would He please try to think of something for me, and, you see, He thought of something."

Anthea looked at her, at the deep and tranquil resignation of her expression, and all at once she envied her her faith. If such an acceptance and a trust has been mine, she thought, things might have been very different for me. She said nothing, however, but continued to stroke the golden hair gently.

Then Mrs. Croft said, "Now, dear Mrs. Carmichael, you must go, I know; I mustn't keep you up all night. But you'll tell Mrs. Anstey, won't you?"

"Yes," Anthea said. "Would you like some coffee before I go?"

209

"No, thank you." Her smile was almost cheerful as she gazed up at Anthea. "I'll just sit here and think my nice, comfortable thoughts. I won't get up, if you can let yourself out. Good night, and thank you."

As Anthea went into the hall Mrs. Croft called her name and she turned back; Marion Croft looked up at her, a little, confused, hesitant smile on her lips.

"You'll think me silly, I know," she said. "George says I always concentrate exclusively on the nonessentials, but you did say you'd do anything I wanted, didn't you?"

"I did," Anthea replied, "and I will, I promise you."

"Well," she said, still looking uncertainly at Anthea, "would you come to the funeral, and would you send a wreath?—not an expensive one—just a little one. It would be a great comfort for me if he had a nice little funeral."

"I'll do that," said Anthea, "but I think you need have no fear, Mrs. Croft; I'm sure hundreds of people will show their regard for you in that way." And, as she closed the door behind her she thought, grimly, Yes, and it won't be my fault if they don't.

When she reached the car she suddenly broke down and wept bitterly for a few minutes, shaking with unrestrained sobbing. Oh, God, she thought, that little creature sitting there alone, wanting him to have a nice little funeral. . . . She felt an ache in her heart that she could scarcely bear. Suddenly lights flashed into the road, and a car drew up opposite her. Someone said, "Who's that?" and a woman came over to Anthea's car. When she saw that it was Margaret Anstey, Anthea said, "I was just coming for you, Mrs. Anstey; she wants you—only you—and I think she needs you very badly. You can ring us at Thornfield if we can help." And, as Margaret Anstey ran up the path, she swung the car round and drove back towards Thornfield.

When she came to the gate Dr. Harding's car had gone and there were fewer lights to be seen from the house. The front door was still open, so she went straight into the living room, where Joady and Mary were sitting, coffee and sandwiches on a table between them. They had heard the car arriving, and her coffee was poured and her chair pulled up when she came in. Her red-rimmed eyes told their own story, and after they had greeted her no one spoke before she had drunk her first cup of coffee.

"Are the girls home?" she asked abruptly.

"Yes," Mary replied. "Eric Harding brought them back just after you left. Dr. Harding gave them a sedative and they're both asleep."

"And Paul?"

"He's still unconscious." Mary's voice was strained with anxiety. "Dr. Harding doesn't know what the result will be. It's concussion—his temple is badly bruised—and we don't know what actually caused it: a rock, perhaps, or perhaps it was just the force of the fall. We'll probably know when it's light and they can go over the ground more thoroughly. At any rate, Dr. Harding says he should be conscious in a few hours, and then he'll be able to tell whether there's any danger of complications —any cerebral injury. But he thinks that unlikely, and, in that case, Paul should be much better in a day or two; I'm glad I waited, Anthea—tomorrow I can write to his mother."

Joady stood up.

"I'll go up to him now," she said. "Dr. Harding said he may need someone when he regains consciousness—there's no knowing what effect the shock will have on him. Good night, Anthea."

When she had gone, Mary said, "How is little Mrs. Croft?"

"Very quiet and controlled," Anthea replied, and told her about Margaret Anstey.

"Well, that's one good thing from the evil; those two were very fond of each other once. But, tell me, Anthea, had she any news? Does she know how this incredible thing happened?"

"No," Anthea said flatly. "It's a complete mystery."

Mary looked at her for a moment.

"Yes," she said, at length, "I see what you mean. Perhaps it will be better if it always remains so."

"I think so," Anthea said. "By the way, it will help if you'll see that someone from here goes to the funeral."

"Of course," Mary said.

"And send some wreaths—not only one, but several—will you?"

"I will," said Mary. "Yes, I'll see to that. Go home now, Anthea, and come down to us tomorrow, when you're rested, dear."

"And you?" Anthea asked.

"Joady and I will manage; we'll have plenty of helpers, and if Paul is no better we'll try to get a nurse."

Mary came to the door with her, and, as Anthea went down the steps, the clock in the hall chimed the hour and then struck four times; weariness dragged at her limbs as she climbed into the car, and she sat for a few minutes in the welcome silence before she lit a cigarette and started for home.

7

SUNDAY MORNING

I

It was still dark when Paul woke to an acute consciousness of pain, pain that throbbed and rattled madly in his head when he turned to look at the dim, shaded lamp on the table beside his bed. They must have got him into hospital quickly. But where? There wasn't a hospital with women in it for hundreds of miles from Chantagong. He tried to talk to the misty figure sitting near the end of the bed, a figure indistinctly feminine in the faint yellow light, but though he knew quite well what he wanted to ask, words would not come as far as his lips: they were there, but deep down in his throat. Bewildered, he closed his eyes and let the blackness drift into his brain again.

When next he became aware of things that were not dreams, he could see two women; they were talking softly, but he could understand nothing. He lifted his hand and put it outside the coverlet, and as they turned to him he could distinguish the face of the one who leant over him. She spoke to him, but the words meant nothing; her tone was restful, however, and some of his anxious desire to question her was soothed by her words. He began to drift off again, more slowly this time, wishing he could have stayed awake long enough to find out what had happened to Rogers, who was just beside him when the dump went up. If only those bloody little Nips had let them put up a Red Cross sign, they would have been safe from the Liberators—but then, the little swine had no idea of how to play the game. It was criminal and suicidal to have a bomb dump beside a hospital

213

camp, but there it was: they never knew the sensible way to do anything. They'd have had their wretched railway constructed in a quarter of the time and with a fraction of the trouble if they'd used fit men to do the work, and if they'd made the smallest attempt to feed and look after their prisoners they could have built up a huge supply of efficient labour to draw on. Besides, they need not have established this reputation for merciless cruelty, which was going to make their defeat so bitter, which would make their names stink in the nostrils of the world, when it was over. But they'd always been the same; in fact, perhaps the most hateful thing about the Jap was his stubborn, blind stupidity; everything was done the hard and wasteful way, and the thing with which they were most wasteful was human life—with the lives of their own poor wretched people as well as with those of their prisoners. Well, no doubt Rogers was gone—it was too much to suppose that two of them would have survived. It was incredible that he should be alive himself, and he began to wonder whether he *was* really alive; but the effort to find out was beyond him and he let it go. If this was being dead, it was very comfortable, except for the pain. Still, he knew that was nonsense; he was alive, all right—no doubt about that.

When Dr. Harding came into the room at nine o'clock on Sunday morning, Paul was asleep. Joady rose from her chair and drew the curtains back a little.

"Not too much light," the old doctor said quietly. "Remember to keep the room dim. Still, it's grey outside—there'll be very little sunlight today. How's he been?"

"He's hardly stirred," Joady answered. "I think he first became conscious about five, but he keeps drifting off again."

"Talking?" asked the doctor.

"A little, but you can't make out the words," Joady replied. "He's said 'Rogers' once or twice—but he's off again the next minute."

"M'm." The doctor looked down at him thoughtfully. As he bent over him, Paul opened his eyes and said distinctly, "How's Rogers? Dead?"

"We haven't heard, here," the doctor answered gently. "We'll tell you as soon as we know."

214

"Good," said Paul, and his eyes closed.

When he had finished his brief examination, the doctor turned to Joady.

"I think he'll do," he said. "I'll come this afternoon. Just a good hearty whack on the head, I hope. No good disturbing him too much, looking for complications, at this stage. He will be aware of things by this evening, if everything goes as it should."

Downstairs, when he had given the same information to Mary, he said, "That lad—didn't you say he was in a confused state of mind before this happened?"

"Yes," Mary said, "there was something a little odd about his behaviour—some anxiety in his mind, I think. He'd do unaccountable things sometimes, and he had a way of being frightfully upset about little things. For instance, he had some notion of things ending today, and if we mentioned plans for anything in the future, he'd become hysterical with anxiety."

"Well, he was nearly right, at that," Dr. Harding said grimly. "Things nearly did end for him today—just a bit closer to that grenade and there'd have been no tomorrow for him. He was lucky—and damned unlucky, too. I went down there this morning; I think he stopped the bomb cap, myself—filthy luck, but better than being peppered with the splinters. Still, it could have been a loose rock, dislodged from the bank he was behind. I don't know. Astonishing, isn't it?" he went on, "that a chap can come through all that hell, and then he has to come to a one-horse place like Ambara to stop a hand grenade—or near enough. How's Mr. Carmichael?" he asked, on his way to the front door.

"Quite calm about it all, doctor," Mary said. "Somehow it's difficult to take in, you know; the whole thing's so unlikely. I know that those two girls were very close to quite horrible danger, and yet my common sense convinces me that it's all nonsense, that I've been imagining the whole thing."

"Nothing imaginary about what happened to Martin Croft," Dr. Harding said settling his hat on his head. Mary was silent. They stood looking out over Ambara, grey-misted with the ap-

215

proaching rain. Then Mary said, "What did happen to him, doctor?"

"He just about fell on the damned thing," the doctor said, briefly. "Got it in the middle—ghastly mess."

"How did—how were you sure it was Martin?"

"Oh, he wasn't blown to bits—quite recognizable. He didn't get it in the head."

A sick wave of feeling surged through her. I must say something, she thought weakly, or I'll go to pieces.

"Have you seen his mother this morning, doctor?"

"I have. Remarkable. May be a delayed reaction, of course, but I don't think so. She's as cool as a cucumber—cheerful, you know. Chatty—almost gay; dressed in a pretty little outfit of some kind—no misery, no mourning. There's something very strange about all this. May have happened for the best—never know, do you?"

As he prepared to descend the steps, he said, "Keep those two girls in bed until lunchtime—longer, if they want to stay; they won't, though. 'Morning, Mrs. Carmichael. That young one sang like an angel last night. Rare talent there."

He was at the bottom of the steps when she called, "Doctor, what about Mrs. Quentin, Paul's mother? You said you'd tell me. . . ."

"Don't bother the woman," he said. "No danger that I can see. Perfectly normal, I hope. See this afternoon."

Mary hurried back to the kitchen. Nothing was spoilt; porridge was cooking gently, bread was cut for toast, eggs were broken for scrambling, and the soup she had made earlier this morning was simmering satisfactorily—there'd be enough until tomorrow, she decided, stirring it slowly. When she had arranged two trays for the girls' breakfasts, she was free to go and help James to dress. When they'd all had some food she would relieve Joady and sit with Paul, she decided; the dishes would have to wait until Anthea came, for Joady must go straight to bed until lunchtime, at least. A subdued knocking at the front door which was standing open, brought her hurrying from the kitchen. Miss Janet Kale stood on the veranda, two large shopping baskets in her hands.

216

"Miss Janet! Do come in," Mary said.

"No, my dear." Miss Janet was the masculine Miss Kale, heavily scowling, black-browed, and sharp-eyed. "Visitors can only hinder; but my sisters and I heard of your trouble and so we rose early; we are, as you know, rather adept in invalid cookery. Please accept these few things, with our regards. What is your news this morning?"

As she told her, Mary looked quickly at the contents of the baskets. How they must have worked! At the sight of the numerous jars filled with expertly cooked and suitable food, Mary decided thankfully that she would not need to bother with any cooking today. Miss Janet cut short her expression of gratitude.

"We were happy to do it," she said shortly. "Strangers are always a nuisance in the house at such times as this, but if there are any chores we can do, you know our telephone number: we'll be here in ten minutes—one, or all of us. Good-bye, now." And she strode off into the now softly falling rain, her hands in the pockets of her good but shapeless macintosh.

There was movement in the kitchen as Mary came down the hall, and she found Megan, fully dressed and looking very competent, stirring the porridge. Her arms around her mother's neck, she stifled her protest.

"No, darling," she said, "I'm all right. I'd have been up hours ago only that old fiend put me to sleep, I know he did. I'll lie down later in the morning. Come on, now, let's get going. Is father up yet? Well, you go to him and I'll take breakfast to Joady and Honor."

When she finally gave in and went hurriedly to the bedroom, Mary found another surprise awaiting her. James was sitting, fully dressed, on the side of his neatly made bed, looking speculatively at his untied shoelaces. He glanced at her astonished face, comically, and said, "Cursed things. Mary, remind me to order some buttoned boots. No, they'd be a nuisance—elastic sides or zip fasteners, that's what I want." And when she knelt to lace his shoes he kissed her hair.

"If only you weren't one of these restless women, always running in and out," he said, "I'd have had both beds made."

When he was ready she handed him his stick and he walked

217

out to the kitchen, and when her own bed was made she followed him, finding him contentedly eating porridge at the kitchen table. Megan seized her and forced her into the chair opposite him, and then she brought their porridge and the dish of scrambled eggs to the table. While they ate, Mary gave them the latest bulletin about Paul and recounted her conversation with Dr. Harding.

When they had finished, James lit his pipe and said, "Now, we'd better apportion tasks for the day. Get some paper, Megan, and write it all down."

Before Megan had reseated herself, Honor appeared in the doorway, still in her dressing gown, looking haggard, but determined not to be sent back to bed. She sat down beside her mother, and laid her head on her shoulder, and methodically they worked out a roster of duties. James was to do vegetables, Megan the washing up, and Honor was to answer the telephone and the door—a very necessary duty, they discovered, for the bells rang all the morning with kind inquiries and offers of assistance. Mary was to sit with Paul, and Joady was to go to bed until after lunch, which was to be prepared by Anthea.

As, glowing with satisfaction, they finished the list, Anthea came down the hall and into the kitchen. She scrutinized the roster and gave it her approval, and then seated herself, demanding coffee, saying that at her last place there was plenty of other help kept and that the cook was never expected to wait on herself at mealtimes, and in the ensuing wrangle James gave notice and Honor organized them into a union with herself as secretary.

"That means," she said, nestling against her mother's shoulder, "that I don't do any work; I just keep in with the boss until I get all the power in my hands, and then I dictate to everyone, the boss included. Lovely job." And she rubbed her cold nose against Mary's face.

They rose and set about their tasks. Megan began to clear the table and Honor went rather slowly up to dress. As she tied on an apron, Anthea said, "I won't stay to lunch. I want to be home about twelve, just to see the family. Libby had one of those queer chewing turns last night, and they both looked a bit off-colour this morning. But I'll be back about two. That do?"

218

James remarked that everyone knew that cooks were a law unto themselves, anyway, and began to shell peas, thinking to himself that this was an excellent thumb exercise.

As she climbed the stairs, a little wearily, Mary felt well satisfied; there had never been a crisis of any kind that they hadn't met in this same cheerful way, for laughter had always been in the background of their life together, and Joady's insistence on orderliness showed its worth at these times. Perhaps it was just that they had never been tried beyond their strength, of course, she reflected, for she doubted her own capacity to endure if she had been in Mrs. Croft's place this morning, if Honor or Megan were dead or disfigured or maimed. Still, no doubt these qualities of cheerfulness and good sense that they all possessed would always help a little, even in the most unendurable circumstances. She opened the door and beckoned Joady to the landing.

"Go and rest until lunchtime," she said firmly. "Everything is in order downstairs, they're all busily occupied. The girls are up and about, and Anthea's there." As Joady looked rebellious, she added, "You'll be wanted later, Joady; come back to him after lunch."

When Joady had gone she closed the door and sat down in the chair by the window. He was breathing evenly, though a little heavily, but he seemed comfortable, his pillows arranged by Joady's expert hand. He looked spent, and his face was a bad colour—yellowish—but no doubt he was in pain, somewhere below his consciousness, and that would be taxing his strength. She determined to try to make him take a little soup when he woke next time, but in the meantime, she had nothing to do except sit here by the window. Luxury, she thought; I should have brought my knitting or my sewing, but I'm glad I didn't. She felt the need to go over the events of the last ten hours, to examine them and think them into some coherent pattern, make them a part of her experience, arrange them into an orderly whole, instead of leaving them lying about, piecemeal, in her mind. The rain came swirling gently down from the hills, dimming shapes and colours, drawing the green from everything and leaving soft greys in its place. The bush won't wear green when the sun doesn't shine, Mary thought; it dons a nondescript, all-over, indistinguishable grey, like a woman's cloak of shot-silk, dull until the candlelight catches it and turns it to brilliant colour.

I feel happy today, she thought. Why is that? I've been through a horrifying experience, my children have been close to danger, this lad, my dead son's friend, is lying here ill and injured, and a hatefully tragic end has come to the child of a woman for whom I feel respect and compassion—and yet I feel strong and content. There was, she realized suddenly, a feeling of contentment generally in the house; James had found a new vigour, he was making efforts at recovery that he had never attempted before, he had come back among them. And she had the knowledge, since yesterday, that he had come back, especially, to her. He has become the centre of my world again, she thought. There was something changed in all of them, she felt; probably there were reasons for these changes, too, reasons just as definite as in her own case, but each one lived a hidden life and no one else could know; yet it seemed as if tensions had been eased and decisions arrived at. Perhaps she was imagining it all, but, if so, it was pleasant imagining and could do no harm. She leant her head against the back of the chair and closed her eyes. Paul slept on.

II

John and Libby were supposedly playing in the billiard room. It was still called by that name, though Anthea had sold the cumbersome and now unused billiard table, and the room, long and spacious, had become an ideal play-room. It was cold and damp outside this morning, so Cassie had lit a fire for them and had given John careful instructions as to how to keep it burning but not blazing. When she had settled the heavy fireguard round it, and had put the tray with their milk and biscuits on the table by the window, she had left them, telling them that she wanted to hear nothing from them until lunchtime. Joseph had gone over to help Mrs. Bowers, whose husband was in hospital at Mitcham. The Bowerses lived over the hill, in the valley on the other side of the main road, and there were chickens to feed, and goats and a cow to milk. He had been gone since early morning, and it was doubtful whether he would get back for lunch.

John knelt on the couch under the long line of windows that ran the length of the room, overlooking the valley. He was in a high state of excitement, for it was half-past ten—nearly time to go. Libby stood behind him, her woebegone face a constant irritation to him.

"It'th raining," she said hopefully.

"Aw, that's nothing," he replied scornfully. "It's only light rain, and I brought our coats down when Cassie wasn't looking."

"I'll get my feet wet," she said obstructively.

He turned from the window in exasperation. "Look," he said, "you stay here; I'm not going to take you."

Her eyes closed and her mouth opened.

"All right, all right," he said hastily. "Don't start howling, for goodness' sake."

She relaxed, her face resuming its former doleful expression.

"Look here," he said desperately, "what do you want? You won't stay here, and yet you're moaning all the time about the rain."

"I want Mumma," she said. "And I'll get my feet wet."

"I told you—" his patience was nearly exhausted—"I've got your goloshes and your coat—and it's got a hood. And anyway," he added scathingly, "whoever heard of a prisoner escaping from the Jap guards wanting his mother and worrying about wet feet. I told you from the start you'd be no good at this. It's a man's game. . . ."

"You're not a man," she broke in witheringly.

"No," John replied hotly, "but I nearly am; I soon will be—and you'll never be, see?"

"I might be," she said irrationally. "I might be the only girl that ever grew up to be a man."

"Oh, stuff!" John said. "You couldn't, it's impossible."

"I might," she said grimly.

"Oh, all right," he said, giving up in disgust, for he knew

221

that she was capable of going on saying "I might" until king-dom come. "Anyway," he went on, "I'm going."

He began to pull on his goloshes, while she sat watching him disconsolately; but when he put on his raincoat and sou'wester, she said, "You do me up, John."

Resignedly, he put her into her raincape, and then stuffed her feet into her goloshes. When he looked at the clock on the mantelshelf, it was a quarter to eleven. They opened the door and listened. The billiard room was on the same level as the kitchen, and they could hear Cassie clattering saucepans, farther along the terrace.

"Come on," John said tensely, and, taking her hand, he hur-ried her across the terrace and down the steps, not pausing until they were in the long grass of the hillside that sloped down to the creek. They were both wet to the knees already, and the fine rain swept across them and down to the trees on the flat. Libby was enduring in dumb misery, only the fear of being sent back checking her from wailing aloud, and even John was a bit uneasy; but he told himself that it would be better when they reached the shelter of the trees. There was a place he knew, within the hiding area allotted to them, where the creek over-hung its bed, with a cavelike space underneath. He'd put Libby there, but he himself would climb the coolabah tree at the bend in the creek, where a cluster of she-oaks grew up to the middle branches, forming a wonderful screen. No one would be able to find him there.

Lifting their feet high and stumbling, they tramped down the paddock, and several times Libby slipped and swung loose by the arm from John's tightly gripping hand. When they reached the wire fence at the bottom of the paddock, he held the wires apart with his hands and one foot, pushing Libby through with the other foot. Then he crawled through after her, and, taking hands again, they ran to the line of trees, Libby swaying and staggering on the slippery, muddy flat. They found the track that led to the crossing, and followed it to the steeply shelving bank, where the red clay was slimy and oozing. As they de-scended the slope Libby's feet shot from under and she sat down and slid a couple of yards. When she came to rest, she made no

222

attempt to rise but, her nerve completely broken, put her head back and wailed loudly.

"Mumma-a-a," she howled. "Ah—ha-ah . . . Mumma."

John was dumbfounded by this disaster. He scrambled down beside her and hauled her up. She stood still, bending forward from the waist. Her hood had fallen back, and her face was lifted into the rain; her eyes were tightly closed and her mouth was wide open. Wail upon wail rose above the soft swish of the rain.

"Shut up, Libby," John said fiercely. "He'll hear you."

Despairingly he pulled her hood down, but too far. It lay across her nose, blinding her.

"My panth are all muddee-ee. . . ."

"Sh!" he said, and lifted up her raincape to see the extent of the damage; underneath the brief kilted skirt she was a mass of wet, red mud.

"Oh, jings!" he said. "I knew you'd spoil everything. Come on home."

The wailing ceased and the open mouth shut firmly.

"Come on, Libby," he coaxed, "it's no use; we're too wet. Mumma will be cross."

"No," she said. "I'm coming with you."

At length, when she showed a disposition to reseat herself deliberately in the mud, he gave up, and, taking her hand, dragged her along the bank to the overhanging part, and here he left her peering bleakly out from under her hood, while he, after showing her where he was going to hide, set off to cross the creek. As he passed her by on the opposite bank he waved to her, and a small, dirty hand emerged from under the raincape and wavered in the air. Poor kid, he thought with compunction, she's only little. She possessed a certain admirable endurance which, even if it was only the outcome of obstinacy, won his grudging respect. He started to climb the tall coolabah, and decided that he had chosen a very wet place to hide. He shivered when he had settled himself uncomfortably into the fork of the tree, and he pulled his sou'wester well down over his eyes. It was tropical rain, of course, and it was always hot in the jungle; and maybe, after a while, he'd begin to feel the steamy, choking sultriness coming up from the ground. As the minutes passed, however, all he felt was a keenly searching little wind, which seemed to penetrate the protection of his coat. He began to listen for the sound of a cracking twig, the stealthy parting of the bushes, but this was hard to do when the rain was making such a row in the branches of the trees and the creek was choking and rattling along over the stones.

After a long while he detected a movement on the opposite bank. He froze to absolute stillness, but relaxed a moment later as Libby called, "John, I'm all cold, and the mudth got right inthide my panth."

"Sh!" he said, waving his arms dangerously. "Go back and hide. Go back, Libby."

Miserably the little draggled figure turned, and he saw her crawling back into her hiding place, where she squatted down and stared hopelessly out at the falling rain.

At last, when a gap seemed to have appeared between the edge of his sou'wester and the collar of his coat, so that a long, cold trickle of wetness was reaching to the bottom of his spine, he decided that the hour was up and that they had won. He slid down from the tree, taking the skin off the palm of his right hand as he did so, and walked along to the crossing.

She was still sitting there when he came for her, and he pulled her to her feet.

"We've won, Libby," he said; "we've won the shilling. He didn't find us, and the hour is up—I think," he added.

She was beyond speech, but she staggered along beside him, and he had some trouble in getting her up the muddy slope to the flat.

"Let's call him," he said, and together they wandered among the trees and bushes, calling, "Paul, Paul—we've won, Paul!"

The rain was falling more heavily now, and at last they gave it up and turned to face the long climb up through the sodden paddocks.

III

Anthea was home by half-past eleven, for there was so much food at Thornfield that she had little cooking to do. She had left the house orderly and peaceful; Honor was dozing in front of the living-room fire with Jenkins beside her on the settee, Megan was lying down upstairs, and James, his chores neatly completed, was at work in his study. Now, as she drove up the hill, the rain was beating heavily against the windscreen and she was glad when she stopped at the porch and let herself into the warm house. Cassie came up from the kitchen when she heard Anthea call, bringing a tray with coffee, but before she could set it down, Anthea said, "No, wait a minute, Cassie. Are the children in the billiard room? I think I'll go down there and have it. I'm still worried about Libby. How does she seem?"

"Well, lovey," Cassie said, following her down the stairs, "they've been playing that quiet and nice, I haven't seen 'em for an hour."

At first she thought they were hiding when she went into the long, still room, but there was a feeling of emptiness there that turned her surprise to a vague alarm. When she turned, Cassie's eyes were staring, and together they looked towards the streaming windowpanes.

"Surely they haven't gone outside, Cassie."

"They'd never," Cassie said faintly. "They'd never do it."

"Well, they must be hiding upstairs somewhere."

"But," said Cassie, in a dazed tone, "they never come through the kitchen; I been there all the time—never moved, I 'aven't."

"Come on, we'll look."

Anthea strode through the kitchen, and they hurried upstairs. In the playroom Anthea paused and again peered through the glass, trying to see through the misty rain; suddenly she gave an exclamation and called Cassie, and after further peering they could both see a movement of some kind in the long grass of the paddock, just up from the flat.

"Cassie, it is—there they are! What in heaven's name possessed them . . . ?"

"My Gawd, they'll be soaked."

"Go and turn the bath on, Cassie, and the radiator in here. And bring towels and blankets." She was still shouting instructions over her shoulder as she ran down the stairs.

When, struggling with an umbrella, she came out on to the kitchen terrace, common sense returned, and she opened the door of the billiard room and stood in its shelter, waiting for them as they progressed slowly towards her. They seemed to be managing, and she would be less useful if she was drenched when they arrived. Though she was angry with them, her heart melted as she watched the gallant struggle. Poor little things, poor little Libby. Something they had planned had turned out wrongly; somehow they had bitten off more than they could chew. Tears smarted against her lids as she watched Libby's staggering steps and John's obvious concern for her. Oh, God, she thought, I love them; they're mine, they're my reason for existing, and everything else in my life is unimportant now, but those two little, wet, struggling figures. I'm a mother, she thought, and suddenly, for the first time, I am realizing that that is what I am primarily.

At last they reached the bottom terrace, and now she watched while John bent down and tried to help Libby to climb on his back. He staggered a few yards with her, but she seemed to slither down the slippery oilskins, and now they were both down on their hands and knees; but he pulled her to her feet and somehow pushed her up the steps ahead of him. They disappeared from Anthea's view for a moment, and then the top of Libby's hood came into sight, and in a minute she had tottered into Anthea's arms, sodden and wailing. Anthea closed the door and carried her through the kitchen and up the stairs, John squelching muddily behind them.

"Straight through to the bathroom," she said. "Get all your clothes off, John, and then into the bath with the pair of you."

It was more than half an hour before she and Cassie had finished with hot water and hot towels and hot milk; then, the bathroom a muddy wreckage, they took them through to the

226

bedroom. When, meekly, they climbed into the beds, warm with hot-water bags, both of them lay exhausted.

"I'll clean up, lovey," Cassie said. "Least I can do after lettin' this 'appen."

"No, Cassie, stop that," Anthea replied firmly. "It's not your fault; there's something here I'm going to find out about, and you, John Carmichael," she added, to the uneasily smiling John, "are the one who's going to tell me."

"It wath the man," Libby said. "We won a thyilling."

Anthea looked at her, frowning.

"What man, darling?" she asked, keeping alarm from her voice.

"The nithe man," she said, blandly explanatory.

"Oh, you go to sleep," John said unhappily. "I'll tell. It was a secret, Mum—Paul made us swear not to tell. I didn't want Libby to come, especially when it rained, but she would come—you know what she is. . . ." His voice trailed off, and he, too, looked at Anthea as if it were all explained now.

"Well, so far I don't understand a word," Anthea said. "You start and tell me slowly, John, right from the beginning."

As she caught the drift of the story, something cold seemed to settle at the base of Anthea's throat. What could he have had in mind, to suggest such a thing? Joady's words came flashing into her mind, and she remembered that Joady had been known, time and time again, to sense danger long before it was apparent to others. As she sat between the two beds, looking from one to the other as they told their story, a fury of fear came to her. No harm was done; they were safe and warm and comfortable. But just suppose he had meant to injure them? No, it was too crazy—what reason would he have had? "Queer in the head." Joady's words came again, and she shuddered with horror once and then again. She mustn't brood on it too much; it would be harmful to everybody to do that. No, just take it as a warning, use it and profit by it. Now I know, she thought triumphantly; now I'm sure that Howard can never have any influence on me again, and nothing which can ever hurt these two, even re- motely, will ever result from any intentional act or any decisions of mine, they are my world now, the limits of that world. No

227

matter what Mannering said, she could defy Howard now; her uncertainty was gone and she knew that she was free of him for ever, that she no longer needed to see him and talk to him to be sure that her madness would not return. He was of no importance to her now, and never would be again.

She bent and kissed Libby, and then rolled her in a bunny-hug. John's eyes were fixed forlornly on her as she turned, for he felt that he had been unwise and he feared her anger. She hugged him to her, tears in her eyes.

"Mum," he said anxiously, "I did try to stop her, Mum, and I tried to bring her back; but she was going to sit down in the mud. . . ."

"I know, darling." She smoothed his hair back and smiled at him. "That's women all over—they're as stubborn as mules. Don't blame yourself, darling. But," she added, "I want a very solemn promise from both of you."

They looked up at her, four earnest, expectant eyes.

"I want you never to do a thing like this without telling me; if anybody asks you to, just say, 'Yes, only I'll have to let my mother into it.' And then perhaps I'll come, too, and we can all play the game. Now, will you promise me that?"

Solemnly they promised, and then she sat and read to them until they grew drowsy.

8

SUNDAY AFTERNOON

WHEN Anthea arrived back at Thornfield at three o'clock the
rain had stopped; the air was cool and still, in the west the
clouds were breaking, and the sunset would give assurance of
a fine day tomorrow. The front door was shut, but the key was
in the lock, so she let herself in and walked into the living room,
where she found Megan and Honor, warm and relaxed, sitting
by the fire. Pulling off her gloves and hat, she went out to hang
them and her coat in the cupboard under the stairs, and when
she came back they had pulled the big settee across in front of
the fire, and Honor was sitting on a cushion on the hearthrug.
Anthea sat down and spread her hands out to the warmth.

"How's things?" she asked. "Anything to be done?"

"No," Megan answered. "Joady's with Paul again, and
Mother's resting. We're to call her at five. Paul's not properly
awake yet, but Joady says he's coming along well. I don't think
we'll need to bother you much more, Anthea."

"No bother," Anthea said. "I've done very little, I'm afraid."

"It's nice to have you round, though, Anthea, when things
come unstuck," Honor said, and Anthea laid her hand on Hon-
or's silky head for a moment.

"Anthea—" Honor turned round and faced her, her eyes
frowning in puzzlement—"what actually did happen last night?"

"You know more than I do; you tell me," Anthea said.

While they told her as much as they knew, she sat silently,
and when they had finished she leant forward, her hands clasped
round her knees, staring into the fire.

"Was he really going to throw that thing at us?" Honor's tone was incredulous.

"What do you think?"

"Of course he was," Megan said impatiently. "He followed us for at least a quarter of a mile—we could hear him. I'm sure it was to avenge himself for the hiding Paul had given him in the morning, that's what I think. The boy's brain was definitely twisted, everyone knows that he wasn't quite normal."

Yes, thought Anthea wearily, and Ambara is a reporter's paradise: everyone knows and everyone is only too anxious to tell. Honor broke in on her reflections.

"Anthea," she said, "the police have been here."

"Oh, and what did you tell them?"

"We told them what had happened, exactly as we remembered it."

"And did they ask about anything else?"

"Yes," Megan said, in a worried voice, "and we don't know whether we've done the right thing. You see, they asked me whether I knew if Martin had any grudge against Paul?"

Oh, Lord, Anthea thought, so much for the poor little secret!

"And what did you say?"

"I took an awful risk," Megan said, "because I didn't know what Mrs. Croft had told them, but Mother told us that she didn't want anything to come out about it, so I said no. In fact, I laughed at them for thinking such things about a boy of thirteen, and I said that it was obvious that the boy was highly imaginative and that he was playing some soldier game he'd read or heard about, pretending to stalk the Japs in the jungle at midnight, and that he would never have dreamt that the grenade was dangerous. I bet he did, though."

"She was marvellous," Honor said, her voice sleepy with warmth. "She was awfully intellectual, and she told them she was a student of child psychology, she even worked in her degree and her scholarship, and the poor coppers became quite humble. Nice, they were, too; there was one that was rather my style."

"She was perfectly dreadful," Megan said, her voice awe-struck. "Do you know what she did, Anthea? After a while she

230

went up and put on those new long, blue earrings she's got, and then she came back and sat down right in front of him and kept on smiling at him. I thought he was going to faint."

Anthea looked from one to the other of them. What a clever pair these two are, she thought; they probably tied the police into knots, between them—and they had done just what was needed, apparently.

"Yes," she said, "that was rather rare. And, after all, no one knows about that scene yesterday morning but Mrs. Croft and us, so it seems as if it might be quite possible, to keep it dark. I'm jolly glad you thought of it."

After another little pause, Anthea spoke again.

"Any newshounds?" she asked.

"You bet!" Honor sat up on her heels enthusiastically and faced Anthea. "I took care of them."

"Yes," Megan said. "I thought I could safely leave them to her; she absolutely swamped them."

"Did you tell them anything?"

"Did she!" exclaimed Megan. "She told them everything—but only about herself. She told them about her plans for the future and the kind of work she was going to do next year, she told them, in excruciating detail, about the homework she hasn't done today; she even asked one of them how to do her trig exercise. She bored them stiff; they didn't get a minute to ask questions and at last they went—jolly glad to get away."

"Well," said Honor reasonably, "one should never let even the smallest chance of publicity slip through one's fingers."

Anthea chuckled. Heavens—what one could accomplish with a little intelligence! She almost pitied the poor newshounds in the hands of these apparently guileless young things. Why, she thought, they're both, in their different ways, as sophisticated as blazes.

"Did they ask very closely about Paul?" she asked.

"Yes," Megan said. "We didn't tell them much, but they have his name, of course."

"Oh," Anthea said thoughtfully. "Then what about his mother? She'll die of fright when she sees the papers, and she'll think we're a lot of heels, not to get in touch with her."

231

"Mother's going to ring her tonight; Dr. Harding is going to tell her the final bulletin on Paul's condition when he comes back about five, so if she books a good long call to Dorrigo she should be able to explain—but I should think she'll need to book about an hour. The poor woman doesn't even know where he is, she doesn't know we exist, and to explain to a complete stranger how it's happened that her son's got concussion through an exploding hand grenade, while enjoying your hospitality— well, I'd sooner it was Mother than me, that's all."

"What a tremendous week end this has been," Honor said, when they had been silent for a few minutes. "I wonder if everyone feels the same as I do: as if dozens of things have happened quickly around me, which might have taken ages to work out, otherwise. Do you, Anthea?"

"Yes," Anthea replied quietly, "that's exactly how I feel."

"So do I," said Megan.

Honor knelt on the hearthrug and looked up at them.

"Would you be willing to tell people about what's happened to you?"

"No," they said, almost simultaneously.

Honor relaxed and sank back against the settee.

"Golly, it's queer," she said, in a wondering voice. "What's done it, do you suppose?"

No one spoke for a moment; then Megan said, "It's that Paul. He's come among our feelings like a whirlwind, he's swept the mists away from our minds and we are seeing clearly—at least, I am. Perhaps we needed him—perhaps he's altered the course of our lives for ever. He's like some painful but beneficial healing process—unpleasant at the time, but leaving healthy flesh afterwards."

"I wonder," Honor said meditatively, "whether we've done the same thing for him; I wonder whether the mists will be cleared from his mind when he wakes."

And now they sat still, preoccupied with their thoughts, respecting each other's desire for remoteness, using this quiet hour to the full, before the time came when they should have to face the return to the even routine of their sane, everyday lives.

232

9

AWAKENING

WHEN Paul woke at four o'clock the lamp was alight again, but he could see that it was daylight outside. He was completely aware of his surroundings, and he felt hungry. The stout, fresh-faced woman who had been there several times before, when he had waked, stood up now and went to the door. He heard her call softly, and a few moments later she whispered to some-one outside the door and then came to his bed. She sat down on the coverlet, and he saw that she held a little tray.

"Try to take some of this," she said gently, and he drank the beef tea gratefully.

"That was good," he said. "What time is it, please?"

"Ten past four in the afternoon."

"What afternoon?"

"Sunday."

"Sunday?"

But it was too difficult to try to remember what day it had been when the dump went up. At any rate, all the days were similar out here. Some of the chaps were very grateful to count them, but he had never bothered. After a few minutes he opened his eyes again.

"What place is this?"

"This is Thornfield." Then, as he looked at her uncompre-hendingly, she added, "At Ambara."

He grappled with this for a moment. It was very confusing. He felt that he should know what she was talking about, that he had heard these names somewhere, at some time, but it seemed a thousand miles, a million years away.

"What's your name, nurse?" he asked.

"My name is Joady and I'm not a nurse," she answered smilingly.

"Not a nurse?" He gazed at her in bewilderment. "What are you doing here, then? Are you Dutch?"

"No," she said, "I'm an Australian, like you, and I've never been outside Sydney Heads."

He stared at her, dumbfounded. What on earth was she talking about? She was far out beyond Sydney Heads now.

"Aren't you with the A.I.F.?" he asked. "Or are you a V.A.? —I didn't know they sent them here."

"No," she replied, "I'm nothing but a housekeeper. You'll remember who I am by and by, but don't bother about it now— I've been told to keep you very quiet. You can talk now and then, but you mustn't move and you mustn't worry yourself, if you can help it."

"All right," he said. "You're the boss. But just tell me this— where is this place? Did you say Ambon?"

"No, I said Ambara. It's a little place on the southern line, beyond Mitcham and Thornfield. This house is the home of Adrian—Major Adrian Carmichael—who was your friend."

"Adrian!" His eyes brightened with pleasure. "Jove, he was a great chap. Did you know him?"

"I knew him well," she said. "I brought him up, from the time he was a baby until he went away to join you at the war."

"Oh, yes, the war," he said absently. "What's the news? Who's winning? Are the Nips definitely on the way out?"

"They're more than that," she replied. "They've been completely and hopelessly beaten. The war's over and the prisoners are home—or they're coming home. You're one of them, and you're home and safe."

"But," he said, gazing at her unbelievingly, "that can't be true; the dump only just went up—oh, only a little while ago. I was hurt, knocked cold—that's why I'm here."

"That was the first time," Joady said. "That was months, perhaps years ago. It's no use telling you just now, but this was something else; it'll all come to you later. You lie there and try to doze off again. Just think over what I've told you: you're

234

home, the war's over, and you're safely in bed at Adrian's place. You'll remember the rest in a while."

He obeyed her and lay gazing at the ceiling; a radiator in the corner by the window cast a softly pink blush on the ceiling, and it was pretty and warm and comforting. He dozed again and woke. This happened several times, and once there was an elderly man there, a big chap who grasped his hand and spoke cheerfully to him.

"You'll do," he said. "Nothing much wrong with you. Been through tougher things than this, haven't you?"

"Yes," he answered, "but I'm a bit worried about things; can't seem to get the hang of them."

"Take it slowly," the big man said. "Can't digest too much information at once. See you tomorrow—you'll know all the answers by then."

When he had gone Joady came back with a woman he didn't know and they talked to him. He replied politely, but when the other woman had gone he called Joady, and when she came to him he said, "I say, will you be able to stay with me?"

"Yes, of course," she said.

"It won't make you too tired, will it?"

"No, I've had plenty of rest. That was Adrian's mother who was here."

"Was it?" he said. "But look, why I want you is—well, I know you now, don't I? And I don't want to start all over with someone else. I mean, I can go on from where we were before and you'll understand, won't you?"

"Yes," she said, "yes, it will be easier. Only you must promise to stop talking when I tell you—and you won't worry, will you?"

"No," he answered, "I don't seem to feel so worried now."

Throughout the night they went on in this way. He would wake from an hour's sleep, his mind clearer each time, and then he would start his questioning, and, patiently, she would give him the clear, slow answers he needed; when the door opened she would go quickly to it and there would be a whispered argument. Several times she brought him food, light food that slid warmly down his throat and strengthened him, and once she sponged him with a soft, warm cloth; after this he slept for several hours, and when he woke it was light outside again.

"Joady," he said, "didn't I go to a long, white house up in some hills?"

"Yes," she answered, and she drew back the curtain a little. "Those are the hills—remember?"

He gazed at them for a moment.

"Cedar Hill," he said at length, in a pleased voice. "That's Adrian's place—where he lived, I mean, his home."

"Yes," she said, letting the curtain fall, "this was his childhood's home, and he bought Cedar Hill when he was married."

"Oh, yes," he said, "he was married, poor chap, wasn't he?"

She said nothing, and he thought, Better not say too much about that. Vaguely he remembered that there was some trouble there; he'd remember it later, but he knew that Adrian wasn't happy, that there'd been something about a letter. . . .

When Joady went to get his breakfast Adrian's mother came in and he greeted her politely, but he didn't know anything about her. He lay gazing at her. She was telling him something, something about some work she had to do in the orchard, when, suddenly, he broke in and said, "James! Mrs. Carmichael, is your husband's name James?"

She nodded. She seemed pleased, he thought.

"He limps on a stick," he said slowly. "He's had some injury."

"Not exactly an injury—an illness."

"Yes, that was it," he agreed. "Now, don't tell me—see if I can remember. I know"—after a pause—"a stroke. He had a stroke."

"Yes," she replied. "That was some time ago, now."

"You know," he said, reflectively, "he was very nice to me at some time or other, he offered—" he frowned for a moment—"oh, yes, he offered me a job. It was a good job, too, specially as I had no qualifications for it."

"Was that why you refused it?"

"Did I?" He was astonished. "I say, that was cheek, wasn't it? No, I don't know why I refused; in fact, it's news to me."

"Well," she said, comfortingly unconcerned, "perhaps when you're better you'll think about it again. I know it would make

236

him very happy if you would change your mind; my husband misses his son very much."

"His son?" he asked, and then went on quickly, "Oh, yes, that would be Adrian; he was a great fellow, Mrs. Carmichael—the men thought the world of him."

She said nothing, but she moved to the window and stood looking out through the half-drawn curtains.

"You won't know about this," she said, "but since you've been with us—just a couple of days, really—we've grown very fond of you. In some way you've stood where Adrian would have been if he had come back. We all feel it. The girls think the same."

She looked at him and repeated, "The girls—Honor and Megan."

But that was beyond him. He lay still, and after a while she went away and Joady brought him his breakfast. She said nothing while he ate, and for a long while afterwards he lay with his eyes closed, disentangling his thoughts. Things came and floated away before he could grasp them and fit them into the pattern, and the idea of time was very difficult, for things could have happened years ago or yesterday, and the present was difficult to see clearly, because the past kept mingling with it. Once he opened his eyes and a fresh-faced, brown-haired girl, a slightly plump, cheerful little person, bent over him and said, "Hullo, Paul—it's Megan. Remember?"

And suddenly he remembered clearly about Alec Kyles. After that things came much more rapidly, but he could not remember Honor—not at all.

"She's thin and fragile," Joady said, "but she's as strong as an ox, really, and she's got a will like a mule; but she's lovely to look at, and she sings like a bird. Thinks an awful lot of herself, too; imagines she's going to take the world by storm. Probably will, too, just to show us."

And then he saw the dairy, in his mind, and he remembered the ride up the beautiful road, with the rosellas flashing in the sunlight. And he remembered that he had kissed Honor—and then he could see her! Oh, Honor, how could I have forgotten you? You, of all of them!

237

Once, late in the afternoon, he asked Joady, "But why did I come here?"

"Nobody knows." Joady's voice was expressionless. "Perhaps you just wanted to see Adrian's home and his people and Anthea —and the children."

As she saw his lack of comprehension, she went on, "Anthea is Adrian's wife, and Libby and John are his children; you seemed very attached to them."

"Yes," he replied. "I must think about that; there's something there I've got to think about."

He told Joady things they hadn't heard about him, about his return to his home and the attempts that had been made to cure him of something.

"I must have been a bit loco," he said. "I can remember a couple of trips to some hospital or mental home or something. They gave me that shock treatment—heard about that, Joady?"

She nodded.

"It made me frightened, desperately afraid, and then I'd forget things for a while, like now; but I know I used to remember them later. I wonder if I'll remember the same things again."

"Just let things come into your mind," Joady told him. "You're remembering fast now; I shouldn't be surprised if things were soon much clearer to you than they were before you were hurt."

When it was growing dark she left him, after she had bathed and fed him, and he was alone for the first time. He missed her, but he was glad of the solitude, for it meant that he couldn't get any more information, and so he had time to go over everything he had had to learn anew. He said their names over slowly, recalling the appearance of each of them, in turn, and their manners of speech. He traced incidents connected with them, and then, methodically, he set to work to recall his impressions of them. Mrs. Carmichael. She was kind, quiet, and pleasant; she seemed perfectly straightforward; nothing teased him in his recollections of her. Then James. He thought about James, and recalled some scene in his study when he, Paul, had been very upset about something, he couldn't remember what it had been, however. As soon as he was better he'd ask James again about that partnership offer in the business—a bookshop, that was it.

It would be a splendid opportunity for him to start anew, and amid friends, people who had loved Adrian and who were, so Mrs. Carmichael had said, fond of him. He felt a little worried for fear he had let the opportunity slip.

He thought about Megan. She had been very kind to him, too. She was cheerful and clever—yes, she'd won herself a scholarship. He liked Megan. And Honor. . . . The memory of Honor filled him with gladness. He thought of her diving into the river, but he couldn't think how long ago that had been. And then he remembered her singing at that little dance. Had it been a dance? It was a . . . a concert. No, it was a Welcome Home to the soldiers—that was it—and she had sung, carelessly, effortlessly, beautifully. Yes, he felt some special, some very happy thing about Honor.

Now what was it about Adrian's wife, Anthea? He closed his eyes and saw himself talking to her in a long white room with gentle colours, a very beautiful room, and suddenly he remembered about the letter Adrian had had from her. It had come, by some freak of chance, to the prison camp, over a year after she had sent it, and Adrian had suffered hell because of it. He recalled, now, that the conversation he had had with her had been about the letter; some fellow, this singer she had fallen in love with, was threatening her. He wanted to marry her—anyway, he was threatening her with something. He felt a little weary and was on the point of giving himself up to sleep, when the door opened and Honor was there.

She came to him and took his hand in hers. Her hair hung forward as she bent over him and her mouth was sweet and her eyes were wide and gentle.

"Honor!" he said, his eyes joyful.

"Paul, you know me."

"Yes, I do. I feel that I know you better than ever before. I've been thinking a lot, Honor; I'm quite fit, now, you know—just a bit hazy about some things. Stay a minute with me."

She sat on the side of the bed, still with her hand in his.

"I'm just going to bed," she said, "but Mother said I could come. I'm terribly glad you're better. We miss you, Paul—we want you back, downstairs."

239

"Oh, I think I'll be up soon," he said confidently. "There's very little pain in my head now. You know, I've been getting to know you all, all over again, lying here. It's been very pleasant. I feel that I want to stay here always, now."

"And perhaps you can," she said eagerly. "Father's still wild to keep you."

"Is he?" He felt greatly relieved. "I've been a bit worried about that. I don't know what possessed me to refuse such an offer—it's what I want more than anything."

"Oh, Paul, isn't life good? It's going to be wonderful for us, I feel certain, now."

When she had gone he fell asleep quickly, and that night Joady was able to rest, too, for he hardly stirred.

She was moving about the room when he woke. It was morning, and he could see the sunlight; the curtains were drawn farther back this morning, but the light did not hurt his eyes.

"Hullo!" he said gaily. "Good morning, Joady—I feel wonderful. What morning is it?"

"It's Tuesday." Joady smiled down at him.

"Lord," he said, "I've given you a ton of trouble, haven't I? You're to go away from me all day today, Joady. I'm well able to look after myself, now."

"We'll see," she said. "I'll be in and out and so will Mrs. Car. Now we'll get you ready for the doctor."

When he was tidy and had had breakfast, Joady brought her darning bag and sat with him awaiting the doctor's arrival.

"There's one thing that's a bit beyond me, Joady," he said. "How did I get this bang? When I first woke up I got it mixed up with the time when I connected with an egg from a Liberator at Chantagong, but I understand about that now. I can't remember anything much about this wallop—it must have been a pretty hefty one, though."

"It was a hand grenade," Joady said calmly.

"Good Lord!" he exclaimed in astonishment. "I thought you told me Ambara was a one-horse, sleepy little place."

"So I did, but I also told you about the soldiers' camp over the hill."

"Yes," he said, still puzzled, "but grenades don't roll down the hills and lob on you, do they?"

"Do you remember little Mrs. Croft?" Joady asked, with what seemed to Paul a fine inconsequence. "You gave her son a hiding."

"Yes, I remember that; little devil—he wrecked his mother's parlour, and he deliberately knifed her, too, I think."

"Well, he had the hand grenade, and when it went off you were quite close and something hit you—hard."

"What happened to him?"

"He was very close to it."

"Good God!" He was appalled. "Then he's dead?"

"Yes," Joady said heavily, "he's dead." And she went on to tell him about what they believed had been an attempt to kill him, and of the reasons that had led to the attempt. When she had finished, he lay very still for a few minutes, and then he began to speak slowly.

"And so," he said, "if I hadn't touched him, he'd be alive." He broke off, his eyes staring in his white, shocked face.

"Don't worry yourself; it would still have happened—or something much worse, perhaps. It's the best thing in the world, as I see it, and his mother thinks so, too. He had a lovely funeral, yesterday, with flowers and cars and a lot of people—Anthea saw to most of that—and his mother is a free and happy woman. No, don't blame yourself, young man, it's far better as it is."

"It's easy to say, when one's still able to enjoy life," he said in a low voice, "that another is better dead—they can't contradict. And you can be so sensible and right about it . . . Oh, God!" he burst out suddenly, "to think of a little kid stopping a hand grenade. . . ." A choking feeling of sickness forced him into silence.

"You'll get me into trouble with the doctor," Joady warned him. "He'll say I've given you a relapse. . . ."

But when Dr. Harding had examined Paul, he announced that he wouldn't waste his time and Paul's money by coming again.

"You can ring his mother tonight and tell her to come and take him home tomorrow," he said. "You'll be glad to get rid of him, no doubt, and mothers are such queer creatures that

241

she's probably longing to get him back. Damn sensible woman, anyhow, to wait until he's better instead of rushing in and crying over him. Good-bye, old chap," he went on, grasping Paul's hand. "You've had yet another narrow escape; keep away from explosives in future—and that means women, too," he added, as he picked up his bag; "they're dynamite, I assure you." And he went away chuckling, well pleased with his witticism.

Mary came back into the room.

"Would you like anything, Paul?" she asked. "You're to have another pillow, so I brought you some magazines to look at. Joady and I are catching up on some chores, so ring this little bell if you want us. We may get you up by the fire this evening if you feel able."

"Good," he said, as she settled him into a comfortable position. "Yes, I'd like that very much."

When he was alone he spent a little time gazing at the hills, of which he could see a glimpse through the gently moving curtains. He could see Cedar Hill faintly, and over to the left was Hester Laing's dairy. A remarkable woman—he'd be glad to go and see her again. The thought that he was to stay among these surroundings and these delightful people was good to contemplate. He'd be glad to go home to Dorrigo for a while, for he felt that he hadn't really renewed his relationship with his parents as yet; he must have been in a queer state of mind when he was there before, for none of it was very clear in his mind— and it must have been hell for them. In fact, he reflected, he seemed to have caused a great deal of trouble to everyone. That poor kid to die like that—no, he couldn't absolve himself from guilt in that manner. . . . Still, better not to go into it just yet.

He opened one of the magazines and looked through it, smiling at some of the cartoons, and as he leant over to take another one from the table, he saw his watch there. Hullo, he thought, the glass is smashed—the explosion, no doubt; but somewhere in his mind was the teasing recollection that it had been broken before, that there was some special significance about the watch. He turned it over in his hand, feeling intensely worried. Eleven o'clock, it said. He put it to his ear, but of course it wasn't ticking. Now, what, what . . . ?

242

When, suddenly, he remembered, something seemed to strike at his brain with terrific force, and he lay back on his pillows and cried aloud. Images and memories came rushing through his mind. I was mad, I must have been insane, insane, he thought frantically. Now he knew why he had come to Ambara. Dear God! . . . The horror of it flooded his mind, overwhelmed him. He felt himself grasping the little bell. . . .

He could taste brandy when he came to consciousness. Joady and Mary were there, their faces twisted with anxiety. His breath was gasping and rattling in his throat, and he caught Mary's hand tightly, painfully.

"The children." His eyes implored her reassurance. "Adrian's children—tell me, for God's sake! Tell me!"

As Mary gazed at him in amazed consternation, Joady leant over him.

"They're fine," she said swiftly. "There's nothing wrong with them. They're back at school."

"Then . . . but are you sure?" Still doubting, his eyes searched her face.

Joady looked up at Mary.

"Leave him to me for a while," she said. "I understand about this."

As Mary, shaken and mystified, left the room, Joady said, "Now I'm going to give you a dose of this sedative stuff, and you're to sleep for a while. You've nothing to worry about; the fact that you've remembered this shows that you're better of whatever ailed you before you got hurt, in fact it seems to me that this is the best kind of shock treatment you've had so far. We've all got a lot to be thankful for, and you musn't brood on what's past. Think of how lucky you are that nothing awful has happened to any of us—and plan for the future."

"But Joady," he said pitifully, "you don't understand. I was going to . . ."

She put her hand on his lips.

"There are things that are better not put into words," she said, her voice very gentle. "I understand about it—enough about it, anyway. I seemed to know, in a vague way, a long time ago,

243

and I don't need you to tell me about it. Just rejoice that whatever it is has gone out of your mind."

"But you do know, Joady, don't you, that I was only doing it for Adrian? I thought it was something I had to do for him. It wasn't at once, not when he died, but later—months later, after the bombing—that I began to imagine it. I used to think he was there, Joady, talking to me, and that he used to tell me what he wanted me to do. It seems just as if I'd dreamt it now, but it was real then, terribly real, and I grew to dread my dreams, I was terrified of them. They came to be real—real things and dreams all came to be mixed up in my mind and I couldn't distinguish one from the other. . . ."

She held a glass to his lips, and when he had drunk, she slipped the extra pillow away from under his head and drew the curtains together. He went to sleep almost at once and didn't wake until Mary brought his lunch. She made no mention of his outburst.

"I rang your mother," she said, sitting beside him as he ate, "and they're coming in the morning to fetch you away for a while; but I've told them that you're coming back and that you're going to take up Anthea's work as soon as you are well. You don't know how happy you're making us all, Paul; James is delighted, and so are the girls. As for Joady—sometimes I think Joady has been missing Adrian more than any of us, so I know she must be feeling very happy about it, though of course she shows less emotion than the rest of us."

After she had gone he lay quietly and thought about it all. He wanted so terribly to stay here. He felt that the only real chance of happiness in his life lay here and that, if he were anywhere else, it would be as an exile. And there was no reason why he shouldn't stay, none at all. He was better. He knew he was completely cured and that the danger had mercifully passed. . . . But no, he could not stifle it! Underneath all his reasoning, his calmness and assurance, was the dark terror of his doubt. You can't be certain, he told himself; you might be quite sane for months and then it will begin to creep back on you, and the first thing you'll do, when it comes, will be to conceal it from everyone. And it will grow and grow in your mind, as it did before, and then, while they're all quite unaware of it, you'll start making your ghastly plans again. And not only will you not try to stop yourself, but you'll see to it, cunningly, slyly, skilfully, that no one else stops you, for once again you'll be completely convinced that it's a good thing you're doing. Oh, yes, you will!

"Yes, I will," he said aloud in a lifeless voice, and tears filled his eyes. It was so much to give up, and for such an apparently nebulous reason—to prevent something so remote that there were a thousand chances to one against its happening. He was going to disappoint them all, refuse to give what help and comfort he could to these people to whom he owed such a great deal. And Honor. . . . Somewhere in his heart he knew he would come to love Honor, for he would never again meet anyone like her, any woman as fine and sweet and delightful, child as she was now. Oh, God, he thought in anguish, I can't give up these things! Yet he knew that he would, that now, in this blessed period of calmness and sanity, which might last for ever and which might vanish overnight, he had sufficient strength to do it, that he must do it; and then, somehow, he must learn to face the future alone.

He rang the bell, and when Megan came in answer to it he asked her to bring him a pen and a writing pad, and a large envelope, if she had one.

He wrote for a long time, slowly and with difficulty, for all the things he recounted were terribly distressing to him, and when at last it was finished he lay back and closed his eyes. He was glad it was done, for the responsibility was not his alone, now; but there were still things he must do, and they must be done tonight. He could not take the risk of waiting a single day, for the mists might begin to cloud over his mind again, and then it would be too late. He felt deeply sad, tremendously alone, and the fact that he was lying in a cosy little bedroom, in a house filled with his friends, seemed poignantly to emphasize his isolation. Yet he could gain peace this way, and he could be sure of peace for them. For such a mind as his, that was the most one could hope to achieve in life, now.

They made a great fuss of him, that evening, when he came slowly down the stairs on Joady's arm. They sat him down in front of the fire, with Jenkins at his feet and Iago wagging his tail violently at him from the hearthrug. They were having high tea instead of dinner tonight, and they drank coffee and ate sandwiches and cakes round the fire. The talk was at first cheerful and general.

"Your parents are making a very early start, Paul," James said, cleverly manipulating a cake fork. "I've been in touch with the Mitcham police, and you can drive over there and sign a statement about this business. You may not have to appear at the inquest, but if you do, you'll come straight here to us, won't you?"

Better, he thought, just to say, "thank you." This was not the time to begin his explanations, which, he knew, would explain little to them anyway, whenever they were made.

Anthea came in when they were packing up the tea things, and when the girls and Joady came in they all settled themselves down by the fire, Megan and Honor sitting one on either side of Iago, on the hearthrug. Suddenly Honor jumped up and went to the piano. She sang "Have you seen but a bright lily grow," and then drifted into the little crooning "Du, du liegst mir in Herzen"; when the last notes had died away they sat for a moment without speaking, and then Honor closed the piano and came and sat down at Paul's feet. His heart bruised with sadness, he touched the lightly curling ends of her hair and said, "Beautiful—you sing beautifully."

For once she did not burst into nonchalant self-praise, but sat very still, feeling the touch of his fingers on her hair.

He raised his eyes and faced them.

"I've got to tell you this," he said. "I've made up my mind that I can't stay here with you as we had planned and as I would love to do."

They all turned to look at him, except Joady, who bit off her cotton fiercely and scowled at the doily she was making.

James said slowly, "That, of course, is a great disappointment to us."

"Yes—and to me."

"Paul—" Honor knelt up and put her hands on his knees, her expression bewildered, desperately pleading—"don't go! Don't go. Stay here with us, for a while at least."

He shook his head, looking sadly down into her eyes.

"Why must you go, Paul?" Megan's troubled voice beseeched him.

"I can see no reason," Mary said.

"There are reasons, though," he said; "good and powerful reasons, Mrs. Carmichael. Try not to think badly of me, nor to accuse me of ingratitude. You're all good enough to say you want me; if only you knew how much I want you and how dearly I would love to stay in Ambara, you wouldn't reproach me."

After a moment James said, "You misunderstand us, Paul; we don't see it that way at all. A man must often do hard and sad things in his life, but if he is doing them because he thinks they are good, then he will always be the better man for making them his choice. You are our friend and our dead son's friend, and you are welcome here at any hour of any day."

"Thank you," Paul said.

"And have you any plans?" Anthea's voice was oddly gentle, pitying. "Any that we may know of?"

"I have relatives in America," he said, "in the south. I think I shall go there just at first."

Joady stood up.

"Bed," she said. "You've got to be up early tomorrow."

"Good night," Paul said, and, turning from their sad eyes, he walked to the door with her. Then he paused and looked back.

"Honor," he said, "you'll be gone early in the morning. I'll see you—at the Metropolitan Opera House. I'll come behind, shall I?"

She looked at him steadily, kneeling on the hearthrug, her hands clasped, elbows resting on the settee; her face was pale and filled with bewilderment and pain. As he went out, she slumped in a little heap and rested her head on her arm, gazing, gazing into the fire. . . .

When he was settled for the night he took the large envelope from the pages of the magazine, where he had hidden it.

"Joady," he said, "come and sit by me a minute." And when she was seated, he went on, "You know about me, don't you?"

"I know enough," she said.

"Well," he said, "I've written it all down here. If I should ever come back here, Joady, or if you should ever hear of my getting in touch with the children again, you're to give this to Anthea and she must act at once. I don't want to burden anyone else with this knowledge—and I'm not mad now and I don't want to spend my days in an asylum. If you should die, leave it to her; if she should die, to whoever is looking after the children until they're of an age to protect themselves. I can't do any more than this, Joady—I hope it will be enough."

"You've done what was necessary," Joady said, "and I'm comforted in my mind about it. But I'll miss you like I did Adrian when he went away, and so, too, will the others. God knows how it's happened so suddenly, but, in different ways, each one of us has come to love you, Paul."

She bent and kissed his cheek, and then went away quickly.

Paul lay in the quiet room. Strain and the sense of fierce endeavour had gone, rapture had been set aside, and now there was only a quiet sadness. He wondered how long they had waited for him, down there at the creek; whenever he felt rebellious and tormented by the awareness of sacrifice, he would quieten himself by imagining what would have been the outcome if he had been able to keep that appointment. He would remember that only Martin Croft, of all the world, had been able to stop him, and in the dark stillness he said aloud, "Rest in peace, Martin Croft—and may God forgive me."